Twin Soul Omnibus

Winner Twins
and
Todd McCaffrey

Books 6-10

OPHIDIAN'S OATH Copyright © 2019 by Brianna Winner, Brittany Winner, and Todd J. McCaffrey. Second Edition.

SNOW SERPENT Copyright © 2019 by Brianna Winner, Brittany Winner, and Todd J. McCaffrey. First Edition.

IRON AIR Copyright © 2019 by Brianna Winner, Brittany Winner, and Todd J. McCaffrey. First Edition.

OPHIDIAN'S HONOR Copyright © 2019 by Brianna Winner, Brittany Winner, and Todd J. McCaffrey. First Edition.

HEALING FIRE Copyright © 2019 by Brianna Winner, Brittany Winner, and Todd J. McCaffrey. First Edition.

TWIN SOUL SERIES OMNIBUS 2: BOOKS 6-10 Copyright © 2020 by Brianna Winner, Brittany Winner, and Todd J. McCaffrey. First Edition.

All Rights Reserved. No parts of this publication may be reproduced, or stored in a retrieval system, transmitted in any form or by any means, electronic, mechanical, photocopying, recording or otherwise without prior written permission of the publisher.
Cover art by Jeff Winner

Books by The Winner Twins and Todd McCaffrey

Nonfiction:

The Write Path: World Building

Books by McCaffrey-Winner

Twin Soul Series:

TS1 - Winter Wyvern

TS2 - Cloud Conqueror

TS3 - Frozen Sky

TS4 - Wyvern's Fate

TS5 - Wyvern's Wrath

TS6 - Ophidian's Oath

TS7 - Snow Serpent

TS8 - Iron Air

TS9 - Ophidian's Honor

TS10 - Healing Fire

TS11 - Ophidian's Tears

TS12 - Cloud War

TS13 - Steel Waters

TS14 - Cursed Mage

TS15 - Wyvern's Creed

TS16 - King's Challenge

TS17 - King's Conquest

TS18 - King's Treasure

TS19 - Wyvern Rider

Books by The Winner Twins

Nonfiction:

The Write Path: Navigating Storytelling

Science Fiction:

The Strand Prophecy

Extinction's Embrace

PCT: Perfect Compatibility Test

Poetry Books by Brianna Winner

Millennial Madness

Books by Todd McCaffrey

Science fiction

Ellay

The Jupiter Game

The Steam Walker

Collections

The One Tree of Luna (And Other Stories)

Dragonriders of Pern® Series

Dragon's Kin

Dragon's Fire

Dragon Harper

Dragonsblood

Dragonheart

Dragongirl

Dragon's Time

Sky Dragons

Non-fiction

Dragonholder: The Life And Times of Anne McCaffrey

Dragonwriter: A tribute to Anne McCaffrey and Pern

Map

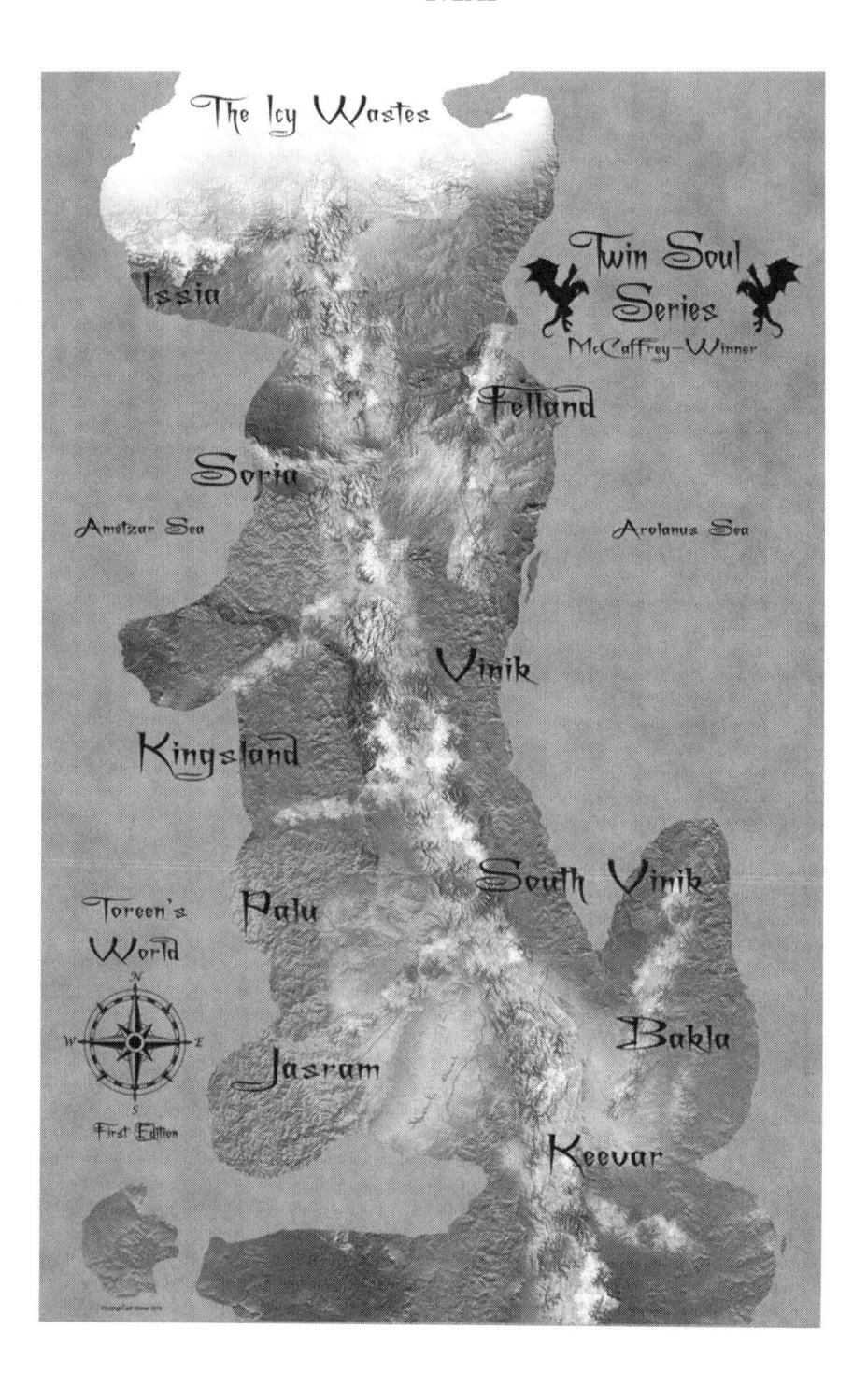

Contents

Twin Soul Series Omnibus 2   1

Map   6

Ophidian's Oath   9

Chapter One: Majestic Meetings   10
Chapter Two: Rabel Revealed   13
Chapter Three: Freedom's Fire   20
Chapter Four: Interlude at Ibb's   24
Chapter Five: Gold Warrior   29
Chapter Six: Ships of the Sky   33
Chapter Seven: Rabel's Oath   38

Snow Serpent   43

Prolog   44
Chapter One   46
Chapter Two   50
Chapter Three   53
Chapter Four   58
Chapter Five   65
Chapter Six   70
Chapter Seven   77
Chapter Eight   88
Chapter Nine   92
Chapter Ten   94
Epilog   95

Iron Air   96

Chapter One   97
Chapter Two   101
Chapter Three   109
Chapter Four   114
Chapter Five   120
Chapter Six   129
Chapter Seven   136

Ophidian's Honor   149

Chapter One   150
Chapter Two   153
Chapter Four   166
Chapter Five   176
Chapter Six   184
Chapter Seven   190

Healing Fire   195

Chapter One   196
Chapter Two   200
Chapter Three   205
Chapter Four   211
Chapter Five   215
Chapter Six   221
Chapter Seven   227
About The Twin Soul Series   231
Acknowledgements   232
About the Authors   233

Ophidian's Oath

Book 6

Twin Soul series

Chapter One: Majestic Meetings

"I have learned long ago that it is unwise to question his majesty's commands," first minister Mannevy said to Captain Nevins as they exited the throne room, the captain shaking with a white-hot anger that was just barely restrained.

"He takes my ship, *my* ship, and tells me to have her gutted to become his flying bauble and *then* he *demands* that I remove all my guns!" Nevins said, the veins bulging in his throat as rage poured through him. "I merely asked what use is a ship without guns and he exploded on me!" He turned to Mannevy. "What use is a ship, first minister, without its guns?"

"It is quite useless," Mannevy agreed affably.

"Then *why* have me remove them?" Nevins demanded.

"It's a question of weight," mage Tirpin, coming up the hallway, answered.

"Weight?"

"There's a limit to how much we can put into the air on your ship, captain," Tirpin told him with a firm nod, pulling up beside them. "Your twelve-pounders —"

"Best guns there ever was!" Nevins interjected.

"They weigh four times the amount of six-pounders," Tirpin said.

"Six-pounders!" Nevins roared. "And what do you expect six-pounders to do?"

"Exactly what Captain Ford and *Spite* did to your ship," first minister Mannevy replied smoothly. "And, as I recall, he only fired one broadside. Imagine if he'd fired more."

Nevins took only a second to absorb that, then shot back, "And what happens when two airships fight each other? Or an airship and a wyvern or gods help us all, a pair of dragons in full flame?"

Mannevy raised a hand soothingly. "All that has been considered, I assure you." His raised hand gestured toward Tirpin as the source of this brilliance.

"It has?" Nevins said, turning to the mage. "And, mage, how often have you commanded a ship at sea? In battle?"

"Captain Nevins," Tirpin returned easily, "how often have you commanded a ship in the air?"

"Never, as you damned well know," Nevins snarled. "But I know enough about war — and those popguns won't save us against a real ship."

"Even when you are firing down and they can't fire back?" Mannevy asked silkily.

That question brought captain Nevins up short.

"You can always add heavier guns later," Tirpin said. "The first thing, captain, is to get your ship airborne."

Nevins pursed his lips and then raised a hand in protest, looking at Mannevy. "Only if my guns are stored at the king's expense."

"Of course," Mannevy said. He smiled. "Captain, if that was your only concern, you merely had to ask."

"Hmph."

"Are there any other issues I can help you with?" Mannevy asked, glancing first to the captain and then to the mage.

"There are going to be two airships," Nevins said. He pointed to Tirpin. "There's only *one* mage."

"Each airship will have one large balloon," Tirpin replied easily. "I need first fill the balloon but after that it will stay full." He shrugged. "So it is no problem to fill two balloons before we depart."

"So why did *Spite* have ten balloons?"

"I am told that was more because of the balloon makers," first minister Mannevy said. The others looked at him so he expanded, "They didn't know how to make such large balloons and so mage Reedis suggested the smaller sizes for safety."

"Safety?"

"Now we know that they can build larger balloons far more efficiently," Mannevy concluded. "In fact, I'm told that the first one will be ready by the end of the week and the second not long afterwards."

"And our engines?" Nevins asked.

"Ready at the same time or within a few days," Mannevy said. "Which is why it's important that we get your ship converted quickly."

"*Spite* was a lot smaller than *Warrior*," Nevins said. "Where do I dock my ship, then?"

Mannevy turned to Tirpin. "Is there any reason *Warrior* needs to be pulled from her slip?"

"Slip?" Tirpin asked.

"Her moorings, where she's docked," Nevins explained to the confused mage.

"Oh!" Tirpin exclaimed. He rubbed his small goatee thoughtfully. Finally, he shook his head. "No, I don't see any reason why she can't stay where she is." He nodded toward Nevins, "Provided we get those guns replaced."

"You'll get that as soon as the first minister here arranges the cartage," Nevins replied.

"Good!" Mannevy said, moving forward to clap each man on the shoulder. "Then we should return to our various duties!"

#

"Where's my daughter?" Rabel Zebala demanded as soon as the dark hood was pulled from over his head. "Where's my apprentice? Why have you taken me?"

"I believe that it is *I* who should be asking the questions," first minister Mannevy said to the manacled man standing before him. The cells of the king's jail were cold with the worst of the winter but air still carried scents and Mannevy found himself raising his perfumed handkerchief to his nose to protect his senses.

"Believe what you want," Rabel snarled. "I demand the king's justice!"

"If you want, I could put you back in your cell," Mannevy said. "*That* is the king's justice."

"I've done nothing wrong," Rabel said. "I'm an old man, I work my trade honestly and all I ask is to be left alone."

"You traded with the mechanical, Ibb," Mannevy said. "Your daughter turned into a wyvern." He paused, catching the other's eyes with his own. "The king has ordered her death."

"What?" Rabel cried. "She's done nothing wrong! She was an outcast, she didn't know better!"

"She grew up within walking distance of a field of wyvern's flowers," Mannevy replied slowly. He smiled when he noticed how Rabel's stance changed. "And why is that? How did that come to happen?" He waited a moment, giving the smith a chance to speak, before continuing, "And how is it that you had such commerce with Ibb, the mechanical?"

"He bought my wares, no more," Rabel said defensively.

"Your apprentice."

"What of him?" Rabel demanded.

"He brought you your apprentice, didn't he?" Mannevy said. "And you supplied Newman the engineer with his boiler and the parts of his engine." Mannevy paused. "How was it that you, with only a bellows-fired furnace could produce what Mr. Newman called, 'The best steel in the kingdom.'"

Rabel had no answer.

Mannevy stood and moved closer to him. In a very low voice, he said, "I don't care, you know."

Rabel twisted his head away from the first minister.

"What *I* care about is that you make more," the first minister said. "That you make it now and that you teach the skill to Newman and his apprentice."

"I can't," Rabel confessed. "I don't know how."

"Oh?" Mannevy said. He took a step back. "Well then, you're no use to me." He turned around, calling loudly, "Guards! Have this man moved to the executioner's cell." He turned back to the old man and said in a dispassionate voice, "And if you're no use to me, you're no use to the king. So I'll relieve him of the need to pay for your keep."

"You do that," Rabel said defiantly. "You just do that."

"Actually, the executioner will do it," Mannevy said. He threw the scented handkerchief to the ground and turned away. "I've no need to do such dirty work."

Chapter Two: Rabel Revealed

They left Rabel free of his shackles and manacles, figuring that he was too old and too feeble to cause trouble. They were right. His white hair was thin and bald on the top. His shoulders were pointy and his arms were like sticks, shorn of their muscle by age.

Rabel sat in the far left back corner of the cell, farthest from the bucket they'd left for his toilet and farthest from sight, lost in the dark shadows of the dark jail.

Krea, he thought despairingly. What a child! Wilful and innocent both at the same time. She had been happy, he thought. At least when the townsfolk left her alone.

He remembered how hurt and sad she looked when they'd taunted her on her birthday for her albinism. White hair, white skin, dark eyes. Her features were good, her body lithe and well-coordinated. If people would look beyond her skin they'd see her true beauty. For a long while only Rabel could see it.

When he took on the new apprentice, when he saw that Angus could see Krea's true beauty, his heart soared and, impulsively, he suggested that the young lad consider becoming her husband. He'd been so happy that he hadn't even considered that Krea might feel otherwise. He was sure that he'd found the solution to all his problems: that he could grow old and feeble in the warmth of his daughter's brilliance and the comfort that he had passed on both his trade and his problems to some stronger back.

Krea had rebelled. Here, in the darkness of the cell, Rabel could see clearly what he couldn't imagine back then. His girl, his little white angel, had her own plans for her future. He should have respected that and, because he hadn't, she'd made her own choices, her own mistakes.

Now she was gone. And soon, unable to care for her, he would face the hangman.

In anguish, Rabel dropped his head into his hands and wept silently, tearlessly. It wasn't supposed to be this way. He hadn't broken his promise; the gods had.

Ametza, he knew, cared for him not one jot. She would be glad to see him gone, forgetting that, however much she hated fire, she loved steel — and there was only one way to make it. She might force rivers off their courses, cause them to rip away earth and expose bare ore but she could not refine it into the steel that she wanted for her plans of conquest.

For that she needed Ophidian's son.

Fire. Dragon fire.

To wield the fire, to smelt the ore into the strong iron, she needed men who could work it. Men like Rabel. Men who'd spent their lives learning all they could of the secrets of iron, the bellows, the flames of the forge, and the care needed to make steel out of iron sludge.

But, because the sea god hated many things, Rabel knew she would discard him whenever she could. That she was inconstant and flighty, that she would smile as the hangman rapped the noose around his neck, cackle as the floor dropped and Rabel's neck snapped with the fall, laugh as he dangled and his soul went to the Ferryman. It was only later, much later, that'd she cry bitter tears as she realized her mistake.

Ophidian, for his part, had forgotten Rabel long ago. He'd lost interest in him when he'd married, had a child, and settled down. Even planting the field of wyvern flowers had only brought Rabel a little favor from the fire god — his child had survived her hard birth.

But not the mother — oh, she had lived — but only as a frail shadow of herself who had only survived long enough to see her baby grow into childhood. Perhaps it had amused the god to see Rabel's mix of anguish and joy. Perhaps the fire god hadn't even noticed.

It was hard to tell with the gods.

Death did not disturb Rabel. He would accept his end when it came. All he wanted was to know that he'd done his best with his life and that he had cared the best for all those he loved.

And he couldn't say that. Krea was gone, twinned to a wyvern and flown far from the grasp of King Markel and his goddess Ametza. But Rabel could not say she was safe. He couldn't even say if she was alive.

And Angus, whom he'd taken in, was gone, too. He had killed Krea at her wish, seen her reborn into the wyvern — and what a beautiful wyvern she was! Angus had told him when they were taken to the jail together, had spoken in hurried whispers, had described — at Rabel's urging — the sort of wyvern Krea had become: snow white with gold filigree on her scales.

In wyvern form, Krea's eyes and white skin were beautiful beyond compare. And she could fly wherever she wanted, fearing nothing.

Except airships and cannon.

And that fool Mannevy had come to him, had come here in the jail to visit Rabel at his darkest moment. The first minister of King Markel had had the *gall* to think that he could force Rabel to build the steel that would be used to hunt down his own daughter! Rabel raised his head from his hands and chuckled bitterly.

No! He would die before he did anything that might cause his beautiful wyvern child harm.

"Why are you laughing?" a little girl's voice called in the darkness.

Rabel's eyes popped open and he searched for the source of the voice. It was a little girl, a street urchin, dressed in less than rags, her body more bone than skin.

"I'm laughing because I'm free," Rabel said.

"You're in jail," the little girl told him. "How can you be free?"

"Free is in your mind, child," Rabel told her. "And no bars can take that away from you."

"You're an old man," the girl said, moving forward to come into sight just outside the bars of his cell. "They say you're crazy with age." She added, "I think they're right."

Rabel chuckled. "Age brings insight. Remember that as you —" he cut himself off. This child would not grow older. She was closer to death's door than he.

"Where are your parents?" Rabel demanded. He glanced around. "Are they in jail?"

"They died. Years back," the girl said. "I was taken in by a gang and they died."

"Died? How?"

"My gang was rounded up by the king," the girl said. Her face twisted in bitter memories. "The boys were sent to the ships. The girls..."

"I understand," Rabel said. "How did you escape?"

"I was out on the street when the guards came," the girl said.

"Lucky," Rabel said. He almost hated himself for his next question. He knew what asking it would bring for him. "What's your name?"

"Ellen," the little girl said.

There, old man, now you know, Rabel thought bitterly to himself. *You had to ask. You had to* care.

"Who sent you?" he said aloud.

"What?" Ellen asked in a tone that might have convinced someone much younger of her innocence.

"You're not here when you could be begging, unless someone sent you," Rabel said. "Someone paid you to be here."

Ellen was silent, rapidly trying to come up with an answer. Rabel almost smiled: the little urchin reminded him of Krea when she tried to lie.

"Who was it?"

"The captain," Ellen said.

"The captain?" Rabel repeated, growing thoughtful. "Which captain, what ship?"

"The captain of the airship," Ellen said, standing a bit straighter. "Captain Ford."

"Captain Ford!" Rabel repeated in surprise. The captain of the airship that had shot the wyvern from the sky. The wyvern who had twinned with Krea on the death of her human half. "Why?"

"He wanted to know about the mechanical man," Ellen said.

"Ibb?" Rabel asked in surprise. "Where is he?"

"Gone," Ellen said. Proudly, she added, "I saw his boot prints in the snow and then they disappeared."

"Disappeared?"

"But there were wagon tracks," Ellen continued.

"But no wagon," Rabel guessed.

"How did you know?"

"It's Ibb," Rabel said. "He would have taken precautions."

He would have taken precautions, the words rang in his ears. He began moving about the cell, searching the corners and the bricks.

"What are you doing?" Ellen said.

"I need more light," Rabel said. "I'm sure that Ibb would have left a message."

"He wasn't in this cell."

"But the cell was unlocked when he left, wasn't it?" Rabel said.

"Yes," Ellen said with some hesitation. "And I didn't see boot prints until he got to the snow."

"So he could have come here," Rabel said, his spirits lifting. "But my eyes are too old, I need light."

Suddenly the bricks were brighter. Rabel turned and saw Ellen holding a small object glowing with a blue-white light. He raced over to her so fast that she lurched back from the cell's bars in fear.

"Where did you get that?" Rabel asked. He looked at it. "It's a witch light, are you a witch?"

"N-no," Ellen said fearfully. "They came to me."

"They're witch-sent," Rabel told her. "Demons ensorceled, which is why they can't escape and they don't burn you."

"I didn't know," Ellen said. "I was thinking about Captain Ford, wondering how I could tell him when they came to me."

"He must have sent them then," Rabel said.

"How could he know I was thinking of him?" Ellen asked in surprised. "Is he the witch?"

Rabel snorted. "Hardly!" He gave the girl a long look before adding, "I think they were looking for you, that your thoughts were what they honed in on."

Ellen absorbed this in silence.

"Can I borrow this one?" Rabel asked, beckoning the girl forward. "I promise I won't hurt it."

Reluctantly, Ellen walked back to the jail and held out the blue demon. Carefully Rabel picked it up, cooing softly, "Oh, aren't you the most brilliant demon of all the gods?"

The demon seemed to appreciate the praise, glowing brighter as Rabel brought it closer to the walls.

"Ibb left something," Rabel said to the light demon. "It might be magic. Can you help me find it?"

The blue demon, nothing more than a blob of blue-white light with no heat, pulsed in agreement.

Rabel went around the cell slowly and carefully. Ellen shrank against the brick wall that separated Rabel's cell from the next, hiding from the bright light.

"Oh, no!" Rabel said when the blue light brightened. Ellen crept around the corner to see Rabel hovering over the only thing in the cell: the bucket left for him to relieve himself. "Metal man, if this is your sort of humor…!"

But it wasn't, much to Rabel's relief. He lifted the bucket and moved it aside. He peered down and saw nothing — but the demon pulsed brighter. With his brows creased in speculation, Rabel reached down to the ground and cried in triumph when he came up with something — something that he couldn't see.

The blue light flared and Rabel grunted in surprise as words appeared in the thin air his hand cupped: *The god will help you if you accept him.*

The words disappeared and the blue-light demon dimmed as if saddened by their loss.

"Here child," Rabel called softly, walking back to the bars. "You may have your messenger back."

"Messenger?" Ellen said, coming around the corner and gently taking the blue-light demon back into her hand. She looked down at it to assure herself that it was unharmed, then up to Rabel. "How does it work?"

"Think of your captain, think of your message and tell it to go," Rabel said. "It will go to wherever he is."

"What if he's dead?" Ellen asked.

"If he's dead I doubt they'll stay with you," Rabel replied, shaking his head. "Their magic was tied to him — and you through him."

"Me?"

"He had to bind them to you," Rabel explained. "So he did it by thinking of you."

"He gave me a shilling," Ellen said shyly, "and promised more."

"Those demons are worth more than your shilling," Rabel said. He gave her a smile. "You must be worth quite a lot to him."

"He told me to spy for him," Ellen said dubiously.

"You must be good," Rabel said.

"I am," Ellen said with no modesty. She gave him a look. "I found you and I found the metal man's boots."

"You are good at finding things," Rabel said encouragingly.

"What did you find?" Ellen asked him. She saw his look and added, "It was my demon that helped you."

"I found a message," Rabel replied.

"What did it say?"

"It said that I have to make a choice," he replied.

"Will it get you free?"

Rabel nodded slowly.

"Then you should take it," Ellen said. "They're going to kill you in the morning."

"Some things are worse than dying," Rabel said.

"Like being hungry?" she asked. Rabel nodded. "And cold?" He nodded again. "And all alone?"

"Those are all worse than dying," Rabel agreed.

"But this is worse than those?" Ellen guessed.

"It could be," Rabel said.

"Well," Ellen said, "I think you should do it anyway."

"Why?"

"Because I'm hungry and cold and if you go to the hangman, I'll be all alone," she said.

Rabel snorted in laughter. He reached through the bars and tousled her hair, dirty and slimy though it was. "I like you, little Ellen."

"I like you too, old man," Ellen said. Shyly, trying it out for the first time, she said his name, "Rabel."

"What do you know of me?"

"Your daughter was the one who turned into a wyvern," Ellen said. After a moment, she confided, "I saw it happen."

"You did?" Rabel asked in surprise. "I was at home."

"Because you were old," Ellen guessed shrewdly. "The man stuck her with this long pin and she cried and then she fell and when she rose again — she was a wyvern. She screeched so loud it hurt my ears and then flew away to the north." Thoughtfully, she added, "Probably to find the gods." She narrowed her eyes. "That message, was it from the gods?"

"It was from Ibb," Rabel replied quickly.

"It was about the gods," Ellen said with surety. "That's why the demon got brighter."

"It was," Rabel replied. "I was told I could get help if I accepted a deal with a god."

"Do gods often offer you such riches?" Ellen asked.

"Just one god," Rabel replied, shaking his head sadly. "And I wished I'd never listened to him."

"Don't say his name!" Ellen hissed in warning, glancing around the place. "Ametza! She likes to hear only about herself."

"Good advice," Rabel said, "and too true." He took a deep breath and let it out in a deep sigh. "I suppose we should leave now."

"Leave?" Ellen said. "How? You're in jail and I'm paid to —"

"Best not say it," Rabel told her, rephrasing her words from earlier. Ellen gave him a startled look which turned into a pout. Satisfied, Rabel continued, "You'll want to come with me anyway."

"Why?"

"Do you want to eat regularly?" Rabel asked. "And don't you want clothes that don't freeze you?"

"They won't do any good if I'm dead."

"That's what I'm talking about," Rabel said. Her eyebrows shot up. "You — staying alive." He didn't wait for her to respond. "Now, back away from the jail. Best go around the corner and close your eyes."

"Why? What's going to happen?"

"I don't really know," Rabel said. "All I know is that we need to leave."

"But —"

"Just do what I say," Rabel said. "I'll get you before I leave."

Ellen shook her head, once, in amazement at the stupidity of old people but, at Rabel's continued gestures, went around the corner of the hallway. She did not close her eyes.

A moment later, Rabel called out, "Close your eyes if you don't want to lose your sight!"

Reluctantly, she closed her eyes.

A brilliant flash, so intense that it glowed through her closed eyes, lit the entire jail. Guards cried out in panic, groping around blindly.

"Come on!" A young man's voice called, and she felt someone grab tightly to her upper arm and tug her after him.

Ellen opened her eyes and tried to shrug off the grip of the man.

"Who are you?" she cried. "Let me go! I'm waiting for someone!"

"You're waiting for me, Ellen," the man said.

"No, I'm not!" Ellen shouted. Then she stopped. "Who are you?"

"We spoke earlier," the man said.

"You said I was too old." He smiled at her and cocked his head. "Still think so?" Ellen's eyes went wide. The voice sounded like the old man's, like Rabel's. But it was much younger. The man in front of her had dark, gleaming hair, not white straggly bits just barely topping his head. The man had energy and vigor and... something fierce lurked behind his eyes. Something that frightened her almost as much as it excited her.

"Rabel?" she said. She didn't need his nod to know the answer. "What did you do?"

"I made a deal," Rabel told her. "A deal to save your life." He tugged on her arm again. "Come on! We're going to have to run very fast if we don't want the guards to see us."

"Why won't they see us?"

"The light blinded them," Rabel said, tugging again. This time, Ellen let herself be led.

They passed the guard at the front who was wandering around, arms outstretched, moaning in pain and fear.

"Don't worry," Rabel said as they passed him, "you'll get your sight back in a few minutes."

"Who are you?" the guard cried. "What are you doing here?"

"I'm a friend of Ophidian's and you've made him very angry," Rabel said. "You and all the guard should leave while you have the chance."

"Ophidian!" the blind guard cried. "Leave?"

"Better than being blind," Rabel called over his shoulder as they left the building.

"Ophidian! Please help me!" the guard cried behind them.

"Ophidian blinded them?" Ellen asked, glancing back to the building from which several guards were running. She frowned. "That's mean!"

Rabel laughed. "*I* blinded them," Rabel said. She looked at him in surprise and fear. "But only for a moment."

"So why did you say *his* name?"

"Because I owe the king payment for all the trouble he's caused me," Rabel said. He glanced at the jail which was almost completely bare of guards. "This is just the start."

"They'll leave?" Ellen said. "And all those locked in the jails?"

"Not so many now," Rabel said, stopping and pointing toward the entrance to the jail. Ellen's eyes nearly popped out of her head as she saw a stream of people fleeing the jail.

Some looked very mean and nasty but too many looked like herself — half-starved and half-dressed: no threat to the king or anyone else in the kingdom.

"Come on," Rabel said, turning down a side street. "We've got to go to the Inn."

Ellen let herself be pulled along. Rabel had exchanged his grip on her shoulder for holding her hand. For Ellen, the grip of an adult's hand was a comfort she hadn't felt in years. Suddenly tears were streaming down her face and she stopped, bawling her eyes out.

"It's okay," Rabel said, turning quickly and bouncing her up into his arms. He held her against him and strode off with renewed speed. "Cry all you need, little one." He pressed her head into his shoulder. "There's no harm in crying."

Chapter Three: Freedom's Fire

"Magic!" the two elderly mages cried as one. "God magic!"

King Markel looked over to them in irritation: he had been having quite a pleasant nap on his throne, dreaming of flying ships and roaring cannons. It took him a moment to gather his wits. "Praise be to Ametza!"

Margen shook his head, and croaked, "'Twas not Ametza, sire."

"It came from the jail," Vistos said in an aged, scratchy voice, pointing toward the far window. "There was a flash of magic, like a bright light and fire."

"So, not Ametza, then," Markel said in a bored voice. He roused himself out of his plush throne and walked down the dais toward the indicated window. He could see light and smoke where the jail had been and people running away from it. "Perhaps a fire was started," Markel guessed. He waved a hand. "The walls are stone, the bars are metal," he considered the notion for another moment, then turned back toward his throne. "The rest is of no consequence and can easily be replaced."

"It was god's work," Margen insisted.

"Why would a god —?" Markel began. And then the answer hit him. "Rouse the troops! Send someone to the jail immediately!"

"I'll send Gergen, Your Majesty," first minister Mannevy said, turning to issue the orders. General Gergen was the head of Kingsland's royal army.

"You do that," the king said. "And have him be prepared to explain how this all happened, too."

Mannevy nodded and waved a hand in acknowledgement.

#

"It happened because we never hired a mage for the jail, did we?" Georgos Gergen, the king's third minister — in charge of the army — growled when Mannevy apprised him of the king's command. "As for the other, I've already sent Walpish and a troop to see what we can learn." He scowled, adding, "We'll know soon enough."

"How soon?"

"Walpish was told to send a messenger —" he broke off as the sound of galloping hooves grew louder and louder in their direction. Gergen nodded at the sound. " We'll know now."

"The prisoners have escaped!" the messenger cried, reining his horse to a halt at General Gergen's hand-raised order.

"Yes, we guessed that from the sight of everyone running away," Mannevy replied with ill-disguised pique. "The question your colonel should have answered is: why?"

The trooper glanced toward Mannevy, recognized him, and bowed in his saddle. "First Minister, my commander sent me as soon as he had appraised the situation. I'm sure —" he broke off, glancing back over his shoulder as another messenger galloped into the courtyard. Wordlessly, he waved toward the new messenger.

"What news?" Gergen called.

The trooper reined his mount to a halt, saluted Gergen and called down, "Colonel Walpish's compliments, sir, —" he nodded toward first minister Mannevy "— minister. The colonel wishes me to inform you that all the prisoners have escaped."

"What about the guards?" Mannevy demanded, turning to glare at Gergen accusingly. "Why did they leave their posts?"

"They say they were blinded," the messenger replied. He opened his pouch and pulled out a roll of parchment which he passed down to the general.

Mannevy moved to take it. Gergen passed it to him without pause. Mannevy scowled as he read the message.

"The locks were melted!" Mannevy growled. "The metal dripped *out* of the cells!"

"One of the gods, surely!" Gergen said. "Has anyone upset Vorg or Veva recently?"

"*Ophidian*," Mannevy said with a groan. The general gave him a questioning look, so the minister explained, "We shot a wyvern, if you recall."

"Oh," the general said. He cocked his head. "But Ametza's protection — we're in her realm, surely Ophidian would respect that?"

"Ophidian is one of the oldest," Mannevy reminded him. "He lives by his own rules."

"I'm sure he has his reasons," Gergen said, careful not to sound critical and trying to avoid glancing nervously to the skies above.

"One of the prisoners said that Ophidian had blinded the guards," the second messenger said in confirmation.

"And they can see now?" Mannevy asked in surprise.

"They have all fled," the messenger said. He glanced toward the general. "Colonel Walpish asks where we can get replacements."

"First we have to get locks, from what you tell me," Gergen said, glancing toward Mannevy.

"It seemed like the doors — at least — will have to be replaced," the second messenger said in agreement.

"You may leave," Gergen said to the first messenger. "Your colonel may need you."

With a nod, the messenger turned his horse around and spurred it into a gallop back out the cobblestoned courtyard.

The second messenger turned to the general, waiting patiently. Gergen glanced toward Mannevy who jerked his head in a dismissive agreement.

"Go," Gergen said to the second messenger. The messenger saluted down to his general from his saddle and nodded toward Mannevy before spurring his horse out the gates.

"I'll let the king know," Mannevy said, turning away. "And I'll talk to Hewlitt." Peter Hewlitt was responsible to Mannevy for spying in — and out of — the kingdom.

"What about Prentice?" Gergen asked. Minister Prentice, the Exchequer and second minister, was responsible for the king's taxes and treasury.

"Of course," Mannevy agreed. "We'll have to dip into our funds."

"And raise taxes," Gergen predicted sourly.

"Which means we'll need the jails for those who won't pay," Mannevy agreed airily. He paused in sudden inspiration. "I have it — an air tax!"

"Air tax?" Gergen said.

"To protect our skies from vermin like wyverns and dragons," Mannevy explained.

"Oh, I see," Gergen replied, not sounding too relieved. "Will it be assessed by acreage of land or per person?"

"Both," Mannevy said, glancing approvingly toward the general.

"That will be hard on the farmers," Gergen grumbled.

"I shall adjust it suitably," Mannevy said, recalling that General Gergen had vast holdings just outside the town. He smiled as he added, "Perhaps I'll include an exemption for those in the king's service."

"I must be about my duties," Gergen said.

"As must I," Mannevy agreed, striding off quickly towards the castle's throne room.

#

"Two weeks, Lord Hewlitt, in two weeks we'll be ready to begin our war," King Markel said to the small, wiry man who knelt before him. "Then, when we make our triumphant entrance into Soria, our queen will suffer a catastrophe."

"At the hands of Sorian spies," Peter Hewlitt agreed, raising his head to meet his king's eyes and smile. "They're in place, they know their duty."

"And the men to handle *them?*" Markel asked. "We can't leave any witnesses."

"I've assigned the troop to hunt them down," Hewlitt replied. "They are troopers in the king's guard, under colonel Walpish."

"But no one *else* knows, do they?" Markel said. "None of the other troopers."

"None," Hewlitt assured him.

"Good," Markel said. "You may go, I can hear that idiot Mannevy returning."

"I shall strive to discover what occurred in the jail," Hewlitt said.

Markel waved him out of the room. Hewlitt left through the secret door that he had discovered years before when Markel had first started to plot the overthrow of his father, King Alavor.

#

"More tea, my dear?" Queen Arivik asked Madame Parkes, hovering the tea pot over the other's fine porcelain cup.

"Indeed, yes!" Suzanne Parkes, the madame of the Inn of the Broken Sun, said with great pleasure.

"It's my own brew, you know," Arivik said with a little giggle. "Guaranteed to fix all that ails you!"

"Oh, indeed your majesty," Madame Parkes agreed easily, raising the now-full cup to her lips and pretending to take a big sip. She knew, from bitter experience, what sort of concoctions Queen Arivik preferred, and Suzanne Parkes wanted a clear head for all her dealings, not one muddied with visions of flying pixies or other small creatures. "You simply *must* let me bring some home for my girls, please say you will."

"I'm sure I can arrange something," the queen returned with an airy wave, raising her cup to her mouth and emptying half of it with great relish. She leaned back in her chair, closed her eyes, and let the visions take her. Some moments later, she opened her eyes again and said, "Now, where were we?"

"I asked if you could supply me with some of your excellent tea," the madame said, careful to not sound irritated with the lengthy delay in their transaction.

"Of course," Arivik said. She waved a hand for one of her servants who approached on her right side from the rear and leaned forward enough to come into the queen's view. "You there, what's your name?"

"Whatever you wish it to be, your majesty," the young lad said with just the slightest hint of fear.

"What was it yesterday," Madame Parkes asked lightly, throwing the lad a warning look. His name was Alain, he was late of the southern lands, and he'd come to Madame

22

Parkes' employment a number of months ago. His features were exotic: blond hair and dark eyes, his build slight and wiry — she knew at once that the lad would be perfect as a consort for the queen.

"Yesterday it was Britches," Alain said.

"Britches! Yes, that was it!" Queen Arivik said. She glanced toward him and smiled with all her teeth. "Tonight I think you'll be 'No Britches!'"

Madame Parkes nodded peremptorily to the young man who swallowed and nodded in return: orders given and received. The Queen would have a pleasant night.

"No Britches," Queen Arivik said, laughing a brittle twinkly laugh, "Madame Parkes would like some more tea."

"No, your majesty," Parkes corrected smoothly, "I misspoke. I asked for some of your marvelous tea to bring back to my girls."

"And why would they want that?" Queen Arivik wondered. The question bored her and she forgot it with a wave of her hand to the young lad. "Just be sure to get what Madame wants, little Britches."

Alain nodded wordlessly and stepped back out of the queen's sight. Madame Parkes followed him with her eyes and give him a slight nod in assurance. Alain had a little sister who was a guest at the Inn of the Broken Sun: he would do everything to ensure that she didn't become an employee. Madame Parkes encouraged him in this notion. She would bide her time: little girls grow and want the pretty things in life; she would ensure that little Lisette would find all the pretty things she wanted at the Inn of the Broken Sun. By then, she knew, Alain would not be in a position to even think to complain, if he were in a position to think at all. The Queen insisted her 'friends' partake of her tea… with very predictable results. Even now, Madame Parkes could see that the sharp young lad she'd sent to the Queen was less sharp than he had been the month before. Soon he would become a vapid, giggling lover of a vapid, giggling queen.

Or perhaps the queen was not so vapid. Just as Madame Parkes was considering ways to make her departure, Queen Arivik reached down to her neck, grabbed her necklace and brought it up to her nose. At the end hung a gleaming red jewel. She sniffed at it and shuddered violently for a moment, before turning, steely-eyed to Madame Parkes.

"What do you know?" Queen Arivik demanded.

"Of what, your majesty?" Parkes asked, trying to sound innocent.

"The jail break, the flight of the airship, the scheming of kings and ministers, what else?" Arivik returned icily.

Madame Parkes took a deep breath and a small sip of her tea.

Chapter Four: Interlude at Ibb's

"The Inn is back that way," Ellen said, pointing back over Rabel's shoulder as he strode briskly down a side street.

"It is," Rabel agreed. "But it is too crowded for us, I think. I know a better hiding place."

Ellen tucked her head against his shoulder to keep from the cold. It was nice to be held, to be warm, even if only on her front. Her backside was exposed to the wind as were her feet, dangling down front and back on Rabel from where he held her single-handedly on his right side. She could feel the strength of him, his taut muscles — he was nothing like the old man she'd met in the jail.

"Why would a god give you gifts?" Ellen asked, not raising her head from his shoulders but trusting her words to reach his ears.

"We made a bargain," Rabel said gruffly. "Now hush and rest. We'll be there soon enough."

#

The maze into the back of Ibb's shop — the *proper* shop — was something Rabel had memorized years before but it still took caution and patience. He made his way slowly, with more caution than he would have used if he'd been unburdened — some of the moves required coordination and his balance was off with the weight of the little girl.

He hit the final touch point and grunted as the shadows in front of him changed. Closing his eyes, he stepped through the portal and gave a small sigh as he felt the air behind him indicate that the 'door' had been closed once more.

"We're safe," he said, shifting his weight to nudge the child.

Ellen blinked and looked around, leaning away from the man to indicate that he could put her down. Rabel did so and she stood, her feet telling her they were standing on wooden floor which had been sanded smooth and coated with varnish. A proper floor. "Where are we?"

"Safe," Rabel repeated.

"Even from the gods?" Ellen asked.

Rabel barked a laugh at her impudence. "Safe enough, then." He took her hand and led the way forward, feeling for and opening a door into a lighter gloom.

Another doorway and they were in a dim light. Rabel moved around, touching some knobs on shapes hanging above them and abruptly the room was much brighter. It took Ellen a moment for her eyes to adjust.

"I know this place!" she said, turning around in excitement. "This is Ibb's lair!"

"And what do you know of Ibb?" Rabel asked.

Ellen's face grew closed and secretive.

Rabel accepted her silence without comment. He pointed forward and to the left. "The kitchen's that way."

"Ibb eats?" Ellen asked in surprise.

Rabel chuckled, shaking his head. "He believes in feeding his guests."

"So what does he eat, if not food?" Ellen asked.

Rabel answered her with a grin and the same silence she'd used earlier. She gave him a sardonic look before gesturing for him to lead the way.

In the kitchen, Rabel rummaged in an icebox — the ice had been replaced by the icemen recently — and pulled out some eggs and milk. He found a well-used pan by the sink and started a fire in the stove.

"How did you do that?" Ellen asked, frowning at the flames glowing under the stove.

"By Ophidian's grace," Rabel told her, raising a finger to his lips to indicate that it was a secret.

"Can you teach me?" Ellen asked.

Rabel frowned in thought. "It's not an easy gift to bear and it comes with a price."

"It'd be nice to be warm," Ellen said hopefully.

"You can be too warm," Rabel warned.

"Fine! I'll bet you can't teach me anyway," she said in a huff.

"The gifts of the gods are dangerous."

"You took them, why can't I?"

Rabel gave her a look then turned back to the stove to scramble the eggs with some of the milk. He put another pot on the stove and set water to boiling.

When the eggs were done, he pulled out some plates and split the eggs between the two. He nodded to Ellen. "Take these to the table. There's salt and pepper there, if you want."

While she was doing that — one plate at a time — her stomach rumbling in excitement, Rabel rummaged through a drawer and pulled out two forks. He waved them at her and she dashed back to get them, placing one beside the far plate and digging in to her food with the other —

"Ahem!" Rabel coughed loudly. She looked up at him. "Say some thanks to the gods. It's only fair."

Ellen gave him a wide-eyed look. "Why? What have they done for me?" Rabel gave her a warning look and she sighed. She closed her eyes and said softly, "Gods, I thank you for this meal. And I thank you for giving me the blue demons. And for the pennies I got from the captain." She paused a long while before adding shyly, "And I thank you for bringing me to Rabel."

"Ophidian…" Rabel began softly, then finished with a deep sigh, "I'm going to regret this, aren't I?"

"What?" Ellen said. "And aren't you afraid to anger the god?"

"Ophidian and I know each other well," Rabel said.

"You know a *god?*"

"I've made bargains with him before," Rabel allowed, turning back to the pot of boiling water and busying himself with making tea. When he was done, he brought the pot on a tray with some milk and two mugs.

Seating himself, he placed a mug in front of her and then himself. He poured the steaming liquid into each cup, adding some milk to his and began to eat his meal.

Ellen had already finished her scrambled eggs and was wondering if she could get more when she noticed her steaming mug. It smelled good. She glanced at Rabel then reached for it. She blew on it as he had and then took a sip.

"Ow!" she cried, nearly dropping the mug to the table. "It's hot!"

"Put some milk in," Rabel told her mildly, gesturing to the bottle.

Ellen glared at him but followed his suggestion. Eyeing the mug dubiously, she tried another sip. When she brought the mug back from her unburnt lips, she smiled at him. "That's good!"

Rabel, who had finished his eggs, sat back in his chair. "What did you learn?"

Ellen gave him a confused look.

"With the tea, and the eggs," Rabel said, gesturing to her mug and empty plate. He turned to gesture toward the stove, "With the stove." He turned back to her. "What did you learn?"

"Huh?"

"How's your tongue?" Rabel asked with a hint of a smile in his eyes.

"It's getting better," Ellen said.

"Good," Rabel said, nodding firmly. "So there's no reason you can't use it." He continued, "So, what did you learn?"

"I learned to let the tea have some milk before I burn my tongue," Ellen said. Rabel nodded and gestured for her to continue. So encouraged, she said, "I learn that you can do something with fire that has to do with a gift from Ophidian." She paused, then asked, "Why not Vorg or Veva?" Rabel gave her a questioning look, so she explained, "They're the gods of fire."

"The young gods of fire," Rabel said in agreement. He shrugged. "It was Ophidian who offered me the bargain, not them." Ellen accepted this with a shrug of her own. Rabel pressed on, "What else?"

"You are friends with Ibb and know your way around his kitchen," Ellen said, feeling on a more solid footing with this, it being close to all the spying she'd done in her past in order to survive. "You don't like the King and you aren't worried about offending our goddess."

"Is she your goddess?" Rabel asked her in a mild tone.

Ellen gave him a worried look, took a breath and let it out, deflated, unused for her answer. Finally, in a small voice, she said, "Everyone says that she is our goddess."

"They do?"

"Everyone except you," Ellen said. She hunched her shoulders and leaned forward to whisper, "She hears everyone and everything."

"Not in this room," Rabel said. "Not in this house."

"How can that be?"

"Ibb," Rabel said. "He made it so that no words uttered in his abode are heard by the gods."

"How did he do *that?*" Ellen asked in wonder.

"I don't know," Rabel told her. "But I know it's true." He nodded toward her. "You can speak freely here."

"I can?"

"And, you should know, the gods usually don't listen to everything we say," Rabel told her. "They listen when you ask and really mean it. Other times they really don't need all the noise."

"Noise?"

"Us," Rabel said, pointing a finger at himself and then at her. "'All that talking is so boring' — those are Ametza's own words. 'Don't you think we've got better things to do with our time?' — that was Ophidian."

"The gods don't listen?"

"Not unless you ask them very carefully," Rabel said. "That's why so many people seek out the shaman. She knows how to get Ametza's attention."

Ellen could only look at him speechlessly. This was an upheaval in her world, in her thinking.

Rabel topped off his tea and gestured to her to see if she wanted the same but she made no response, unmoving.

After a while, Rabel got up and put another pot on to boil while putting the dishes in the sink. When the water was hot, he washed the pots and the dishes, drying them with a towel that he found under the sink. He put everything away, made a gesture to the stove that killed the fire and sat back down in front of the still wordless child.

"What do you know of the gods?" Rabel asked her softly.

Ellen jerked in her chair and met his eyes. "The gods?"

Rabel nodded.

"I know about Ametza, and Ophidian, and Vorg and Veva," Ellen said.

"What about Arolan?" Rabel asked.

"Who?"

"Arolan, Ametza's husband."

"She's married?" Ellen said in surprise. "Does she have any children?" A moment later, she added, "Where is he?"

"Gone," Rabel said. "He's been gone for at least two hundred years now."

"Two hundred years?" Ellen said, trying to imagine such a long time. "Are you that old?"

"No," Rabel said with a chuckle and a shake of his head. "Most people only live sixty years or so."

"You're older than that," Ellen declared stoutly. She saw Rabel's reaction and said, "You made a deal with Ophidian, so you've lived longer."

"I have," Rabel agreed softly.

"What happened to Arolan?" Ellen asked. Before Rabel could continue, she said, "Can you teach me about the gods?" Rabel nodded and she turned to the stove and back to him, asking in a smaller voice, "And how to make fire?"

"I can teach you," Rabel said. Ellen heard the note of caution in his voice and gave him a hopeful look. "But there are rules."

"I'll follow them!" Ellen promised immediately. "I'll be good, I promise!"

"Oh, I doubt you'll be good!" Rabel told her with a laugh. "Just be sure to follow the rules."

"I'll be good anyway," Ellen promised.

"Don't make promises you can't keep, child," Rabel told her sternly. He pointed a finger at her. "*That* is the first rule."

"I'll *try* to be good always," Ellen corrected herself.

"Good enough," Rabel agreed. He rose from his chair and stretched a hand toward her. "First thing, we've got to get you cleaned and dressed."

"Dressed?"

"New clothes," Rabel told her. "Where we're going it will be cold." He led her out of the room. "Have you ever had a bath?"

"I can have a *bath?*" Ellen asked, eyes as wide as saucers. "I heard about them. Rich people at the Inn, they get them." In a smaller voice, she said, "And I can *really* have one?"

"Yes."

#

Rabel had filled the tub with warm water, shown her how to use soap and had left her to her own devices. When, three minutes later, Ellen had brightly declared herself all done, Rabel had entered and had given her a lengthy description of getting into the water, getting wet, soaping up, and rinsing herself off. He'd also pointed to the two very dry towels sitting on the back of the chair and had explained how she would use them to dry herself off. He told her that he'd have clothes for her when she was done. He'd left immediately afterwards. Ellen eyed the warm water airily. She put a finger into it. She put her hand into it. It took her a good while before she was willing to put a toe in.

Thirty minutes later, she came out of the bathroom, dressed in warm clothes, her hair only slightly damp. With a huge smile on her face, she began pledging herself to the goddess of water and the gods of fire.

"Can I do that again?" Ellen begged.

"Later," Rabel told her.

"But it's so much fun!" Ellen squealed. "I see why the rich pay so much to have baths!"

Rabel, who had experience with converts to the glories of warm baths, said nothing.

Chapter Five: Gold Warrior

"So, Mr. Newman, what is it you wish to see me about?" Captain Nevins said, gesturing for the other to sit himself at the other side of his captain's table aboard *Warrior*. He allowed himself a grim smile. "I got the impression that it was neither good news nor the sort you wished to share with minister Mannevy."

"Oh, it's —" Newman began airily.

"I'm not a fool," Nevins cut across him. "Spit it out man, it'll just fester in the dark."

"We had planned on using steel for the engines," Newman said.

"And?" Nevins prompted. He knew what the other was going to say but he wanted to see the mechanic squirm — payback for trying to weasel his words earlier.

"You heard about the jail?"

Nevins snorted. "Who hasn't?"

"I understand that Rabel Zebala is among those missing," Newman said.

"And *he* made your steel!" Nevins declared. "So you don't have any, or enough, so now what?"

"The engines will be built, rest assured," Newman promised, spreading out his hands in assurance.

"That's not my problem," Nevins said. He nodded curtly to the other. "Say on."

"It'll mean that the engines will be heavier," Newman said.

"Just as long as they move the ship, I don't care," Captain Nevins declared.

Newman looked relieved and started to stand only to halt as he saw Nevins' hand waving him back down.

"But if you don't want first minister Mannevy to know…" Nevins said, leaning back in his chair and crossing his hands behind his head, "well, I'm open to persuasion."

Newman dropped back into his chair. "How much persuasion? I have a case of some good port wine, if you're interested."

"That's a start," Nevins said. "But I've in mind something more… flashy… something bright… and gold."

"How much?" Newman asked, figuring he could just include the loss in his price for the engines.

"Say a chest the same size as a good chest of your port wine," Nevins told him. He sat up in his chair and nodded. "Yes, that should be shiny enough for me."

"Very well," Newman said. "I'll be happy to oblige."

"Good," Nevins said, rising from his chair and extending his hand. "Then, Mr. Newman, if there are no other problems, I'll wish you good day."

#

"Newman gave your captain Nevins a cask of port wine and another cask," Peter Hewlitt, the spymaster, told King Markel the next evening.

"Did he?" the king replied. "Care to wager on the contents of the second cask?"

"Gold," Hewlitt said. "Clearly, Mr. Newman was looking for some favor from the captain."

"And my prisoners?"

"We've had no luck in recapturing them," Hewlitt confessed.

"And Rabel Zebala?"

"He is highest on our list, as you ordered," the king's spymaster assured him. "We've offered a reward, of course —"

"For him?" the king asked in a dangerous tone.

"No, for any prisoners who've escaped the king's justice," Hewlitt replied. "And we've got a list of names."

"How much are you offering?" the king asked. Before the other could reply, he said, "Double it."

"Your Majesty?"

"Double it," King Markel said. "Dead or alive."

"Rabel is no use to you dead, sire."

Markel shrugged. "He's no use alive, either."

#

"They're building more airships," Rabel said two days later, as he returned from the docks. He and Ellen had taken turns, dressed in different clothes every day, to spy on the king's men.

"I should tell the captain," Ellen said, reaching for one of her blue demons.

Rabel stopped her with a raised hand. "Wait," he said. "He can't do anything yet and you only have two of them —"

"Three," Ellen corrected.

"Two," Rabel said. "The third will only go if something happens to you."

"What?" Ellen asked.

Rabel said nothing but his eyebrow twitched.

"If I die?"

"That way he'll know," Rabel told her. "Wait to send your demon until you have something important to tell him."

"And if I never find out anything important?"

"Then you'll have three demons to give back to him," Rabel told her with a grin.

"How do you know they're building more airships?" Ellen challenged, not convinced of his reasoning.

"I helped them before," Rabel told her. "I can make steel, dragon steel."

"Dragon steel?"

Rabel nodded. "I can use Ophidian's fire to make iron into steel. Those who use it call it dragon steel because only a dragon's fire is hot enough."

"What about a wyvern's?" Ellen asked. Instantly she regretted her question. Rabel stiffened and shook his head as though he'd been hit. "Sorry."

Rabel raised a hand and shook his head. "It doesn't matter," he told her. He added, "And you're right — I imagine a wyvern's fire would be hot enough. But no one has ever called it wyvern's steel, only dragon steel."

"I'll bet no one ever tried," Ellen said. Rabel cocked his head thoughtfully, then nodded. Ellen took this as encouragement, so she asked, "And if they don't get your dragon steel, they can't make the airships?"

"No," Rabel said, shaking his head. "They have to use iron and that's not as strong."

"And?"

"So they have to use more iron and that adds weight," Rabel said. His eyes gleamed as he added, "I'll bet they're not thinking of that."

30

"What does it mean?"

"It means that their ships will be harder to lift into the air and slower to move in the sky," Rabel told her. He chuckled, saying, "And they haven't pulled the ships out of the water. They're going to get a surprise!'

#

"What's wrong? Why doesn't it fly?" Mechanic Newman demanded of mage Tirpin when they stood under the new balloon aboard *Warrior*.

"I don't know," Tirpin admitted wearily. He tried once again to reproduce the lifting spell. The balloon above them bulged with the lighter air and pulled on the ship… but *Warrior* remained firmly waterbound.

"Gentlemen?" Captain Nevins prodded irritably. "Why are we not flying?"

"Mage Tirpin seems to be having some trouble with his spell," Newman said, nodding toward the blue-robed mage who stood, sweating in the morning cold, under the straining balloon above him.

"Could there be a leak?" Captain Nevins asked, pointing to the huge balloon above them. Under his breath, he added, "Maybe that's why they used so many on *Spite*."

"That was an inferior design!" Tirpin cried, lowering his arms to his side and glaring up at the balloon above him. "Ten balloons meant ten times more weight of fabric! This is much more efficient!"

"What's weight got to do with it?" Captain Nevins demanded.

"The balloon is designed to lift the proper weight," Tirpin said. "If we had more balloons, we'd have to adjust our lift to account for the added weight."

Captain Nevins turned toward the mechanic, who was turning an interesting shade of green. "Ah… Mr. Newman, is there something that you perhaps forgot to relay to our blue-robed acquaintance?"

#

"Here," Rabel said to Ellen in the kitchen. He pointed to the sink which he'd filled halfway with water. "Take this glass, dunk it in the water and turn it so that it's pointing upside down." Ellen, frowning, did as he instructed. "Now pull it up, slowly, from the water." Ellen pulled it up until the glass was halfway out of the water, even though it still had water inside. "The water sticks to the sides of the glass. It'd stick to the sides of anything," Rabel explained. "Slowly, now, pull the glass all the way out of the water. Concentrate on how hard it is."

"It's not that hard," Ellen said, pulling the glass out triumphantly.

"Now, try lifting it," Rabel said. Ellen did as told, giving him a perplexed look. "It's easier, isn't it?"

"But… that's because of the water!"

"Exactly!" Rabel agreed. "Water has a weight of its own but it's also got one other thing."

"What?"

"It likes to hold on to things," Rabel said. "It takes more effort to break free from water than just pulling up the weight."

"And?"

Rabel smiled. "Think about what that pull would be like on something really big."

Ellen thought. And her eyes widened as she said mischievously, "Like a ship?"

"Exactly!"

"It's harder to lift a ship out of water than it is off the ground?"

"On the ground, a ship is only resting on air," Rabel pointed out. "There's no water clinging to its sides."

"So they won't be able to get their ships into the sky?" Ellen asked, smiling at the thought of the king and all his men running around screaming in confusion and rage.

"No," Rabel said, "they'll just need more magic than they imagine."

"When I pulled the glass out, it jumped as it left the water," Ellen said. "Will that —"

"Indeed," Rabel said with a chuckle. "They're going to get quite a surprise!" He took the glass from her and cleaned it with a towel, putting it back into the cupboard gently. "But we won't be here to see it."

"We won't?" Ellen asked in surprise. They'd been at Ibb's for over a week and she'd only just learned how to start the fire in the stove — the normal way, without any magic whatsoever.

"We need to go north," Rabel said. "First we'll stop at my house."

"You've got a house?"

"I did," Rabel said in a sad voice. "We'll get what we need there and then —"

"Then?"

"We'll head north," Rabel told her.

"To the captain?"

"Perhaps," Rabel agreed. "But certainly to keep our word."

"Our word?"

"Well," Rabel said, with a smile, "you did promise to abide by my rules."

Ellen accepted this with a nod. "But that's just *my* word, isn't it?" Rabel nodded. "So what's *your* word?" Before he could answer, she guessed, "The bargain you struck with Ophidian?"

Rabel nodded firmly. Then he raised a finger to her, warningly. "Remember, outside this house, the gods will be listening."

"Well, sometimes," Ellen agreed.

"I should have said: 'The gods *can* hear us,'" Rabel corrected himself.

"What are we going to find at your house?"

"Memories, mostly," Rabel told her in a sad voice, looking down to the ground. He looked up at her. "Memories, and seeds."

"Seeds? What for?"

"For beginnings."

Chapter Six: Ships of the Sky

"*Now* what is it?" Captain Nevins asked tetchily as *Warrior* strained once more to leap into the skies. He pointed to the dock where King Markel and Queen Arivik looked on with ill-concealed despair. "Your King does not look at all happy, mage."

Mage Tirpin shot Nevins a look of pure hatred. The past several days had done nothing to improve Nevins' opinion of the blue-robed mage and his language had reflected that with the result that he had driven Tirpin to rage and despair far too many times.

Nevins wouldn't have done it except that the blue-robed Sorian was so much fun to tease. But he'd thought they'd finally worked out all the kinks in the magic — and the mechanics — necessary to get *Warrior* into the skies. He'd even removed another pair of canon — six-pounders — from his much-reduced armory to facilitate matters.

"I can't — I don't — it's like this damned water is holding us down!" Tirpin cried, gesturing to the sea below.

"Well, of course it is!" Nevins returned hotly. And then he paused. "Are you trying to say you didn't know that?"

"What?" Tirpin barked. "Are you saying that Ametza —?"

"Praise be her name," Nevins interrupted quickly, before the mage brought a flood upon himself — and them. "I am telling you that water holds onto things and you have to account for that." He paused. "Make your spell half again as strong and we should leap to the skies."

"*Half again?*" Tirpin shouted, veins bulging in his head. "Half again, how do you imagine I can do something like that?"

"I imagine you can do it immediately," Nevins returned smoothly, waving his hand toward the royal party at the dockyards, "or his majesty will doubt your skills." He paused, adding silkily, "Perhaps enough even to lighten your shoulders of their burden." He saw that the mage was too flustered to follow him, so he explained, "That is, of your head." He turned toward the stern before the mage could react and bellowed, "All hands! All hands grab tight!"

"Grab tight?" Nevins heard one of his slower 'airmen' — a certain Gates — grumble in confusion. "What's he — *urp!*"

Warrior leapt into the skies, pulling free from the water as though scorched.

Nevins smiled as he raised himself back to his feet and turned to Tirpin. His words of praise were swallowed in alarm when he saw that the mage had collapsed to the deck.

#

"How soon can you get the other in the air?" the king demanded of Mannevy as they watched *Warrior* soar above them.

"Tomorrow, maybe the next day," Mannevy replied suavely. "I understand that mage Tirpin may need some rest —"

"I'm not happy that we've only got the one mage," Markel said. "We need more."

"Indeed," Mannevy agreed. "However we're having trouble finding those with the right sort of abilities —"

"*Mine* are utterly useless," Markel grumbled in agreement, referring to Margen and Vistos, the two ancient mages he had inherited from his father.. He pursed his lips sourly. "That Reedis fellow really was rather special, wasn't he?"

"Mage Tirpin seems more talented to me, sire," Mannevy said. "He can lift *two* ships at once."

"So he says," the king returned mildly.

#

"It's a simple spell," mage Tirpin said, "any half-trained apprentice should be able to do it."

"Sorry, sir," apprentice Tortin Borkis said miserably as the blue-robed mage turned the full power of his scorn upon him. "I tried, sir, I really tried!"

"Try again!" Tirpin screamed, moving right up to the young lad's face, brushing the lad's blond hair back with the power of his breath.

Borkis swallowed. He closed his eyes. He took a deep breath. He raised his arms and executed a slow turn, all the while chanting under his breath.

Above him, the balloon's taut walls grew slack and *Warrior* lurched downwards.

"No, you idiot!" Tirpin shouted, slapping the apprentice, hard. "Now I have to raise it up again!"

"I tried," Borkis said, crumpling to the deck. "I really tried."

"You're useless!" Tirpin said, closing his eyes and raising his arms. Magic flowed from him to the balloon above and *Warrior* ceased her slow descent. She did not, however, regain her lost height.

"Mage Tirpin," Nevins said, his voice taut, "you told us that, once filled, the balloon would remain filled."

"The weavers or balloon-makers or whatever you call them," Tirpin said irritably, "must have botched the seams."

"That's not what you said yesterday," Nevins replied. "You said that the balloon was perfect."

"Don't tell me what I said!" Tirpin barked. He kicked at the crumpled apprentice. "It's all his fault. Get him off your ship."

"And his replacement?"

"I don't have time for that," Tirpin said, glowering at the captain. "I'm to lift *Parvour*—"

"*Vengeance*," Nevins corrected with relish. "The king changed her name when he took her into his service. She's the royal airship *Vengeance*."

Tirpin growled and shook his head. "I'm to get the *other ship* into the air today." He gestured toward the ground below them. "Prepare to land, captain."

"And once we're on the ground, how do we get back into the sky?" Nevins asked. He gestured toward the sad apprentice cowering on the deck. "He's no use, clearly."

"I can say the spell from the deck of *Vengeance* as easily as I can from this deck," Tirpin assured him haughtily.

"Will you have the strength?" Nevins asked, genuine concern in his voice.

"Of course!" Tirpin snapped. "This is child's play!"

Nevins nodded to the limp form of Borkis. "It seems that only *some* children can play this game."

#

"What's the delay?" King Markel demanded testily as they watched the re-named *Vengeance*, waiting for her to leap into the sky and join — well, repeat the flight of — *Warrior*. The king frowned at the frigate, she was supposed to be above *Vengeance*, ready to greet her sister ship to the skies, not hunkered down just above the water, like she was too heavy, wallowing.

"I think it's… mage Tirpin, your majesty," Mannevy said, peering to the deck of the ship beyond. "I think he's having some trouble —"

"He'd best *not!*" the king growled. "He told us that this would be child's play!" A shout from the crowd caught his attention and he looked to see *Vengeance* rise — slowly — into the sky above them. "Is she carrying too many stores?" the king asked his first minister. "She's not nearly as sprightly as *Spite*."

"I imagine they're just being cautious, your majesty," Mannevy said soothingly.

"I suppose it won't matter how fast they get into the sky, just that they fly above everything else," the king allowed.

"Indeed, sire," Mannevy agreed. He turned his attention to *Warrior* and hid a frown. Tirpin had promised that he could lift the two ships by himself but then he'd demanded an apprentice — the same hangdog lad who was now skulking back toward town at the edge of the crowd — and now he seemed incapable of filling *Warrior's* balloon with lift.

"Rise!" Tirpin's voice carried from the rear of *Vengeance*. Mannevy had a brief glimpse of a man dressed in expensive blue robes — lined with gold filigree, no less, as the treasury had pointed out quite needlessly earlier — before Tirpin collapsed from sight.

Mannevy turned his attention to *Warrior*. The larger ship moved upwards. It was painful to watch, like a drunkard falling from the sky… only backwards. Finally the frigate steadied up, a good five hundred feet below *Vengeance* — too low to safely deploy her propellers.

King Markel turned his head and beckoned Mannevy to lean close. "We need to find another mage."

#

"Ah, that's a sad sight, isn't it?" Rabel said, pointing back to the town far in the distance.

"What?" Ellen asked, craning her neck to peer behind her.

"Here," Rabel said, lifting her to his shoulders and turning back to the town that they'd left hours ago aboard the northbound train.

The crew on the train had greeted Rabel like a hero and had allowed him to show Ellen the boiler and blow the whistle before the train sped away from the town and out into the country.

Now, many miles north, they were trudging the final two miles from the station to Rabel's farm.

"I see a smudge," Ellen said.

"And a bump," Rabel said. "That bump is one of the airships." He chuckled. "But where's the other?"

"I see it!" Ellen said, bouncing up and down on her perch. "It's there, it's there! It's just — lower than the other."

"Lower?"

"Yes," Ellen said. "And it doesn't look the same. The higher one has some big white things at the end and they're spinning slowly."

"The propellers," Rabel told her. "Slowly?"

"Very slowly," Ellen said. "Not like *Spite*."

"I suspected as much," Rabel said, turning back to head toward his farm.

"What's it mean?" Ellen said, looking down at the top of his head with its full mane of black hair.

"It means the king has made a fool of himself," Rabel said with a laugh. "It's a good thing we got out of town when we did or he'd be after us."

#

Rabel's farm was covered in a thick layer of snow as was the surrounding countryside. The kitchen door was unlocked and opened easily. Rabel dropped Ellen from his shoulders before they entered.

"Start the fire," he told her.

"Which way?" Ellen asked.

He smiled at her and shook his head — he'd leave that up to her.

Ellen smiled back and moved forward, her hands hovering over the iron of the stove, her eyes closed as she said the words he'd taught her. Nothing happened. She opened her eyes and looked up to Rabel.

"It's always best to see if there's fuel," Rabel told her, his eyes twinkling. He moved forward and opened the grating. He gestured and she saw that it was empty. "It's never a good idea to leave the start of a fire untended."

Chastised, Ellen reached for several likely logs and put them into the grate. She closed it and then repeated the spell. She gave a cry of delight when light and heat erupted from inside the grate. "I did it, I did it!"

"Yes, you did, child," Rabel assured her, patting her on the shoulder. "So, what's next?"

In the past few days, Ellen had learned that Rabel was always teaching, always had a lesson in mind. She also discovered that she *loved* learning. Especially magic — or witchcraft — whichever worked best for the job.

"The difference between witchcraft and magic is whether you're using your heart to reach the gods or whether you're using your head," Rabel had explained to her.

"But if you do witchcraft you need something special, like blood," Ellen had said.

"You need energy to do magic," Rabel countered. "There's always something you must offer the gods for their favor." He pursed his lips. "A witch can do her magic all day long if she's got the supplies —"

"— like blood —"

Rabel accepted her interjection with an approving nod. "— but a mage can only do so much magic every day or he'll —"

"— she'll —" Ellen corrected.

"— *he* or *she* will collapse from fatigue," Rabel had finished, giving her a sardonic nod.

Now, in the kitchen, he looked at her and asked again, "So what's next?"

"We need food, hot food, hot water, and supplies," Ellen said. She glanced around the kitchen. "Is there anything here to eat?"

"Why don't you find out?" Rabel asked, turning to close the split doors of the kitchen entrance and moving toward the stairs at the far end of the room.

"What are you going to do?"

"I'm getting us supplies," Rabel said. His lips quirked. "First, I'll see to the gods."

"What, are they here?" Ellen asked in surprise.

"They're always with us," Rabel reminded her. He pointed up the stairs. "But this is personal." He turned back to her. "Get us something to eat, Ellen, while I get this done." He frowned. "We might stay here the night but not longer."

"Because the king will come looking," Ellen guessed.

"Or worse," Rabel agreed.

"So we'll set wards?" Ellen guessed, allowing herself a smile when she caught Rabel's pleased expression. "Should I start now?"

"No," Rabel said. "Usually, wards should be done before fires, but we've a bit of time and we'll need the food to stoke our spirits."

Ellen nodded, turning to the cupboard and pulling open the door to peer inside.

#

"We've got him!" Vistos cried as he rushed into the king's bedchamber.

"What?" the king huffed, disturbed in his sleep. "What is this? It had better be good!"

"Rabel, sire!" Vistos crowed. "My wards detected him at his home."

"Good," the king said, coming to his senses. "And the trap?"

"Set, ready to be triggered," Vistos promised.

"Get General Gergen, have him send a troop at once," the king said. "And leave me!"

Minutes later the courtyard rang with the sound of iron hooves on hard cobblestones. King Markel grunted at the noise, rolled over in his bed, and was soon back to sleep.

Chapter Seven: Rabel's Oath

Rabel paused at the entrance to Krea's room, his face a mix of emotions. With a sigh, he pushed the door fully open and moved toward the window. He knelt down, found her sacred place and gently took the figurines from the shelves and put them in the small wooden chest, saying their names as he deposited each one. Ophidian he kept for last.

"I am here," he said, picking up the figurine. "I have done as you required. The wards are not set. We shall be ready to depart. Send him."

The dragon-god's red eyes opened and Rabel felt the full power of the god's intent upon him. *You must call him yourself.*

Abruptly, as though burnt, Rabel dropped the figure — only to catch it with his other hand before it hit the floor. With a scowl, he transferred the figurine into the chest.

She should learn the calling.

"What?" Rabel barked in surprise. "The bargain — our bargain —!"

She must learn the calling. You cannot do it alone.

"We have to eat, to set wards —"

They are coming. If you do not call him, you will die. The red eyes, partly obscured by the soft black velvet of the chest, closed and Rabel felt the god's presence disappear.

With a shout, he bundled up the chest, put it in the sack he carried over his shoulder and bolted back down the stairs.

#

Ellen looked up at the loud shout and the sound of Rabel barreling down the stairs. "What is it?"

"Trouble," Rabel told her, pushing past her and dropping a bar across the kitchen door. He raced away and she could hear him doing the same to the front door before he appeared once again in the kitchen. "They're after us."

"Now?"

"Now," Rabel said, nodding. He took a breath. "I've got to teach you something. Something I thought you could learn later."

"What?" Ellen asked. She glanced around the kitchen, her eyes on the two windows that looked down the road. "Do we have enough time?"

"If we don't, we die," Rabel said. He frowned, looking to the ground, then looked up to catch her eyes. "What do you know of dragons?"

"They're not wyverns," Ellen said quickly, "they have four limbs and two wings, they breathe fire, and they're enemies of Ametza." She put a hand to her mouth in worry and glanced toward the ceiling, fearful that the goddess had heard her.

"They're children of Ophidian," Rabel told her. "And, like wyverns, they're twin-souled."

"Like your daughter?" Ellen asked in a soft, awkward voice.

Rabel nodded. "Like her," he agreed. He looked up to the ceiling. "We're going to summon one." He lowered his head to catch her eyes again. "I'm to teach you how."

"Why would anyone want to summon a dragon?" Ellen asked in surprise. Rabel gave her *that* look — the one that told Ellen she had to find the answer herself. "Are we going to *ride* the dragon?"

Rabel smiled and gave her a pleased nod. "It's that or be taken by the king's men." He gestured her toward the stairs.

"But the food!" Ellen protested. Rabel sniffed at the pot, smiled at her, and ducked into the pantry, pulling out a large sack which he threw to her. Ellen caught it in surprise and nearly staggered under the weight.

"Always keep travel rations handy," Rabel told her. "They taste awful but they'll keep forever."

Ellen, who'd eaten many strange things, merely to keep body and soul from meeting the Ferryman, rather doubted that they tasted *that* bad.

"Come on," Rabel said, pushing her toward the stairs. "You can see my daughter's room before we burn it."

"Burn it?"

"There are too many secrets here," Rabel told her. "And the fire will help attract the dragon."

Ellen was too rushed to take in the various pieces of artwork hung on the way up the stairs. She paused just long enough to brush her hand against one piece.

"Redwork," Rabel said, pulling the piece off the wall and handing it to her. "Put it in your bag. You can give it to Krea, maybe, someday."

"Krea made it?" Ellen asked, clutching the piece tighter to her chest. She wondered what it would be like to meet the wyvern, the union of Rabel's daughter and something much different.

"She did," Rabel agreed. He pointed toward a door. "That's her room, we go there."

Ellen entered the room and saw treasures beyond her imagining. "It's beautiful!"

Rabel snorted. "It did its job," he allowed. "But it was a small room, when all's said."

Ellen, who'd never seen a prettier bed, nor a nicer coverlet, kept silent.

Rabel stopped her by the window. "When the time's right, we'll open it," he told her. He put down the sack he was carrying. He turned to the chest of drawers and opened them. "See if there's anything that might fit you while I set the kindling downstairs."

"Kindling?" Ellen squeaked. "For a fire?" Rabel nodded. "But we're still in the house!"

"That's what the king's men will say," Rabel agreed, bounding out of the room and down the stairs. His voice carried back up the stairs. "There's a chest there. Find Ophidian and pull him out."

Ellen felt odd pawing through Rabel's sack but she did as ordered. She found the chest. It wasn't all that big, not much larger than her two hands but thick. She pulled it out and opened it, pausing to gasp as she took in all the carved figurines that gazed up at her.

"Ophidian," Ellen said to herself, looking at the figures and wondering which one represented that god. She saw a scaled creature with folded wings and grabbed it. She felt a warmth from it. She pulled it up to her face and said, "Nice to meet you."

The figurine's eyes flared red for a moment then closed again.

"I found him!" Ellen called out, hoping to catch Rabel's ears. "Now what?"

"We're to summon his son," Rabel called, his voice climbing up the stairs. He was in the doorway just as Ellen turned to him and said, "His son?" Rabel nodded. "Gods have sons?"

"And daughters," Rabel said, moving to stand beside her. He gestured for her to place the figurine just under the window. "And the sons and daughters have children of their own."

39

"Are they all gods?" Ellen asked in awe.

Rabel shook his head. "No," he said firmly. "But they have more ability than those who don't carry a god's blood."

"Am… I…?"

Rabel shook his head. "I don't think so," he told her softly. "But — remember — I said *ability*. Ability is a chance, not a guarantee."

"But… the fire…" Ellen said, feeling both surprised that discovering she was not a child of a god upset her so much, and amazed that she could even be so bold as to *hope* for such a thing.

"Tonight you will learn how to summon a dragon, Ellen," Rabel said. "Most people cannot do it."

"So how do you know I…?"

"I made a bargain with Ophidian," Rabel said, nodding toward the figurine. "And he told me." He gestured again to the god and then moved beyond to open the window. Cold air with bits of snow rushed in and froze the room. "Close your eyes and think of fire," Rabel instructed. Ellen closed her eyes.

"Ophidian has made a bargain with me," Rabel said. His tone changed and his voice rose above the wind as he continued, "Ophidian, I, Rabel Zebala, wielder of the dragon's fire do accept your bargain. Life given, lives guarded." He nudged Ellen who opened her eyes to peer up at him. "Three lives I'll guard for you, even beyond death." Ellen's eyes widened at his promise. Who could promise beyond death? He smiled down at her. "Ellen Unnamed is under my care, with your blessing, to guide to her doom or destiny as the gods decree. By my word, she will not starve. By my word, she will not sicken. By my word —"

Get on with it! The words were raspy in Ellen's brain; it took her a moment to associate it with the dragon figurine in front of them, its eyes wide and flaring with red.

"Touchy, touchy!" Rabel chided the god with a half-smile. "My word, then. And my word for my daughter, Krea —"

Already given — get on with it!

"And the third life — your son, Jarin," Rabel said. "I so pledge my word to provide the same."

Call him! Both *of you!*

"Jarin, son of Ophidian, I call you," Ellen said now, loudly, looking out into the night sky. Suddenly she found words inside her that she'd never imagined. "Red and black dragon of pure flame, I call you! My aid for your aid, my blood for your blood —" she winced as she felt her finger pricked and looked to see Rabel holding a small pin against her finger "— I so promise."

"Jarin, dragon, friend of wyverns, I call you to us," Rabel said, pricking his own finger and letting the blood drop on the dragon figurine, indicating that Ellen should do the same. "I am pledged to your father and by his bond to you, your debt to him, I call you for your debt to me." He glanced to Ellen. "To us, fire-born. Come and carry us away, as your father wishes."

Ellen closed her eyes, trying to ignore the pain of the prick in her finger. She imagined the bright red dragon, imagined his flaming breath, imagined him swooping —

"Open up! In the king's name!" A voice boomed loudly outside in the snow.

"And hurry up, please!" Ellen added in a small voice.

"Fire and flame!" Rabel shouted down the stairs. Ellen felt his magic fly past her and, a moment later, the bottom of the stairs brightened in the red of flames.

40

"Out the window, now," Rabel said, urging her up, dropping the figurine back into the chest and thrusting it into his sack. "Careful, the snow is slippery!"

#

Colonel Walpish reined in his horse as his troops dismounted outside the farmhouse. He nodded as they stood guard around the two doors and he marched up the steps to the front door, pounding loudly. "Open up! In the king's name!"

He waited a moment then waved his men forward to smash in the door. They started forward but he stopped them with a raised hand — he'd heard something inside. And then he leapt back as the inside of the house brightened.

"Fire!" One of his troopers cried unnecessarily, jumping back from the farmhouse.

"Stand away, men!" Walpish called. "Stand back!"

"There's a well, sir," a trooper called out, pointing. "We could get some buckets —"

His words were cut off by a cry of surprise from one of the mounted troops. He pointed to the sky. "Look!"

Flame flared above them and they heard a harsh cry from the sky.

"A dragon!" a trooper called. Walpish frowned at the man. *Really, was he stupid?*

"Stand back!" Walpish ordered, directing his words toward the oaf who had twice stated the obvious.

The dragon descended toward the house, breathing fire over the eaves, stooped, seemed to pause for a moment, and hauled itself upwards, back into the dark night and the white snow.

#

"This better be good," Jarin growled as he heaved himself up into the night sky. "I am not *summoned* by mortals like I was a pet."

"I think you're wonderful!" the little girl said as she draped herself over his back, nuzzling her chin against his shoulder. "And thank you for saving us, son of Ophidian!"

"Well," Jarin huffed, "I might let *you* stay." He flicked his shoulders, feeling the weight of the man riding on him. "Him, I don't know about."

"He swore an oath to your father," the girl said. She continued quickly, "He's Rabel, and he used to be old but your father made him young again so that —"

"So that I could be of service," the man interjected smoothly.

"To me?" Jarin asked in surprise, though the notion pleased him.

"And your father," Rabel added with a bow from his waist — Jarin could feel the change in weight above him. "And Ellen here. And one other."

"Very pleased to meet you, Ellen," Jarin called over her shoulder.

"Thank you!" the young girl said in a light piping voice that irrationally pleased Jarin no end.

"Who's the other?" Jarin asked Rabel.

"You've met her," Ellen said. "She's his daughter, only she's a wyvern now."

"You know Wymarc?" Jarin cried.

"Wymarc?" Rabel repeated in surprise. "No, I know Krea. She's my daughter."

"Well, well," Jarin said, "this *is* interesting." He paused a moment, changed course and resumed climbing at greater speed. "I can help you find her."

"Thank you," Rabel said. "But your father has a different journey in mind for us."

"Does he?" Jarin asked in a defiant tone. "And what journey is that?"

"He wants us to go north, to Soria," Rabel said. "He wants us to warn them that Markel is sending airships their way." He paused. "He wants us to prepare to defend them."

Jarin was silent for a long while. Finally, he said, "I can take you there."

Snow Serpent

Book 7

Twin Soul series

Prolog

"Rest, you're going to need your strength," mage Reedis said as he lowered captain Ford to the snowy ground. Although, given the smoke and flames rising from the distant wreck of captain Ford's command — the once-proud royal airship *Spite* — the injured man was, at this moment, captain of nothing.

Spite had been destroyed by a wrathful wyvern — the same sort of beast it had been built to destroy — and the accidental explosion of the guns firing from its bow.

"Pfah!" Ford said, making a face. "We're leagues from anywhere, we're going to freeze before the dawn."

This was true: they were resting on hard-packed snow, centuries old. All around them there was nothing to see but frozen plains and, rising in the distance, a threatening mountain range with a forlorn — and very high — pass somewhere in it midst.

Of course, even before her destruction, *Spite* was a dying ship: an airship lost in the frozen north without fuel. In desperation, Ford had ordered the crew to fire off the remaining shot and powder for the guns in the hopes of attracting attention.

They had. They'd attracted the attention of the wyvern. Which would have been an entirely different proposition had not one of the two bow guns not suddenly exploded, probably from improper — or too hasty — handling.

The wyvern's wrath on seeing the explosion had included destroying as many of the airship's ten lifting balloons as it could before turning her attention to the ship's wooden hull, setting it alight with her wyvern's flames.

Captain Ford had done all he could help his crew abandon ship — hundreds of feet in the air falling into a frozen waste — but was himself trapped in his cabin after seeing to the safety of his cook and his friend, mage Reedis. Reedis had surprised himself by ordering Annabelle to destroy his safety balloon and falling back to the crashing stern of *Spite* in a bid to rescue captain Ford from his trap. He'd failed — at least until crown prince Nestor had surprised everyone by charging the stern with an axe and cutting away the window frame that had trapped the captain. But the vengeful wyvern had carried Nestor off in its talons before he could complete the job. He'd done enough, however, and Richard Ford had flown out of his cabin on the bottom end of another of mage Reedis' magical safety balloons. Reedis had grabbed on hastily and they'd floated to the ground, falling faster than desirable and landing — hard — on the cold plains below.

"We won't freeze until our fire dies," Reedis said, surprising Ford by throwing a bundle of broken planks onto the ground and setting it alight with his magic.

"You should leave me here," Ford said. He pointed to his splinted leg. "There's no way I can walk far. You could, though."

"I didn't come back for you on the ship to leave you here on the frozen ground," Reedis said testily.

"The fire's warm," Ford said thoughtfully. He glanced to Reedis. "I'd be safe here. You could go on, maybe find some help —"

"Richard, that's enough!" Reedis snapped. "We are either going to get through this together or we're going to die together!"

"Why —" Ford's brow creased. "Do you know, mage Reedis, I don't think I ever learned your first name."

"That's because I don't like it," Reedis said sharply. "It was my father's, I think —"

"Think?" Ford interrupted. An awkward silence grew between them and then Ford waved a hand at the mage. "Oh, I'm sorry. I didn't know."

"No reason you should," Reedis said. He stared at the fire for a moment before looking up. "It's Karol."

"Karol?"

"My first name," Reedis said.

"Oh," Ford said. He glanced to the fire. "It's not a bad name, all things considered."

"I go by Reedis," the mage said curtly.

"Very well," Ford said. He raised his eyes to meet the mage's, saying, "It has been a pleasure working with you, mage."

"So what's next?" Reedis said. "You said we should avenge Nestor, I believe."

"We should," Ford said. He roused himself, leaning up on an arm, wincing as the movement jerked his broken leg. "I have no respect for a King who wants me to commit the murder of his own son."

"His son?" Reedis asked mildly.

"I've heard the rumors," Ford said with a wave of his hand. "If the prince is a bastard, I guarantee this — he's Markel's bastard."

Reedis snorted with laughter. "Yes," he said when he'd recovered. "I can see why you would say that."

"You know," Ford said thoughtfully, closing his eyes to concentrate better on his words, "I could see how, with some training, some guidance, someone to mentor him, he might turn out to be a good king, even better than his father."

"You do?"

"I do," Ford said. "In fact —"

"Richard," Reedis interrupted him in a frightened voice — a voice that didn't come from the direction of the last voice.

Ford opened his eyes and glanced toward the mage. Reedis gestured with wide eyes toward where Ford had heard the other voice.

"I'm glad to hear that," the owner of the voice said. "Because I have a job for you two. One that deals directly with crown prince Nestor."

Ford glanced at the speaker, frowning. He knew that face.

The owner of the face saw his confusion and smiled. "Imagine me with a beard. Older." He paused as he saw Ford's continued confusion. "Frozen."

"And as large as a mountain," Reedis said in a very small voice.

"Exactly," the god Arolan said with a nod and a smile. He gestured to the distance. "I think this conversation is better carried out —"

And suddenly there were in a white room, warm, and both of them were in adjoining beds as the god Arolan continued —

"— when you've had a chance to rest and recover."

Chapter One

"Really, Arolan!" a woman's voice cried in disgust as she burst through the doorway. "Don't you ever think to *knock!*"

"Sorry, Avice," the water god replied. He gestured toward Ford. "This one has a broken leg and I know that you're the only one to handle them properly."

"Flatterer!" Avice said with a smile. She moved over to Ford and ran her hand over his leg where it lay under the sheets. She frowned and said to Ford, "That's a nasty one." She closed her eyes. "All better now." She glanced at Reedis. "You heard the god. You should be resting." She expanded her gaze to include Ford. "*Both* of you."

She motioned Arolan to the door, leaving the two men fast asleep behind them.

Arolan glanced around the corridors as they left the infirmary room and said to Avice, "It's a bit *white* isn't it?"

"Feeling cold?" Avice asked him with a grin. "Two centuries of snow a bit much for you, water god?" Avice had no problem teasing him: she was a god even older than himself. Arolan was one of the younger gods. He was the god of water just as Ametza, his much-estranged wife — two centuries is long enough to qualify as estrangement, even for an immortal god — was the goddess of water. Arolan preferred the sea somewhat more than Ametza, who preferred to spend her time with rivers and lakes — and the humans who had slowly spread out across the expanse of Toreen's World. Mother Toreen was said to be sleeping — leaving her children, the gods, to play in comfort in the world she had created for them. Humans had been created a very long time ago and had proven endlessly amusing — to some gods more than others.

"I'd like to see some blue," Arolan confessed. Avice snorted and shook her head at him in amusement, waving a hand in a go-ahead gesture. "And some green," Arolan added as he nodded graciously to her. The corridors were suddenly decked out with the colors of the sea, sea-foam, and white breakers, artfully added to the pure white marble décore.

"Ophidian has decorated the main corridor up by the hall," Avice informed him. "Apparently your artistry inspired him."

Arolan snorted. "He and I shall have words."

"I expect," Avice said, guiding him toward the dining hall. "In the meantime, you should eat. You're probably hungry after being frozen for so long." She stopped before a door which was now decorated in light green accents with deep blue hues. "I have to prepare some concoctions for the others —"

"Others?" Arolan said. "Some of Ophidian's?"

Ophidian was an older god, like Avice, but quite different in outlook. Arolan and Ophidian — the dragon god — had had more than one encounter in their long lives. Arolan had rarely enjoyed the outcome.

"And others from the wreck," Avice said in agreement. She turned back the way they'd come, saying, "I presume you have plans for your two."

"Some," Arolan said in agreement, his eyes twinkling with amusement. "Though I've no doubt that dear Ophidian has something in his mind." He paused a moment and added in a different tone, "Not to mention Ametza."

"You haven't talked to her yet," Avice guessed, watching the younger god shrewdly. Arolan shook his head, "I'd like to keep my return a secret for a while."

"You came to the wrong place for that!" Avice told him.

"With your help, then," Arolan said, bowing toward her. "You and Terric were always discreet."

"Very well," Avice said, opening the door to her apothecary. "Do see Sybil, she's got something especially tasty for you. Fit for a god."

"I should hope!" Arolan said with a laugh, waving in farewell and moving quickly to the dining hall.

#

"Sybil!" Arolan cried in joy as he jumped over the counter to the kitchen, hugging the goddess tightly. "How I've dreamed of you!"

"Why, Arolan! And what will your charming wife say?" Sybil said, hugging him back with all her might.

"She'll probably say '*urp!*' when I squeeze her traitorous neck," Arolan growled in response.

"Lover's quarrels!" Sybil said, pushing herself away from him and eyeing him critically. She grabbed a tray and pushed it on him. "Eat this, you'll feel better!"

"More ambrosia?" Arolan asked, eyeing the god-sized bowl of orange simmering stew in front of him.

"And what else?" Sybil said with a laugh. "I put this on the stove especially for you when mother said you'd returned."

"Join me?" Arolan said as he started back to the dining hall, looking for a table.

Sybil shook her head. "I'm going to leave you to your food and your murderous thoughts."

Arolan smiled at her, saying, "You're always looking out for my best interests!"

Sybil laughed. "How many thousands of years has it been and you *still* haven't killed her?" She waved him away. "Admit it — she is your soul mate."

Arolan gave her a sour look but took his tray to a table and began eating with a murderous intensity. He turned back to shout to Sybil. "Where is Ophidian?"

"He's around," Sybil said, turning back to her kitchen. "You can kill him later. Eat first."

"I wasn't *planning* on killing him," Arolan said, knowing that Sybil would hear, adding in a different tone, "but it's a thought."

"So if you weren't planning on killing him," a different voice spoke up, right beside Arolan, "and thank you for that — why do you want him?"

Arolan smiled at the god seated next to him. "Hello, Terric, and you're welcome. I wouldn't want to put you and Bryan to unnecessary trouble." The god of death nodded and raised an eyebrow, imploring Arolan to answer his question. Arolan sighed. "I've been out there in the frigging snow for the past two centuries because I did a good deed."

"That's not my department," Terric said with a wave of his hand. "But as you're obviously *dying* to tell me, pray, what good deed was that?"

"One of Ophidian's get came my way," Arolan said, scooping up a large spoonful of the orange stew and swallowing it loudly. "A twin soul. Only with one soul."

"Oh?" Terric said, eyebrows going high on his forehead. "That's dangerous. We had that trouble with another just recently —"

"A dragon," Arolan said, shaking his head. "Matched him up with a child, as I understand. And the twin soul calls itself Jarin, after the boy." He frowned, shaking his head. "Just Jarin."

"And how do you know that?" Terric asked him sharply. "Weren't you a frozen ornament these past two centuries?"

"I still have followers," Arolan said, tapping his forehead knowingly. "They worship me, tell me things."

"You've got one at least in the infirmary," Terric allowed. "A most interesting young man."

Arolan smiled. "Richard Ford. I like to keep good ones around."

"You and Ophidian, both," Terric said with a note of disapproval in his voice.

"You're not complaining are you?" Arolan asked in a tone of alarm. "I thought you'd be glad not to have the extra work."

"No, I'm not complaining," Terric said. "But it's a circle, you know." He made a circling motion with the forefinger of his right hand. "Life. Death. Life. You and Ophidian are stretching it all out of shape with your favorites."

Arolan stirred unhappily in his seat. "Didn't I pay the price?"

Terric burst into a grin. "So you noticed? Two centuries as frozen stone got your attention, did it?"

"It was rather hard to ignore," Arolan said with a grunt. Then his expression changed. "But I had a lot of time to think."

"Yes, I would imagine," Terric said. Wistfully, he added, "Must be comforting, all that time."

"Like your garden," Arolan agreed with a nod.

"And what did you grow in your frozen garden of thought?" Terric asked him.

"Ideas," Arolan said. He gave the god of death an unhappy look. "Something is not right. Something is out of balance."

"Agreed," a boy's voice added. Aron, god of judgement.

"Well, hello," Arolan said, reaching out his free hand and ruffling the young boy's head. "Did you miss me?"

"You paid your price," Aron said.

"And Ophidian?"

"He paid his price long ago," Aron said, a sad look on his face.

"We need a soul for that dragon," Arolan said firmly. "It'll be moving soon, without me to keep it frozen. It's been nearly a week, now."

"Yes," Aron agreed. "And we've got another imbalance."

Arolan quirked an eyebrow upwards in question.

"A *kitsune* twin soul was betrayed," Aron said.

"A *kitsune* found a twin?" Arolan asked in surprise. The land-based twin souls rarely called for his attention but he liked to keep up with the works of his siblings. The *kitsune* had become interesting not just because they were Moon-born but because they'd famously never found a human soul twin. "Why didn't I hear of this?"

"I'm not saying that you might want to gather more followers," Terric muttered sardonically, "but it is obvious none of them were close enough to the matter to learn of it."

Arolan frowned. He nodded to Terric, tacitly accepting his suggestion. "What happened?"

Quickly Aron sketched the events that led up to the judgement in the hall of the gods that left the girl, Hana, behind and her *kitsune*, Meiko, bound to Lyric, twice-murderer.

"We should have words with Ibb," Arolan said. "He has much to answer." Ibb the mechanical had spent thousands of years learning knowledge. Arolan had heard some mutter that he knew more than any other god except the Mother herself.

"If you bring him here, I shall have to judge him," Aron warned.

"He has warped the circle of life," Terric added sternly.

"You know why he does it," Arolan said to them.

"None the less," Aron said.

Arolan threw up his hands. "I'm not doubting you, little brother. But Ibb has become... interesting."

Aron smiled. Terric pursed his lips tightly but, at Arolan's prodding look, unbent enough to nod in agreement.

"You should talk with Ophidian," Aron said as Arolan emptied his bowl of stew.

"I shall wait for the mortals to wake and recover," Arolan said. He'd left his two in the good care of Avice who'd mended Ford's broken leg before sending them to sleep.

"And Ametza?" Aron asked.

"I have been thinking of her a great deal," Arolan said, smiling. It was not a pleasant smile.

Chapter Two

Annabelle was shivering with the cold. She didn't know how long it had been since she'd last seen anyone. The snow was blinding her and her breathing hurt. Worse, it seemed that no matter how hard she tried, she couldn't get enough air into her lungs. The strange belt that Ford had given her had transformed itself into a magical lifting balloon and hauled her free from the wreck of the *Spite*. At mage Reedis' urging, she'd used her knife to puncture the mage's own lifting balloon so that he could fall back onto *Spite* and attempt to free Captain Ford. But that had been hours back.

Ice clung to her eyebrows and the tops of her ears. Her nose was nearly frozen, and she couldn't feel her fingers or toes.

Suddenly, the cold seemed to vanish from her. She glanced around hopefully in the dimness of the snow storm. Was help coming her way?

You are dying, a voice said to her. *The air is too thin for you to breathe. Your body is saving you the pain as you freeze to death.*

Are you Terric, the god of death? Annabelle thought.

No, silly, came the quick reply, *I'm just your mind. Terric is too important a god to waste his time on you personally. The gods have no time for you!*

That's not true! Annabelle thought heatedly. She knew better. All her life she had used her devotion to the gods to create spells, build potions, make her witch craft. And Reedis had used magic — 'the brains of the gods' as Richard had so aptly called it — to make the airship fly. The steam engine was magic, too: built with the steel that only Ophidian's flame could create. *The gods care.*

So why is it that you're floating higher and higher, freezing to death?

I don't know, Annabelle admitted. If she had a knife, she could puncture the balloon like she'd done for the mage. But, she realized, she was very high in the sky. The fall would kill her. *There must be a lesson here*, she thought after a moment. She already knew that cold air would freeze her. What else was she learning floating so high in the sky?

The air gets thin up here, Annabelle realized. *Too thin to breathe.* The revelation pleased her and she thought, *I must tell Reedis.*

"If you want to do that, you're going to need help," a voice said in her right ear. Annabelle twisted her head around. The voice continued, "What will you do for it?"

Ophidian, Annabelle thought. *What is your game?*

To know, little one, you'll have to bargain, Ophidian said in her head.

"You don't have permission to be in my head," Annabelle croaked out loud.

You've been asking for warmth and life, that *was my permission.*

Trickster!

Of course, the dragon god replied with pleasure. *Now, what do you offer?*

Nothing, Annabelle said.

Ophidian was shocked at her refusal… and intrigued. He left the question floating between them.

You want something from me, Annabelle said. *Or you wouldn't be here.* She was silent in her own head for a moment as she thought rapidly. *It's Richard, isn't it?*

Arolan has him, the fire god admitted.

Annabelle would have smiled if she could move her lips that far. *Very well, hear my bargain: I will help Richard for a week, if you save me.* She imagined bargaining with the dragon god from her initial offer for a good while before they reached agreement. Ophidian was a notorious haggler.

Done!

Annabelle had just enough time to blink in surprise before she found herself in a bed, in a white room, in a place she'd never seen before.

"You used this one hard," a woman's voice said sternly to someone out of Annabelle's sight — Ophidian, she was certain. The woman turned to Annabelle and said one word: "Sleep."

#

Arolan found Ophidian in the Hall of the Gods at the end of the main corridor in this, the House of Life and Death. The Hall of the Gods contained statues of all the known gods and, given that it was part of the building created by Avice and Terric — the gods of Life and Death — Arolan had no reason to imagine that it didn't contain images of *all* the gods. Except their Mother, of course.

"You've got some explaining to do," Arolan said to Ophidian when he met him.

"Always," Ophidian agreed. He gave Arolan an amused look. "You're a bit slow, so I expect no less."

Arolan ignored the taunt. He'd gotten better in dealing with the older god over the course of thousands of years.

"What are going to do?" Arolan demanded. His lips twitched as he taunted, "You can't me expect to shed dragon tears over *this*."

Ophidian snorted at the younger god's attempt at humor.

"I don't want it killed," Arolan offered as a starter.

"No," Ophidian agreed with a snort that hid a threatening growl, "you *don't* want it killed."

"So we need to control it," Arolan said.

"And there's only one way to do that," Ophidian agreed. He sighed, glancing over at the sea god. "King Markel had *Spite* made into an airship with the hopes of winning wars and killing wyverns."

"And dragons," Arolan said. He raised an eyebrow as he added, "And didn't he get some help from the gods?"

Ophidian grinned slyly. "He might have."

"I don't understand why you would want him striking at the wyverns and dragons," Arolan muttered.

"That was merely a means to an end," Ophidian said, reaching over to pat the sea god on his head patronizingly.

"You were trying to *help* me?" Arolan asked in surprise.

"Well, you're free now, aren't you?" Ophidian asked him with a smirk. "And we have lots of choices when it comes to the sea serpent."

"Sea serpent! Just a wyvern in the water!" Arolan said with a snort. "So your problem became *my* problem and you're claiming that you *helped* me?"

"Well, I got you away from your wife," Ophidian added, his eyes glowing red.

"For which I will properly thank you at some later occasion," Arolan promised, his eyes glinting. He turned toward the exit. "I brought Ford —"

"One of your pet projects, as I recall."

"— and the mage," Arolan said. "Your *pet* wyvern is here and there's that half-*kitsune* —"

"More like *kitsune* remains," Ophidian corrected. "The bond was sundered."

"Your doing?"

Ophidian shook his head. "No," he said firmly. "And that concerns me."

"You're a god, you'll cope," Arolan told him scornfully. "But the half was bound once —"

"She might do," Ophidian agreed. "She's loved by the moon and your siblings touched her."

"That's three," Arolan said, "unless you're planning on making Wymarc renounce her bond —"

"No," Ophidian said shaking his head vigorously. "I tried that once."

Arolan laughed. "I remember! *She* showed you."

"Let's not talk of it," Ophidian said, almost pleading. It was an old, bitter memory for him and a source of constant amusement to his sibling gods. "But we've got more than three."

Arolan raised an eyebrow.

"I collected the witch, Annabelle," Ophidian said, sounding smug. "And," he added in a different tone, "I suppose if the serpent's hungry, there's the crown prince."

"Nestor?" Arolan said without much fervor. "Isn't he —?"

"Well, he's here," Ophidian said. "Apparently Wymarc's new girl didn't want him dead when the airship crashed. So that's four. And then there's Rabel's apprentice —"

"Rabel?" Arolan asked sharply, shaking his head.

"Not your concern," Ophidian said, waving a hand aside. "He was the father to Krea, Wymarc's new half."

"Oh!" Arolan said. "And you use first names with him!"

"I've made his acquaintance, yes," Ophidian added slyly.

"So that's six," Arolan said. "Five if you don't count your wyvern's half."

"Four," Ophidian agreed. "Ford, Reedis, Annabelle, and Angus, the apprentice."

"What about Nestor?"

"Him?" Ophidian said with a snort. "He's just an appetizer."

Chapter Three

"You're alive!" Crown Prince Nestor cried joyfully as he spotted captain Ford and mage Reedis seated at a table in the huge dining hall. He'd been led there by Avice, the goddess of Life herself. He guided Krea Wymarc — the winter wyvern and the cause of his quest to the bitter north — to a seat and then rushed over to grab the two startled men in a big hug. "I'm so glad!"

Reedis looked at the prince in surprise. "Nestor, is that really you?"

"It is!" Nestor replied. He gestured toward another young woman who came in with Angus Franck, lately *Spite's* steam engineer. "This marvelous young lady took it upon herself to rescue me." He leaned in to add in awe, "Her name is Hana. She can fly, you know!"

Hover, only! Wymarc snorted to Krea. Krea was growing more used to sharing her body with another — her twin-souled wyvern half. Krea sent Wymarc a soothing thought.

"Your food is growing cold," Sybil, the cook, growled from her counter, waving a hand toward the many trays waiting on it.

"It's best to do as she says," Krea told the others meekly.

Soon, Krea, Hana, and the four survivors of the wreck of the *Spite* were all seated and eating contentedly.

Avice, who wandered nearby looked at the group, and scowled. "We're missing someone," she said, waving a hand and creating another place setting. She glanced up. "Waiting to make an entrance, Ophidian?"

"She was tired and slept in," Ophidian said, suddenly standing in front of Avice and gesturing toward the now-filled eighth seat.

"Annabelle!" Richard Ford cried, leaping from his chair and rushing around to hug the witch tightly. "I was just going to ask about you!"

Annabelle, still seated, allowed him to wrap her in his arms and hugged his arms back, before releasing them, saying, "Ophidian offered me a deal."

Richard stood up and glanced at the suave man with dark straight hair, dark cinnamon skin — and eyes that glowed brightly with an inner heat. Ophidian, in one of his more common human guises, regarded the captain with veiled amusement. He dismissed Ford immediately, turning to Reedis, "Are you responsible for that floating magic that saved her life?"

"Y-yes, Lord Ophidian," Reedis stammered.

Ophidian frowned at him and moved toward him, hand upraised. Reedis quivered in his seat, ready for the wrath of the dragon god. At the last moment, the god smiled at Reedis and extended his hand to him. Awkwardly, Reedis rose from his seat, made a hasty bow, and gingerly took the god's proffered hand.

"That was a very nice piece of magic," Ophidian told him with a smile. Reedis responded with a smile of his own which Ophidian destroyed when he added, "The same magic that caused the death of Annora Wymarc."

"The mage is blameless," Nestor said rising in Reedis' defense. "I ordered the guns fired, the shot was mine, the blame was mine." He glanced toward Krea Wymarc and bowed deeply, "My lady Wymarc, I regret all the harm I caused you." He swallowed and added, "I put my life in your hands."

The sound of sullen clapping distracted him and he turned to see Ophidian, a sour expression on his face. "Very noble," Ophidian said, sneering at Nestor. Then he smiled. "Your offer is accepted."

Nestor's eyebrows rose and he glanced back between Krea and the dragon god, at a loss for words.

"Ophidian, stop playing with the boy," Wymarc said. "He's pledged his life to me, that's enough for you."

Ophidian's jaw clenched and he looked ready to argue the point but Wymarc lifted Krea's head haughtily and… stared the dragon god down. Ophidian, unwilling to concede his defeat in the battle of wills, shook his head irritably.

"They need to eat," Avice said to the dark-haired man who glanced at her, eyes flaring gold, before glancing back to the group.

"Very well," Ophidian said, taking in Reedis, and Nestor in turn, "eat." He dropped himself into a waiting chair and sat, legs crossed, the upper leg jerking in a steady, impulsive beat.

Reedis found himself unable to eat until Avice moved to his back and touched his shoulder. "You need your strength."

Ford kept glancing to Annabelle, Nestor, and Reedis as he crunched his way through his warm bowl of gruel.

There were all just about done their nervous breakfast when Arolan appeared. The sea god nodded tersely to Ophidian, smiled at Avice, and bowed to Sybil who called from the counter, "Can I get you anything?"

Arolan shook his head. He stood by a wall, tapping his finger nervously on his leg and watching the humans impatiently.

"Why do I get the feeling that the gods are anxious?" Ford said to Annabelle as she took the last spoonful of her breakfast.

"Because we are," Ophidian shot back.

"We haven't much time," Arolan said in agreement.

"They won't do you any good until you tell them what you need, you know," Wymarc told the two gods.

Ophidian smiled at her. "Daughter, you're being irreverent."

"And you're being obtuse," Wymarc snapped. She leaned Krea's body back from her chair and glanced to the fire god and then to Arolan. "I've been around long enough to know when there's trouble."

"Perhaps not so much trouble as… opportunity," Ophidian allowed with a twitch of his lips.

Wymarc snorted derisively.

"More like both, one after the other, providing the one is handled," Arolan said, moving toward Ophidian. He looked at Ford and nodded solemnly. "The day of reckoning is at hand."

Ford's eyebrows shot up and he leaped up from his seat. He moved away from the table toward Arolan to whom he knelt, head bowed. "I made oath to you, my god," he said firmly. He glanced up. "What is your will?"

"Oh, *do* get up!" Ophidian cried, waving a hand toward Ford while glaring at the sea god. Arolan gestured for Ford to rise. "The one thing I do know, is that nothing will work unless they undertake it willingly."

"What have you two done now?" Wymarc asked, rising from her chair to better glower at the two gods. She looked at Ophidian, frowning thoughtfully, then to Arolan and then she groaned. "It's another tear, isn't it?"

"A tear?" Annabelle said, making a ripping gesture with her hands. "Like the world is sundered?"

"A tear, like a god crying," Wymarc said in a strange tone, staring toward Ophidian with an unreadable expression.

Ophidian frowned then nodded to her. "Tell them, they'll know soon enough anyway."

Krea Wymarc moved to where the wyvern could address the group easily.

"I don't know everything," Wymarc said with a frown toward Ophidian. "The gods like to keep their secrets."

"It's better that way," Arolan said in agreement. Wymarc cocked her head at him, then nodded.

"Long, long, long ago," Wymarc began, "when the world was formed and the gods walked it, when men were created and the gods began to rejoice in them, something happened." She paused. "I don't know what, my father —" and she nodded at Ophidian "— was in a battle." She frowned at him, an affectionate look on Krea's face. "Or maybe something made him very sad —"

"Or maybe both," Ophidian added cryptically. Wymarc waited a moment until he nodded to her to continue past his interruption.

"And he cried," Wymarc said in a soft voice. She pursed her lips. "He didn't cry much but his tears fell from the heavens." She smiled at the dragon god. "He doesn't like showing emotion, I think he feels that it makes him weak —"

Ophidian coughed warningly but Wymarc just smiled at him.

"— so when he cried, he let some of his emotions, and himself, fall to the ground," Wymarc said.

"And where they landed, a wyvern was born," Reedis finished softly. All heads turned to him and he flushed, embarrassed. Reedis gestured toward Krea Wymarc. "But the tears were so unhappy, they needed something more to make them whole. So they found a human who was willing to bond with them and became a twin soul."

"How did you learn this?" Wymarc asked.

Reedis shrugged. "I didn't, quite," he admitted. "I've been thinking on it a long time. Something that Ibb said —"

"He says entirely too much!" Arolan growled.

Reedis nodded to him. "I think you're very much correct in that," the mage agreed. "In fact, I think he has been thinking deeply on matters for a very long time."

"Since I was born at least," Wymarc said, glancing toward Ophidian, her father. Ophidian gave her a look through half-lidded eyes and she smiled.

"So the serpent that attacked my ship," Ford said to Arolan, "that's another wyvern?"

"Indeed," Arolan said. "Eveen Pallas was betrayed and the twin soul killed." He frowned angrily. "Dark magic was used."

"Like Lyric," Krea guessed suddenly.

Arolan glanced at her. "I know nothing of this."

Krea gestured to Hana and explained quickly how Lyric had tried to kill her to steal Wymarc, then succeeded in stealing Hana's twin-souled *kitsune*.

"A hatpin?" Arolan said when she was done. "She used a hatpin? On a wyvern?"

"It was my mother's," Krea explained.

"It was a gift to her from your father," Ophidian said. He sighed. "I told him how to use dragon fire to make steel." His lips twitched and his eyes dimmed in some old memory. "It was his first piece."

"Dragon steel, with dragon magic, couldn't destroy a twin soul," Wymarc said, turning Krea's head toward Hana questioningly.

"It was your blood that finished the deed," Ophidian said to Wymarc. He frowned, looking toward Avice. "How did the murderer — Lyric — learn that?"

"She was in the library a lot," Krea said. To Avice, she added, "Could she have learned it there?"

"Or from Ibb," Avice allowed. She shrugged as she took in the others' expressions. "Or he could have told her something enough to make her curious, and she could have found the full answer here."

"I think I should like a long talk with Ibb," Arolan said with a menacing look on his face. He turned back to Ford. "Pallas, with her twin soul destroyed, went mad with the pain and grief of the loss."

"The serpent attacked my ship, killed everyone aboard but myself, Knox, and Havenam," Ford said, shuddering in recollection. He looked up to the sea god. "We prayed to you, swore our lives to your service —"

"And I took pity on you, and dragged Pallas to the shore," Arolan said. He glared at Ophidian. "She was one of your get but she'd landed in my seas so I had some control."

"Not enough," Ophidian said with a smirk.

"You set me up!" Arolan growled.

"I had help," Ophidian admitted. "Besides, I merely took advantage of the situation that presented itself."

"Did Ametza arrange Eveen's destruction?" Annabelle spoke up. The two gods turned their gaze on her but she met it with a shrug. She gestured to Ophidian. "You said you had help: she has been rejoicing these last two hundred years without her husband."

"And how would you know?" Ophidian asked in a dangerous tone.

Annabelle snorted. "People talk, dragon god."

"To subdue Pallas, I had to get it away from the sea, to someplace where I could calm it down," Arolan said. "I brought it to the frozen north."

"And you froze," Ophidian said with a smirk.

Arolan nodded, turning his head slowly toward the other god. "Did you know what your pet tear could do?"

"What?" Ophidian taunted.

"I took Pallas to the frozen north because it was the only way to contain the serpent's power," Arolan told him coldly.

"I have so many children," Ophidian said with a wave of his hand. "I don't keep track of their powers."

"Pallas, being shed into the cold waters of the north, learned the gift of freezing," Arolan said. "If I hadn't brought the serpent up here, it would have frozen all the seas."

"And that's bad?" Ophidian asked snidely.

"Ophidian," Avice said warningly. Ophidian gave the goddess a guarded look. "*Think* for once."

"If she froze the seas, the land would not be long in following," Annabelle said with dread. "And everyone would perish."

"So you kept the serpent here, and allowed it to freeze you, too," Ophidian guessed.

"And now it's loose," Reedis said, rising from his chair.

"And you want us to stop it," Wymarc guessed. Krea could feel her dread.

"We've got a week," Annabelle said, nodding toward Ophidian. "I know because that was our bargain."

"Actually," Ophidian said with a nod toward her, "we've got three days."

"Less if the serpent finds any water leading to the sea," Arolan corrected.

"How do we kill the serpent?" Angus asked with an apologetic look toward Krea. "It's just a wyvern with no legs, right? Can we use your hatpin?"

"You can't kill a wyvern," Wymarc said testily. "Pallas needs a twin soul. One that can control the serpent's rage and grief."

Arolan nodded firmly and waved at Ophidian, throwing him the last word.

"You really want *me* to say it?" Ophidian said to him testily. Arolan nodded firmly. Ophidian let out a long sigh. Finally, he turned to the humans gathered around him. He muttered to Arolan, "You know, we're going to regret this."

"Your rules, old god," Arolan said without any sympathy.

"Very well," Ophidian said. He nodded to the humans in front of him, the nearest to a bow the arrogant god could make. He cleared his throat and said, "Annabelle, you are bound by your oath."

"Get on with it," Arolan prompted. "A little humility doesn't hurt, you know."

"Says the newly-thawed god," Ophidian griped. Arolan merely shook his head sternly. Ophidian took a breath. "Very well."

Silence.

"You want us to pledge to you that we'll meet the snow serpent and give our lives to help it find a new twin soul," Nestor said into the silence.

Ophidian shot him a sharp look but the crown prince didn't flinch. Ophidian held his eyes for a moment longer then shrugged in grudging admission of the prince's integrity.

"My lord Arolan, god Ophidian," Nestor said carefully, rising from his chair and bowing deeply to each, "I accept."

"I've got no choice," Annabelle said, rising from her chair with a sigh.

"I will do what I can to help," Hana said in a small voice, rising from her chair.

"My lord, you have but to ask," Ford said, nodding to Arolan. "My life is yours."

"I will do what I can, father," Wymarc said to Ophidian.

"I agree," Krea said. "We cannot allow Pallas to continue to suffer."

Reedis looked around at the others standing above him and rose slowly from his chair, glancing first to Ophidian and then to Arolan. With a sigh, he stepped forward to join the others.

"We're all going to die."

Chapter Four

"Well, certainly, some day," Terric, the god of Death, said to the mage. "It's the way things are. Nothing to get upset about." He glanced to his wife, Avice, the goddess of Life. "Do they complain to you when they get born?"

"Of course!" Avice told him emphatically. "All new babies cry! Why do you think that is?"

Terric thought about it and shrugged.

"It's the time in between that's important," Ophidian said.

"And what you do with that time," Nestor added.

The dragon god gave him a piercing look. "You know," he said after a moment, "it's possible that I may have misjudged you."

Nestor's lips twitched as he shrugged. "Don't worry: I think I misjudged myself."

"I'd certainly say so!" Ford cried loudly, turning to the crown prince. "You saved my life, your highness."

"And I'll gladly do it again," Nestor told him. Ford reached out and grabbed his arm with his.

"So…," Reedis said, glancing around the room, "all we have to do is find someone to bond with this snow serpent, pierce their heart with that ever-useful hatpin, and our problems are solved!"

Ophidian shook his head, his eyes dimming to near-normal.

"The way to a bond is different for every one of father's tears — wyvern or serpent," Wymarc said. She smiled bitterly and gestured to Krea's body. "And sometimes the way is different for each soul mate."

Reedis frowned, then brightened, turning to Avice, "My great goddess, did you not mention a library?" When Avice inclined her head in agreement, he continued, "And would not the answers be held there?"

"They would," Avice agreed with a sour look, "if there had ever been anyone to record how Eveen Pallas was first twinned."

Arolan glanced in surprise to Ophidian. "Eveen Pallas was that old?"

Ophidian nodded.

"I hadn't known," Arolan said in surprise. He glanced toward Krea Wymarc, addressing his question to the wyvern. "That's a very long pairing, isn't it?"

Wymarc nodded. "There were stories about Eveen Pallas going back thousands of years."

"But wouldn't there be *something* in the library?" Hana asked, glancing to the gods nervously.

"Lyric found something," Krea noted.

"It's possible that she only found something to confirm her guess," Wymarc allowed, twisting Krea's expression into a sour look. She glanced toward Ophidian. "We don't know how much she learned from Ibb."

"She left her caravan here," Avice said, gesturing toward some place in the distance, beyond the walls of the dining hall, "perhaps there might be a clue."

"I'll take a look," Annabelle said. "Where is it?"

"In the stables," Avice replied as though it were obvious.

"Where are the animals? Is someone taking care of them?"

Avice smiled, shaking her head. "There were no animals, the contraption was driven by magic." She smiled at Krea. "Some sort of steam engine. I smell your father's hand in it." She lidded her eyes as she glanced toward Ophidian but said nothing.

The dragon god chuckled. "I *may* have had a hand in it. Through Rabel."

Krea was amazed at this news. *Children rarely know their parents*, Wymarc told her.

"Richard, come with me," Annabelle ordered. She saw his consternation and added, "Reedis will go with the children —"

Children! Wymarc snorted bitterly. *Shh*, Krea thought, *I want to hear.* Wymarc subsided.

"— to the library and see what they can learn," she glanced to Angus. "Can you read?"

"Yes, but not well," the apprentice smith admitted. *I knew that!* Krea thought to Wymarc smugly.

Shh! I want to hear, Wymarc shot back to Krea, her amusement evident in her thought. Krea fumed but said nothing more.

"I'd be better with Lyric's caravan," Angus admitted. Annabelle accepted this with a shrug and gestured for him to follow her. Angus glanced toward Hana who smiled at him encouragingly.

"I'll come with you," Nestor said to Krea Wymarc, glancing nervously to Ophidian and Arolan, "if that's all right."

"We'll stay here and confer," Arolan said, gesturing for the humans to proceed.

"Wouldn't you be able to read much faster than us?" Krea asked in surprise.

Arolan made a shushing gesture and Ophidian gave her a faint look of pain.

"Gods don't read," Ophidian said. "Our humans write thing in our praise, we don't need to read them."

"Knowledge is strength," Sybil said, her eyes flashing, "*some* of us read."

"Not the really important ones," Ophidian said.

"But, while I read, I have great speed," Sybil confessed. "Many eyes will find your answers quicker." She glanced toward Krea Wymarc, adding with a crooked smile, "Besides, Wymarc is the fastest reader I know."

Krea could feel the wyvern preen with pride. Hana grabbed her arm, tugging her out of the dining hall, "Come on, Krea Wymarc. We haven't much time."

#

They arrived at the library and went through the doors to find Ophidian waiting for them, an angry look on his face.

"Smoke!" Wymarc said with Krea's lips. Ophidian, eyes hooded, pursed his lips tightly and nodded.

"And recent," Ophidian said, stalking around the library briskly. He stopped in a corner at the far right back. "Ashes."

Wymarc rushed Krea's body to join him, the other three on their heels. She held up a hand and turned to Reedis. "What can you scry of this?"

Reedis closed his eyes, stretched his hands — and opened his eyes, shaking his head. "I'm good with hot and cold magic, not so much with detection."

"Excuse me," Hana said, pushing herself forward. She knelt down, put her head nearly to the ground and sniffed deeply. She put a hand over the pile of ashes for a long moment before pulling it back and standing up, saying to the others, "The ash is still warm, the book but newly burnt."

"Not just one," Reedis said grimly nodding toward the shelves above. "Almost the whole row."

"It's a wonder the whole library didn't burn!" Nestor said.

"We put it out," a pair of voices said in chorus. The others wheeled to find Vorg and Veva standing behind them. They smiled at Reedis in greeting, nodded to Krea Wymarc, gave Nestor a speculative look, and bowed to Hana.

"It started when you brought the witch here," Veva continued.

"Did she —?" Ophidian began hotly.

"It was set for your presence, brother," Vorg said. Veva frowned, shaking her head, "Perhaps not *just* his."

"Who else?" Ophidian demanded, then guessed at the answer, "Arolan?"

"Only you two would know the dangers of the half-soul," Vorg said.

"She wanted a distraction," Wymarc said through Krea's lips. The others looked at her. "She wanted to hide her tracks, slow us down."

"Lyric?" Hana asked in a small voice, looking sick. She gestured at the books. "Why would she destroy such treasures?"

"Because they would teach us how to defeat her," Krea said, putting a comforting hand on Hana's shoulder. "She means to keep Meiko for herself."

And if they are bound too long, she might succeed, Wymarc warned.

How long? Krea asked worriedly.

Weeks, no more than months at best, Wymarc said. *Especially if she can call upon spells to speed the bonding up.*

Spells?

Horrid things, Wymarc said with a shudder. Krea got the impression that her other half knew from first-hand experience — and decided not to press the issue: Wymarc would tell her in her own good time. *Also, if Hana dies or is bound to another twin soul — the connection will break, naturally.*

"Collect all the books that we can carry from here and make a list in order," Nestor said decisively. He paled as three gods, one wyvern, one witch, one mage, and one god-touched girl all gave him affronted looks. Stammering, he added, "I-I m-mean, if that's all right with you."

"I think it's a capital idea!" Reedis exclaimed, clapping Nestor on the shoulder. "Wherever did you come to it?"

"Well, it just seemed sensible," Nestor allowed. "It was something that first minister Mannevy would say on occasions like this —"

"Does your library burn often?" Ophidian interjected drolly.

"Just the once," Nestor added, turning red. "After that they wouldn't let me bring candles in."

"Ah!" Ophidian said, enlightened. "So from personal experience, then."

"Father," Wymarc said through Krea's lips. "Let the boy speak. He is talking sense."

"Rare," Ophidian allowed. Wymarc arched Krea's eyebrows at him warningly. Krea cringed internally: *You're telling a* god *what to do!*

Get used to it, child, Wymarc told her. *Because if we don't tell him what to do, he's liable to go off on his own.* Krea could feel Wymarc shudder at some memory. *And that's never a good idea.*

"We can't help you," Vorg said, shrugging with a flick of flame.

"Not unless you want more books ruined," Veva added ruefully.

Another reason gods don't read, Wymarc added devilishly.

"Yes," Nestor said, nodding to them respectfully. "Perhaps it's best if we let you depart."

Veva smiled at his choice of words and gently tapped him on the nose, leaving a small red mark. "Well said, lordling, well said." And the two fire gods disappeared.

"We don't have to worry about father," Wymarc said, nodding toward Ophidian. "Fire is only one of his aspects and he can control himself." Krea could hear the slight emphasis on the word 'control'. Ophidian allowed her a sardonic look, crossing his arms, and saying, "Besides, gods don't do menial labor."

Liar! Wymarc thought to Krea alone. Krea moved to grab the nearest stack of half-destroyed books.

"Do we have any paper?" Nestor asked, looking to the others. "And a pen?"

"I *always* have paper," Reedis said, pulling a small notebook from his pocket. "But I can't carry a pen." He pulled out a small thin rod from his pocket. "I have this instead."

"A wand?" Hana said, looking askance.

"A pencil," Reedis corrected. He passed it to her. "It's wood wrapped around graphite."

"Graphite?" Hana said, frowning.

"A particularly hard form of coal," Ophidian explained. He gave Reedis an approving look. "I hadn't known you were so capable."

Reedis shook his head. "I got it from a friend many years ago."

Nestor frowned at the pencil. "But when the graphite wears down, what do you do?"

"Cut the wood away, sharpen the tip, and continue writing," Reedis said. He nodded to Hana. "You're the smallest, can you write?"

Hana smiled and nodded. "My father said it would make me more suitable for the gods."

"The gods don't write!" Ophidian growled. Hana flinched at the force of his words but replied meekly, "And wouldn't you like a twin-soul who could, oh great god?"

Ophidian cocked his head thoughtfully before nodding and smiling at the young girl.

"Can you write Kingspeak?" Nestor asked.

"Kingspeak?" Hana repeated in confusion.

"Of course not!" Wymarc said, frowning at the crown prince. "Why would she write in such a barbaric script?"

"Barbaric?" Nestor said, affronted. "What other script, what other language is there?" He frowned. "It's clear that Hana speaks my language, or else how could we communicate?"

"You're in the house of Life and Death," Ophidian told him with a droll look. "Everyone can understand you here."

Language is tricky, Wymarc said to Krea in confirmation. *Fortunately, I know them all so you won't have to worry.*

"Is that why Ophidian created the twin souls?" Krea asked out loud. "So that they could talk to everyone?"

"No!" Ophidian said hotly, his eyes flaring up. "It had nothing to do with it."

"It was a happy accident, is all," Wymarc said, nodding fondly at her father god.

"But if I can understand what she says while we're here, won't I be able to understand what she *writes* as well?" Nestor asked. He was greeted with a stunned silence. Finally, Reedis said, "It's worth a try."

Hana, feeling all eyes upon her, took a seat at the center table and started to write the number and title of the first book:

Fire Magic for mages.

"I can read that!" Reedis said. He glanced at the book and his eyes widened. "I can read this too!" He reverently spread open the first mostly-whole page and skimmed it quickly. He pushed it toward Hana. "Can you read this?"

"'Magic comes from the understanding of the gods'," Hana read, "'Fire magic comes from understanding the need of all things to return to their elemental states.'"

"So it doesn't matter what language the book was written in, it can be read by anyone here," Nestor said. He turned to the back of the library and headed toward the burnt section purposefully. Krea Wymarc followed him.

Slowly they collected all the books and brought them out to the table, then when there were too many, to the next table and the next. At the end of it all, they counted over a hundred burnt or partly-burnt books.

"And there are ashes of at least a dozen more," Reedis said sorrowfully as they finished clearing the shelves. He glanced to Ophidian who had chosen to stay with them throughout the whole lengthy task. "My lord god, is there perhaps any knowledge you have that could rebuild the original wood and words from these ashes?"

Ophidian shook his head. "I don't doubt that one day a witch, mage, sorcerer, or twin-soul might discover some way but I know of none living today or before who had this power."

"There's not been that much cause for it," Wymarc said through Krea.

"It would have helped me in the library," Nestor muttered ruefully. He glanced up to Reedis. "I would have paid *gold* for such a spell."

#

"I've never seen the like!" Angus exclaimed when they found the abandoned caravan in one of the stalls in the stables. There were no horses anywhere but several other strange contraptions that, from the look of them, had been abandoned hundreds — if not thousands — of years before.

The caravan had large spoked wheels. The wheels themselves were made of metal and studded. They were mounted on half-springs that attached to the caravan proper. The caravan was painted in brilliant colors. On top was a small contraption and a smoke stack — Angus decided that it was the engine, although he could see no boiler from where he stood. The caravan was almost twice as tall as a man and many times as long. At the front was a tiller, like on a small boat, which seemed to connect to the front wheels. At the back there were steps up to two wide double doors which could each be opened separately.

The driver's bench seat was covered in leather and a bright red that seemed to show no signs of wear. There was a blanket — thick and comfy — draped on one arm where Lyric must have thrown it on her arrival. There was a small split door leading back from the front to the cabin inside.

"I'd like to look inside," Ford said from the back as Angus poured over the front.

Intrigued, Angus climbed up onto the bench seat and pushed open the split door behind it. Peering inside, he expected to see Richard peering back from the other end. Instead, he saw only darkness, illuminated by what little light escaped from outside around him.

"Richard?" Angus called in alarm.

"I don't know how anyone could sleep here!" Richard's voice came back dimly. "There's a great big table and — fresh food! — and books and crafts, tools, too!"

"Where are you?" Angus called.

"Don't you see him?" Annabelle asked from her position at the middle of the caravan, peering to Richard at the back and Angus at the front.

"No," Angus said.

"There's a door up front, you should be able to open it," Richard called back.

"I *have*," Angus said.

"It's closed, I can see," Richard told him.

Angus frowned, stepped back, closed the door and opened it again. Inside was a well-lit room with a large bed and many, many large comfortable quilts. It looked like a perfect place to snuggle on a freezing night. A lamp hung at the far end filled the room with a warm light.

"I see a bedroom," Angus said, glancing to Annabelle who looked at him thoughtfully.

"Try again," she said.

Angus tried again. This time he got the darkness. He sniffed and crawled inside. He'd smelled coal. And fire.

"Angus?" Annabelle called.

Angus reached up and found a knob. He turned it and suddenly a small storm lantern lit. He glanced around, his jaw dropping in amazement.

"There's an engine room here! It's incredible!"

"There's enough food for an army," Richard's voice called back. "Where is this engine room of yours?"

"Both of you get out *now!*" Annabelle cried. Her voice rose to a shout. "Now, now!"

Angus started to protest but Annabelle cried again. "Richard, Angus! Before it's too late!"

Angus rushed out of the cabin, back into the light.

"Jump down! Run away!" Annabelle cried as soon as she saw him. *"Richard!"* she shrieked. "Run!"

Richard broke into a run and followed Annabelle out of the stall and into the long wide corridor of the stables.

"Don't stop!" Annabelle called over her shoulder, pumping her legs as fast and as hard as she could.

"But —" Richard began.

Whoosh! The sound shook their insides and seemed to both pull and push in on them with some tremendous force. In the distance they heard horrible crashing sounds — like the stables were crashing down all around them.

They kept running, stopping only when they dashed through the door into the main corridor of the House of Life and Death.

Avice met them, her expression grim and furious.

"Really!" she scolded them. "I've *never* had guests behave so —!"

"It was Lyric," Annabelle gasped out, her hand clutching the stitch in her side. "It was a trap."

Avice stopped her tirade and took on a faraway look, as though seeing through the walls. "Sybil?" she said. The goddess appeared beside her. "It appears that the stables have suffered a mischief." Sybil took on the same faraway look and scowled, turning her angry gaze on the three humans.

"It was the murderer, Lyric," Avice said before Sybil's look grew more menacing.

63

"Oh," Sybil said. "Yes, much in keeping with her ways."

"What happened?" Richard asked.

"It's like the caravan turned into a hole and sucked the rest of the stables after it," Angus said.

Avice and Sybil both gave him a sharp look and asked in unison, "How did you know?"

Angus shrugged. "I could feel it."

"I felt something, too," Richard said. "But not like that."

"Sorcery," Annabelle said, her fists clenched and eyes flashing. "Dark."

"Ungodly," Avice said, turning to Sybil with a sick look on her face.

"Ibb?"

Angus shook his head. "No," he said even as the two gods glared at him angrily. "He wouldn't condone such." As Sybil started to shake her head, he held up his hands defensively. "He's not like that," Angus said. "What he wants, I don't know. But I can't believe he'd bring destruction here."

"He wouldn't be so foolish as to declare a war on Life and Death itself," Annabelle said in Angus' support.

"Oh, but he has, dear, he has," Avice told her with a shake of her head. "For quite some time now, in fact."

Richard raised his head and met her eyes. "My lady Life, I have met Ibb. I know the quarrel he has with you and your esteemed husband but I do not think he would so bold, so brazen, so disrespectful, and so *arrogant* as to try to harm your home." He shook his head, his lips twisted. "He protects homes — this one above all."

"I believe you are right," the voice of Terric — who suddenly appeared beside his wife — spoke up. "You, who still owe a reckoning, have the right of it." He looked at Avice. "This is not Ibb's doing."

"But it *is* the doing of his apprentice," Sybil said with a sour look. "It will take some time to rebuild the stables."

"Then it's just as well we have no livestock at the moment," Terric said, patting her on the shoulder. "Besides, dear, you were getting a bit stale, admit it."

Sybil snorted in amusement.

"I think I know how she did it," Angus said, glancing quickly toward the gods, then away in awe.

"How?" Sybil asked encouragingly.

"The caravan, it had many rooms," Angus said. "Like it was ensorceled to have the rooms hidden inside each other."

The three gods exchanged grim looks. Sybil gestured for him to continue.

"I think she caused the rooms to collapse inside each other, creating a hole in the world," Angus told them.

Sybil closed her eyes, concentrating on the ruin outside. When she opened her eyes again, they were dark and flashing — like they held the stars and lightning inside them. "I think this mage is correct."

"I'm not a mage, goddess," Angus said demurely.

Sybil smiled at him. "If you say so."

Annabelle laughed at his slack-jawed expression and clapped him on the back, "Angus, you should to listen to the goddess. She *might* know a bit more about such things than you!"

64

Chapter Five

"I felt it," Reedis said when Annabelle, Ford, and Angus joined them in the library minutes later. "What happened?"

Angus sniffed and frowned as he spotted all the burnt books. "What happened here?"

"Lyric," Wymarc said with a frown. "She burnt the books she's used to learn how to murder Krea and Hana."

"Didn't do too well, by the looks of thing," Angus said, nodding to the two girls.

"She stole Meiko," Wymarc told him. Angus' look fell. Wymarc waved the issue aside, saying to him, "And what happened to you?"

"Lyric," Angus said grimly. "She broke Ibb's magic and managed to crush the caravan."

"There were at least three rooms all crushed together," Annabelle added by way of explanation.

"That is very special magic," Wymarc said, frowning with Krea's face. "I'm surprised that Ibb loaned it to her —"

"I have a feeling that she betrayed him," Annabelle said. "Or she played a role to confuse him."

"Ibb is not very good at reading emotions," Krea said in unison with Ford. The two exchanged amused looks.

"He's been trying to rid himself of his for several thousand years now," Wymarc said with a grimace. "I kept trying to tell him that he was making a mistake…"

"I think he may have learned that," Ford said to her. "But too late."

"He thought for the longest time that emotions were the curse of mortality," Wymarc added in reminiscence. "That if he could banish them, he would live forever."

Annabelle snorted and shook her head. "He knows nothing of the gods, then!"

"Or too much," Reedis added with a frown of his own. He glanced toward Angus and his brows furrowed. "Is there more?"

Angus started to shake his head in vigorous denial but Annabelle stopped him with a hand on his wrist and a snort. "Sybil said that he's a mage!"

"A mage?" Nestor said, looking up from his reading. He jerked as he took in the new arrivals and said, "Who's a mage?"

"Me," Angus said, glancing toward Hana fearfully. "The goddess Sybil said so."

"Well," Nestor said matter-of-factly, "wouldn't you have to be to handle those infernal engines?"

"And you were apprenticed to Rabel," Wymarc added with a sniff.

"And Ibb recommended you, didn't he?" Krea added in her own voice.

"He was always good at spotting talent," Wymarc added sagely.

Reedis and Ford exchanged looks and the mage said to the former captain, "You know, I actually had *no* trouble following that, strange though it seems."

"Following what?" Nestor said, looking at the mage in confusion.

"When Wymarc speaks and when Krea speaks," Reedis explained.

Nestor shrugged. "I *never* have trouble separating them."

Krea found herself beaming at him, even as she experienced a moment of surprise when she realized that Wymarc *also* approved.

But he killed *you!* Krea thought.

And now he's sworn his life to me, Wymarc replied smugly. *And he's a prince. With a little guidance and a little help, he could become* something, *you know.*

The thought warmed Krea's heart and she smiled at the prince. Nestor smiled back for a moment before flushing and hastily bending back to his reading.

He was blushing*!* Wymarc giggled.

Krea couldn't believe the wyvern and shook their head vehemently. Nestor glanced up at that with a worried look, then back to his reading when he felt her — their — gaze on him.

"You should go to the Hall of the Gods and see which one favors you," Reedis said to Angus, oblivious to the by-play between Nestor and Krea Wymarc.

Ford glanced around the library and started wandering away.

"Where are you going?" Annabelle asked sharply.

"I was wondering if there might be books on different types of wyvern and sea serpents," Ford replied absently.

"Yes, there is!" Hana said, jumping up from her chair and leading him toward the section where she and Krea Wymarc had seen the book that Terric had pointed out to them. She frowned as she searched for the book and then brightened when she found it and passed it to him.

"Thank you," Ford said, gesturing for her to precede him to the table, even as he opened the book and began scanning the pages.

"Maybe there are others there," Reedis said, retracing Ford's steps.

"We're going to need to take a break soon," Nestor said. "My eyes are watering from all this smoke."

"I can help with that, maybe," Hana said. The others looked at her and she smiled, shyly. She waved a hand toward the double doors and a gust of wind opened them, pushing them gently all the way back against the outside wall. And then a swirling gust of wind picked up from the back of the room and gently wafted the worst of the dust and smoke up the far corridor and curled it around and out into the hallway.

"We'll take it from there, dear," Hissia's voice came from outside the library.

"Of course!" Hanor, her partner, agreed affably.

"Thank you!" Hana called to them, smiling at their kindness. She caught Angus' look and whispered, "The gods of air." When his eyes widened, she added, "They kindly gave me the power of air when I lost my Meiko." Her voice caught on the *kitsune's* name.

Angus gave her a worried, sympathetic look. "We'll get her back, I'm certain."

A moment later the winds dropped and the door closed.

#

"You've wasted a day and we've learned nothing!" Ophidian growled as they all collected for dinner in the dining hall that evening.

"On the contrary," Wymarc said, "we've learned quite a lot."

"Two days," Arolan said grimly. "We've only got two more days to stop Pallas."

"We know that Pallas is the only ice serpent there is," Reedis said slowly, wiping his eyes to remove sleep from them — he'd been found asleep over his book only ten minutes before.

"We know that fire is its nemesis," Angus said.

"We know that of the hundred damaged books, only two mentioned twin souls," Hana murmured, glancing toward Krea Wymarc.

"And we guess that Lyric's magic destroyed at least a dozen books," Krea said.

"And we know that twin souls are created in many different ways," Reedis said.

"Including *eating*," Angus muttered, still in shock at the discovery.

"Yes," Wymarc said with Krea's voice. "Among some of the twin-souls, man flesh is considered a delicacy."

"Among some gods, too," Ophidian added, happily observing Angus twitch in response.

"Father!" Wymarc said with a half-groan. "Please stop tormenting the lad."

"We have no idea how to find the creature," Nestor said with a frown.

"And no plan of what to do when we do," Hana added with a sigh.

"We should bring the hatpin," Reedis said brightly. The others all looked at him. He threw up his hands. "What?"

"I think it goes without saying," Ford said lightly to his friend. He glanced to Ophidian. "This child of yours is fire-born?"

"Perhaps not," Arolan said. "Pallas was known more for snow and ice than fire or steam."

"The tear fell in icy waters," Wymarc said. "Where a tear falls influences the twin soul that it becomes."

"So if piercing a heart with a dragon-fire hatpin works with you," Angus began — and stopped, giving Wymarc a horrified, repentant look.

"My dear," Wymarc said with a sniff and a toss of Krea's long white tresses, "if you're going to keep apologizing every time for binding us to life, we're not going to get anywhere."

"What else could work?" Annabelle asked, breaking the awkward silence. She held up a hand, flicking up her index finger. "Food. Water, earth, blood."

"Blood usually works well," Ophidian said, with a sly glance toward Angus.

"Lightning," Angus said suddenly.

"Lightning?" Ophidian said with a snort. "I've never heard —"

"But is it possible, great god?" Angus asked quickly. "I just wanted to list all the possibilities."

"A sleeping draught," Annabelle suggested. Ophidian glared at her. "It worked once."

"Once," Ophidian agreed.

"I think we've learned all we can about how to bind the serpent," Richard said. "I think we should concentrate first on how to find it."

"Pallas will still be mostly torpid," Arolan said, glancing toward Ophidian for confirmation. "It won't have gotten far."

"How far, sea god?" Annabelle asked.

"No more than two or three thousand miles," Arolan said. "Maybe less."

"It would try for the sea," Ford said.

"Or some body of water," Arolan agreed.

"We need a map!" Reedis declared.

"Eat first," Sybil said. "You'll need your strength."

"And then your rest," Avice said in agreement. "You can start again in the morning." She glanced toward Angus. "Except for you," she said. "When you're done, you must make your choice."

"Choice?" Richard asked.

"He needs to go before the gods," Hana said in a small voice.

67

"And you all need to find rooms," Avice said. She glanced toward Hana and Krea Wymarc. "You two have yours already but the others…"

"Rooms, goddess?" Nestor asked respectfully.

"Unless you want to sleep in the halls," Avice said.

"We find rooms in the house," Krea told him.

"The infirmary is for the sick," Avice agreed. "And you're all better now, so you need to move out." Under her breath, she muttered, "I've got to clean them and get them ready for the next lot."

"Are you expecting them soon?" Annabelle asked.

"Ten, maybe twenty years from now," Avice said with a shrug. "Although sometimes someone *will* appear uninvited."

"Do you need help cleaning?" Ford asked.

"Not from you, my dear," Avice told him.

"Us?" Krea asked, gesturing to Hana.

"You've already done the dishes," Avice told her with a kindly shake of her head.

"I'd be happy to help," Annabelle said.

"And I," Reedis added.

"I will do whatever I can, goddess," Nestor said.

Avice snorted and said in a low voice, "No doubt you will." She nodded to Reedis and Annabelle. "You two can help. Once you've all found rooms." She made a dismissive gesture.

The humans took the hint. Nestor bowed deeply to each of the gods in turn and the rest followed suit.

#

"You'll know your room when you find it," Krea Wymarc assured Nestor after the prince had tried the tenth door without luck.

"They all seemed locked against me," Nestor said miserably. "There can't be that many more people here — we would have seen them, right?"

Krea shrugged. "I don't know if the rooms work that way."

"Well, maybe I'll be sleeping in the dining hall," Nestor muttered. "Or the library." He brightened and motioned to Krea who followed him in surprise as he made his way back to the library. Her eyebrows rose as he tried the door to the library. The doors opened easily but Nestor closed them again, crestfallen. "Just the library," he told her glumly. "Although if I find the right room, maybe I can borrow a book or two."

"You like reading, don't you?" Krea asked.

He smiled at her. "When I'm reading, I'm not a prince, nor a disappointment to my father. I'm just a person in a different place or learning something I never thought to know."

"I like that," Krea said, placing a hand on his. "It sounds comforting."

"It is," Nestor agreed, covering her hand with his. "It's like spending time with friends." He frowned. "I don't have many friends." Shyly, he glanced up at her. "Would you be my friend?"

"Of course!" Krea said, squeezing the hand she'd covered with her own. Nestor squeezed his hand over hers, lightly, and then let go, turning around. "I didn't see a door there before!"

There was a regular door just opposite the library's double doors.

"It wasn't there before," Krea said. "I think the house makes them." She pulled on his hand. "Go on! Try it!" She told him. "Maybe this is *your* room!"

The door opened at Nestor's touch and he peered inside. He turned back to Krea and called excitedly, "Come, have a look!"

He led her into a well-appointed study. There was a large desk, a plush, comfortable chair, a crackling fire with two chairs arranged on either side, and bookshelves all around. A hallway led to another room and bathroom.

"Look!" Nestor said as he returned to the large study desk. There were several book spread on it. Nestor sat down and picked up the first book. The light on the desk brightened, illuminating the words evenly. "It's another book on twin souls."

"Is it?" Krea asked, taking the one chair by the fire that let her observe him.

"It is," Nestor said. He started reading steadily, out loud to Krea. She smiled at him and closed her eyes to better hear his words.

Some time later, she found herself being gently shaken. "Krea?" Nestor said. "Wymarc?"

Krea opened her eyes blearily and found Nestor crouched worriedly beside her.

"What is it?" she asked. "Oh, did I fall asleep?" she said, flustered. "I didn't mean to! You were reading and —"

"I think you need some rest," Nestor said. He stood and lowered a hand toward her. "May I escort you back to your room?"

Krea took his hand and nodded thankfully.

Chapter Six

The next morning, Ophidian met them all at breakfast, along with Arolan.

"We've only two days left," Ophidian said.

"I think we're going to have to split up," Nestor said. "We don't know where the serpent went, except that it probably went to some water —"

"If it got to water, we'd know," Arolan said. The others gave him dubious looks, so he continued grimly, "Because the world would be frozen."

"We need maps," Reedis said, repeating his demand from the night before.

"I have them," Nestor said, yawning mightily. He held up a rolled parchment triumphantly.

"Didn't you sleep?" Krea asked in alarm.

Nestor shook his head. "I couldn't," he confessed. "I needed to know."

"Very good, my prince," Ford said, moving to sit beside him and gesturing for the map. "And what did you learn?" he asked, moving plates to make room for the map and spreading it in front of them.

Nestor pointed to a spot on the map. "This is the House of Life and Death," he said. He moved his hand to the far end of the map. "And there is the ocean," he said. He moved a hand further up, back toward Issia. "There are streams here," he said. He pointed to another place. "And here." Then he frowned. "But beyond that, I see no water."

"So we've only got to search three places," Ford said. He looked over at Arolan. "Can you take us there?"

"Yes," Arolan said. "But all those are vast expanses, it would take time to search all the lengths of the rivers — even more to search all the sea."

"I think, my lord, I can help," Nestor said. He pointed to the maps. "Wouldn't the wyvern try to make the quickest approach?" He glanced to Ford. "Can't we draw straight lines to the nearest parts of the rivers and the ocean?"

Ford frowned for a moment then nodded emphatically. "Indeed!"

"And we could split up from there to cover a greater area," Krea Wymarc said.

"But only you and Hana can fly," Angus protested. "And if you found the serpent, what then?"

"I could carry someone," Krea Wymarc said, glancing toward Nestor.

"I don't know if I could," Hana said shyly to Angus. "But I could try."

"That leaves the three of us on foot," Ford said to Reedis and Annabelle.

"Actually," Reedis spoke up, "if there is any chance of making things here, I believe I might be able to create some lifting balloons."

"Could you?" Ford said in surprise. Then his expression changed. "That would get us in the sky but how would we move?"

"Or get down again?" Annabelle added.

"I can help on the moving," Arolan said. He grinned as he added, "You might recall I provided your airship with a little push a while back."

Ford smiled at the memory of the frozen sea god blowing the royal airship *Spite* onward to the bitter north.

"I think I can arrange a spell that will let us ascend and descend on command," Reedis said. He nodded to Annabelle. "I could teach you as well, if you wish."

"I'd be delighted!"

"Good," Reedis said with a sigh, "because I'm pretty sure that five balloons will take a lot of effort!"

"Five?" Annabelle asked in surprise, gesturing to herself, the mage, and the captain.

"Because I believe that the prince and the apprentice might also benefit," Reedis said. "If only to give their hosts a rest from their weight."

"Very well," Ford said. "So now we have to learn how to build these balloons of yours."

"Yes," Reedis agreed with a laugh. "I know nothing of the sewing or assembling of the balloons themselves!"

#

Reedis claimed Angus and Annabelle for his spellwork, leaving Nestor, Ford, Hana, and Krea Wymarc to do the sewing.

Unsurprisingly, the prince knew nothing of the art.

"Good!" Ford exclaimed, clapping him on the shoulder, "Now's the time to learn!"

Ford, to Wymarc's surprise, was quite adept with the needle. He smiled at her expression as he explained, "I grew up on ships. I learned to mend torn sails and make my own clothes."

"My mother taught me," Hana said with a sad look. "She made me make father's burial gown."

Avice appeared in the room, waving to a corner. "There's ten bolts of fabric. Let me know if you need more."

"Thank you," Wymarc said, dropping into a deep curtsy and motioning for the others to imitate her.

Avice sniffed and left the room.

"Usually she uses the door," Ford said in a small voice as he looked at the place where she so suddenly *wasn't*.

"No, dear," Wymarc corrected him, "usually she doesn't."

Ford quirked an eyebrow at her. "She was just being nice, earlier. She told me, once, that her sudden appearances had caused her dear husband some unexpected increases in his workload so she'd stopped in respect of him." Krea Wymarc smiled. "She must be feeling comfortable with your constitution or she wouldn't indulge herself now."

"How big are the balloons to be?" Hana asked, moving toward the nearest bolt of fabric. It was nearly twice as tall as she was, and topped Ford's head by a good few inches.

"They need to be man-sized," Ford said. He moved past her and hefted the roll, carrying it to one of the nearby tables. He closed his eyes for a moment, recalling Reedis' balloons. "And then we'll have to rig a rope netting around the balloon to which we attach ourselves."

"Oh," Krea said, "that sounds difficult."

"Didn't Annabelle wear one of these when Ophidian found her?" Wymarc asked, glancing to Ford. Ford quirked his eyebrows in thought but before he could answer, the door burst open and Annabelle rushed in, a large bunch of fabric bunched in her arms.

"I thought you could use this," she said, placing the bundle on an empty table. "It's the balloon I used."

Ford rushed forward, spreading it out and eyeing it critically. He turned to the witch. "Did Reedis examine this?"

Annabelle nodded and sighed. "He did," she said. "He said that the fabric is too worn to use again." She eyed the bolts of cloth lining the far corner and went to the table where Ford had placed a roll, fingering the fabric critically. "This is a much better weave, it will be best to work with it."

"So we've got five balloons to make," Ford said to the others.

"Three will do in a pinch," Wymarc said. Ford raised an eyebrow to the albino woman who maintained the wyvern's soul. Wymarc held up Krea's left hand and began flicking up fingers as she counted, "You, Reedis, and Annabelle. Hana can take care of herself —" she shot a smile to the dark-eyed girl who nodded back with just the least signs of worry "— and I'll take Nestor on my back."

"Five would be better," Ford said. "If anything happens to you, it would be good to give Nestor some safety."

"Five, if we can make them," Wymarc agreed. She waved a hand toward the tables. "But we're wasting our time dawdling."

Annabelle looked at the others. "Karol needs me —"

"Who?" Wymarc demanded.

"She means mage Reedis," Ford said drolly. He winked at Annabelle. "Apparently, she's managed to cajole from him his much-loathed first name."

"Whatever," Wymarc said with an irritated shrug. She pointed toward the door, motioning for Annabelle to leave. "Just let them know that we'll need help."

"We'll come as soon as we can," Annabelle promised as she rushed out of the room.

Ford rummaged through one of the cabinets just to the right of the fabric rolls and pulled out a set of small knives. "First, we should pick the seams to separate one of these sections for a pattern," he said, gesturing toward the crumpled balloon.

"Enough talk," Wymarc said, gesturing for a pair of scissors. "You're slowing us down."

Ford gave her an irritated look and shook his head, pulling up the dead balloon and deftly picking apart seams.

When he'd finished separating a section, Krea Wymarc took it from his hands with an irritated noise and placed it over a piece of folded fabric. She used a stick of charcoal to make a quick outline and said to Hana, "If you're able to cut through the two layers, we'll get it done quicker."

In short order they had eight pieces cut and ready for sewing.

"You're best at that, I'm sure," Wymarc said to Ford. "Can you start stitching while Hana and I continue with the sections?"

Ford wiped the sweat from his brow and nodded, aligning the seams of the two pieces he'd just cut and started sewing from the top half to the bottom. When he'd completed joining those two sections, he found a third and carefully joined it to the free half of one of the originals —

"How about you make pairs and we'll handle joining them," Wymarc's voice broke through his concentration.

"Better, let's have you make more pairs and then we'll put Hana to make halves by sewing the two pairs together," Ford countered.

"And then?"

"When we're done with that we'll join the halves," Ford replied.

"Sounds efficient," Wymarc said approvingly.

"You learn things aboard ships," Ford allowed.

"So leave off with this and get started on pairing," Wymarc told him with a small smile.

#

"I'm not sure they'll be able to finish the balloons in time," Annabelle reported as she re-entered the long study to which the mage had brought them earlier.

"I'm not sure we'll be able to do the spells needed," Angus said with a nod toward Reedis who sat in a chair, eyes closed, appearing to be sleeping deeply.

"Don't touch him!" Annabelle said, moving to stand between the mage and the smith. "He's conjuring, can't you feel it?"

Angus started to shake his head and stopped, eyes narrowing. "Does it feel like a buzzing in my eyes?"

Annabelle smiled. "To you, perhaps," she said. Seeing his chagrin, she added soothingly, "Magic feels different to everyone. And it changes over time."

She motioned Angus to take a chair, moving toward one herself. "Just close your eyes, breathe, and listen."

Angus shot her a worried look but she waved his worries aside with a finger and firm nod. Reluctantly, Angus did as she said.

"The trouble," Reedis' voice came out in a thin, thready squeak, "with working with others is that they always *talk*."

"Sorry," Angus said, opening his eyes to glance at the mage. Annabelle shook her head at him, made a shushing gesture with her finger to her lips, and closed her eyes suggestively.

"Every spell is different for everyone," Reedis said. When Angus opened his eyes again, the mage glared at him and with a resigned sigh, closed his eyes once more. "The first spell I used on the balloons was a heat and expansion spell." He paused a moment, letting his words sink in. Angus could hear the mage's clothes rustle and guessed that he was gesturing. "I take my hands, pressed together and pull them apart quickly, imagining heat and void in the air of the balloon."

Angus' brows creased as he tried to imagine that. He moved his hands —

"*Don't* do anything!" Reedis said warningly. "Annabelle, you know what to do."

"It's different for me," she said. "You want to use the air and fire, don't you?"

"Very good," Reedis said, with a smile in his voice. "Fire and anything, really. I could do something similar with water —"

"To make steam," Angus exclaimed.

"Silence, please," Reedis said but he sounded pleased with the smith's observation. "And I can use earth, but it is much more difficult to manage."

"And you can't make a balloon with it," Annabelle murmured.

"You can be quiet, too, I believe," Reedis suggested.

Angus could hear Annabelle's clothes rustle as she waved an apology.

When he seemed satisfied at their silence, the mage continued, "That pocket of thin, warm air, wants to reach its own level in the air above it and so the air rises," he paused a moment to let them reflect on his words. "If that air is surrounded by something or even contained in something, it will strain against the extra weight. If it strains hard enough, it will lift the weight with it." He paused again and moved in his chair, Angus could tell by the sounds of the upholstery. "You may now open your eyes and observe." He turned to Angus. "In your case, observe closely."

"Why thank you," Annabelle said, lowering her eyelashes in a flattered look.

"This —" Reedis held up a small piece of cloth. Its ends were tied together in a lump. "Inside this knot there's a small rock." He passed it to Angus to feel, then grabbed it back and passed it to Annabelle for her inspection. She returned it with a frown. Reedis smiled at her. "Observe." He threw the bundle up. The rock pulled it down but the cloth billowed and the bundle fell slowly through the air.

"I've seen those!" Angus said in surprise, glancing to Annabelle and then Reedis. "We used to make them as kids and use them to —"

"To what?" Reedis asked testily.

"To distract passersby," Angus said in a small voice.

"To pick their pockets," Annabelle guessed. She caught Reedis' look and told him, "Angus was found by Ibb."

"And brought to Mr. Zebala to apprentice," Angus said.

"I've used the trick much the same way myself," Reedis admitted with an amiable nod to the apprentice. "Sometimes one must supplement one's income."

Annabelle snorted derisively.

"It was while I was attempting just such a subterfuge," Reedis said with a nod toward Angus, "that I discovered I could do *this*." He threw the bundle up again and, as it started its descent, he waved a hand and muttered a spell. The cloth seemed to bulge a moment and then bundle stopped — suspended in mid-air.

The others gasped.

Reedis beamed at their reaction before waving his hands once more and saying, "And *this*."

Nothing seemed to change for a moment and then, slowly, the bundle started to rise above them. Reedis smiled at their reaction and continued his incantation until the bundle touched the ceiling.

Then, still smiling, he waved his index finger toward the bundle and, with the motion of his finger, slowly lowered it and raised it again.

"That requires some practice," he allowed as he sent the bundle back to the ceiling.

"And that's our spell, isn't it?" Annabelle said thoughtfully.

"Except that we'll need to tie the spell to words," Reedis told her. "That way the others can simply say, 'Up' or 'Down' and their balloon will rise or fall."

"How fast?" Angus asked. The other two looked at him, so he explained, "We might need to rise very fast or drop just as quickly."

Annabelle exchanged a glance with Reedis who nodded and sighed.

"I suppose we shall," Reedis said. He waved his hand at the bundle and it fell to the ground. He smiled ruefully as the rock clattered against the wood floor. "And probably not like *that!*"

"By preference, certainly," Annabelle agreed with a half smile.

"*That*," Reedis said with a sigh, "is where the problems begin."

"Shouldn't we first learn your spell?" Annabelle said.

"You can't *learn* my spell," Reedis said testily. Annabelle quirked her eyebrow up questioningly. "You have to learn how to do my spell *your* way."

"Witchcraft?"

"No," Reedis snapped. Then he shook his head and added doubtfully, "At least, I think not." He waved a hand at her. "Where would you carry all the supplies? Or would you prick yourself and get blood?"

"For *that?*" Annabelle said, shaking her head. "No, blood would be too much for a simple spell like that."

"Simple?" Reedis said, sounding affronted.

"Let me see…" Annabelle said, rummaging through her front pockets. She pulled out a rock, frowned at it and let it slip back into her pocket. A thimble followed it, as did a dead insect, and a thin bit of string.

"You can do magic, can't you?"

"I can," Annabelle said slowly, "but I prefer witchcraft." She sat back in her seat, sighed, and closed her eyes. With her eyes still closed she gestured in the direction of Reedis. "Throw it up, please."

Reedis obliged and sat back in his chair with a pleased expression as the cloth bundle stopped its descent and hovered, wobbling up and down as though not quite sure whether it would fly to the ceiling or drop to the floor.

"Can you make it go up?" Reedis asked after a moment. In answer, the bundle dropped to the floor and Annabelle let out a long, slow breath, opened her eyes and shook her head.

"That's hard, that is," she said with feeling. Reedis lifted his head and looked pleased with himself. "I don't know if I could lift a person."

"Once you get the hang of it, it gets easier," Reedis promised.

"But we're going to need this spell tomorrow!" Annabelle snapped. "I haven't got *time* to get the hang of it."

"Could you do it with witchcraft, then?"

Annabelle shook her head. "I doubt it," she said. "At least, not by tomorrow."

"Well…" Reedis said slowly, turning his head toward Angus. 'Why don't you try?"

"Me?" Angus cried in surprise. "I haven't got any magic!"

"Angus, my boy, when a god says you've got magic, you've *got* magic," Reedis told him firmly, gesturing to Annabelle for confirmation.

"He's right," she said. She gave Reedis a frown. "Although no one said what type or how quick he'll be."

"I'd say you'll be strong or the goddess of strength wouldn't have told you," Annabelle told him brightly.

"You're good with fire, aren't you?" Reedis asked. Angus nodded. "And you've made dragon steel?" Again, Angus nodded. "I don't know much about it but it would seem that for you to do that you must get your magic from Ophidian."

"No, he doesn't," Ophidian said in response. The others started and located the god — he was standing near the door, leaning against the wall, looking somewhat bored. Ophidian smiled — that is, he showed many teeth — and said to Angus, "It's true that you can use the fire, but I don't claim you."

"Then who does?" Reedis asked. Ophidian locked eyes with him silently and Reedis grew pale, adding quickly, "If you'd be so kind as to tell us, great god."

"Or you could turn him into ash and let the serpent freeze the world," Annabelle said, buffing her nails on the top of her blouse.

Ophidian turned his gaze to her, his eyes glowing brighter. "I *like* you," he told her, showing more teeth. "How tasty are you?"

"I'm a better cook than I am cooked," Annabelle replied coolly. "Mage Reedis — as you doubtless observed — was showing us his spell."

"Yes," Ophidian said, "so I saw."

"Invisibility is one of your things, isn't it?" Annabelle said, pursing her lips and shaking her head. "Must make you *very* popular at parties."

75

Ophidian's nostrils flared and he blew out a breath… smoke came out and curled upward huffily.

"That might work," Angus said, pointing to the dragon god. "Your breath could fill the balloons."

"And turn them into ash," Annabelle said, "his breath is too hot, as you should remember."

Angus' face fell.

"Go to the Hall of the Gods, apprentice of Zebala," Ophidian said. "The sooner you learn your fate, the sooner you can help here." And with that, he vanished, leaving Annabelle and Reedis looking nervously at the young smith.

Angus rose to his feet slowly and seemed to wobble for a moment before he collected himself. "I'd better go."

Chapter Seven

Outside the study, Angus found Hana rushing toward him. "You're not going alone!" she swore, grabbing his hand and leading him up the long main corridor. Accents of blue and green gave way to accents of yellow and orange.

"Wymarc told me," Hana explained as she tugged him along. "Krea was there for me, so I wanted to be here for you."

"Thank you," Angus said with feeling. "That's very kind." He added, in an attempt at levity, "At least we don't have to worry about hatpins."

Hana turned back to him, reached into a long pocket in her robe and pulled the hatpin out. "Actually," she said, "I thought we might want it. For defense."

"It won't do any good against the gods," Angus said. "I wouldn't even try."

"I don't think we need to worry about them," Hana agreed.

The walk up the main corridor to the Hall of the Gods did not really take forever, it only seemed so. Even so, Angus was glad of the company and found himself glancing at Hana out of the corner of his eye until she caught him at it and pushed against him, laughing. "Am I close enough now?"

Encouraged, Angus draped an arm across her shoulder and hugged her tightly. They finished the long walk together.

#

At the double doors, Hana pulled away. "You need to go in first."

Angus made a face then nodded. He drew one of her hands up to his lips and kissed it. "For luck."

"I'm going to be right behind you," Hana pledged.

Angus pushed open the door and stepped through. As soon as he entered the hall, the door behind him clanged shut. He turned and pulled on the handle but it wouldn't budge. He tried the other door with no better luck.

Resolutely, he turned back to the long line of statues of the gods. He squared his shoulders and marched forward.

He stopped in front of the statues of Hissia and Hanor, the gods of air and bowed deeply to them. "Thank you for helping Hana," he said. Silence. "She saved my life."

When they made no motion, no response, Angus rose and, with a final nod, turned to continue his journey.

He paused at the statues of Vorg and Veva, bowing. "I thank you for all my time at the forge," he said to them. "The flames kept me warm even while I was working steel."

Again, nothing.

He smiled at Arolan and nodded to Ametza.

He just barely recognized the statues of Geros and Granna — the earth gods. Rabel Zebala — Krea's father — had spent several hours drilling Angus on the names and appearances of the gods. "Although they can choose any form they desire, most gods have a preferred form," Rabel had said so many months ago.

He saw the figures of Hansa, god of fate, of Kalan, the god of justice, and continued onwards until he reached the very end of the hall with the gods of the Moon and the Sun. None of them stirred.

As he turned back toward the doors, he noticed a stone basin mounted on a raised pedestal. Water shimmered in it. As Angus approached, the surface of the water changed. He peered into it. The water darkened and then he saw flashes of lightning flare across the surface. A moment later, the water stilled. Angus waited for minutes but nothing else occurred.

Slowly he retraced his steps toward the double doors. He pushed on one hopefully and was surprised when it sprang open. Hana was pulling frantically from the other side.

"What happened?" she cried as she rushed into his arms and hugged him frantically. "I tried and tried to open the door but it wouldn't budge!"

"Nothing," Angus said. "None of the gods spoke to me."

"But what did you see?" A voice asked from behind Hana. Ophidian.

"See?" Angus said. He started to shake his head but stopped. "There was a basin with water."

"And?" Ophidian prompted, moving to Hana's side, opposite Angus.

"It looked like there was lightning, and then nothing," Angus said.

"Lightning?" Ophidian repeated, his expression intent. "How many bolts?"

Angus frowned at the dragon god. "Two. I think."

Ophidian nodded. "That makes sense." He stared at Angus for a moment, then moved and touched the smith's forehead with an outstretched finger. "I shall give you this, for the present."

Angus felt a burning sensation and a jolt shoot through his head and he tried to jerk away from the dragon god but couldn't.

Smiling, Ophidian pulled his finger back and blew on the tip as though it were on fire. "Now, you need to get back to work." And he was gone.

"He touched you," Hana said in awe. She raised her hand to his forehead but didn't touch it, checking for warmth. Her eyes widened as she said, "I swear he burned you but there's no sign, no heat, not even a mark."

"You don't have time to dawdle," Ophidian's voice echoed in the hallway. They looked around but could not find him. Ophidian chuckled. "I'm a god. I can send my voice where I will."

"We'd better get back," Angus said, glancing around nervously. Hana nodded jerkily and let Angus lead them down the corridor. Outside the study, Hana said, "We've got the balloons almost ready."

"We're still working on the spells," Angus told her. He made a face. "Reedis showed us his magic."

"Can I see?" Hana said.

Angus shrugged and pushed open the door.

"Which god calls you?" Reedis asked Angus excitedly, rising from his chair. He caught Angus' look and frowned. "Surely there's a god?"

"Ophidian touched me," Angus said, "but I don't think he claims me."

"Correct," Ophidian said, pushing himself away from the wall where he was suddenly standing.

"Not everyone is called by a god," Annabelle said, glancing up to the ceiling where two bundles were bouncing, trying to rise higher.

"Some are called by many," Reedis said in agreement. "And some use their knowledge of many gods to create their magic."

Ophidian gave the mage a very toothy smile. Reedis glanced away, relieved to spot Hana, and said to her, "How are the balloons?"

"Almost done," Hana said. She looked up to the ceiling. "Those are flying?"

"Floating," Reedis said. He glanced to Annabelle. "She's got two of them floating by herself and is about to try a third."

"It's Angus' turn," Ophidian said. He vanished.

Reedis looked at the spot where Ophidian had been and blinked in astonishment.

Annabelle waved her hand in a strange gesture —

"That's magic," Angus said even as Annabelle completed her motion and one of the cloth bundles fell toward the ground. She grabbed it before it hit the floor and tossed it to Angus.

"It is," she agreed. She nodded toward the bundle. "Now it's your turn."

Angus eyed the cloth tied at its corners around a small rock doubtfully.

"Throw it up, close your eyes and imagine it floating," Annabelle suggested.

"Or close your eyes, throw it up and imagine," Reedis countered. Annabelle gave him a look and the mage shrugged. "The order doesn't matter, only the result."

Angus sighed, closed his eyes and threw the bundle up. *Clunk!* It hit the ground.

"Again," Reedis said.

Angus tried again. And again.

"Maybe you should open your eyes," Annabelle suggested. "At least that way you can catch it."

Angus tried. This time he caught it. And the next time.

"If Ophidian touched you and left the mark as Hana here says, then I would imagine he's given you some fire magic," Reedis said. "Can you imagine the air getting hotter, holding up the bundle?"

"Here," Hana said, holding up a hand and twisting it quietly. With a *whoosh* a small hand-sized funnel of air appeared right above her hand. She gently moved her hand toward Angus and released the funnel. "Try making this hot."

"I don't know how," Angus said.

"It's different for everyone," Reedis told him. He glanced toward Annabelle, adding, "Sometimes it can take days to learn the first spell."

"Or months," Annabelle said with a frown. She pursed her lips. "If Angus can't make the spell, can you and I do it ourselves?"

Before Reedis could answer, there was a bright flash and a loud burning sound as the bundle Angus had thrown up burst into flame and turned into ash.

"Well, it's a start," Reedis said as the ashes rained down onto the floor in a small pile.

"I got so mad at everyone thinking I couldn't do it," Angus said in a tight voice.

"Try the funnel," Hana said in a kind voice, pointing to the funnel of air hovering near Angus.

Angus frowned and clenched his jaw. He raised a hand and pointed a finger at the funnel. A moment later it became a roaring jet of hot air that thrust to the ceiling and punched a hole in it. Angus dropped his hand in horror.

"Ophidian's flame!" Reedis exclaimed, staring at Angus with alarm. "You have Ophidian's flame!"

"I'm sorry," Angus said. "I was just —"

"Don't be sorry!" Annabelle said.

"This is amazing!" Reedis said, shaking his head. "I never expected to be able to work with Ophidian's flame directly —"

"You're welcome," Ophidian's voice came quietly from the corner where he'd last been. He appeared long enough to wink at Angus, saying, "It won't last. Use it while you can."

He was gone before Angus could open his mouth.

"Yes," Reedis said, "I think we should start to work now."

"Thank you Hana," Angus said to the dark-eyed girl.

Hana shook her head. "I didn't do anything."

Angus shook his head. "You believed in me."

Hana smiled, "Always."

"Ahem," Reedis interjected.

"Hana, perhaps you can see how the others are doing," Annabelle suggested, rising from her chair, stepping over the pile of ash, and guiding the young woman to the door. "I think we can finish on our own."

Hana gave Angus a nervous look, then expanded it to include Reedis. "I-I didn't mean to —"

"And you didn't," Reedis assured her. "You were a great help."

Annabelle escorted her out the door and stayed long enough to tell the younger girl, "I think Angus is a bit nervous around you."

"But — I —"

"He's a sweet lad," Annabelle interrupted, smiling. "But with you here, he won't get any work done." She nodded to Hana. "And neither will you."

"I… yes," Hana said. "It's just that —"

"You like him," Annabelle said. Hana blushed. "It's okay to like him. He seems to like you, too."

"He does?"

"He'd be a fool if he didn't," Annabelle assured her fiercely. She waved a hand down the corridor. "If we can conquer this serpent, you two will have years to see each other. But if we don't…"

Hana nodded firmly and turned away, walking briskly back down the corridor.

#

"Perfect!" Reedis cried in joy at the end of the afternoon. "I can't believe I hadn't thought of this before."

"It's because you needed help," Annabelle told him.

"And because I hadn't your —" and Reedis nodded to Angus and Annabelle in turn "— brilliant skills and aid." He waved to the table. There were five stones on the table. They had started the day as regular stones picked up outside the rebuilt stables. Now they were quite a bit more. "With these, we shall be able to make any balloon fly."

"Float," Annabelle corrected. "Ophidian is quite firm on that distinction."

Reedis waved a hand dismissively. He stood up, scooped the stones into his pocket and gestured the others out. "Let's see if the others are done."

Angus needed no prompting and headed quickly out and down the corridor to find Hana and the others.

"Five!" Ford called proudly to the others when they entered the sewing room that he occupied along with Krea Wymarc, Nestor, and Hana. He pointed in turn to the five separate bundles. "We're done, how about you?"

"Done," Reedis told him, moving closer to inspect one of the completed balloons. He examined the seams critically, felt inside for the circular cap at the top, and grunted in satisfaction. "Looks good."

"The test will be in the using," Krea Wymarc said.

"We should eat first," Hana said, moving toward Angus and smiling at him.

"It will be getting dark soon," Ford warned. "Perhaps we should try them now and eat after."

The others reluctantly agreed. Ford grabbed a balloon, gesturing to Annabelle, Reedis, Nestor, and Angus to get theirs.

"The front doors are closest," Wymarc said, holding open the double doors and pointing in their direction.

"We're not dressed for the cold," Hana said.

"There's a coat closet near the entrance," Wymarc told her. "There should be something there for everyone." She jerked her head toward the exit, commanding action.

The others hustled out in front of her. As she closed the door, she said, "Ophidian, no doubt you'll want to observe."

A chuckle followed her out of the room.

#

It took them longer to bundle up in great coats, grab fur-lined caps, wrap scarves around their necks and find warm gloves which fit than Ford would have liked but, at last, they were ready to brave the cold of the frozen world outside the House of Life and Death.

Wymarc frowned as the cold winds chafed them when they moved out of the courtyard. She turned Krea's head to Hana and said, "Hana, dear, you'll want to be ready if anyone gets blown away." Hana's eyes widened in alarm. "Anyway, you'll need the practice."

"I'll go first," Reedis said, unfolding the harness of his balloon. It was not what he expected and he gaped at captain Ford. "Richard...?"

Ford smiled. "I recall my previous experience," he said with a wince. "Krea Wymarc and I came up with a more secure fastening." He wrapped the belt around his waist. Two straps dangled down and these he wrapped around his legs, fastening them up to the belt. Two other straps went over his shoulders — one on either side — and tied into the center part of the belt. "This is much more secure and less..." his smile grew strained "... constricting, shall we say?"

"Oh, what a brilliant idea!" Annabelle said, adjusting the straps around herself. The balloon hung down from her shoulders.

With a frown at the new development, Reedis struggled to get himself harnessed in, muttering, "But the other way was easier."

"Quicker, too," Ford agreed affably. "But not, my good mage, as safe or comfortable."

"There is that," Reedis conceded as he finished his fastenings. Defensively, he added, "The original was intended for emergencies only."

"Indeed," Ford said. "And now that we're all safely strapped in, Reedis, how do we proceed?"

Reedis lifted his thick coat and fumbled in his trouser pocket with much effort and grunting before retrieving the five stones. He frowned as he passed one to Ford, saying, "Can you tie that securely into your harness?"

Ford looked at the small stone quizzically.

"You'll need to be able to touch it," Annabelle warned.

"Can we put it in a pocket?" Ford asked.

Reedis shook his head. "It must touch the harness or the balloon."

"Why not sew it into the balloon?" Hana asked.

"Actually," Reedis said, "it really only needs one touch to the balloon or the harness when you use it." He touched his stone to his belt and said, "Fill."

The balloon above him suddenly rose and stood taut at the top of his harness.

Ford, Hana, Nestor and Krea Wymarc gasped in astonishment. Annabelle and Angus both looked pleased.

"That's the readying spell," Reedis said proudly.

"And to empty it?" Ford asked.

Reedis smiled at him, touching the stone to his harness and saying, "Empty." The balloon went limp and folded back down over the mage's shoulder.

"And to go up?" Nestor asked, eyeing his balloon respectfully.

"'Up,'" Annabelle said.

"So, 'down' to go down?" Ford guessed. He frowned. "But how fast? And how do we rise faster?"

"Repeat the word," Reedis said. "Each time the speed will double." He placed his stone against his harness once more. "Fill." The balloon inflated. Then he smiled at the others. "Up." And a moment later, his feet left the ground.

"Reedis!" Ford cried angrily. "Get back down here!"

Alarmed, the mage looked down.

"The wind is blowing you into the building!" Ford called.

"Oh!" Reedis said, suddenly realizing his plight.

"Fill," Ford commanded his balloon. "Up, up, up!" And Ford soared into the sky.

"Hana!" Wymarc cried in Krea's voice, pointing to the two balloons. "Blow them away!"

Hana frowned, raised her hands and shot winds toward the two errant balloons. The first caught Reedis and pushed him back towards them but the second missed as Ford's balloon zipped past her aiming point.

With a cry, Krea Wymarc ran out into the snow, took two steps, leapt — and flew upwards in wyvern form. With Krea's urging, Wymarc banked sharply and beat their wings mightily pulling their body up higher and higher until they were well above Ford.

"Don't puncture the balloon!" Reedis' voice carried up to them in warning.

With a screech of disgust, Wymarc fell down toward Ford, talons extended. Triumphantly, Wymarc grabbed the man's feet and then cried in surprise as the man and the balloon tried to pull the wyvern upwards.

"Empty, Richard, empty!" Reedis called from far below.

"Empty!" Ford dutifully shouted. The balloon became limp and the man immediately fell below Krea Wymarc, tugging the wyvern earthwards alarmingly by his feet. A moment later, Ford said, "Fill." They stopped falling, the balloon pulling Ford upright, tight against Krea Wymarc's chest.

"Now, just one 'down'," Reedis ordered. Ford said the word and could feel his ankles pushing against the wyvern's talons. "Wymarc, can you bring him back down closer to the ground? Then you should be able to let go."

Krea Wymarc screeched in agreement and started a slow descent, matching the pull of the charmed balloon until she was just above the humans. With another cry, she released Ford and pulled upwards and to the right, sharply. She completed her turn in time to see Ford touch the ground and his balloon droop, unfilled, over his shoulders.

"I suppose it's best if you remain aloft," Reedis called from the ground up to the wyvern. "In case we have any more accidents."

Wymarc screeched in agreement, circling easily over the others.

With much less excitement, Annabelle, Angus, Reedis, and, finally, Nestor, all completed quick trials and returned safely to the ground. Only Nestor had to be wafted back to safety by Hana, as the winds had started to pick up with the last of the evening's light.

"That went well," Reedis said when they'd returned inside, depositing their outdoor garb back into the changing room.

"Except for the beginning," Ford said ruefully. He glanced to Krea, saying, "Wymarc, I'm sorry to have caused you such trouble."

"It *does* seem to be your nature," Wymarc said with Krea's voice. She quirked Krea's lips upwards, adding, "It was rather enjoyable, all the same. I like a challenge."

"Well," Ford said, "I'll do my best to be more boring tomorrow."

"I don't know if that will be possible," Wymarc warned. She gestured toward the dining hall. "But, in the meantime, we should eat and rest."

#

After dinner they went to the library. Books were piled four high on the center table. Nestor had consumed most of them, followed by Reedis, and, surprisingly, captain Ford.

"So what do we know?" Richard said as they gathered near the table. He glanced toward Krea Wymarc. "Wymarc, is there anything you remember about Pallas?"

Krea's lips formed a frown as Wymarc's response. "Eveen Pallas was one of the kindest twin-souls I'd ever met," Wymarc said with Krea's voice. "But I got the impression that most of that was due to Eveen who was a sweet soul and wouldn't hurt anyone."

"The serpent we saw killed eighteen men before Arolan intervened," Richard said grimly. "The water around our ship was red with blood."

Krea Wymarc shuddered and nodded slowly. "I'd heard that about Pallas," Wymarc said. "The serpent had acquired an appetite for human flesh thousands of years ago and never quite repented of it." She cast Ford a worried look. "She scents and remembers smells." She paused, wrestling with herself before adding, "She'll remember your scent."

"Can we use it to lure her?" Richard asked. Before the others could protest, he raised a hand. "I can't see that we have any other choice, particularly if she's near the sea."

"You make a good point," Ophidian's silky voice said in agreement. He was standing opposite Ford, giving the other a speculative look. He bared many teeth in a what could not be mistaken as a smile. "There was a time when *I* would have relished your flesh."

"You've gotten over that, father," Wymarc reminded him sternly, raising one of Krea's hands dismissively.

"I know," Ophidian said. "But Pallas was before that time."

"You've cried many times, haven't you?" Annabelle asked.

Ophidian glared at her for a fulminating moment, then turned back to Ford. "She would want you, maybe more than anything."

"Then we shall give her what she wishes," Ford said lightly.

"Richard!" Reedis cried in surprise.

Ford raised a hand, palm out. "We shall lure her with my scent," he said. He nodded to Hana, "Perhaps you could help in spreading it?"

"I could blow a wind behind you," Hana agreed reluctantly.

"And when she strikes?" Ophidian asked.

"She is very fast," Wymarc added in warning.

"I'll float upwards, out of her reach," Ford said, "leaving the rest of you to capture her."

"I could help with that," Hana said.

"And I," Wymarc added, glancing toward the dark-eyed girl, "can snatch you if need be."

"That'll leave you four," Ford said, pointing to Annabelle, Angus, Reedis, and Nestor in turn, "to deal with her."

"You can't *deal* with her," Ophidian said testily. "You have to find a soul mate for her."

"And if we can't?" Ford asked the god directly.

"I will not destroy her," Ophidian declared, shaking his head slowly.

"If she freezes the sea, she will destroy every human and twin soul," Arolan said from behind Richard's shoulder. Richard tensed but forced himself not to turn at the surprise arrival of the sea god.

"If need be, I will help," Sybil spoke up from beside Annabelle. "Father has spoken with Hansa and said that that much we can do."

"And your father?" Wymarc asked. She heard Ophidian's hiss and turned to him. "I'm sorry, father, but it must be asked."

"My father cannot act until the time is right," Sybil said. "Nor can Bryan."

Richard rose from his seat, moving to the side and turning to Arolan. "I will do whatever is needed to keep my oath."

"I'd prefer if you did it without dying," Arolan told him. "I'm told that I have far too few followers as is."

"Isn't a death always required when a twin soul is mated?" Annabelle asked, looking to Krea Wymarc for an answer.

"Not always," Nestor spoke up, surprising everyone who turned their gaze toward the young royal. Nestor flushed and took a breath before continuing, "As far as I can tell, there have been four times in the past five hundred years when death was not required."

"Four?" Reedis said, impressed.

"And how many others?" Angus asked the prince.

"All the others," Nestor said in a small voice. Angus bent his head demandingly. "About two hundred or so."

"What happened those four times?" Annabelle wondered.

"Three of them involved life-threatening wounds," Nestor said with a grimace. His expression changed as he added, "The fourth involved a red rose."

"We'll bring a dozen roses then," Arolan said, clapping Ford on the back.

"And wyvern's flowers," Ford added, nodding toward Krea Wymarc. The twin-souled pair nodded in response. "If nothing else, the scent of them and me should bring the serpent more quickly."

"Add the roses," Reedis implored. Ford smiled at him and nodded.

"It does seem to be a plan a trifle short on specifics," Annabelle said. "We use the captain as bait and then hope for the best."

"I'll bring the hatpin," Angus said.

"To use on who?" Wymarc asked him. Angus had no answer for that.

"Where did Ophidian go?" Nestor said, glancing around the room.

"And Arolan?" Annabelle added.

"All the gods are gone," Angus said. The others looked at him and he shrugged. "It's something I know now."

"A very useful gift, if it works when they don't want you to see them," Wymarc said. She yawned and had Krea's body stretch suggestively. "We should get our rest while we can."

"May I escort you?" Nestor said, rising from his chair and proffering an arm gallantly.

Krea Wymarc shook her head. "No, I think I need to be alone."

Nestor tried to hide his dismay. Krea patted him on the arm, saying, "It's been a long day and we're very tired."

Nestor gave her a jerky nod and sat back down at the table, pulling a book toward himself.

"Richard?" Reedis said. When Ford looked up, Reedis jerked his head toward the doors. "A word, if I may?"

Ford gave the mage a surprised look but, nodding a good evening to the others, rose and followed the mage outside.

#

"What is it?" Ford asked when the doors were firmly closed behind him.

Reedis held up a hand, begging for indulgence. "Follow me, please."

Ford followed, his curiosity piqued. Reedis led him to the large study where he, Angus, and Annabelle had perfected their lifting magic. When they were inside, Reedis gestured for Ford to take a seat and took one himself facing the captain at an angle.

"You may die tomorrow," Reedis said without preamble. Ford pursed his lips and nodded slowly. Reedis gave him a quizzical look. "That doesn't trouble you?"

"I've faced death many times," Ford said with a shrug. "It hasn't come to me yet."

"The serpent attacked your ship," Reedis began. Ford nodded. "And Arolan saved you." Again, the captain nodded. Reedis frowned. "But that was two hundred years ago."

"More, actually," Ford said pensively. "I think about two hundred and twenty, maybe two hundred and thirty."

"You're surprisingly well-preserved!" Reedis exclaimed.

"No," Ford said. Reedis' brows rose questioningly. "How old do you think I am?"

"Late thirties, maybe early forties," Reedis said.

"Yes," Ford said, "something like that."

"So you're *not* two hundred... two hundred and twenty years old."

Ford shook his head and the mage spluttered in exacerbation.

"I'm tied to the tide," Ford said slowly. "I think Arolan must have made some deal with the moon." He paused a moment, then continued, "I grow old like all men." He waited to see Reedis' reaction but the mage merely gestured for him to continue. "When I am too old, the sea calls me."

"The sea?"

"Yes," Ford said. "It calls me when the tide is out. I have to go into it, into the water —"

"No matter where? No matter when?" Reedis demanded. Ford nodded. "Even in winter?" Again, the captain nodded.

"I go out all the way and swim into the surf," Ford said. "And then, when I'm under the water, I die."

"Die?"

"I can feel myself becoming undone," Ford said. "It hurts but it doesn't last."

"And then what?"

"I come back with the new tide," Ford said. "I come back as a young boy, usually five or six years old."

"Do you remember everything that happened before?"

Ford shook his head. "Bits, things that seemed important or particularly poignant," he said, his eyes bright with sorrow. "I forget a lot."

"Do you have children, Richard?" Reedis asked in a low voice.

"If I do, I don't remember them," Ford said. He shrugged. "Sometimes, sometimes I meet someone and I think I know them, might have been their parent or grandparent in lives past."

"Or great-grandparent," Reedis muttered. He shook his head. "This gift of Arolan's is a mixed blessing."

Ford's lips twisted ironically. "Don't they always say: 'Be careful what you ask the gods! They might listen.'"

"Do you want to die?" Reedis asked.

Ford shook his head. "Never. Every time, I held off as long as I could." He met Reedis' eyes. "But I am sworn. And I will not lose the world."

"If you die, you will," Reedis said.

Ford shook his head. "If I die, I will meet Terric and his son, and go on to a new life."

"If you die," Reedis said vehemently, "I shall be most peeved."

"I'll bear that in mind, purple mage," Ford said, rising from his chair. He stretched and turned back. "And with that said, I'll bid you a good night."

Reedis snorted in displeasure. He sat in silence for a long time. And then, with a cry of exaltation, he jumped from his chair and moved to the large table, dragging paper and pencil to hand.

#

"Why are you still awake?" Annabelle asked as she entered the library late that night. Nestor was slumped in a chair, a pile of books surrounding him.

"Why are you?" Nestor replied.

"Couldn't sleep," Annabelle admitted.

Nestor nodded. "Much the same."

"Did you find anything interesting?"

"I found three different ways to put my arm to sleep and two different ways to crick my neck," Nestor said sourly. "Besides that, I am no more enlightened than I was earlier."

"I see," Annabelle said, skirting the table and heading to the back part of the library where the fire had been set.

"Are you looking for anything in particular?"

"I realized that we hadn't spent any time examining her spell," Annabelle said abstractedly.

"How will that help?"

"I don't know if it will help tomorrow," Annabelle said. "But I plan on finding this person and I want every advantage I can get."

"Good idea," Nestor said, stretching and yawning. He rose and walked back to her. "Is there any way I can help?"

"I don't think so," Annabelle said, shaking her head. She gestured toward the table. "You should go back to work."

"Very well," Nestor said and turned but stopped mid-stride and turned back again, eyes bright.

"What?"

"I was wondering, would you know how to make a love potion?"

"A love potion!" Annabelle spluttered in outrage and raised her balled fists at him. "Do you plan on ensnaring some poor girl —" and she thought of Hana "— with your charms?"

"No," Nestor said, raising his hands defensively, "I was thinking of the serpent."

Annabelle's eyes went very wide. Slowly, she nodded. "I think that's a very good idea, my prince."

Chapter Eight

"It was Nestor's idea," Annabelle said when everyone praised her the next morning at breakfast.

"It's a very good idea!" Reedis said, turning to nod firmly at the blushing prince.

"Well done," Ford added, clapping Nestor on the back.

"The only question is who to put it on," Angus said grimly.

"Don't put it on me!" Krea Wymarc declared firmly. Beside her, Hana shook her head in agreement.

"Nor me," Ford said firmly. The others looked at him. "I can't be bait and lover both."

"Why not?" Annabelle asked him sardonically. "It worked in the past, didn't it?"

Richard gave her a look.

"Anyway, we can't put it on everyone or the affect will diminish," Annabelle said.

"So we see what transpires," Ford said. "See what works best at the time."

"Everyone should carry some, in that case," Reedis declared. The others nodded in agreement.

Annabelle frowned at them for a long moment. She turned to Nestor and passed him a small vial, "This is made for the serpent only."

"I understand," Nestor told her with a curt nod. "That's what we wanted."

Annabelle snorted and shot a glance toward Hana but Nestor merely shook his head in response.

"If you are all done with your games," Ophidian spoke up, appearing suddenly at one corner. Wymarc noticed the odd smile on Angus' lips: the smith had known of the god's arrival.

"We'll start playing yours, father," Wymarc said.

"Daughter," the dragon god said in a dangerous tone. Wymarc gave him a quick nod, even as she comforted Krea's inward anguished cry. *He needs us,* Wymarc assured her. She could feel Krea's alarmed gulp and then felt the young woman calm herself. *He also needs to remember his place.*

He's a god! Krea said. Wymarc said nothing in reply.

"Arolan?" Ford called politely.

"Here," the sea god said, appearing at Ford's side. He glanced to the others. "Are you ready?"

"We should go to the cloakroom and get dressed for the weather," Nestor said. He didn't quite meet the sea god's eyes when he said, "Shall we meet you outside?"

Arolan disappeared. So did Ophidian.

"We should make our way," Reedis said to the others.

"A moment," Ford said, raising a hand. He moved to the kitchen counter in the dining hall. "Sybil?"

"Yes, dear?" the goddess appeared, wearing an apron and wiping sweat from her brow. "What is it?"

"I wanted to thank you for all that you have done," Ford said.

"Oh! Well, very well," Sybil said, reaching across the counter to shake his hand. "It really was my pleasure. I rarely get a chance to cook for so many for so long."

Ford nodded and smiled at her. He moved away, first in a sudden line of others. He turned back to their table and said, "Avice, Terric! I wish to thank you for your hospitality."

"Our pleasure," Avice said, suddenly appearing in front of him. Impulsively she hugged him. Terric nodded at him mutely.

When the rest were done with their farewells, they marched down to the cloakroom and wrapped themselves in warm winter gear before strapping into their balloon harnesses — all except for Krea Wymarc and Hana who had their own means of flying.

"I want you to stick close to Ford," Reedis said in a worried tone to Hana as they turned to leave. Hana turned to look at him. "He might try something stupid."

"We all might," Ford said drolly, proving that the mage had not been as quiet as he'd hoped. He clapped Reedis on the shoulder. "I'll do my best."

"That's what I'm afraid of."

#

"Where first?" Ophidian asked when he met the others outside of the House of Life and Death.

"I think the shore, nearest the ocean," Ford said, pulling out his scroll and unrolling it to point at the lines they'd drawn for the serpent's possible courses. He pointed at a spot. "If you could put me here and the others a bit further —"

— before Ford could complete his sentence, he was standing in the exact spot he'd indicated.

"— away," Ford completed in a smaller voice. He turned and saw the others arrayed behind him. "Hana? If you would…"

The dark-eyed girl nodded and gestured with her hands and Ford found himself the center of a light breeze.

"We should get aloft," Reedis said. "Fill."

"Fill," Ford added, feeling the balloon on his back lift and go taut.

"Up," Annabelle said, followed by Angus, Nestor, and Reedis.

"I'll stay here," Krea said, glancing toward Hana and Ford.

Ford glanced at her and nodded. "But not too close, if you please. Give yourself enough distance to get airborne."

"Of course," Wymarc replied with mild affront.

Ford glanced to Hana, pointing to the others, slowly rising in the morning sun. "Can you spread them out so that they can scan a greater distance?"

Hana nodded and raised a hand, fanning it upwards back and forth between the others while keeping one hand pointed toward Ford, to maintain the wind.

"Nothing!" Reedis called down impatiently.

"Arolan?" Ford said. "Could she get here by now?"

"No sooner than now," Arolan said, standing beside Ford and scanning the frozen plains stretching eastwards away from them. "Of course, she might have been distracted —"

"Distracted? How?"

"She might have stopped…" the god's voice tapered off.

"For something to eat!" Ophidian swore in surprise.

"Where's the nearest village?" Ford demanded. He glanced up to the others. "Any sign?"

"No!" Nestor cried down. His answer was followed by a chorus all saying the same thing.

"She might still be coming…" Arolan said.

Ford turned to Ophidian. "Can you take me there?"

"Alone?"

"And Hana and Krea Wymarc," Ford said suddenly. He turned to Arolan. "Keep the others here —"

"Leave Krea Wymarc," Ophidian said, "and take the prince."

"The prince?" Ford asked in surprise.

"That gives her a choice, at least," Ophidian said.

"The prince?" Arolan repeated, looking at the dragon god as if he'd grown another head.

"We can bring the others if we find Pallas," Ophidian said testily. "But I don't want to leave you without choices if the serpent comes here after all."

"Very well," Arolan said, waving his hand dismissively.

Ophidian frowned up at Nestor and turned to Arolan. "I can't move him against that magic, can you?"

Arolan looked up and turned back to the dragon god, his eyes wide with surprise.

"Then send me and Hana," Ford said testily. "Send the others when they get down."

"So be it," Ophidian said.

#

Ford heard screams all around him. "Hana!"

"I'm here," the dark-eyed girl called from behind him.

"I'm going up," Ford said, saying the magic word, "Up."

Hana rose with him and they scanned the village spread out in front of them with growing horror.

There were fires in several of the houses. And bloodstains on the snow. Here and there, Ford could see a dark smudge or something torn in half. His ears were filled with cries of despair, overshadowed by a roar of triumph.

"Hana!" Ford shouted, pointing to the distance. "Blow me over there!"

Hana gave him a worried look, he was pointing to the center of destruction. Ford repeated his gesture emphatically and, looking worried, Hana complied.

"Stay back!" Ford called to her. "If this doesn't go well, I'll need you to —" He cut off sharply and suddenly clasped his hands to his ears. "Arrr!"

"Ford!" Hana cried, blowing herself closer to him.

Ford waved at her frantically with one hand before bringing it back to his head. "The serpent!" Hana gave him an uncomprehending look. "It's screaming in my head!" He turned back toward the ruins of the village. "Arolan! Arolan!"

He can't hear you! A voice roared gleefully in Ford's head.

"I heard it!" Hana cried in pain. "Ford, I heard it!"

"Go!" Ford screamed to her. "Get away from here! Warn the others!"

"I don't know where!" Hana cried in despair.

Ford pointed behind her. "Go to the shore, then head north!" he shouted. "Quickly, before it kills again!"

"What are you going to do?"

"Don't worry about me," Ford shouted, gesturing again with one clenched fist. "Just go!"

Hana twisted around, torn between helping Ford and alerting the others. Finally, with a sob, she thrust herself away as fast as she could toward the shore, leaving a blast of wind behind her.

In his harness, Ford felt the wind blow on him. In a flash of inspiration, he rolled up his sleeve to the bitter cold, pulled his knife from its sheath and slashed down quickly, letting the wind blow his blood far and fast.

"Here I am!" Ford shouted, as he floated with the wind. "Come and get me!"

In the distance, the snow serpent roared with the joy of the hunt.

#

"Hana?" Angus cried when he spotted a figure in the far distance moving toward them up around the seashore. The figure seemed to falter, falling, and then lifted once more, moving in a serpentine line northwards.

"Ophidian!" Angus shouted. The dragon god appeared beside him, his expression furious. Angus pointed to the distance. "Is that Hana?"

"What if it is?" Ophidian asked in a surly tone.

A screech distracted them and they both turned to see Krea Wymarc dive toward the distant figure. It was falling, lifeless, toward the ground.

"Take me to her!" Angus ordered. Ophidian's eyes glowed red with anger. *"Please?"*

And they were there. Angus dove, using abilities that he didn't think about and grabbed Hana by the arm, then dropped further and wrapped his other arm around her.

"It's okay," he said to the limp form. "I've got you."

"Ford," Hana said in a whimper. "It's after him."

"Ophidian!" Angus bellowed, causing the others to turn toward him.

"I heard," the dragon god said. "But I can't take you there with this magic —"

"Empty!" Angus ordered, glaring at the god.

"That's one way to do it," Ophidian murmured. The next moment they were gone.

Chapter Nine

Ford was tired. He'd covered his arm with his jacket as soon as he had the beast's attention but he was still dripping blood and he was freezing from its loss. He'd managed to lure the serpent from the village up to the foothills and now into the mountains as the breeze that Hana had sent, slowly dying, had wafted him further and further away.

At least they're safe, Ford thought as he glanced to the ruined village in the distance. He imagined it was some Issian outpost, a new settlement that wasn't on his map. *If it had been, I might have thought to come here first.*

"Up, up, up!" Ford ordered the balloon as the serpent gained altitude climbing among the hills. The balloon pulled him upwards. Ford grinned and shouted back down to the blue-white shape slithering below. "I'm up here!"

The serpent bellowed in rage and anger, increasing its speed and climbing further upwards and further away from the village.

"Up!" Ford called again to the balloon. His eyes narrowed as he gaged his progress: was the balloon rising slower? How long would Reedis' spells last? He knew that the balloon might stay inflated forever but the spell to rise or fall, that was something that would wear off, wouldn't it?

The beast below was everything Ford remembered from his distant past. It was a serpent which slithered and writhed with four legs set at great distance along its bulk. The head was huge, nearly as large as its body, and it had no neck, the head joining directly to the sinewy body. Atop its head were curled horns and small ears. Its eyes were huge and dark, its mouth wide — it looked like it could open its mouth as wide as its body.

At least it can't fly, Ford thought thankfully to himself.

Fly? The word was scarcely in Ford's brain when the world erupted in a maelstrom of motion.

"Ford!" A distant cry came even as Ford felt something rip into his midriff, tear him and suddenly he was streaming upwards and in pain, pain, *pain!*

You taste good! The beast shouted triumphantly.

"Ford!" It was Reedis, crying in terror and alarm. Ford tried to turn toward him, but found it hard. He tumbled in his harness and found himself looking straight down into the dark eyes of the serpent as it leaped straight up for him, chewing mightily on something —

The lower half of Ford's body.

#

They burst out into the sky just as they heard a shriek of triumph and saw the blue-white serpent leap upwards, snapping its jaws tightly around captain Ford's lower half.

"Ford!" Annabelle cried in terror. She shrieked in horror as the beast's jaws tore the captain in half. Ford's head and torso lurched upwards as the serpent fell back.

"Ford!" Reedis added his pained voice to Annabelle's.

"Hana!" Angus cried to the girl he was holding in his arms. She groaned at his words. "We need you!" He turned in his balloon harness and snarled at the serpent below. He waved his hands and threw a venomous curse its way. It streaked from him as a bolt of fire.

92

The serpent shrieked in pain as the bolt hit just behind its foreleg and it turned to face its attacker, bellowing in rage and vengeance.

"Krea Wymarc!" Nestor cried toward the wyvern. The winter wyvern turned red eyes toward him. He smiled at her. "I love you," he said. Then, to his balloon, he said, "Empty." With that, he plunged downwards.

"Hana!" Angus cried, seeing the prince fall and instantly guessing his intentions. "Blow him toward the serpent!"

"Fire!" Reedis cried furiously, throwing a fire bolt of his own toward the serpent.

"We can't kill her!" Annabelle cried in warning.

"It killed the captain!" Reedis shouted back, hurling another bolt toward the enraged serpent.

"But we *can't* kill her," Annabelle shouted back. "Now matter how hard we try."

"That is for the gods," Ophidian added, eyeing the purple mage with disgust.

Reedis pointed back down the mountain to the village, still burning in the distant. "What about them?"

"You do not want Pallas dead," Ophidian said. In the distance, Krea Wymarc screeched in agreement. He waved toward her. "Trust us on this."

"Then help us!" Angus bellowed.

"I am," Ophidian said, surprised. He gestured toward Nestor who lurched even closer to the serpent.

With a jolt, Nestor landed on the serpent's back. He clung on for dear life even as the serpent bellowed in rage. It jerked upwards, trying to shake him off and catch the upper half of Ford at the same time.

With a cry of horror, Nestor saw that Ford was hanging upside in the remains of his harness.

"Captain Ford!" Nestor cried, straining to reach one hand upwards toward the dying man.

"My King," Ford said, glancing at Nestor with a pained look of surprise on his face. "Promise me —"

"Anything!" Nestor shouted back.

"Promise me you'll forgive her," Ford called down. He groped his hands against the harness and pulled free from it. "She is *so* sorry."

And he plummeted down, falling into the gaping jaws of the triumphant serpent.

"Richard!" Reedis cried down from the heavens above.

Nestor slammed his fist against the heavy scales of the serpent in anger and fury. He wanted to hurt it, to kill it. He reached around his person, looking for anything, any weapon — and found the vial that Annabelle had given him.

With a snarl, he pulled it out and plunged it deep into the serpent's hide, feeling the glass vial shatter and give way as he did so, cutting his hand to ribbons and —

"Nestor!" dimly the cry came to his ears over the roaring, the pain, the joy, the —

A screech followed and he landed hard on something soft.

And then he knew no more.

Chapter Ten

"Shh, shh!" a voice came to him. "You're not to move!"

Where am I? Who am I?

Dimly he remembered falling. He remembered crying in horror. The cold, he'd been freezing cold.

I am so *sorry! Can you ever forgive me?* The words were not his. They were strange in his head and he grew frightened. *I was mad with terror and rage. I didn't mean it!*

"My King," a voice came back to him. Richard. Captain Ford.

Nestor opened his eyes. And closed them again just as quickly. The room was spinning.

"It will take a while," a voice cautioned him. "You must give it time."

"Wymarc?" Nestor asked, his eyes still closed. His voice was just above a whisper.

"We're here," Krea's voice came back to him with a deep warmth. *Krea.* The name brushed at Nestor's memory and he winced.

"I didn't mean to hurt you," Nestor said with all his heart. "I didn't know —"

"You must hold onto that, my prince," Wymarc said with Krea's voice. "It is important that you hold onto that."

Important?

Krea. She was important.

He loved her flowing grace, her kind smile. How could he have ever thought to hurt her?

I'm so sorry. I didn't know, the other voice said in his head.

I *didn't know*, Nestor repeated the thought. And then his eyes jerked open and he found himself looking up at Krea's body, saw the concern on her face. "What happened?"

"It was a very strange choice," Ophidian's voice came back from another part of the room. Nestor twitched his head in the god's direction and regretted it as the world spun behind his eyes and his stomach protested.

"What was?"

"I'm sure the love potion helped," Ophidian continued, ignoring his question. "But I never would have guessed."

"Father!" Wymarc scolded in Krea's voice. Nestor could always tell when the wyvern spoke and when Krea used her voice herself. There was something… something in the tone.

Nestor went rigid in thought and fear.

I am so, so sorry. The thought was in a different tone.

"What happened to the serpent?" Nestor asked, his voice gravelly and hard.

A hand patted his shoulder soothingly.

"*You* happened, Nestor," Ophidian told him approvingly.

Pallas? Nestor said to the other voice he'd been hearing.

Your friend, the serpent replied miserably. *I only meant —*

You're a girl! Nestor thought in surprise.

Epilog

"Feeling better?" a man's voice said above him.

"I was dying, I was cut in half —" Captain Sir Richard Ford said in surprise. He realized he felt no pain. "And now I'm not."

"Of course," the man said.

Ford opened his eyes and smiled. "Hello, Terric," he said to the god of Death.

"Balance has come," a small child's voice piped up from Ford's other side. He turned and realized that he was seeing Aron, the god of Judgement, for the last time.

"You were on the ship," Ford said, suddenly remembering all the other times he'd seen the lad.

Aron smiled and nodded at him. "You remember now."

"The others?" Ford said, first to the boy and then to Terric.

"They continue," the god of Death said.

"They are needed," Aron said, smiling and bouncing on his feet.

"I thought as much," Ford said. He glanced around. "Arolan?"

"This is not his territory," Terric said sadly.

"Did I fulfill my oath?" Ford asked, glancing to the god of Judgement. Aron nodded. Ford sighed. "Good." He said to both of the gods, "Please convey my respects to him."

"You served him well," Aron said. "That is all he asked."

Ford nodded and glanced to Terric. "Can I stand?"

"If you wish," Terric said. He helped Ford to his feet for the last time.

Ford gestured to the two gold hoops in his ears. "Will they suffice?"

"They will," the god of Death agreed. He waved a hand. "Bryan, please escort our friend onwards."

"With pleasure," the Ferryman said.

"Please give my regards to your mother and sister," Ford said as the Ferryman grasped his hand and Terric placed gold coins in his eyes.

"Certainly," Bryan replied.

"It was interesting, wasn't it?" Aron said to Terric in the silence that followed.

"I don't think he could have done better," Terric said, pocketing the two gold coins once more.

Iron Air

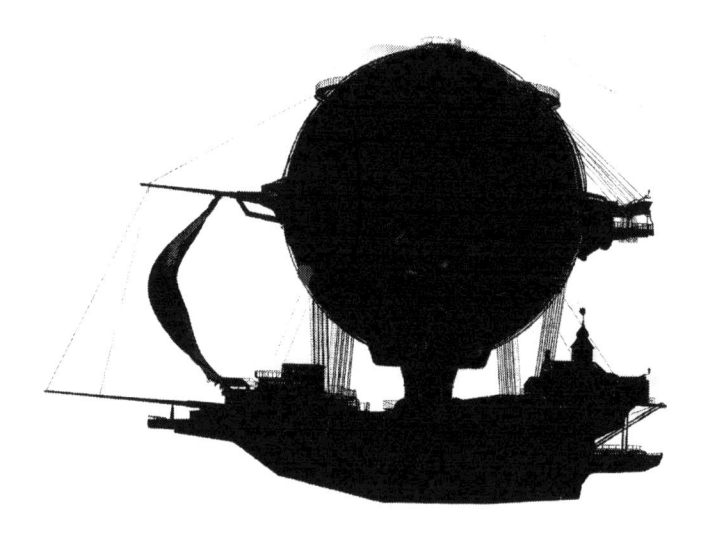

Book 8

Twin Soul series

Chapter One

Rabel Zebala opened his eyes to a world of white. He closed his eyes immediately, dazzled by a brilliance that threatened to blind him. The sun. The sun was just on the horizon, rising — he guessed — and it filled the room with a fiery white light.

Finally the sun rose high enough that the world beyond his closed eyes was only bright, not blinding, and he took the chance of opening his eyes, narrowed to merest slits.

The room was white. In fact, Rabel realized, the room was ice. He stood up, letting the blankets wrapped loosely around him fall away. He was still in his clothes.

Then he remembered. He had been riding a dragon. They'd been fleeing, flying in the night through a blizzard and… there was a girl as well.

Ellen. The little street urchin.

He raced out of the white room into the brilliant morning air, crying, "Ellen!"

A small form appeared over the crest of a hill. She waved at him and Rabel's chest eased.

"We were just getting food," she cried, waving behind her. Another form came into view: a young man, in his late teens or early twenties, striding along behind her with a glum expression and a heavy sack on his back.

"Who are you?" Rabel demanded irritably. He was annoyed with himself over his fear for the child, more annoyed that she was with a stranger, and relieved beyond imagining that nothing untoward had occurred. Unless the stranger was dangerous.

"What? Don't you remember?" the young man called back. His expression changed, as he said gruffly, "You summoned me."

"Oh!" Rabel said, enlightened. He cocked his head apologetically. "I didn't recognize you."

The young lad nodded and guided the little girl over to the ice cave.

Rabel turned back to examine it, then back to the lad. "Your doing?"

"With the last of my strength," the lad agreed. He placed a hand on Ellen's shoulder. "She's quite a taskmaster, in case you didn't know."

"I only begged him," Ellen said in her defense.

"She's got ability," Rabel said, half apologizing.

The lad nodded in agreement and gestured for Rabel to precede them into the cave.

#

Inside, the sack was poured out onto Rabel's bedding to reveal bread, cut meats, a jar of butter, a couple of bottles and a few herbs.

"Eat," the lad said. Rabel nodded gratefully, tearing up a piece of the bread and handing it to Ellen.

"We've had some already," Ellen said, shaking her head and pushing it back to him.

Rabel didn't need further encouragement, chomping down the slice and reaching for some meat.

"Where are we?" he said when he'd swallowed. He eyed the bottles warily.

"Right where you told us to be," the lad replied.

"You're Jarin," Rabel said, examining the young man carefully. In human form, the dragon had dark hair and green eyes. He seemed younger than his body, as though he was less matured than his years would indicate. Rabel thought for a moment, then asked, "And where did I tell us to be?"

"You told us to land just after we were across the border," Ellen said. "We did and Jarin made this cave and we slept."

"So now what?" Jarin said. "Tell me why I don't leave you right now."

"He's Krea's father," Ellen said, grabbing his head to get his attention. "She's the winter wyvern."

Jarin turned his gaze on Rabel. "You can't be," he said finally, "you're not old enough."

"I *told* you," Ellen said in irritation, "he made a deal with Ophidian." She glanced toward Rabel and gave him a look, worried that perhaps she should not have revealed that secret.

"Your father had us call you," Rabel said.

"My *father?*"

"Ophidian," Ellen said.

"The god?" Jarin asked. He glanced to Rabel for confirmation. "You're saying that I'm the son of a *god?*"

"That's what he told me," Rabel said.

"Annora Wymarc said —" Jarin stopped and closed his eyes in pain. "Annora is no more."

"She is not," Rabel agreed. "Wymarc twinned with my daughter —"

"Your daughter!" Jarin exclaimed. His brows furrowed. "Krea? Krea is *your* daughter?"

"You're repeating yourself," Ellen said.

"If I am, little girl," Jarin replied sharply, "it's because I cannot believe the words themselves!"

"What did Annora Wymarc say?" Ellen prompted. Jarin gave her a questioning look. "You were saying…"

Jarin frowned. "Annora Wymarc said that I am twin soul, that she was sent by my father to help guide me." He closed his eyes in sorrow as he continued. "I didn't listen to her when she said not to play with the airship. They nearly killed me."

"They got her instead," Rabel said. "She died for you."

"Yes," Jarin agreed in a small voice. "But I got revenge."

"You stole from the prince," Ellen said.

"It was nothing," Jarin said, waving it aside. He opened his eyes and glanced to Rabel. "Your daughter was oathsworn twice."

"I know," Rabel said sadly. "I had hoped to spare her, to —"

"Why?" Jarin demanded angrily. "You're young! You could take care of her —"

"He's young *now*," Ellen interrupted. "When I met him, he was old and bald."

"Old and… you made a deal with a god!"

"Your father," Rabel said in agreement. "'Life given, lives guarded.'"

"You?" Jarin said incredulously. "You're to replace Annora Wymarc?"

"Just as my daughter replaced Annora," Rabel said.

"You can't fly," Jarin said. "Why don't I just leave you here?"

"Your father is a god," Rabel said slowly. "I have a feeling that perhaps I know him better than you."

"You do?" Jarin challenged. "And how is that?"

"Because I knew Annora Wymarc," Rabel said. Jarin's eyebrows twitched upwards. Rabel twitched a grin. "Did you know why she brought you here?"

"She said we were going to see someone," Jarin replied. "You?"

Rabel shook his head. "Ibb."

"The mechanical?" Ellen asked. "The one who helped you get away?"

"If this Ibb helped you get away, why did you need my father?" Jarin asked shrewdly.

"That *was* Ibb's help," Rabel replied with a twist of his lips. "I sometimes wonder how much Ibb truly means it when he says he has no use for the gods." He shrugged to dismiss the question, then said to Jarin, "Do you know why you were to see Ibb?"

Jarin shook his head. "Annora wouldn't tell me much."

"She learned that from Wymarc," Rabel muttered.

"Learned what?" Jarin demanded.

"Being obtuse," Rabel said. "And Wymarc learned it from your father."

"The god," Jarin said, shaking his head.

"You can turn into a dragon," Ellen told him. "What makes you think that your father *isn't* a god?"

Jarin mulled that over and spread his hands in acceptance.

"How long did you know Wymarc?" Rabel asked.

"All my life," Jarin said immediately.

"How many years?"

Jarin frowned in thought. "I don't count years that much," he said. "Four? Maybe five?"

"You're *younger* than me?" Ellen said looking up at the tall man and shaking her head.

"Ophidian tasked me to guard you," Rabel said to Jarin. "He wouldn't have done that if you were of age."

"How do you know?" Ellen demanded.

"I have dealt with him before," Rabel said. "He believes that his children should take care of themselves."

"Then I should leave you," Jarin said, rising to his feet.

"When they're of age," Rabel added hastily, gesturing for Jarin to sit back down. "He won't leave his children unguarded in the world when they can't guard themselves."

"Annora Wymarc was my guardian?" Jarin said, sounding betrayed. "I thought she was my friend."

"There's no reason the two can't be one," Rabel said, flicking a hand toward the dragon man.

"And *you're* to take her place?" Jarin asked. Rabel nodded. "I'm to be treated as a baby?"

"If you're only four or five years old, you *are*," Ellen told him primly.

"Dragons mature very quickly," Rabel said to the little girl. He turned to Jarin. "It's not your age that determines your abilities. It's your experience."

"Well, I wish to experience being my own master," Jarin said in a huff.

"And I wish no less for you," Rabel said. "But Annora Wymarc is no more. And we have enemies."

"Enemies?"

"Those who built the airships," Rabel said.

"You helped," Ellen piped up, "you said so."

"*You* helped?"

"I was working with Ibb," Rabel said. He raised a hand before the dark-haired lad could fume at him, adding, "And, I think, your father."

"Who's a god," Jarin said, shaking his head again. He glanced up to Rabel. "If he's a god, why doesn't he just— just—?"

"Just what?" Ellen asked, shaking her head. "The gods can't be everywhere. And they don't seem to care about us all that much." She glared at Jarin. "You're lucky that your father cares enough about you to give you friends."

"Friends?"

"If you're smart enough to have them," Ellen said, her jaw clenched in anger. She nodded to Rabel. "He could have died, could have ended everything but he gave his oath for me, for you, and for Krea Wymarc."

Jarin absorbed the fierce girl's words silently. A long moment passed before he turned to Rabel, "So what am I to learn?"

"Usually," Rabel replied slowly, "I have found that the *teacher* is the one who learns the most."

Chapter Two

"The house was completely destroyed, burnt to cinders," Colonel Walpish reported as he bowed deeply before King Markel and gave his report to General Gergen. "My men formed a bucket line and threw what water we could but we were too few, the fires too hot."

"Ophidian's flame," Vistos, the mage, pronounced sagely.

"Did he die?" King Markel said to his mages.

Vistos frowned. Margen, the other aged mage, looked doubtful.

"If not in the fire, the dragon would surely have consumed him," Vistos declared. "He was an old man."

"He managed to break out of the jail," Markel growled. "Scarcely the action of a man too old to take care of himself."

"I think," first minister Mannevy interjected suavely, "your Majesty, that we should not concern ourselves further with this man."

"And the dragon?" Markel demanded. "It was the same one which attacked *Spite*, wasn't it?"

"But it's gone now, sire," Mannevy replied. "I think we can safely assume that it was only drawn by the fire and the wyvern's flowers in the field nearby."

Markel gave him a doubtful look and then, with a flick of his fingers, dismissed the issue. "That still leaves us in need of someone who can make steel, does it not?"

"Engineer Newman assures me that it will not present us with an insurmountable obstacle," Mannevy replied smoothly. "We have two airships commissioned and more under construction."

General Gergen frowned at the first minister. Mannevy noticed and flicked two fingers in response, cautioning the general from any outbursts.

"That's true," King Markel said after a moment. "General, how stand your troops?"

"My first echelon is ready now, sire," Gergen replied, drawing himself to attention. "We could begin the invasion in a week, with scouts committed tomorrow if the order is given."

"And Soria?" King Markel said to Mannevy. "Do they suspect?"

"They've sent an inquiry about their ship, the *Parvour* —"

"*Vengeance*," the King interrupted with a chuckle. "And they'll see it soon enough."

Mannevy nodded at the king's jest. "Our spies —" and he nodded to Peter Hewlitt, the King's spymaster who nodded back "— have reported nothing indicating that King Wendel or any of his ministers have the least suspicion of our actions."

"Good!" the king said firmly. "And our airships, are they ready?"

"The first two, as you know," Mannevy said with a nod. "The next four are still working up."

"I wanted two dozen!"

"We'll have six in two weeks, sire," Mannevy replied calmly. "The other eighteen will take longer, particularly as we're having trouble finding hulls."

"Build them!" the king barked.

First minister Mannevy gave his king a pained look. "Sire, as you no doubt recall, it takes a good two years to build a ship."

"It doesn't have to be a ship, does it?" the king said. "Just a deck for the cannon."

"And the supplies and a place for the crew to sleep," Mannevy replied with a shrug. "All our builders are convinced that a ship is the best starting point for an air*ship*, sire."

"Will six be enough, general?" the king demanded.

"Sire," General Gergen replied slowly, "as you know, my expertise is on land." He gave the king a small bow. "I would expect your admiral to know better about this than myself."

"Pfaw!" the king grumbled. He couldn't trust his admirals — they were far too likely to blubber about the loss to their fleet and, besides, the high admiral had been known to spend far too much time with the queen. He turned his gaze back to Mannevy. "Two years?"

"Actually, your majesty, we're planning to levy another six from the fleet and the merchant fleet," Mannevy said. "Our planning is that should give you an even dozen in another three months. The rest…" he shrugged "… well, we could hope that our sea fleet might capture enough hulls for our needs."

"I'm sure Admiral Kettner will be happy to oblige," the king murmured.

"Certainly," Mannevy agreed. "I shall draw orders for him to be given as soon as we commence hostilities."

"See to it," king Markel said with a wave of his hand. He gestured to Colonel Walpish. "Rise, colonel," he said. "I understand you and your men are to handle our initial scouting?"

"It is my honor, sire," Walpish replied with a quick bow. "My men are keen for the work."

"I hope they are better suited to that than to apprehending aged men," the king replied drolly. Colonel Walpish kept his expression rigid. The king decided that he was going to get no joy in goading the man so he waved a hand in dismissal. "You may go about your preparations, then."

"Sire," Walpish replied, bowing once more and backing away diligently.

#

"I understand that his majesty was much put out at the failure to capture a prisoner," Josiah Prentice, the King's Exchequer, said to first minister Mannevy when they met for tea later.

"Sadly, true."

"One prisoner?" Prentice prodded.

"One who was instrumental in the steel used for *Spite*," Mannevy explained. "We were counting on his skills."

"Is this not the same man you were going to have hanged?"

"If he's no use to us, there's no point in feeding him," Mannevy said with a shrug. "Too many useless mouths in the kingdom as is."

"His majesty will surely fix that," Prentice said, pointing to a map laid out before them, "when he commences this expansion."

"Surely," Mannevy agreed. He gestured to the map. "Now, you're here to tell me about what we can expect to acquire with our conquests."

"Overall?"

"No, town by town," Mannevy said. "You know our expenses, tell me how we'll meet them."

Josiah Prentice smiled. "My pleasure."

Ellen, with the younger ears, heard it first. Jarin and Rabel were too busy sniping at each other to pay attention to the noises outside the snow fort.

"Listen!" Ellen cried, interrupting the two men, flinging a hand toward the entrance.

Rabel held up a hand to silence Jarin who glared at him. The two turned to the girl, then the entrance.

"I don't hear anything," Jarin said.

Rabel frowned and moved to the entrance, out into the warming sunshine. The other two followed him. Rabel turned to Ellen, "Get our things." She gave him a look, nodded and rushed back in to gather everything in the fort. To Jarin he said, "How angry are you?"

"What?"

"Are you angry enough to burn this fort to nothing?" Rabel said as Ellen rushed out of the fort with their meager belongings in the large sack Rabel had provided when they'd fled his burning home.

"*What?*" Jarin repeated, his jaw clenched.

"Perhaps I should start," Rabel said. He turned to Ellen, "Do you think you can conjure up fire?"

"What are we going to do?"

"We're going to send a signal," Rabel said. Jarin's expression changed and he said, "Do we really want to attract attention?"

"Dragon-child, do you think there is anything that can harm you?" Ellen said with a half-suppressed grin. Jarin's eyes glowed at her jibe.

"Ellen, watch," Rabel said. He raised his hands, pressed the tips of his fingers together in a wide tent, then pulled them apart slowly, revealing a large glowing ball in the air which his hands had enclosed.

"Wow!"

"You try," Rabel said, as he batted the flaming ball toward the entrance of their snow fort.

Ellen licked her lips and pursed them tight in concentration, putting her fingers together the way Rabel had and pulling them apart. Nothing.

Jarin chuckled. Ellen scowled at him. The dragon-man relaxed his expression to one more sympathetic.

"Try again, now that you're mad," Rabel said, nodding toward Jarin. "Think of heat, of flame, of a ball of fire that can consume water."

"Ametza will be mad," Ellen said.

"Good," Jarin said with feeling.

Ellen glanced at him, at the snow fort and raised her hands once more.

"You are using Ophidian's power," Rabel told her, "don't forget."

"Ophidian," Ellen said, pressing her fingertips together. She took a deep breath and pulled her fingers apart. In the middle of the air they had enclosed was a small ball of brightness. She laughed, raised a hand and batted it —

"No!" Rabel cried, too late.

"Ow!" Ellen said, clasping her burnt hand to her side.

"Put it in the snow," Rabel told her. "I should have warned you not to try to hit it."

"You did!" Ellen said accusingly, as she put her hand in a pile of snow. The cold ice eased the pain of the burn in the center of her hand.

"Jarin," Rabel said to the dragon-man, "you can help her."

"What?"

"Ellen, show him your hand," Rabel said. Ellen, with a grimace, complied.

"That's a nasty burn," Jarin said as he looked at the mark in Ellen's palm. He glared at Rabel.

"You can fix it," Rabel said.

"How?"

"Touch it — gently! — with your fingernail and think to draw the fire back to you," Rabel said.

Jarin frowned but did as Rabel ordered. Ellen gasped in surprise as Jarin's fingernail barely brushed the surface of the burn and the burn vanished, turning into a stream of brilliant flame that was absorbed by Jarin's fingernail. Jarin gave Rabel an amazed look.

"Just as you can throw fire, you can draw it," Rabel told him. He nodded toward the snow fort. "Now, can you throw the largest, hottest fire to the center of our fort?"

"To do what?"

"To create a vent of steam that rises high in the sky," Rabel replied.

"And attracts attention all from miles around," Jarin warned.

"That's the idea," Rabel agreed. "But we won't be here."

"Where will we be then?" Jarin asked grumpily. "I haven't the strength to fly us far."

"The flame?" Rabel repeated.

With a growl, Jarin drew himself up, stood away from Ellen and Rabel, and whipped his body around to throw a huge glowing fireball right inside the snow fort. Instantly, the fort collapsed into a huge gout of steam, blowing first out of the entrance and then billowing up into the air as the entrance and the fort collapsed from the heat.

The three of them stood in amazement as the resulting steam rose higher and higher in the sky. Finally, Rabel turned to Ellen, "Do you still hear the noise?"

Ellen turned to listen. Her brows creased. "The noise has stopped," she said after a moment. "But there's something else. Odd. I've heard it before."

"Lead the way," Rabel said, throwing the sack over his shoulder and nodding to Jarin.

"There's a road that way," Jarin said in warning. "It leads to the village where we got the food."

Rabel nodded to show that he'd heard the younger man but said nothing. They walked for about five minutes until they crested a low hill and saw the village in the distance and the road just beside them. Rabel stopped for a moment, passed the sack to Jarin who took it with ill humor, and knelt to the snow, making a quick snowball.

"What's that for?" Jarin demanded.

"Attracting attention," Rabel said, throwing the snowball to the roadside.

"What are you —" Jarin began.

The snowball hit something several feet above the road and fell to the ground. Ellen giggled, knelt and made her own snowball which she quickly sent after Rabel's.

"What are you…?" Jarin said again glancing between the two before dropping the sack and making his own snowball.

"Attracting attention," Rabel said. "Though I don't doubt we're expected."

"Who?" Jarin said, throwing another snowball to the invisible thing on the road.

"Ibb," Ellen said, still giggling. "He rode away in an invisible wagon."

"Which you are making visible," a voice spoke from behind them. They turned and saw nothing. Rabel grinned and threw his snowball at the voice. The snowball clunked against something and fell to the ground.

"And now you're —" the voice of Ibb was cut off as Ellen's snowball hit at mouth level. The invisible mechanical man spluttered as he spit out bits of snow and then said, "This is most indecorous."

"On the contrary," Rabel said, "it is our decorations which are enlightening." Rabel hit the mechanical with another snowball, aimed higher.

"If I release the spell —" Ibb began only to be hit in the mouth again by Ellen's expert throw.

"Is your caravan big enough for the four of us?" Rabel asked, gesturing toward the invisible object on the road.

"I'm sure I can find a room that will suit," Ibb replied, moving toward them.

Now that she knew what she was hearing, Ellen had no trouble following the clanking motion of the mechanical man as he marched ponderously toward the caravan. Rabel gestured for the others to wait until Ibb had passed them and then fell in behind the invisible man.

Jarin gave Rabel a challenging look, to which Rabel replied, "He knows how to get in and where to enter."

Jarin accepted this with a wary shrug. He fell in at the rear of the group. They reached the road and Jarin was surprised to see a dark door-sized opening appear in the air above them.

"Watch the step," Ibb warned.

"I can't *see* it," Jarin returned hotly. Ellen gave him a reproving look over her shoulder, reaching forward and feeling for invisible steps in front of her. The young dragon-man tried not to feel chagrined at her expression.

"Shut the door," Rabel's voice carried back to Jarin as he felt for, and found, steps leading up to the darkness. Ellen vanished and then Jarin followed her.

#

"This is new," Rabel said as he stepped into the large well-lit room. Ibb the mechanical man, turned to him and nodded agreeably.

"A little something I've been saving for emergencies," the mechanical man allowed.

"I thought you didn't like emergencies," Rabel said.

"I don't," Ibb agreed. "And this one even less."

"Trouble?"

"Many troubles," Ibb corrected.

Rabel grunted in acknowledgement. Ibb glanced toward Jarin. And Rabel groaned in apology. "Ibb the mechanical, may I make you known to Jarin the dragon?" he said, waving a hand from one to the other. "And Jarin, may I introduce you to Ibb the mechanical man?"

Jarin gave Ibb a guarded nod of recognition.

"You're the thief," Ibb said. Jarin glared at him. "You helped Krea —"

"Krea…?"

"Now Krea Wymarc," Ibb said, "if I remember the namings aright."

"The girl who turned into the wyvern," Jarin said in sudden understanding. He looked at Rabel. "She was your daughter but you were an old man!"

Rabel nodded. "As I said, I gave an oath to your father."

Jarin turned to Ibb. "I'm not a thief." He glanced at Rabel. "She took the money for you."

Rabel patted a pocket. "And I have it, mostly."

"How did you keep it from the guards?" Ellen asked.

Rabel gave her a sly look, as he said, "There are ways to keep things hidden."

"I thought her man — that apprentice —" Jarin began.

"My apprentice," Rabel corrected with a nod. "Angus Franck. He passed it to me when we met in the jail." Rabel added, "I made sure he took some for himself."

"That's *my* money!" Jarin cried. The others looked at him. "I took it for Wymarc!"

"And now we have it, where we need it," Rabel said.

"Need it?" Jarin said. Rabel nodded. "What for?"

"War," Ibb said heavily.

"And more," Rabel agreed.

"War?" Jarin said.

"Markel intends to take Soria," Rabel told him.

"He and Ametza are plotting together," Ibb said.

"How do you know that?" Jarin demanded.

"I have been watching this land for many years," Ibb said. He glanced to Rabel. "You may remember some of it."

Rabel shook his head. "I have not your years, old man."

Ibb made a grinding sound that might have been a snort. "No, you are still a sproutling." The glowing eyes of the mechanical man turned to Jarin and Ellen. "And you have become a teacher once again."

"I learned from a master," Rabel said, with a nod toward Ibb.

The sound this time from the mechanical man was harsher, less happy. "I hope that none of your students are as bad as mine."

"What do you mean?" Rabel asked, tensing.

"I have mislaid my latest apprentice," Ibb said with a grinding sigh.

"And?"

"And she had your child in her care," Ibb said heavily.

"Ophidian!" Rabel shouted at the top of his lungs.

Wymarc is an adult, she can handle herself, Ophidian's voice echoed through the heads of the three humans. *Tend your business!*

"He sounds testy," Jarin said glancing worriedly toward Rabel.

"Who?" Ibb asked. "I heard nothing."

"You didn't hear the *god?*" Ellen asked, amazed.

"He can't hear the gods," Rabel told her, glancing apologetically to the metal man. "He gave that up when he gave up his body."

"Oh," Ibb said. A moment later, he added, "Doubtless he reminded you that Wymarc can take care of herself."

"Except when she gets hit by a cannonball," Jarin grumbled.

"Wymarc survived," Ibb said.

"Half of her was killed."

"Wymarc lives," Ibb said. "It is Annora for whom we grieve."

"They saved my life," Jarin said in a low voice.

"She is much like Rabel in this," Ibb said.

"You don't know where they are?" Rabel asked the mechanical man.

"I had given her directions to head north, toward a sanctuary I knew," Ibb said. "I have just recently received word that they did not arrive."

"You can track your work, can't you?" Rabel said.

"I could except that the tracking device has been disabled," Ibb replied, his words spoken in a harsh mashing tone, as though he was grinding gears. "I would seek after them but…"

"What?" Jarin demanded.

"Markel intends on Soria," Rabel guessed. "Using the airships —" he glanced toward Jarin "— that you, I, and Ophidian conceived —"

"Not without help," Ibb added.

Rabel accepted this with a nod. "— for a different purpose."

"What purpose?" Ellen asked.

"I was not told," Rabel said with a sour look toward Ibb.

"I can only guess," Ibb said. "I believe that there are great changes coming, changes that perhaps frighten even Ophidian himself."

"What does this have to do with Soria?"

"I don't know," Ibb said. "What I know for certain is that Markel has many schemes in motion."

"What do you suspect?" Rabel challenged.

"I suspect that Ametza is using this king as she used the last," Ibb said.

"Someone is giving you information," Rabel said.

"Many people," Ibb agreed. "But, in particular, the madame of the House of the Broken Sun has been most helpful."

Rabel grunted in satisfaction: he had guessed as much.

"I find myself concerned more with Ametza's actions than I like," Ibb confessed. "She has not behaved well since…"

"When?"

"Since Arolan was lost to her," Ibb said. The mechanical was silent for a moment, then whirled as though thinking rapidly. "I believe that perhaps one of her plots had worked out too well —" he glanced toward Jarin "— perhaps aided by your father."

"Who's Arolan?" Ellen asked.

"He is her husband, the god of water, ice, and steam," Ibb said. "He has been missing for a while now."

"How long?" Jarin asked.

"Two hundred years or more," Ibb said.

"If we're not going after Wymarc," Jarin demanded in irritation, "what are we doing?"

"Tending business, according to your father," Ellen said with a shrug. She caught Jarin's fuming look and smirked.

"Ellen," Rabel said reprovingly. She glanced at him. "It's neither nice nor wise to irritate fire-breathing dragons." The little girl's eyes widened in alarm. Rabel smiled as he added, "At least until you know how make yourself flameproof."

Jarin snorted. To Ellen, he said, "I promise not to turn you to ash for your impudence."

"Always?" Ellen said, pressing the issue with a pleading, half-fearful look in her eyes.

Jarin regarded her for a moment. "Always."

"Markel will march his forces and sail his airships in the next two weeks," Rabel said to Ibb.

"He plans to murder his wife and marry the queen of Soria," Ibb added. Jarin hissed angrily.

"That's not nice," Ellen said. The others glanced at her. "Couldn't he just divorce her?"

"That would seem wise," Ibb agreed in melodious chimes. His tone shifted as he continued, "But this king is not known for his wisdom."

"Soria is an earth kingdom," Rabel said to Ibb, "why would Ophidian want to help it?"

"I do not know," Ibb said. "As you have noticed, I do not hear the gods."

Rabel snorted in derision. "As I have learned, old clanker, there is little you *don't* hear."

"What's your game?" Jarin demanded of Ibb. He glanced to Rabel suspiciously. "And how do you know this mechanical?"

"I've worked with Ibb for most of my life," Rabel said with a reminiscent sigh. After a pause, he added, "Lives."

"There are changes coming," Ibb said. "They are great changes." The mechanical's innards whirled thoughtfully. He turned his glowing eyes to Jarin. "In this, your father and I are in accord." He paused with the sound of wheels slowing down, then speeding up. "As I have said earlier."

"Ibb has had thousands of years to perfect the art of lying without appearing to do so," Rabel said drolly to Jarin. To Ibb, he said, "And what do you propose?"

"I think that it is not wise to allow king Markel — and Ametza — to acquire too much power," Ibb said. "I fear that they will make war in the air." There was another moment of whirling before the mechanical continued, "I cannot say what will be the outcome."

"More airships would put dragons and wyverns both in danger," Jarin said with a haunted look.

"And Markel plans to build fleets of airships," Ibb said.

Rabel chuckled. "They'll all be slow and poorly armed."

"That will not help the people on the ground," Jarin warned. The others looked at him. "Imagine cannonballs falling from the sky."

"So what can we do to stop him?" Ellen asked. She glanced toward Ibb. "I'm learning how to make flames."

"And you have an excellent teacher," Ibb's voice boomed inside his body as his gears turned his head and he raised a hand toward Rabel.

"Geros and Granna are the gods of the earth," Rabel said to no one in particular. "They will have no defenses against an attack from the air."

"Or the water," Ibb said in agreement.

"So we must teach them how to fight in the air," Jarin said.

"Would you raise the earth up to the sky, then?" Ibb asked.

"Yes," Rabel said, his eyes gleaming. "We'll do just that!"

"What?" Ellen said.

"How?" Ibb demanded.

"Well," Rabel said, "we're going to need a *lot* of help." He nodded toward the mechanical man. "Particularly yours."

"I eagerly await enlightenment," the mechanical man responded.

Chapter Three

"My dear madame, it is so good to see you again!" Queen Arivik called cheerfully to the madame of the House of the Broken Sun. She was followed by a handsome young man who was plainly fawning on her, a silly smile plastered on his face.

"And good to see you and —?" Suzanne Parkes returned, fishing for the lad's name.

"No Britches, madame," the lad supplied with a smile. Suzanne Parkes nodded to him in thanks while keeping a tight smile on her face. Not too many weeks ago, the lad had been Alain, a very smart orphan from the southern lands who had traded his body for the safety of his younger sister, Lisette.

Lisette was still young and learning the ways of a maidservant at the House of the Broken Sun. She asked after her brother regularly but her inquiries had grown less frequent of late, as her duties kept her always on her feet and exhausted — as Madame Parkes had planned. Lisette was already getting envious of the ladies of the House — how they seemed always to be sleeping or a-bed. In another year she would be anxious to take on the less strenuous duties but Madame Parkes would tell her no… and in another six months the girl would beg to take up the trade, forgetting her brother, her former life, forgetting everything. Suzanne Parkes had seen it had been before, many many times.

Alain would not inquire after his little sister: he had drunk too much of the queen's special 'tea' and now had only one thought on his mind — pleasing queen Arivik.

Queen Arivik seated herself and nodded for Madame Parkes to join her. She lifted the pot of tea that had been placed between them.

"Tea, my dear?" the queen said. "Let me pour."

"Just a little," Madame Parkes said, gently placing her cup under the teapot's spout.

"A little is never enough," the queen giggled as she filled the cup generously. She poured for herself and drank deeply, closing her eyes and — for a long while — closing her mind to the world around her.

When she opened them again, she had a beatific smile on her face. But she reached for her necklace and clenched the red jewel hanging from it — and her expression suddenly sharpened as she took a quick, painful gasp.

"Now," she said, "what do you know?"

Madame Parkes raised her cup to her lips and pretended to drink.

"I have heard many disquieting things, your majesty."

#

Peter Hewlitt, the king's spymaster, knelt down before the king, thinking quickly. He had been sent for an hour before but it had taken time for the messenger to find him, more time for Hewlitt to collect his information, and finally he was here.

"I just had a very uncomfortable interview with the queen," King Markel said. "She knows far too much of what is going on in my kingdom and I want to know why."

Spymaster Hewlitt remained prostrate before his king.

"Oh, *do* get up!" Markel said testily.

Hewlitt picked himself up from the floor, keeping his eyes from meeting Markel's.

"Well?" Markel demanded.

"It would help, sire, if I knew more of the nature of her knowledge," Hewlitt replied.

"She knows about the invasion," Markel said.

Peter Hewlitt allowed himself to relax, at least internally. "I thought we had planned for her to know about it, sire."

"If so, why am I spending so much on that infernal tea and all those special 'spices' she keeps drinking?"

"The effects of her tea and spices vary, your majesty," Hewlitt temporized. He was lying, and he hoped the king wouldn't call him on it — as far as he knew the drugs and the tea leaves the queen used should leave her both addicted and mindless. Certainly all the test subjects he'd seen had lost their faculties with alarming ease. Admittedly, there were some circumstances in which they could regain *some* of their former mental prowess but it was very rare. That boy the town's madame had provided, for example, was now just a little better than a gibbering idiot. "We were hoping that the queen would be happy to ride in the van of the army with you," Hewlitt reminded the king. "Has that changed?"

"It has," the king said sourly, glowering at his spymaster. "As you should know."

"Sire?"

"The queen," the king said heavily, "said that she would be glad to ride with me and the army providing the crown prince accompanied us."

"Did you remind her of his journey?" Hewlitt said.

"I did," the king replied. "She said that she would wait until his return, then."

Hewlitt kept his expression blank. "Does she suspect something?"

"I don't know," the king said. "But if we can't get her to go north with the army then all our plans fail."

"We could arrange an assassination here, sire," Hewlitt suggested mildly. He'd argued before that the king's plan was too complex but had been overruled by the king with Mannevy's support. "We could make it look like a Sorian spy."

"No," the king said, shaking his head. "She must go north." He impaled Hewlitt with a gimlet stare. "I have my reasons."

"Sire, if you would share those reasons with me —"

"No!" Markel barked. He waved a hand dismissively. "Your job is to ensure that she goes with me, willingly. Make it happen."

Peter Hewlitt bowed and nodded, backing away from the king and through the open doors out of the throne room.

Outside, with the doors closed, Peter Hewlitt stood, rubbing his chin as he thought furiously. The only reason, he decided, for the king not to share his plans with *him* — the king's spymaster — was because the king had plans that he did not want Hewlitt to discover. And what plan would a king hide from his spymaster?

Hewlitt dropped his hand to his side, his eyes burning angrily as he turned down the corridor. He had to make plans of his own.

#

"How are we going to get through Korin's Pass, sir?" Colonel Walpish asked when General Georgos finished outlining the battle plan.

"We're going to have help, Colonel," the general replied, nodding toward Nevins and Morel. He allowed himself a wintry smile. "From the air."

"Once we've got the pass, we'll pour our troops through and send the cavalry charging through the mainland and up to Sarsal," Major Taplan, in charge of plans said, pointing to the long line inked on the map in front of them.

"Cavalry against a fort, sir?" Walpish said, glancing to the general once more.

"Again, you'll have help," the general said, nodding to the two airship captains once more.

"Sir, I hate to sound critical but we've only the *two* airships," Walpish said. "What if something were to happen to them?"

"The king is building more and they will be ready shortly after we start the war," first minister Mannevy spoke up for the first time. Frostily, he added, "But, Colonel, if you still find this assignment too onerous, I'm sure there are others who will be happy to take over your command."

Walpish gave the first minister a dirty look but shook his head in a quick jerk. "First minister, it is customary when viewing war plans to ask questions and to be doubtful."

"Really?"

"Better to find fault ourselves on paper than pay for errors in blood," General Georgos said in agreement. He nodded toward Walpish. "Still, Colonel, if you would prefer…?"

"No, sir," Walpish replied firmly. "I merely wanted to ensure our success, nothing more."

"Good!" Georgos said. "I'm counting on you."

"With the airships, I'm sure we'll be victorious," Walpish said, nodding toward the first minister in particular. He turned back to his general. "How soon will we begin?"

"Two weeks," Georgos said, glancing to Mannevy for agreement. "That will give us time to get to the pass, drill the troops, and deploy the airships."

"And the infantry, sir?" Taplan asked.

Georgos smiled. "We're going to use our new railroad to move them and our artillery to the pass. When Walpish storms through, they'll deploy and follow up."

"Taking Sarsland with only cavalry…"

"Actually, Colonel, you'll just be a distraction," first minister Mannevy said.

"Sir?" Walpish said, glancing to his general.

Georgos nodded to the first minister and then to the two airship captains. "*Vengeance* started her life as a merchant ship, Colonel."

Walpish looked confused.

"She's good at carrying cargo," the general explained, "including infantry and artillery."

"We will be able to provide three hundred crack grenadiers and two light cannon," Major Taplan said.

"While you're demonstrating outside the capital, the troops will be lowered in under the cover of night, storm the gates — from the inside — and let you in," General Georgos expanded.

"A night attack?" Walpish said. "With surprise?" He smiled. "It will be a pleasure to lead such an attack."

"And with the king and capital secured, Soria will be ours," Georgos said.

#

Peter Hewlitt had spent several days keeping the queen under surveillance before he discovered her secret. He had used the old secret passageways himself and had waited until the queen had invited Madame Parkes over. Then he had stood there, in the darkness above her day chamber, watching and listening. His eyes had narrowed in pleasure when he'd seen her grab her necklace and finger the red jewel on it. Her countercharm had been simplicity itself. Dealing with it would also be simplicity itself. And, Hewlitt decided, he would gain control over Madame Parkes at the same time.

"Your majesty!" Peter Hewlitt called out affably as he entered Queen Arivik's quarters.

"Do I know you?" the queen said, taking another sip of her tea.

"I was wondering if I might have a word with your lad, here," Peter Hewlitt said. "It would only take a minute or two."

"Britches?" the queen said, frowning. She waved a hand. "Go with this man."

"Yes, your majesty," the boy known alternately as 'Britches', 'No Britches', and 'Come here!' said, looking up toward the king's spymaster with a glazed expression.

"Come along," Peter Hewlitt said, grabbing the lad's hand and leading him away.

#

"Your queen is in danger," Peter said to the lad when they were safely in his office.

"She is?" the lad asked. "What can I do?"

"She has a necklace," Peter said.

"She has several."

"The one she wears when she meets with Madame Parkes," Peter said.

The boy made a face.

"What?" Hewlitt demanded.

"I don't like madame," the boy said, shaking his head. "She's mean. My sister —"

"Tell me about your sister," Peter said.

"I — I — her name is Lisette," the boy said, groping for words in his fogged mind. "She's my little sister. She's pretty."

"I see," Peter said, digesting both the boy's sparse description and his foggy-headedness. "And where is your sister?"

"Madame — madame —" the boy spluttered, frowning, straining through the fog that the tea had created in his mind.

"She is with Madame Parkes?" Hewlitt guessed. The boy strained to focus, smiled blearily, and nodded.

"How would you like to help your sister?" Hewlitt asked. He had no more intention of helping the boy's sister than did Madame Parkes but it would provide him with more leverage on the half-addled lad. Indeed, the lad smiled at him and nodded quickly. "I think that your majesty's necklace — the one she wears when she takes tea with Madame Parkes — I think that we should give her a new one."

"A new one?"

"Prettier," Peter said. "Shinier." He opened a drawer and pulled out a carefully made duplicate of the queen's necklace. He placed it in front of the lad. "Isn't it pretty?"

"It is," the lad said, fondling the necklace and smiling at Peter.

"Do you think the queen will like it more than her old, dull necklace?"

"Yes," the lad said, "she'll like it."

"So why don't you trade this necklace for her old one," Peter said. "You can trade it when she's sleeping so she'll be surprised in the morning."

The lad giggled at the thought.

"Put it in your pocket and swap it tonight," Peter said. "You can give me the old one in the morning."

"The morning," the lad said. He took the necklace and pulled it toward him. He stopped halfway, his brows creased, his face screwed up in thought. "And my sister?"

"This will help her," Hewlitt said. He smiled. "You want to help your sister, don't you?"

"Yes," the lad agreed, pulling the necklace all the way toward him and stuffing it in his pocket.

"The queen will be pleased," Peter promised.

"Pleased?"

"Happy," Peter said.

"Happy," the lad agreed.

"I'll take you back to her now," Peter said. "Just remember, swap it tonight."

"Tonight."

Chapter Four

"We're going to need a forge — a big one — and several apprentices," Rabel said after Ibb had started the caravan forward once more. Jarin had agreed to go up front to ensure that the caravan did not stray off the road — rather, off the snow which lay over the road.

"To make steel, I imagine," Ibb said. "But then what? Do you propose to harden the walls or put up steel shutters to protect the towns?"

"Neither," Rabel said. He turned to Ellen. "How well do you know Soria?"

Ellen's brow creased in a frown.

"What do you know of Soria?" Rabel asked.

"It's to the north of us?" Ellen asked. Ibb made a mechanical grinding noise that the little girl was beginning to consider his laugh. She turned to glare at him. "Mr. Ibb, everyday I spent begging for food or freezing. How am I supposed to learn?"

Ibb made a noise Ellen had never heard before: a wheezing, plaintiff noise that reminded her of all the cold days she'd endured.

"And *that* is why I am sad," Ibb said, turning his glowing red eyes to Rabel. "Children shouldn't freeze or starve."

"I know, my friend," Rabel said.

"And that's why I'm apprenticed to Rabel," Ellen said, sliding over toward the dark-haired man and hugging herself against him.

"Ophidian's will," Ibb said with a mechanical grumble.

Rabel nodded and sighed, glancing down to Ellen. "Soria is north of us," he told her. "We are just north of Korin's Pass which is one of two passes through the mountains of Geros —"

"Geros the god?" Ellen asked. Rabel nodded. "He made the mountains?"

"That is not known," Ibb replied. "They were there long before I was born."

Ellen accepted this with a nod and looked up to Rabel. "Two passes?"

Rabel smiled at her and tousled her hair affectionately.

"Near the coast — to the west — is the Sea Pass," Rabel said.

"What's a pass?"

"It's a gap between mountains," Ibb said. "A place where it's possible to 'pass' through the mountains without going too high."

"So people want to go through the passes," Ellen guessed. Rabel nodded, smiling. "If the king wants to invade Soria, he would go through the passes." She thought for a moment, then asked, "Both of them?"

"Sea Pass is the traditional route for attacks," Ibb said. She cocked her head at him, so he continued, "There have been wars between Soria and Kingsland ever since Ametza and Alavor conspired to flood what they now call King's River and drive out the Sorians."

"They *stole* the land?" Ellen said. She sounded more impressed than outraged.

"Gods and people have been fighting over lands since time began," Ibb said.

"So the king is planning a surprise," Rabel said, "by attacking through Korin's Pass and using his airships."

"Without his airships, he wouldn't be able to take the pass," Ibb said. "The East Peak Fort commands the center of the pass and his troops would be destroyed by the fort's canon."

"With the airships, he can pound the fort into submission," Rabel said.

"He'll probably use only one airship for that," Ibb said. Rabel gave him a questioning look. "He'll use the other to prevent any warnings from going north to the king."

"And there's a new king, untested," Rabel said.

"Did the old king die?" Ellen asked.

"He was killed when the new king, Wendel, attacked from the lands near the Pinch," Rabel said. "And Rassa switched her allegiance when Wendel promised to keep her son, the crown prince Sarsal, in succession to the throne."

"Rassa was the queen before?" Ellen asked. Rabel nodded. In a rush, she asked, "And Sarsal is their son? What was the name of the king?"

"Yes, and the old king's name was Sorgal," Rabel said.

"What's the Pinch?"

"The Pinch is the name given for the bit of land that is pinched between three mountain ranges at the far east of Soria, right next to Felland and Vinik."

"Felland and Vinik?" Ellen asked, looking slightly overwhelmed by the names.

"The kingdoms to the east and southeast of Soria," Ibb said.

"You mean there's more than *two* kingdoms?"

Ibb chuckled mechanically. "There are very many more than just *two*. In this northern land alone, there are ten, not counting the barren lands in the bitter north."

"We are getting far from our topic," Rabel said sternly. He looked down at Ellen. "What matters is the attack on the fort."

"So we have to defeat the airships," Ibb said.

"How?" Ellen asked. "Didn't they kill a *wyvern?*"

"They didn't *quite* kill it," Jarin's voice came back from the front of the room. He'd stepped through the thick canvas curtain that separated the caravan from the driver's compartment. "And we are approaching the town."

"Korin's Pass," Rabel said with a nod. He turned to Ibb. "How well do you know this town?"

"Not as well as some," Ibb said evasively.

"Can we get help here?"

"I know a better place further north," Ibb said, "particularly well-suited for what you plan."

"You don't know what I plan," Rabel said.

"I am certain you will soon correct that deficiency," Ibb said.

Rabel snorted.

"What plan?" Jarin said.

"The plan to save East Peak Fort and keep Markel's men from taking Soria," Ellen told him. Jarin glanced her way, his head cocked to one side. "Because if the airships can destroy the fort, there's nothing to stop them from taking the pass."

Jarin grunted, turning to Rabel. "And what about me?"

"Do you want to risk the canon's fire?" Ibb wondered. "You saw what happened to Wymarc."

"I think you could destroy any one airship easily," Rabel said before Jarin could speak. "But the other one would be firing at you, too. And the two of them together…"

"Didn't you say the king was building more?" Jarin said after a moment. Rabel nodded. "So what's your plan?"

"The fort is vulnerable because the airships can fire down on it," Rabel said.

"And?" Jarin challenged.

Rabel's lips twitched. "What if we made it so that the fort could fire down on *them?*"

There was a long moment of silence as the other three considered his proposition.

"And what magic could lift a fort?" Ibb said.

"Are you familiar with magnets?"

"The bits of metal that twist to point north?" Jarin said.

"They're used on ships," Ibb said. Ellen's brows rose, so the mechanical said, "If you know where north is, you can set a course to go anywhere." He turned to Rabel. "But I cannot imagine how that could help a fort to fly?"

"Not fly: float," Rabel said. "You know what happens when you try to push the two north ends of magnets at each other?"

"They push against it," Ibb said. "Somewhat forcefully, as I recall. I could imagine…" the mechanical stopped suddenly. A moment later the room was filled with the sounds of gears turning swiftly, and the mechanical's glowing eyes flickered like candles in a strong breeze. Then silence. And suddenly, the mechanical man's innards gave a grinding rumble. "You can't possibly hope to use magnets to lift a fort," Ibb exclaimed. "How can you hope to make them strong enough?"

Rabel smiled and pointed at Jarin. "Dragon's fire to make dragon steel, dragon steel to make dragon magnets."

"You'll tame Ophidian's flame for your purposes, once again," Ibb said approvingly. "How high would the fort have to be to shoot down on the airships?"

"That's the joy of it," Rabel said with a chuckle. "These airships aren't built with steel —"

"So?" Jarin demanded.

"So they're heavier and slower than the one that shot at you," Rabel said. "I think they can rise just about two hundred feet above the East Peak Fort as things stand now."

"So if we get the fort to float up two hundred feet…" Ibb suggested.

"Three hundred feet might be better," Rabel allowed, "so that the fort can fire down on *them*."

"I think, my friend, that we should stop here, in Korin's Pass," Ibb said.

"Why?" Jarin asked.

"Because we're going to need help," Ibb replied.

"But you said you'd get better help further north," Jarin said.

"I did," the mechanical man agreed, "but now that I understand my good friend's plan further, I realize that we're going to need local help, too."

"It's a small town," Jarin said, he nodded to Ellen, "we were there this morning. I doubt there's more than a thousand people all together."

"Above ground," Ibb said with the mechanical rumble that was his laughter.

#

Hamo Beck was a middle-aged, well-dressed man who was growing portly in his old age. His hair was thinning, his dark eyes piercing, and his expression genial. He was shorter than most and wore a long beard which he would stroke whenever he was deep in thought. He had been the mayor of Korin's Pass — the town that grew up tending the traffic through the pass — for over thirty years. Korin's Pass had prospered under his guidance as much as he had himself. He wore a waistcoat from which depended an intricately machined gold watch. A marvelous red jewel adorned the gold pin with which he held his fine cravat around the collar of his fine red shirt. No one would mistake him for a man without means.

"Mr. Ibb!" he said when he saw the mechanical at his door. "What marvels have you for us this day?"

"If I may, sir, we should talk in private," Ibb said in gravelly tones.

"By all means!" the mayor said, waving Ibb inside. "You remember where my office is, I presume?"

"I do," Ibb said, "unless you've changed it again."

Hamo boomed with laughter. "Oh, ho! I remember you knew it when we were doing renovations twelve years ago!"

"That soon?" Ibb said. "How little changes."

"On the contrary," Hamo said with another boom of laughter. "Since you last came, the town's almost doubled in size and more than doubled in wealth." He bowed Ibb into his office, bustled quickly past him to the plush chair set behind his broad wooden desk and gestured for the mechanical to take the seat opposite only to crinkle his brow in worry, as he said, "You *do* sit, don't you?"

"Not when I can avoid it," Ibb replied, moving the proffered chair gently aside and standing in its place. He nodded to the mayor. "But please do, I recall it pleases you."

"You won't be offended?"

"No," Ibb said, "I shall not."

Hamo started to relax, let out a grunt of annoyance, bounced out of his seat, bustled back to the office door, closed it quickly and just as quickly resumed his seat, saying, "Sorry, I recall you said you wanted to speak in private."

Ibb stroked one of the gleaming jewels on the bracelet encircling his left wrist, and said, "There are other ways to ensure privacy."

"As I recall," Hamo said, glancing wonderingly at Ibb's bracelet, "but I wanted to ensure that no humans would think to intrude."

"Ah," Ibb said, "good idea."

Hamo leaned back in his chair and stroked his beard in thought, before saying, "So, what would you like to tell me?"

"I would like to ask for your help," Ibb said. "It would be mutually beneficial —"

"Always has been," Hamo interjected with a pleased look and nodded for the mechanical man to continue.

"It involves some danger but less than would occur otherwise."

"That sounds ominous," Hamo said. He stroked his beard again. "You come from the south. What do you need?"

"I need to find a working forge, equipped with enough supplies to make about four tons of steel," Ibb began.

"Four tons!" Hamo cried in surprise. "What in the world would you need that much for? An army?" He stopped himself, stroked his beard again and said more thoughtfully, "An army."

"No," Ibb replied, his mechanical neck creaking as he moved his head back and forth. "I shall also need as many apprentices or workers as you can muster to help in the construction of magnets."

"Magnets?" Hamo said, his eyes going wide. "And what would you need with magnets?" He paused, stroking his beard once more before exclaiming, "You're not hoping to use four tons of steel to make magnets, are you?" Before Ibb could answer, he added, "And how is it possible to make magnets from steel?"

"You beat it into shape," Ibb said. "And, yes, we are."

"'We'?"

"I have some aid in this matter," Ibb said.

"You usually do," Hamo said, more to himself than to the mechanical man. "How many and what sort of lodgings?"

"There are three," Ibb replied, "a man, a lad, and a girl."

"So food and lodging for four," Hamo said to himself. He shrugged. "That I can do." He stroked his beard. "Near the forge, then?" Ibb nodded. "So they're going to help you with this project."

"We'll also need about four tons of cable," Ibb said.

"Rope, like for ships?" Hamo asked. When the mechanical man nodded, the mayor said, "That might be difficult. We would have to send for it."

"We can buy it from Kingsland," Ibb said, "the new railroad would deliver it in two days from Kingsport."

"That fast, really?" Hamo said more in surprise than in question. He thought to himself, shifting in his chair and propping his bearded face in one hand. "We've done well with that railroad. There's been talk of extending it through the pass and onward to Sarskar."

"That might be premature," Ibb said. "And unwise."

"I thought so," Hamo Beck agreed. "But King Wendel seems to have different —" he stopped, eyes going wide. "This is about the king, isn't it?" Before Ibb could react, the mayor exclaimed, "Markel is planning an invasion!" The mayor leapt out of his chair, sending it sliding backwards, ready to charge out of his office and spread the alarm.

"Which we are going to stop," Ibb replied spreading his metal hands out, palms down, gesturing for the mayor to return to his seat.

"I still have to warn the king," Beck replied. He frowned. "Do you know when they'll attack?"

"Within a fortnight," Ibb replied. "They're moving their troops to the border."

"And they have those blasted *locomotives* and railroads," Beck muttered sourly. He pulled on his beard fiercely. "I wish you'd never thought of them."

"They are efficient," Ibb said, "and they aid commerce."

"As much as they aid war," Beck said.

"I had not considered that," Ibb admitted.

"It will take at least two weeks for our army to mass and move here," Beck said. "Even the cavalry will take six days from the moment king Wendel gives his orders."

"And there are no soldiers closer by?"

Beck shook his head. "They have a garrison at the Sea Pass but they expect the fort to stop any attacks here."

"And it will," Ibb said.

"So why is your king so foolish as to plan an attack here?"

"He is not my king," Ibb said. "I place allegiance with no one."

Beck waved the issue aside. "Again, why?"

"Because he is going to use airships to attack the fort," Ibb said. "The airships fly in the sky and can fire their cannon *down* on your fort."

"But that's disastrous!" Beck cried, jumping from his chair. "They could take the Pass and rush their troops through to the capital before the army has even formed!"

"Just so," Ibb agreed.

"Can we build our own airships in time to stop them?"

"No," Ibb said. "We have a better plan."

"Which is?"

"Which is why we need the steel, the rope, the forge, and the help of your distant kinsmen."

"You want me to contact the Zwerg?" Hamo Beck asked, returning to his seat and stroking his beard furiously. After a moment in silence, he looked back up to Ibb and said, "They built the fort. Are you planning to get their aid to build another one?"

The mechanical man creaked as he shook his head from side to side. "We want their help to unhinge the fort."

"Unhinge?"

"From the mountain," Ibb said, his joints creaking differently as he nodded up and down.

Beck's eyes bulged. "But then it would fall down into the pass!" He frowned. "Do you hope to use it to block the pass?"

"No, to guard the pass," Ibb said. "And it won't fall down."

"It won't?"

"No," Ibb said. "With the help of the Zwerg, it will fall *up*."

Chapter Five

'No Britches' really thought that the new necklace for the queen was much prettier than the old one. He was happy to make the switch. He knew that the queen would be pleased and surprised at how shiny the new necklace was. She would reward him — and he liked rewards.

He left her room to find the nice man who'd given her the new necklace. The necklace didn't look nearly as nice in the light of the torches lining the hallways. 'No Britches' stroked the red jewel, hoping to brighten it —

— and gasped as the spell took hold.

#

Peter Hewlitt was angry. *The stupid fool! Was he so lack-witted that he forgot his task?*

The queen was to meet with the Madame in less than an hour and Peter wanted to be able to report that she had lost her resistance to her special 'tea.'

He *needed* that necklace! At the very least, it would be worth no small amount of money to him. At best, if he could get one of the mages to recreate it, he would have a valuable weapon in his spy arsenal, something that could let his agents go undetected wherever he needed.

He was out of time. He would check on the queen — on the off chance that the lad had made the switch but had been too fuddled to remember to bring him the old necklace. He moved out of his office and toward the secret passageway he'd discovered. He had just reached the location when he heard the queen call out, "Britches! Where are you, Britches?"

#

Madame Parkes was happy to follow 'Britches' through the hallways of the castle until the lad, giggling vacuously, led her down a corridor she hadn't seen before.

"Where are we going?" she asked. "The queen isn't this way."

"She's in here," the boy said, giggling. "She wanted to show you something special."

"She did?" Madame Parkes said in surprise. She wondered if Queen Arivik was sober or tea-dazed. "What is it?"

"She wants it to be a surprise," the boy said, pushing the door open and gesturing her through.

Suzanne Parkes gathered her dress as she stepped through the narrow doorway and stopped suddenly as she peered at the interior. The boy pushed her roughly the rest of the way in. "What are you doing?"

"I'm repaying your kindness," Alain said forcefully. Madame Parkes turned quickly but stopped as she saw the sword in his hands.

"Wh-what are you doing?" she demanded. She peered at the sword in his hand and scoffed, "You don't know anything about swords!"

"Actually," Alain Casman said, stepping forward a pace, placing the sword against her throat, "I do."

Before Madame Parkes could say another word, Alain Casman, son of a knight, lunged — and repaid her cool kindness with cold steel.

#

"Guards, guards!" Peter Hewlitt shouted. He heard the thunder of feet responding to his call and stood back, away from the door where he'd found the body of the madame of the House of the Broken Sun, lying quite broken in a pool of her own blood. The sergeant of the guard saluted when he recognized the spymaster. Hewlitt gestured to the door. "There's been a murder!"

"It's Madame Parkes," the sergeant said as he peered inside. "She was supposed to be taking tea with the queen."

"The queen!" Hewlitt cried, racing out of the room and down the corridor, calling back to the sergeant, "Follow me!"

The sergeant detailed a man to stay with the corpse and hurried after Hewlitt. They tore down the corridor and into the queen's morning chambers, Hewlitt bashing the door open and stopping only when he was beside the queen.

"Who are you?" Queen Arivik asked crossly. "And where's my tea?" She glanced around the room. "Am I supposed to be meeting someone?"

"No, your majesty," Peter Hewlitt said solemnly. She wore her red-jeweled necklace around her neck and Peter kept his expression unchanged as he realized that the jewel and chain were brighter than before — the lad had made the switch. "I believe you were just here for your tea."

"And where is it?" the queen demanded.

"Here, your majesty," he said, raising the pot to her eye level. "May I pour?"

The queen giggled. "Why, yes, please."

#

"But I don't want to leave," Lisette said, struggling against her brother's grasp as he pulled her out of the House of the Broken Sun, a sack of hastily packed clothes thrown over his shoulder.

"Lissy, you need to come with me," Alain said to her. He held the necklace in his hand. "The queen, Queen Arivik herself, gave this to me for you."

Lisette's eyes grew wide as she saw the necklace. Alain turned to her, placing it easily over her head.

"Doesn't it look good?" he asked her.

"It does! It does!" She beamed and pranced with it clung in her hands. Alain moved to stand beside her, a hand on her shoulder, urging her along.

"I've got us a carriage and we're going south, back to our home," Alain said.

"Can we really?" Lisette asked in awe. "Will we see mamma and poppa?"

"I hope so," Alain said. "But we have to go now or there will be trouble."

"Trouble?" Lisette's pretty brows creased with worry.

"I'll explain when we're away," Alain said. "Come along, now."

"Okay," Lisette said. She rushed forward eagerly. "Did the queen give you the carriage?" She asked in a rush. "And did you get to spend much time with her?"

"I did," Alain said, hiding a grimace. "I'll tell you all about it!"

"It must have been wonderful! I'm dying to hear it!"

#

"The queen's carriage is missing," Peter Hewlitt said to the king when he had managed to put most of the pieces together. "It was traced to the House of the Broken Sun and reported to have left the town heading south."

"Indeed?" King Markel said.

"We could send troops after it, or even an airship," first minister Mannevy suggested silkily.

"Why bother?" the king asked. "There was a murder, we know the suspect, send word with the regular couriers and we shall see what occurs."

"Sire?"

"I have need of those troops," the king told his first minister icily. He turned his attention back to his spymaster. "And the House of the Broken Sun?"

"Madame Parkes' rooms and office were ransacked," Hewlitt said. "I imagine that any wealth she had went with the murderer and his sister."

"Was there much?"

"I would imagine that she had quite a great deal of savings, your majesty," Hewlitt said. "She ran a profitable institution for a very long time."

"Profitable, eh?" the king repeated. "And who will run that institution now?"

"Without any capital, it's bankrupt," Mannevy said.

"Then we should find someone with capital, shouldn't we?" the king said. "Someone who has a good eye for business and won't forget favors given." He turned to Mannevy. "Sounds like something in your bailiwick."

"Sire," the first minister licked his lips, buying time to consider his words, "I —"

"Of course," the king said, turning from his first minister to his spymaster, "if you don't want it, I imagine that Peter here would be happy to take charge."

Mannevy looked from his king to the spy and back again.

"I could increase our intelligence by at least half," Hewlitt said, looking toward the king.

"Fine, then!" the king said, waving a hand toward his spymaster. "It's settled. Peter gets the ladies and their custom." His expression grew sly as he added, "I get ten per cent."

"Of course, your majesty," Hewlitt said, bowing his head in acceptance.

"What of her majesty?" the first minister said, looking at the spymaster.

"I believe —"

"Darling!" Queen Arivik's voice came bellowing through the room. "Oh, boopsie! I've been looking for you!"

"She never called me boopsie," king Markel said, glancing to Hewlitt. "What happened?"

"She got a new necklace, your majesty," Peter Hewlitt said. "I imagine she's grateful."

#

The steam engine slowed as it came to the station, pulling the eight carriages behind it. They were empty. The locomotive had stopped earlier, out of sight of the village and disgorged its passengers before continuing on to its destination empty. It would refuel with water and coal and then turn back for the return journey, taking on some trade goods to bring to the capital.

From a distance, Colonel Walpish watched as the engine slowed and stopped. He waved to his troops and pointed in the direction of the mountains. The sixty-three horsemen of his special troop spurred their mounts to follow behind him.

The opening moves of the war with Soria were about to begin, and Colonel Thomas Walpish was proud to be at the forefront.

One of his ensigns pulled up next to him and nodded in salute. Walpish gestured toward a hillock and the ensign nodded, signalling for a pair of troopers to follow them. They would remain unseen and unreported — the dead would not betray them.

#

The spy was well-armed and well-placed. His hiding place was high up in the hills just beyond the town of Korin's Pass and his mission was easy: he was to stop any messages leaving the town to the north.

Jenthen Barros was thrilled to have received training from King Markel's two mages. They taught him the spells for the bow to increase the range of his arrows, they taught him how to make the killing poisons that acted too quickly for words. Already a skilled archer of long standing, he reveled in the way his new arrows flew through the air.

The first he sent diving on the magical demon that had been sent northwards. It vanished in a burst of light, confirming its extinction.

The second was more satisfying — he loved the way the courier tried valiantly to spur his horse onward as the poison wrenched his body and darkened his eyes. But, Barros noted with delight, the courier was no match for his arrow. A moment of panic, a moment of death, and the courier fell from his saddle. The horse — well-trained — continued onward toward its destination, riderless.

Jenthen Barros followed the riderless horse with his eyes for a long moment before knocking another arrow to his bow. He hated to have to do it but a riderless horse was too much warning. The arrow found its mark — the horse faltered, took four steps, stumbled, its hind legs splaying out behind it, tried ardently to stand back up and fell, neck stretched outwards, legs twitching in agony as the poison killed the muscles of its brave heart, steadfast lungs, and tormented brain. With one final spasm, the horse lay motionless, barely two hundred yards from its rider.

If they were found, someone would know that something tragic and sinister had befallen horse and rider. But Jenthen Barros would be there to ensure that such discoveries also caused no alarm. He had plenty of arrows.

He scanned the snowy plain for a long moment then, satisfied, crept back into his hideout.

#

"I do not *care* what you say, I will take only the girl," Hamo Beck told Ibb firmly when the mechanical man brought the issue up for the fourth time. Ibb started to reply but Hamo raised a hand to forestall him. "They are short people and shy. Your little Ellen won't seem like a threat to them."

"Are you okay with this?" Rabel said to the girl.

"They're shorter than me?" Ellen asked Beck.

The bearded man smiled at her. "Some are, some are just a bit taller than you."

Ellen looked up at Rabel and said, "I know the shield spell and I can make fire. I'll be fine."

Rabel smiled back and tousled her hair. "I'm sure you will."

"If not, you know what to do," Jarin said with a hint of a growl in his tone.

Ellen smiled at him and touched his arm. "I'll give the signal and you'll come to the rescue, right?"

"Exactly," Jarin said with pleasure.

"Because I'm just a little girl and I can't take care of myself," Ellen said, her tone going brittle.

"No," Jarin said hastily, "not because you're little, but because I don't want anything happening to you." Then, as if abashed by his admission, he added, "It would upset Rabel."

"I swear she will be safe with me," Hamo Beck said, nodding to the dragon and the god-touched man. He gave a shorter nod to Ibb. "Besides, they know I am meeting under your authority, they won't want to upset you."

Ibb rumbled approvingly.

"There, it's all settled, everyone knows what's going to happen," Ellen said, reaching to grab one of Hamo Beck's hands and dragging the man behind her to the cave. In a lower voice she implored him, "Come on, before they think of *more* things to worry about."

Rabel snorted in amusement.

Hamo moved ahead of the young girl, keeping her hand clutched in his. "When you make your flame, be careful not to frighten people."

"I'll make a little flame," Ellen promised. Again.

In front of them, in the darkening night, was a large entrance at the base of the hills. Hamo turned to Ellen and said, "Last chance."

Ellen snorted and tugged him forward. "They're smaller than me."

"Most of them," Hamo warned her. They entered the cave and were soon lost from view.

#

"Shouldn't we be seeing something by now?" Ellen asked for the third time as they made they way deeper and deeper into the caves. "It's getting too dark to see."

"For you, maybe," Hamo told her, leading her firmly forward. "Mind your step there's —"

"Ow!" Ellen cried as she stubbed her toe on a rock.

"A rock," Hamo finished lamely. He could see Ellen glare at him but pretended not to notice.

A moment later a light flared beside him.

"Too bright!" Hamo warned. Ellen dimmed the flame even as she caught sight of dozens and dozens of eyes reflecting the light back. Ellen clutched Hamo's hand more tightly. He paused and told her, "Don't worry lass, they're friends."

"Provided you don't blind us," a voice growled nearby.

"Sorry," Ellen said before Hamo could react. "My eyes aren't as good as yours."

"Get the mechanical to fix that, if you want," another voice observed.

"Fix what, sir?" Ellen asked.

"Those eyes of yours," the voice replied. "'Tain't no good to have sky eyes down here."

"Sky eyes?"

"Granno means your eyes, child," Hamo Beck said. "Eyes that are built for the surface."

"Rabel's daughter Krea had sensitive eyes," Ellen said, "she wore special dark lenses when she went out, would they work for you if you went out above?"

"Why would we ever want to do that?" another voice asked.

"We have others to do our bidding above ground," Granno said, "we don't need to fix our eyes."

"Is my light too bright now?" Ellen asked. "I can make it dimmer."

"Too bright?" Granno exclaimed with a snort. "No, child, it's not too bright for us." He raised his voice and seemed to turn away from them as he called, "Lights!"

Suddenly Ellen's little light was lost in a blue-green brilliance which filled the entire cave. She gasped as she took in the size of it, saw the vaulted arches way above her, the carefully laid cobblestones on the path, the marvelous stone dwellings all around.

And the people!

She cried with delight as she caught her first sight of one of the underground people — she guessed it was the one named Granno because his voice had come from the same place. His face was smooth, his eyes big, his ears tall and pointed, his shoulders broad, his feet huge on the end of sturdy thick legs and his belly was huge. She just wanted to run up and hug him. He was shorter than she was!

Beside her, Hamo Beck grumbled, tightening his hand on hers. "Granduncle, may I make Ellen Unnamed known to you?"

"Unnamed?" Granno rumbled in response.

"Ellen Zebala, if you please you, sir," Ellen said, pulling her hand away from Hamo and curtsying toward the small man. She turned her head up to Hamo, adding, "I am apprenticed to Rabel, you know."

"No, I did not," Hamo replied, bowing his head toward her. "My apologies if I offended."

"You were unnamed, why?" Granno asked in his deep voice.

"My parents died when I was little," Ellen said, surprised at how tight her throat had become. "I survived on the streets of Kingston, first with a gang and then on my own until I met Rabel."

"Alone?" a high-pitched voice cried. Ellen turned toward the sound and was delighted to see a person shorter than her marching toward her. Her features were startlingly similar to Granno's, so Ellen guessed they were related. "Did no one take you in?"

"They leave children starve, aboveground," Granno said disdainfully. He pointed to Ellen. "This one was lucky —"

"No!" Ellen cried. "I fought for my food. I earned my years."

"Of course you did," the young Zwerg woman said, glaring at Granno and then at Hamo Beck. "These two big oafs don't know any better." She seemed satisfied with the looks on their faces for she strode past them and held out her hand. "I am called Diam."

"You're amazing!" Ellen said, smiling and shaking the other's hand eagerly. She leaned down a little and asked, "Can I hug you?"

Diam gave her a wide-eyed look but before she could react, Ellen rushed forward and hugged the young Zwerg woman tightly. After a moment's bafflement, Diam started patting the taller girl on her back and then hugging her.

"Ahem!" Granno growled angrily.

Ellen stepped back, eyes wide with fear. "I'm sorry, don't you hug?" she asked Diam.

"It's not often a person hugs the queen on their own, is all," Granno grumbled.

Ellen's jaw dropped. "You're the queen?" Ellen said to Diam. A dimple appeared in Diam's cheek and she nodded. Ellen's face crumpled and she dropped to her knees. "I'm sorry," Ellen sobbed, "I'm so sorry, I've ruined everything and now you won't help us and they'll come for us and they'll — they'll *kill* Rabel and I'll be homeless again!"

Ellen's wailing stopped only when a hand gently reached for her jaw and pulled her head up. She saw queen Diam looking down at her, shaking her head.

"Oh, child!" Diam told her, pulling her back off her knees. Ellen rose to wobbly feet and suddenly found herself embraced in a tight hug. "Oh, sweet child, you must never think that we of the earth would treat you the same harsh ways the topsiders do!"

Ellen bawled, feebly reaching her arms around the smaller person and nuzzling her head into the crook of her neck. After what seemed forever, she caught herself, pushed herself back from the queen and curtsied. "Your majesty, I'm sorry. I didn't know —"

"Shh!" Diam said, raising a finger to Ellen's lips to silence her. "You are welcome here, bright and loud as you are. You are like one of our shinier jewels." Ellen was aware of a tense, expectant silence around her and gave the queen a worried look which Diam met with a smile. "I declare you a friend of ours, Ellen bright-eyes," Diam said, her voice rising. "Friend and hugger of queens." Ellen's eyes bulged with amazement and Diam laughed, raising a hand in caution. "There is but one condition —"

"Your majesty?"

"You have to meet my children," Diam said with a devilish grin. "Show them your flame and see if you can get them to behave."

"Don't do it!" Hamo Beck called from behind Ellen. "No one could ever get her to behave, how can you hope that you'll get her children to do any better?"

"I'm sure Ellen will rise to the challenge," Diam shot back. She caught Ellen's look and chuckled. "Hamo is my distant cousin."

"My sister married a sky-toucher," Granno said in a tone of mock annoyance. "And they've been afflicted with height ever since."

"Momma, momma!" a pair of twinkling voices cried out and Ellen laughed with delight as two young Zwerg girls rushed up to grab at their mother, the queen.

"Ellen Bright-Eyes, I introduce you to my daughters," Diam said, gesturing with each hand to the child on either side of her. To the girls she said, "Introduce yourselves, please."

"I am Imay," the taller girl, the one on Diam's left said, curtsying gaily.

"They call me Missy," the shorter one said without curtsying, "but that's not my name."

"What is your name?" Ellen asked, kneeling down and bringing herself as best she could to the girl's eye level.

The little girl's eyes grew huge in her head and she glanced up anxiously to her mother, the queen. Queen Diam beamed down at her, saying, "Go on, then, you can tell her."

"Mother named me Lissy," the girl confided shyly.

"And why do they call you Missy?" Ellen asked as clearly was intended.

"Because my sister says that I'm so loud that no one would ever miss me," Lissy replied, cocking her head around her mother's knees to glare up at her older sister.

"And which do you prefer?" Ellen asked. She added quickly, "No one ever gave me a nickname."

"I like Lissy," the Zwerg girl replied shyly. She glanced around her mother's knees to stare back up at Imay. "But Missy isn't so bad."

Imay smiled back at her sister and reached a hand out to pat Lissy on her head. "As sisters go, you'll do."

"Your mother the queen says that I have to get you to behave," Ellen said. She glanced to the two girls and motioned them toward her. Still holding on to their mother's hands, the two moved a few steps closer. "She said I'm to show you my fire."

"You can make fire?" Lissy asked with awe in her voice.

"Rabel taught me," Ellen said. "And sometimes I don't get it right, so maybe I won't be able to do it now."

"Please try," Imay said.

"Only not too bright," Lissy added.

Ellen shook her head. "I'm not so good that I can make it bright or dim, most times." She took a deep breath, closed her eyes, gathered her strength, opened her eyes and held out her right hand, palm up. "Fire."

And a small pool of blue light began to bounce above her palm. Ellen's eyes widened in amazement. "I've never done blue before!"

Lissy pranced with delight. "It's beautiful!"

"It is truly amazing," Imay said, sounding much more mature. "I have not seen blue light in a very long time."

"Nor I," Diam said, moving closer to peer down at it. "How did you come by this magic?"

Ellen screwed up her face and shook her head. "I can't say," she replied. "I have some demons that are blue —"

"Demons?" Diam said imperiously. "Show them!"

Ellen gave her a worried look and doused her hand. Then she reached into herself where she'd hidden the demons and pulled one out.

"It was sent to me," Ellen said, "by Captain Ford so that I could report to him."

Diam looked down at the small blue-white demon and frowned. "May I hold it?"

Ellen responded by gently dumping the demon into the queen's outstretched hand. Diam lifted it up and examined it carefully, then swung it around to Granno on her side.

"It is not one of ours," Granno said knowingly. "I'd say it comes from the south." He peered forward and made a gesture with his hand. The blue demon responded by stretching upwards, stroking his hand with its head. "It is not here against its will."

"How did you get this?" Diam said, returning the demon to Ellen's palm.

"As I said, three were sent to me to let me report to Captain Ford —"

"Who is he?"

"He is the captain of the royal airship *Spite*," Ellen said, drawing herself up to her full height with pride. "He paid me to spy on Ibb and sent me these three demons to report back if I had anything of interest."

"And you had nothing?"

"Nothing that Rabel thought was necessary to report," Ellen said. She frowned. "Although now…"

"Does this captain have magic or witchcraft?" Granno asked. Ellen shook her head. "So it was a witch that ensorceled them and sent them."

"Do you know a witch?" Diam asked.

Ellen shook her head. "But Rabel says that he'll teach me sorcery, more than just the fire." She did not add that she'd sworn an oath to Ophidian: it seemed to her that the Zwerg were nervous around fire and would not like knowing that they were in the company of the fire-touched.

Granno grunted a laugh and moved toward her waving genially. "She's fire-touched, for certain," he said. "The flames prove it, although given that she's ward of Rabel, it would take a fool not to guess."

"Sworn to Ophidian, no doubt," Diam said.

"Is that a problem?" Ellen asked, trying not to sound nervous.

Diam shook her head. "I trust you to keep your oaths, little spy," Diam said. "I will not try to force your will against Ophidian — we respect him and his — but I trust that if ever your oath to him goes against your pledge to us, that you'll give us fair warning."

"I won't hurt you," Ellen said.

"Even if one of us is hurting one of yours?" Granno asked.

"Granno, leave off!" Diam said. "She's too young to have to worry about cross-sworn oaths."

"I know about them," Ellen said. "Rabel's daughter is the winter wyvern. She was pledged to be married to his apprentice but she swore an oath to the dying wyvern."

"So she did," Granno said with a nod. "And, last I heard, she's gone up to the bitter north." He exchanged a dark look with his queen.

"Well, enough of that," Diam said, waving a hand dismissively. She turned her attention to Ellen. "You were sent with others, including Ibb."

"I came with Rabel, Jarin, and Ibb," Ellen said. "King Markel is planning to invade Soria —"

"So?" Granno asked gruffly. "Sky-touchers are not our concern."

"Granno!" Diam said quellingly. The taller Zwerg pursed his lips but said nothing more. Diam turned to Ellen. "Say on."

"Rabel says that you traded with him some time back," Ellen said. "And that you did not regret it."

"We did well," Diam agreed. She cocked her head. "And what does he want to trade with us this time?"

"Ask the price first," Granno said warningly.

"The price is your help in lifting the East Pass Fort into the sky," Ellen said.

"What?" "That's not possible!" "He's mad!" The cries came from all around them.

"How?" Diam asked.

"There's a way to make magnets from steel," Ellen said. "Rabel plans to set them so that the magnets oppose each other."

"They push away," Diam said.

"Set them under the fort and push it up into the sky," Ellen said. All around her she heard the Zwerg gasp in surprise.

"Just to see *that* would be payment alone!" Granno swore.

"We'd need your help in undermining the fort as well as making and placing the magnets," Ellen said.

"And how soon must this be done?"

"A little over ten days from now," Ellen said in a small voice. She was certain that even the Zwerg could not work so fast.

"We'd need steel," Granno said to Diam. "We've got the ore but we'd need fire, hot fire —"

"Dragon-fire," Ellen said, raising her hands up, palms together, fingertips pressed tightly. She closed her eyes and drew a deep breath. When she opened them again, she drew her hands apart, fingertip by fingertip until she pulled her two index fingers apart and held one tip up, smiling at them. The tip of her finger burnt with a brilliant white light. A pleased smile touched her lips as she said, "Like this?"

Chapter Six

"Oh, we can get there all right," Captain Nevins told General Georgos sourly, "but we'll be just about out of coal, where will we refuel?"

"Korin's Pass," the general replied gruffly. "They've got a vast coal field there and supply both much of Kingsland and southern Soria."

"But to get the coal, we'll have to *take* the town," Captain Martel pointed out, glancing to Nevins who nodded in agreement.

"Your two airships and my cavalry will be certain to sweep all before them," General Georgos said airily. "After that, you'll have no problem finding 'volunteers' to load your fuel."

"Sounds iffy," Nevins said slowly. Beside him, Captain Martel nodded.

"It is the plan," General Georgos replied stiffly. "If you cannot follow it, you may take it up with the King."

Nevins and Martel exchanged sour looks.

"We'll go," Nevins said at last. "But I'm worried just as much about our mage as I am about our coal."

"He is not my department," General Georgos said, waving away the issue with a stern hand. He rose from his chair. "You have your orders, gentlemen." With a final, curt nod to the two airship captains, he strode out of the briefing room.

Martel and Nevins turned their attention to the fourth man in the room.

First minister Mannevy gave them both a languid look and said, "Has not mage Tirpin always managed to deliver on his promises?"

"Only halfway," Nevin said.

"If there's trouble —"

"I'm certain that the two of you can manage until the rest of the fleet joins you," first minister Mannevy said, rising from his chair to end the conversation. "The flags and signals will be delivered to your ships — they should be there already." He paused. "All it takes, gentlemen, is for you to seize the victory that will shortly be presented to you." He smiled at them. "The King will be pleased to then grant you your just rewards." He brushed past Nevins and nodded to Martel. "I await the news of your victory." And, with that, he followed the general out of the room, leaving the two captains seated.

"It shouldn't be that hard," Captain Martel said with a wave of his hand to the other captain.

"Have you ever heard of a plan that worked?" Captain Nevins replied sourly.

"Not at first, perhaps, but with the two of us…" Captain Martel said with a half smile. He raised his cup to the other. "To success!"

Nevins glowered at him a moment, then raised his cup and clinked against the other's.

"Success and damnation to Soria!" Nevins was pleased to see the Sorian turncoat pale at his words. He dropped his cup back on the table, pushed himself out of his chair and headed toward the door. "One way or the other, we've begun."

#

"Very well, general, you have your orders," King Markel said as he met the general at the train station with a steaming locomotive waiting anxiously for its departure. The station was to the north and west of Markel's castle, far enough away that the journey was tiring but also far enough away that the king was not disturbed by the whistles of the locomotives at night. The station was finished with red brick and some utilitarian stone work. It looked brash and ugly to the king's eyes. He didn't complain: he'd been the one to fund the construction of the station and all the railway lines that connected it to the rest of his kingdom. Two only were finished, strategically — the one leading to South Pass and the other leading past Korin's Pass. The two lines joining the south and east of his kingdom were being slowly constructed — more slowly now that much of the treasury was being used to support his army and navy.

"The navy supports us, Sire," General Georgos agreed with a firm nod. "Admiral Iskin has been the sole of discretion and support." He gestured toward the train. "This is the last of the troops to be sent to the Sea Pass. When we arrive we shall be prepared assault the Sea Pass from both the land and the sea as soon as we see the Sorians drawing off."

Georgos commanded the left wing of the King's Army: seven brigades of musketeers supported by two squadrons of horsemen. The right wing, tasked with taking Korin's Pass, was lighter in numbers — only three brigades of musketeers supported the five assault squadrons of horsemen including the two squadrons under Colonel Walpish's direct control. The general in charge of the right wing, General Tashigg, had been told by Georgos that he was to leave Walpish to his own devices and conform his actions to the colonel's. General Tashigg was getting on in years and still visibly jerked when a musket was fired, so he was more than willing to obey Georgos' order.

"Good," the king agreed. "And when you have South Pass…?"

The general smiled. "By that time the bulk of our troops will already be marching from Korin's Pass to trap King Wendel's forces between us. We shall encircle them and force them to surrender."

"And then Soria will be ours."

"As you say, your majesty," the general agreed. "With the enemy destroyed it will be a quick cavalry ride to reach, Sarlas, the capital and receive Wendel's surrender."

"Then I wish you fair travels and fair seas," king Markel said, waving the general away. "I will see you in Sarlas!"

General Georgos saluted one more time, turned and strode briskly to the car at the head of the train.

"This had better work, Mannevy," King Markel said to the first minister arrayed at his side. "We have emptied the treasury to build these railways and our airships."

"As you say, sire," Mannevy replied with a courteous bow.

The steam engine's whistle blew and the train started slowly out of the station. Kingsland was going to war.

#

Little Ellen whimpered in her sleep. Rabel looked over to her, saw that she'd kicked off her blanket and put it back on her before turning from the room where the Zwerg had lodged her to begin his shift.

The girl had been a marvel: her abilities growing by leaps and bounds. She insisted on working as hard as Jarin or Rabel. Giving her the day shift had been Rabel's solution — allowing her to sleep most of the night. Queen Diam had assigned her daughters to make sure that the young girl didn't overwork herself. They were not as good at the task as Rabel would have hoped — Ellen had seen to that in the first few days by bribing each of them with the "loan" of a blue fire demon. The two were delighted by the brilliance of the little creatures who thrived in the dark underground caves of Zwerg and seemed to return the zwerg girls' affection.

"How is she?" Ibb said in a low clank as Rabel joined him outside the room and they made their way to the underground forges.

"Sleeping."

"Doesn't she seem… thinner than she was?" Ibb said carefully.

Rabel sighed. "It's all we can do to keep her fed."

"She has an amazing amount of energy," Ibb said. "I do not think that she was well-fed before which may explain why she is not gaining weight proportionate to her feeding."

Rabel jerked his head to one side, negating the mechanical man's observation. "She's working too hard and I can't stop her."

"There's been no word from the north," Ibb said as they entered the huge hall that glowed with the bright heat of metal being poured into molds.

"We're on our own," Rabel agreed, pausing in his walk as a brilliant light flared in front of them. He nodded to the source of the flame, Jarin in his dragon form, melting a cradle of iron ore in an instant. "Not that we don't have sufficient help."

"He's enjoying this," Ibb said. His tone was wary.

"And?" Rabel prompted. "What aren't you saying?"

"What happens when we're done?"

Rabel shrugged.

"That's the last of the melts," Ibb said. "We've got the first eighteen magnets ready, with Jarin and the girl — and you — we should have the last eighteen done in a few days."

"And the mining?"

"They'll be ready for the magnets by then," Ibb said. "What I don't know is how to keep the magnets from pushing apart while we're placing them."

Rabel smiled and patted the metal man on the shoulder. "I have a plan."

"Yes," Ibb said, "you've told me so repeatedly." The mechanical man rumbled unhappily. "What you haven't said is what your plan entails."

"What, where is that vaunted patience of yours?"

"I am patient when I know what is to come," Ibb rumbled. "When the situation is… 'in the air', shall we say?… then I am not patient."

Rabel snorted at the mechanical man's witticism.

"Let's get the last of the magnets made, then we'll talk."

"Why is it, old friend, that I suspect you do not wish to tell me your plan until we're committed?"

"Because I'm an old friend," Rabel assured him smoothly.

Ibb rattled in response. "Time is of the essence," he said finally. "There will be no time to make other plans."

"I know," Rabel agreed heavily. "But the fort will fly, as you no doubt have planned."

"It was *your* plan."

"Oh, yes," Rabel agreed. "But you have been known to plant an idea or two in another's mind and let them take credit for it."

Ibb said nothing.

"Knowing you, this is part of a greater plan that you've been working on for a number of centuries," Rabel said. "And if *you* will tell me nothing of *your* plans, I don't see why I can't let you have a taste of your own medicine."

"I do not take medicine," Ibb said.

"Except this time," Rabel said, smirking.

"The excavation is complete," Diam reported two days later. "All the magnets are made, tested and ready for transportation."

"And the enemy is only one day from us," Granno said. He gave Rabel a dark look. "It will take hours to place your magnets, more if we have to constantly fight to keep them from pushing each other away."

"There must be some way to neutralize your magnets while we place them," Diam said.

Rabel turned to Ibb. "*Now* I will tell you my plan." He beckoned the mechanical to lean down so that he could put his lips near a metal ear and spoke quickly.

"*WHAT?*" Ibb bellowed when Rabel was done. "However did you think —"

"Can you do it or not?" Ellen asked, moving forward from her place by the two zwerg girls to stare challengingly up at the metal man.

"Do what?" Diam and Hamo Beck asked in unison.

"He will absorb the magnetic force into himself," Ellen said. She held out her arms. "He will hold the north force in one hand and the south force in another."

"This is madness," Granno swore. "How can you separate the ends of a magnet?"

"Magic," a new voice boomed up from the outskirts of the group. Everyone turned as a small form bustled forward into the light.

"Down," Rabel said to Ellen, dropping to one knee. He turned to Jarin. "You, too."

"What?" Jarin snapped. "I bow to no man."

"He is not a man," Rabel said, pointing a finger imperiously to the ground. Jarin's eyes went wide and then he fell to his knees.

"Who —?" Granno demanded of the approaching figure only to stop as Diam thrust a hand to his arm.

The queen of the Silver Mountain Zwerg dropped to her knees and lowered her head. "Geros, god of the earth, I greet you!"

The small figure stopped, put his hands on his hips and glanced down at the young zwerg queen. Hearing her words, the rest of the zerg went to their knees before their god. Geros smiled at them all and chuckled loudly.

"Well met, well met!" his voice filled the cavern. "Rabel, fire-touched, I greet you!"

Rabel looked up and rose when the god gestured for him to rise.

"And Ibb — you should know that there are many who are looking for you," Geros said to the mechanical man who had not bowed.

"Geros," Ibb rumbled in his deep voice. He inclined his metal head just a touch. "It has been many a year."

"It has," Geros agreed. He moved forward, knelt in front of Ellen and reached a hand out to lift her chin up to meet his eyes. "Little one, I greet you."

Ellen's eyes bulged in her head and she gasped for air but could not form words.

"Great god of the earth, this little one is very tired," Ibb said.

"I know," Geros said, moving his hand to Ellen's shoulder and somehow causing her to rise up with it. "I have watched you, little one."

"Y-y-you —?" Ellen squeaked.

"You are very powerful, young one," Geros told her. He glanced toward Diam and her two girls, gesturing with his eyes for them to rise. "And you are well-regarded by those I hold dear."

"Th-th-thank —" Ellen could say no more. Released by the earth god's gesture, Missy and Imay rushed over to either side of Ellen wrapping their arms around her and talking to her soothingly.

"Take a breath, fire-touched dragon-friend," Geros said, with a nod toward Jarin who rose immediately and took a step closer to the girl. Geros raised a hand to show Jarin that he meant no harm. "And then explain how you will make earth fly."

"It was my plan, god Geros," Rabel said.

"I know," Geros said with a swift nod. "But this is the one who must explain it."

Rabel drew breath to reply but stopped, nodding in understanding.

"We're going to use magnets," Ellen said, finding her voice and her strength. "We're going to use the power of their attraction against them and push the fort into the sky."

"But?" Geros prompted.

"But we need to trap the magnetic forces while we place the magnets," Ellen said. She glanced to Rabel, looking for approval but his face betrayed nothing. "So we're going to put the forces into each hand of Ibb and have him put them back when we've got the metal plates in place."

"And why am I here?" Geros prompted gently.

"Because, great god, you are the god of earth and this is a matter of the earth," Ellen said. Her lips quirked. "And I don't think we could do it on our own."

Geros smiled at her and turned to Ibb. "This is a new thing for you, isn't it, immortal one?"

"The girl or the magic?" Ibb asked.

"Both," Geros laughed. He turned to Diam. "And what do the Zwerg get from all this?"

"Safety," Diam said. "And knowledge." She nodded to Rabel and Jarin. "We know more of making steel now than we ever did."

"And?"

"And we're going to show them that the earth can defend itself even from the air," Diam replied.

Geros grinned. "Excellent!" He turned to Rabel. "So what is needed?"

"If you would consent to use your powers, great god, we could accomplish this and show the king Markel the error of his ways."

"At least some of them," Geros said, his lips pursed tightly. His eyes flashed and he bounced off the floor. "Very well! This will be fun!"

"It will!" Ellen agreed, rushing forward and grabbing the god around the waist, hugging him tight. All around her the others gasped in astonishment but Ellen didn't hear them at all, babbling excitedly, "Thank you, thank you! I just knew you'd agree!"

Arms like rock patted lightly on the back and then pushed her away. Geros glanced down at her. "And you're ready to pay the price?"

Ellen's expression fell. "I'm sworn to Ophidian."

"That's not at issue," Geros told her.

"We promised Ophidian that we'd help here," Ellen said, her eyes troubled. She glanced over her shoulder toward Rabel and then back to the god of the earth. "What do you wish, god Geros?"

"A favor for a favor," Geros replied. "Today the Zwerg help you. When the time comes, you help them."

"That's fair," Ellen said. She dropped to one knee and looked up at the earth god. "This I swear: to repay your kindness as you request with regards to my previous oaths."

Geros grunted in agreement. "One can't ask for more."

"And get away with it," Ophidian's voice came from behind Ellen.

Geros raised his eyes and nodded to the dragon-god. "We are in accord, then."

"The oath binds them to me," Ophidian said. "Her oath binds all three to you."

Geros smiled. "Of course."

"So you agree to train them in exchange for their training your people."

"What? You want an earth god's training for the fire-touched?"

"And why not? Is not fire-hot lava one of your creations?"

"Hmm," Geros said. He gave Ophidian a probing look before dropping his eyes back to Rabel, Jarin, and, finally, Ellen. Then he glanced to Ibb. "And what of the metal man?"

Ophidian laughed. "He is not sworn to me."

"I make no oaths to the gods," Ibb said in a deep, uncompromising tone. "But you know me of old; I seek no quarrel with you."

"Good enough," Geros rumbled in agreement, his voice coming out lower than Ibb's, rumbling as though it were the very earth speaking. Which, of course, it was.

"Ophidian," Rabel said, turning to the dragon-god. "What of my daughter?"

"What of Wymarc?" Jarin demanded.

"And Captain Ford, how is he?" Ellen added.

"My wyvern daughter and your daughter are alive," Ophidian replied, nodding to Jarin and Rabel in turn.

"And the captain?"

"What do you know of the captain, child?" Ophidian asked, his tone strained.

"He saved me," Ellen said, thrusting her jaw out emphatically. "When I was starving and cold, he gave me a copper to spy on Ibb and Rabel —"

"And that saved you?" Ophidian interrupted.

"It did," Ellen replied with a firm nod, her dark eyes flashing. "If it weren't for him and his demons —"

"Show me these demons," Ophidian demanded.

Ellen's eyes grew wide and she shook her head. "I can't."

"What?" the dragon-god demanded.

"I-I lent two of them out," Ellen stammered. "One to Imay and one to Missy, the queen's daughters."

"You lent them," Ophidian repeated slowly. His brows furrowed a deep groove in his face. "Were there not three?"

"How did you know?" Ellen asked in surprise.

"I've met your captain," Ophidian said. "He struck me as a prudent person." He gestured toward her chest. "The third?"

Ellen swallowed hard and reached to her skirt, pulling out a small blue-white ball of light and raised it toward Ophidian. Even as she did so, she cried, "There's something wrong with it!"

"Yes," Ophidian agreed gravely. "I'm afraid there is." He knelt down on both knees in front of the little girl. "Actually, I'm surprised that there are still here with you."

"I would have sent them to the captain, to tell him about what was happening but there hadn't been anything… until now," Ellen said in a defensive rush of words, a worried look on her face.

"Did you know that Captain Ford was sworn to Arolan?"

"The god of water?" Ellen asked. When the dragon-god nodded, Ellen shook her head. "No, I didn't."

"He has fulfilled his oath," Ophidian said gravely, glancing up toward Rabel and Jarin in warning. He gestured toward the little demon. "The demon is freed of its bond to him."

"Freed?" Ellen repeated, confused. "But why is it still here then? And why didn't the captain tell me himself?"

"Because he couldn't, child," Rabel said, kneeling down behind her and placing his hands on her shoulders.

"He couldn't?" Ellen said and then — with a sob — she said, "Is he dead?"

"He was taken by Death and given to the Ferryman," Ophidian said, nodding slowly. He glanced up to Rabel and Ibb. "He showed great courage. It surprised me."

"Arolan is free?" Ibb asked. When Ophidian nodded, the metal man began, "And the —"

"There are some things that should not be spoken at this time," Ophidian said, standing up once more. He looked down to Ellen. "I am glad he trusted you, young Ellen."

"He was kind to me," Ellen said in a small, lost voice. "I was an orphan, I had nothing."

"He was much the same," Ibb said, "long ago when I first met him." The metal man creaked his head toward Ophidian. "I am glad to hear that he kept his oath. The sea god has been distracted from his duties for too long."

"I came only because I felt you near, brother," Ophidian said, turning to the earth god. He turned back to the three human forms, adding, "And because I wished you to know that they were sworn to me."

"And through this little one — Ellen Zebala — to me in turn," Geros said, stretching out a hand toward Ellen.

"Ellen Ford," Ellen said firmly. She turned around to glance up to Rabel. "If you don't mind?"

"Of course not," Rabel said, tousling her hair. "It's only fitting."

Ophidian gave her a strange look, his eyes going brighter, before nodding. "I will tell my brother, he will be pleased." He nodded once more to Geros, saying, "I shall see you soon." And then he vanished.

"Well, then," Geros said into the stunned silence, "I think we've got the oaths all sorted." He nodded to Rabel, Ellen, and Jarin. "And now, I think it's time you learned some earth magic."

"We shall be honored," Rabel said dropping to a knee. Ellen and, a moment later, Jarin, followed suit.

Chapter Seven

"I don't like spies," Colonel Walpish said as he surveyed the grubby man on horseback in front of him. The man had come down from the mountain and none of Walpish's troops had seen him until he'd turned up in the middle of their camp.

"That's the same with me," Jenthen Barros said, spitting into the snow to the side of his horse. His spit colored the ground brown so Walpish guessed that the man made a habit of chewing on herbs or such like. "Killed five of them just the past two days, truth be known."

"So why are you here?"

"Lord Hewlitt told me to come down and meet with you," Barros replied. "Let you know the lay of the land, pick up some fresh arrows and grub."

"He'd warned me that he'd placed spies on the far side of Korin's Pass," Walpish admitted with obvious distaste.

"Had to, to keep them from reporting north and rousing their army," Barros agreed tersely. "But I'm out of arrows and could do with some grub as well."

"Very well," Walpish said, gesturing for one of his aides. "I'll see that you're taken care of."

"Don't you want my report?"

"Didn't you give it already?" Walpish replied.

Barros chewed on his herb a moment more, spat down again, and bobbed his head. "I guess I have at that."

#

"We should be seeing the airships any moment now," Walpish said to his gathered lieutenants early the next morning.

"How many, sir?" Lieutenant Marless asked.

"Two at the outset," Walpish said. "But I'm told that one by itself captured two warships some weeks back."

"And then, sir?" Ensign Berry asked anxiously.

"We wait for the fort to fall," the colonel replied, "and move through the pass. By then the musketeers will have arrived and they and the pioneers will complete the passage to the north."

"And once we're through and the infantry are with us, we head west," Lieutenant Marless said with a fierce grin. "And we'll trap the Sorians between us and the General coming up from Sea Pass."

"Exactly," Walpish said, clapping the young lieutenant on the back. "There'll be plenty of loot for all of us."

Marless nodded to the young ensign, "No doubt the king will make you Baron Berry!"

"And you Count Marless," ensign Berry returned with a grin. He turned to Colonel Walpish. "Duke Walpish, sir?"

"First, we take the pass," Walpish said sternly. "After that, we'll see."

"She needs food!" Queen Diam shouted angrily when she caught sight of Ellen and the way she was shaking.

"That's not it, your majesty," Jarin said, "it's the charge she's holding."

"Is it too much?" Diam asked, giving the dragon-lad a wide berth.

"We have to get it out of her soon, your majesty," Rabel said in a strained voice. "We all need to do it."

"The slabs are in place," Granno said. "All that's needed is the word and we can start charging them."

"Ibb and Hamo are supposed to be talking with the garrison commander," Diam said testily. "What is taking them so long?"

"We won't have much choice, soon," Rabel said, nodding toward Ellen. "She'll have to release her charge or she'll die."

"I'm afraid Geros didn't consider your mortality when he taught you the spells," Diam said with a worried look toward the little girl. "Perhaps Ophidian shouldn't have praised you so highly."

"We're almost there," Granno said as they made their way through the underground caves. "They can release their spells the minute they get to the metal."

There were thirty-six inert slabs of high-grade steel all placed strategically in a pair of concentric circles under the base of the East Fort Pass. All they needed were their magnetic charges and they would repel each other, forcing the fort and the earth on which it rested to rise into the sky.

"We don't want to raise the fort too early," Rabel warned. "If the airships see it too early, they'll not attack."

"Isn't that the point?" Granno asked.

"If they think they can defeat the fort and learn otherwise, they'll think twice before attacking again," Jarin said, nodding toward Rabel.

They had discussed the plan and revised the plan several times in the past few days. Geros, in particular had added twists that neither Rabel nor Ibb had considered, although, to be fair, neither of them had known the sort of magic the earth god could teach them.

Geros seemed delighted to surprise the metal man and almost as delighted to discover that of the three of them, Jarin was the most adept.

"It's easy enough," Geros had said, rubbing his hands in glee. "When metal cools in alignment with the earth, it takes a magnetic charge."

"If it's hammered when aligned with the north, it will do the same thing," Ibb had said.

"Ah! But that's forcing what comes naturally," Geros had said. He glanced to Rabel. "You'd charged the magnets and were going to transfer the charge to Ibb." Rabel nodded in agreement. Geros shook his head. "That won't work."

"It won't?"

"The charge would be too great, even if you could transfer it," Geros said. "Even our metal man here would be hard-pressed to keep the north magnet in one hand from slamming into the south magnet in the other."

"If we did it one magnet at a time?" Ellen had asked.

"It might work but you've got thirty-six magnets," Geros said, shaking his head. He chuckled. "No, this way is much better!"

"It is?" Rabel had said.

"It is, and you each know half of it already," the earth god agreed gleefully.

It had taken over a day for the god to teach the spell to the three. Jarin found it the hardest to learn, Ellen the easiest but, surprisingly, Rabel was the strongest.

And so now they were making their way, charged up with their first spells, ready to magnetise the steel slabs that had been placed by the Zwerg in the chambers mined under the fort.

The spells were exhausting so they had agreed that they'd charge themselves up with all the necessary spells and release them all at once.

Only now, it seemed that the spells were too much for little Ellen. Her teeth were chattering and little spurts of lightning sprang from one finger to the other.

"Is she supposed to do that?" Diam asked worriedly. "She's almost glowing with the power."

"So are they," Granno said, pointing to Rabel and Jarin.

"I imagine we must look quite a sight," Rabel said with a strained grin.

"Your teeth are glowing," Diam said by way of agreement.

#

"Where are they?" Colonel Walpish muttered testily as he and his men scanned the skies at sunset. The airships had been expected all day and he'd had his men stand to for most of it. They were now all tired and listless in their saddles, murmuring quietly to themselves as the sun crept to the horizon on the west.

"Maybe the wind held them up," Lieutenant Marless suggested.

"I thought they could sail against the wind," ensign Berry said.

"But a harsh wind will push against them and it will take more time," Marless replied.

"Wherever they are, it will be dark soon," Colonel Walpish said. He shook his head sourly. "And we can't see them with the sun in our eyes."

"Can they attack at night?" Berry asked.

"I don't know if they'll be able to see their target," Walpish grumbled. He turned to the mountains and the dim lights of the fort in the far distance and then turned back to his officers. Bitterly he said, "Have the men stand down."

#

"It'll be too dark to see," Captain Nevins grumbled as he scanned the skies to the north.

"As you say, sir," Lieutenant Garrett said. "Although we should be able to pick up any torches they light as the night falls."

"Can you fire at torches?" Nevins growled.

"Actually, sir, if the weather holds, we might just be able to do that," Garrett replied.

"Won't that be a surprise for them!" Nevins chuckled. "Iron will be falling on them from the sky and they won't have a clue how."

"They'll think the gods are angry," Garrett agreed.

"And they'll be half right, I'm sure," Nevins said. He gestured peremptorily to someone in the distance. The figure approached warily. "And how are you today, mage?"

"Please sir, I'm just an apprentice," Tortin Borkis replied, ducking his head nervously.

"You're better than that fat-headed lout on *Vengeance*," Nevins said, gesturing to the airship that followed along behind — and below them. "*Mage* Tirpin is not half the man you are, lad."

Borkis gave *Warrior's* captain a doubtful look.

"You've only to see how much higher our *Warrior* is in the sky to know that, lad," Nevins said. "That mage back there might think he knows a thing or two but you are showing him up."

"He's helping, sir," Borkis said, swallowing nervously. "I'm only adding my magic to his."

"And he doesn't suspect a thing," Nevins chuckled. "He thinks he's doing it all himself."

"On deck!" the lookout shouted from above. "Lights to the north!"

Nevins turned to the sound and grabbed a telescope from the cabinet near the helm. "I'm going forward."

#

"Lie still!" Queen Diam ordered when Ellen opened her eyes and struggled to rise to her feet. "You fainted."

"I did?" Ellen repeated. She struggled again. "I didn't mean to."

"No, of course not," Diam agreed. "Nor did Rabel or the dragon but they fainted all the same."

"Are they all right?"

"Yes," Jarin's voice came to her ears from somewhere close by. "Rabel took it the worst, being the oldest."

"And carrying the most spells," Rabel's voice added testily.

"I could have taken three more," Jarin replied.

"I wanted you to save your strength," Rabel reminded the dragon-man.

"Drink this," Granno said from beside Ellen, thrusting a mug into her hands. Ellen sat up, aided by the queen and heard the other two do the same by the rustling of their clothes.

"That was close," Rabel said after a moment. He glanced around and looked above him, his eyes going wide. "Did we do it?"

"Can you not feel the stones straining to break free?" Granno asked in surprise. "It will only take the least —"

"But they're held for the moment?" Rabel asked, his voice full of worry.

"For the moment," Queen Diam agreed. She glanced around the large cavern that had risen between the two sets of magnets. She glanced down to Ellen. "Can you stand?"

Ellen considered the notion and rose slowly to her feet. Diam raised a hand up to support her.

"We've got eighteen of the thirty-six magnets charged," Rabel said, rising to his feet and nodding to Jarin. "We'll need to know when to charge the final half."

"Ibb said something about a signal," Granno said dubiously.

"Until then, can you three rest?" Diam asked. She looked over to Ellen as she added, "I've sent Imay and Missy to get some comforters."

"That would be a good idea," Rabel said. "But we should also eat and prepare our spells." He glanced upward at the gleaming bands of metal above him. "We can't say how soon we'll need them."

#

"I've heard of you," Ellas said to Ibb. He glanced to Hamo Beck. "You vouch for him?"

"I do," Hamo said with a curt nod. "I've known him most of my life."

"They say that you don't die," Ellas said to the metal man.

"I've heard it said as well," Ibb replied.

Captain Ellas Berold snorted in amusement. "And what is it, metal man, that has driven you to climb all the way up here this night?"

"You are going to be attacked," Ibb said.

Ellas shook his head. "Not tonight," he swore. "Any guns powerful enough to reach us we'd would have seen hours ago." He gestured to the other two and they began climbing to the heights above the thick walls of the fort built into the peak of the eastern hill of the pass.

"They will not be coming where you look," Ibb said as he clanked his way up the steps.

"Then they'll do no good," Ellas said. He guided them toward the west end of the fort overlooking the opening of the pass that led from south to north. "My guns cover the pass and we're too high for them to hit us from below."

"What if the guns that fired on you were higher?" Ibb asked.

"Higher?" Ellas repeated in surprise. He looked above them. "This is the highest point right where we stand."

"What if you could be higher?" Ibb asked.

"And how do you propose we do that?" Ellas demanded. He stuck his thumbs under his armpits and flapped his arms. "Fly?"

"No... float," Ibb said.

"Hamo," Ellas said turning angrily to the mayor of Korin's Pass. "Why did you bring this clanking fool to waste my time?"

"Sir, sir!" A sentry shouted from the highest tower. He pointed south into the gathering gloom. "I saw something!"

"Well, what is it?" Ellas demanded irritably.

"It... it looked like ships!" the man said.

"Ships in the sky?" Ellas roared. "Sergeant of the guard! Have that man relieved he must be —"

Boom! Boom! Boom!

"Duck," Ibb ordered, pushing both the captain and the mayor beneath him.

"We're being attacked!" Captain Berold cried, ducking out from under the metal man. "Man the walls! Prepare the cannon! Fire at will!"

"I'm afraid that won't do any good," Ibb said from above him.

"Why not?"

"Because the ships are in the air, above you and firing down," Ibb replied. "Your guns cannot reach them."

Ellas went to the wall and looked up into the darkening sky. He turned back to Ibb and Beck even as the first of his gun crews rushed to their stations.

"What do we do?" Ellas asked the metal man.

"We must rise to the occasion," Ibb replied, lifting a hand, palm out, upwards.

#

"Well done, hit them again!" Captain Nevins roared as the first broadside fell on the fort below. He could see large chunks of stone — and a few soldiers — fall down to the valley below. "We've got them right where we want them!"

Not too far away, the guns of *Vengeance* flamed in the night.

"Mannevy was right, by the gods!" Nevins said, dancing with delight as his guns fired once more. "There's no way they can stand against us, not even with our six-pounders!"

#

Dimly, in the cavern they heard the heavy percussion of cannon roaring well above them.

"That's our signal!" Rabel said, gesturing for the other two to rise from the comforters they had lain in just a few minutes before. He glanced over to Ellen. "Are you up for this, little one?"

"Of course," Ellen replied stiffly, pushing herself to her feet and moving toward her position.

"As am I," Jarin said, pushing his comforter off him.

"Don't do anything until I say," Rabel warned. "We all need to be in place and we can't be late with our spells."

"Or what?" Jarin asked.

"Or the fort will wobble and maybe fall on one side," Rabel said.

"With us underneath?" Jarin asked, eyes wide.

"Your majesty, perhaps you and your people should leave us, just in case," Rabel said, glancing toward queen Diam.

"No," the diminutive queen said after a quick glance toward her children and her guards, "we prefer to watch this glorious moment." Beside her, Granno let out a resigned sigh.

#

"Cease fire!" Captain Berold called loudly. "Gunners, cease fire!"

"Sir?"

"Stand to, though," Captain Ellas warned. "When I give the word, you're to give the nearest ship a full broadside."

"They're too high, sir!" a gunner called back.

"Not for long," Ibb said. He turned to the captain. "Tell them to aim flat, straight and level."

#

"We beat them!" Lieutenant Garrett cried in awe when the guns of the fort fell silent.

Captain Nevins eyed the silent fort critically before snapping, "Get me a glass!"

A seaman — Nevins didn't have *air*men on *his* ship — handed him a telescope and he brought it up to his good eye, scanning the fort hurriedly even as another broadside from *Vengeance* roared out, brightening the night sky.

"They've raised no white flag," Nevins said after a moment. He turned to Garrett. "Keep firing."

"Sir," Garrett said, turning to the gun crews. "Continue the action!"

#

Rabel, Ellen, and Jarin fanned out in a circle midway in the large chamber. The queen and the others were safely in the center.

"Are you ready?" Rabel said, lifting his hands up to his waist and glancing to see that Jarin and Ellen had done the same.

"Ready," Jarin said.

"Ready," Ellen added.

"On three," Rabel said, closing his eyes and imagining his fingers tingling with power, each pointed toward a different steel slab. "One… two… *three!*"

He opened his eyes as power arced from him into the inert cold steel of six stones. He heaved a great sigh as the power drained from him. To his left, he heard Jarin grunt at the effort as he also magically magnetized six stones. From Ellen, who only had four, he heard nothing. Nervously her turned toward her. "Ellen?"

"This is fun!" the little girl cried as the air around her glowed with her magic and her hair flew up and out from her body, each strand standing straight and away from the others.

"Is it working?" Granno asked from inside the circle.

Around them, the ground shuddered and groaned.

#

"What's happening?" Captain Ellas cried as the stones of the wall shuddered and jerked.

"Magic," Ibb said.

"I can feel it," Hamo Beck confirmed. He glanced over the parapet to the ground below.

A huge rumbling sound came from below them and the fort shook more and more.

#

"Listen!" Lieutenant Garrett called. The guns stopped and everyone strained their ears in the night sky.

"What's that rumbling?" Nevins said, coming to the railings at the side of the ship, his telescope clutched tightly in one hand.

"The fort's shaking!" the lookout cried from above.

"We must have shaken it from its foundations!" Lieutenant Garrett cried in awe.

#

"Mount up!" Colonel Walpish cried as the huge rumble of groaning earth came to his ears. "We ride the pass and no stopping!"

Behind him, his squadron of cavalry leaped to their saddles and formed up in two columns.

"The airships did it, sir!" Lieutenant Markless swore in delight.

"We'll be in the village by daybreak!" Ensign Berry crowed.

"Sound the trot!" Colonel Walpish ordered, spurring his horse forward.

#

"Steady men, steady!" Captain Ellas Berold cried as the fort wobbled once more.

"About now, I believe," Ibb said with some satisfaction.

"Sir, sir!" the guard in the tower cried. "We're rising!"

#

"Look up!" Ellen cried as the rumbling grew quieter. Everyone in the cavern looked up. A giant circle of earth tore, with dirt falling to the ground as the magnets above strained to free themselves of the forces of the magnets below.

"I can see night!" Granno shouted. "There's a gap between the top above us."

"It's working," Queen Diam said in a voice filled with awe.

"I had hoped so," Geros said from beside her. She looked at him in surprise. "This is quite something, you know. I wouldn't miss it for jewels."

"Ellen, Jarin," Rabel called, "how are you?"

"Tired," Jarin admitted. He glanced upwards as the dirt and the fort above it rose slowly into the night sky. He turned to Geros, the god of the earth. "Has this ever happened before, earth god?"

Geros shook his head. "No, never in all the life of the world."

"Ellen?" Rabel repeated, worried that the girl hadn't spoken.

"It's beautiful," she swore in awe. She giggled. "This is so amazing!"

"We must be prepared, in case the magnets slip or move from alignment," Rabel warned.

"What do we do then?" Jarin asked.

"If we can, we use our magic to increase or lower the power of the magnets to level things up," Rabel replied.

"And if we can't?" Jarin asked.

"Run," Rabel said grimly. He turned to queen Diam. "It might be best if you retired now, your majesty."

"You can see this safely from one of our burrows," Granno added in a tone of repressed anxiety.

"Your children will be safer," Jarin said, gesturing to Imay and Missy.

"What about you?" Diam said.

"I'm a dragon," Jarin said with a shrug. "I'll burn my way through."

"That's an awful lot of rock to melt," Granno said dubiously.

"It will be easier to concentrate if we don't talk," Rabel warned.

"We shall leave you, then," queen Diam said, waving for the rest of her retinue to follow her down the newly-dug cavern which led back to her kingdom — and a nearby burrow to the surface.

#

"Steady men, steady!" Captain Berold called as the East Pass Fort slowly rose in the night sky. "Wait for my order!"

#

"What's happening?" Captain Nevins said, glancing northward in the growing darkness. "Why aren't they firing?"

Lieutenant Garrett shrugged and shook his head.

"Mage Tortin!" Captain Nevins shouted. "I need you here, now!"

A rush of footsteps heralded the arrival of the nervous mage. Nevins thrust his telescope into the mage's hands and gestured to the fort in the distance. "What's happening? Is it some magic?"

#

"Mage Tirpin, what is it?" Captain Jacques Martel of the royal airship *Vengeance* said to the royal mage, gesturing toward the fort in the night's gloom. "Are they doing something to float their torches because I swear they've gotten higher."

Tirpin looked out into the distance and stared at the flames from the fort. After a moment he shrugged. "Probably just some trick to throw off your aim, captain. I wouldn't let it —"

143

"Fire!" Captain Berold roared. Six heavy cannon all belched fire and smoke into the night sky, their twenty-four pound cannon balls racing through the air like a wall of iron.

"Reload!" the captain cried. "Fire at will!"

#

"By the gods!" Captain Martel shouted as the night flamed in front of him. "They're on our level!"

Three balls struck the airship's hull, smashing it to pieces. Two balls missed completely. But the sixth — the sixth hit the airship's balloon in the middle and torn it into tiny shreds in the blink of an eye.

Vengeance fell from the sky, crashing onto the plains below, a shattered, lifeless hulk.

#

"Tortin!" Nevins cried as he saw *Vengeance* plummet to its death. "Get us out of here!"

The apprentice mage looked at his captain in complete surprise. "Captain?"

"Take us up!" Nevins bellowed, pumping a hand upwards in emphasis. "Get us above those bastards!"

"But —"

"They can't get much higher," Nevins shouted. "Do it!"

#

The gunners on the fort yelled in excitement as the first airship fell from the sky. Captain Berold shouted with them.

"They still have one," Ibb warned. "We should take care of it."

"In a moment," Ellas said, waving to the cheering soldiers. "Let them cheer!"

"Sir!" the guard in the lookout tower cried.

"What?" Ellas shouted back.

"The second ship is *rising*, sir!"

"If it gets above you —"

"All guns, fire on the second ship!" Ellas roared, gesticulating wildly toward the ship in the distance.

#

"Sir, sir, look!" Ensign Berry cried, pointing to the battle in the distance. "They got one of the ships, sir!"

Colonel Walpish jerked his head to the right just in time to see one of the flying ships plummet from the sky and shatter on the ground below.

"What do we do?" Lieutenant Marless asked in anguish. "Sound the charge," Walpish replied. "The pickets will be too distracted by the fighting and the fort's guns can't range on us. We'll be through before they can react."

"Bugler!" Lieutenant Marless called. "Sound the charge!"

#

The earth shook from some impact in the distance. Rabel looked above him, his brows furrowed.

"It's wobbling!" Jarin called, confirming his fears.

"Steady it!" Rabel said, raising his hands and seeking the proper spot to expel his magic.

"Don't push too hard!" Ellen cried in warning.

"It's like a top trying to teeter to one side," Jarin cried.

"Let's just steady it up," Rabel said, forcing himself to sound calm.

"It's rising higher," Geros commented. "If the top gets too far from the bottom, it may become even more unstable." The earth god sounded rather pleased with the thought.

#

"It's rising more!" Lieutenant Garrett cried, pointing to the fort.

"It's wobbling," Captain Nevins said as he watched the fort rising in the night sky. He turned to the apprentice mage who was sweating with the effort of making *Warrior* rise higher in the cold night sky. "Mage Borkis, what happens if the fort wobbles too much?"

"I don't know, sir," Borkis replied, shaking his head. "But if it was a top that wobbled, it'd fall on its side."

"It would, wouldn't it?" Nevins said to himself. He turned to his lieutenant. "Garrett, have the gunners aim for the spire."

"The spire, sir?" Garrett repeated in surprise.

"We're going to see if we can topple the fort over," Nevins said with a calm he didn't feel. If this plan didn't work, he was certain that the fort's twenty-four pound cannon balls would make short work of his poor ship — just as they had done with Martel's *Vengeance*.

"Aye, sir," Garrett replied nervously.

"A guinea to the first to hit the spire," Nevins called out loudly.

#

"Another hundred feet and they'll be too high for us to hit," Captain Berold swore bitterly as the second airship continued to fire on the fort.

"He's aiming for the spire," Ibb said, seeming surprised.

"Maybe he can't see too well," Hamo Beck suggested.

Captain Ellas said, "Then he shouldn't be —"

A ball hit the spire and the whole fort tipped in the air, wobbling back and forth.

#

"What happened?" Jarin cried as the earth above them suddenly teetered to one side.

"It's wobbling!" Ellen cried, screwing her eyes tight and shooting spells out of her fingers.

"Ellen, no!" Rabel shouted. "That's too much!"

The earth above them rolled back away and further over.

"We can't hold it!" Rabel said. He turned to Jarin. "Jarin —"

But above them the night sky suddenly grew larger on one side as the floating fort tipped on its side.

#

"We got it!" Nevins shouted, pounding the deck with his feet and pumping the air with his fists in triumph. "We got the damned thing!"

The fort lurched away from the shots, lurched further and further until it seemed certain to fall over and then —

It swung back again. Upright. More than upright. It started tipping toward them. Faster and faster.

"It's going to hit us!" Garrett cried in alarm.

"Throw the guns overboard!" Nevins cried. "Throw everything over! Make us lighter!"

"Slash the rigging and fire the guns!" Garrett roared. "Stand clear and let the recoil take them overboard!"

The confused gunners looked at him in amazement until he and Nevins both pulled their swords and started slashing with all their might. The moment the first gun was unleashed, Nevins took the match and lit it off, standing back as the recoil shot the gun across the deck, through the railing on the other side and down into the dark night.

"Get them all!" Garrett roared. One gunner was unlucky and got hit by a flying gun, screaming as it smashed into him and took him through the railing and into the darkness beyond but the rest of the guns soon followed it into the night.

"We're rising!" Nevins cried in delight.

"The fort's falling!" Borkis shouted, pointing as the fort tipped toward them.

#

"By the gods!" Lieutenant Marless swore as the night was filled with the sounds of crashing rocks in the distance. Colonel Walpish jerked his head around and spied the fort as it fell into the night, its spire tearing a huge gash into the hull of the remaining airship as it scrambled upwards in the night sky.

"Bugler!" Colonel Walpish called. "Sound the trot!"

"Sir?" Marless turned to him in shock.

"We're through their pickets," Walpish replied. "We'll go to the walk and rest the horses." He gestured ahead of them. "We'll be in the village by sunrise."

"Yes sir," Marless said in a different tone.

"Bugler," Walpish called, "sound walk."

The slower tones of the walk trumpeted in the night and the heavy hooves of the cavalry squadron slowed and grew more quiet, drowned out by the huge booming crashes in the distance behind them.

#

"Are you all right, your majesty?" Granno asked as the last of the horrendous noise died away around them.

"Yes," Queen Diam said, rising to her feet and dusting herself off. She glanced around to find her daughters and reached for their hands. "And you?"

"That was rather louder than I'd anticipated," Geros, the god of the earth, said as he stood beside them. "Does anyone know what happened?"

"The fort fell over," Missy said, pointing to the edge of the hill. "I think it hit the airship, too."

"But the airship is still there," Diam said, glancing up into the night and picking out the dim white of its balloon high above them.

"The pass is unguarded, the enemy can take the village," Granno said solemnly.

Diam accepted this with a nod. She glanced toward the large hole that had just moments before been the cavern of magnets. She could see some glinting of the steel that girded the bottom of the cavern still.

"Where is Ellen?" Diam asked, her voice going chill.

"And the others," Geros said with academic interest. He looked at the mess of the cavern and muttered, "They're human and rather delicate."

Missy turned to her mother and buried her head against her thigh, bawling.

"Are —" Imay began slowly, looking up to her mother "— are they dead?"

"They knew the risks," Geros said, nodding to the ruins.

"But — but —" Imay couldn't say any more.

"We will mourn them," Granno said, moving toward his queen. "Their deeds will be sung by the bards forever."

"They were sworn to Ophidian," Geros said idly, "I'm quite surprised that he —"

"Look!" Diam cried, pointing to up to the sky just as a flame burst from under the airship.

"Ophidian's flame!" Geros swore.

"It's Jarin!" Diam cried in joy. "Look, children, it's Jarin!"

"It's not *just* Jarin," Granno said as two more bolts of flame joined the first.

#

"Fire! Fire!" a seaman shouted as *Warrior* rose in the night sky. Nevins turned to look toward the man, ready to berate him but —

A gout of flame erupted from below.

"It's a dragon!" another man cried. "It's a dragon and it's flaming!"

"Stand by the —" Nevins began, turning to the gun crews but cutting himself off as he saw the empty gun ports. "Get bows and arrows! We'll show this thing!"

Lieutenant Garrett turned to him in absolute amazement. "Sir? Are you mad?" Before Nevins could reply, Garrett turned around and shouted. "Abandon ship! Abandon ship! All hands, throw ropes over the sides and go down them." He turned to the young mage. "Can you start us down?"

Borkis' jaw fell.

"Well?" Garrett demanded. "Can you?"

Mutely, the mage nodded.

"Then do it!" Garrett shouted. "Do it or we'll all burn!"

Borkis turned imploringly to Captain Nevins. Nevins looked at the flames rising from below and sighed. "Do it. It's our only hope." The captain turned to the man at the wheel. "Turn us south."

Epilog

The sun rose brightly the next morning over a huge plain of destruction. East Pass Fort lay shattered and broken under a pile of rock where it had tumbled down the slopes of the hill on which it had once rested.

It was joined by the shattered remnants of one airship and the burnt timbers of another.

A small group of battered men were making their way south, toward the railway.

An exhausted Jarin stood in human form at the top of the hill, with Rabel and Ellen standing beside him. Shortly, they were joined by Queen Diam, her daughters, and Granno.

"What do we do now?" Diam asked.

"The King's cavalry broke through the pass," Granno said. "By now they've taken Korin's Pass. The whole pass is open to Markel and his men."

"So we failed," Ellen said miserably.

"We destroyed two of their ships," Jarin said. "Isn't that something?"

"And we know how to build floating forts," Diam said. "And we can build them fast."

"With Geros' help," Jarin said. He glanced toward Rabel who had said nothing. "Rabel? We can build more, can't we?"

Rabel nodded glumly.

"What's wrong?" Ellen asked him.

Rabel raised his head and looked at the others. "Where's Ibb?"

Ophidian's Honor

Book 9
Twin Soul series

Chapter One

The sun rose over a huge plain of destruction. There was no sign of life among the rubble. East Pass Fort lay shattered and broken under a pile of rock where it had tumbled down the slopes of the hill on which it had once rested. The huge guns were buried under the mass of the rock-built fort and the hill on which it had been constructed.

Nearby were the shattered wooden remains — just a bare skeleton — of what once had been proud airship. Further were the blackened timbers of a second airship — all that remained of King Markel's surprise attack on Soria.

A small group of battered men were making their way south, toward the railway. Survivors from the fort or the airship, it wasn't clear from this distance.

#

The dragon Jarin stood in human form at the top of the hill, with Rabel and Ellen Ford standing beside him. They were joined by the queen of the underground Zwergs, Diam, her daughters, Imay and Lissy, as well as Granno, her trusted general.

"What do we do now?" Diam asked.

"The King's cavalry broke through," Granno said. "By now they've taken Korin's Pass. The whole pass is open to Markel and his men."

"So we failed," Ellen said miserably.

"We destroyed two of their ships," Jarin said. "Isn't that something?"

"And we know how to build floating forts," Diam said. "And we can build them fast."

"With Geros' help," Jarin said. He glanced toward Rabel who had said nothing. "Rabel? We can build more, can't we?"

Rabel nodded glumly.

"What's wrong?" Ellen asked him.

Rabel raised his head and looked at the others. "Where's Ibb?"

The others looked at him in alarm and then they all craned their necks back to the rubble that had once been the East Pass Fort… and the last known location of the metal man, Ibb.

"We have to find him!" Ellen said, breaking free of the others and starting determinedly down toward the ruins.

"He's dead!" Diam said, "You'll only be wasting your time!"

"He's made of metal, he may have survived," Rabel said stoutly. He turned to Jarin. The tired teen met his eyes briefly, turned away and called over his shoulder, "Climb on!"

In the next instant he had turned into his dragon self. Rabel called to Ellen who turned, spotted the dragon, and raced back happily to throw herself on his back. Rabel climbed aboard more leisurely.

"What are you doing?" Queen Diam shouted as strong dragon wings lifted the three up to the sky.

"We're saving our friend!" Ellen called back down, waving a hand toward the fort.

Diam fumed and turned expectantly to Granno.

"Do we help them or leave them to their own devices?" the older Zwerg asked.

Diam scowled, shaking her head. "We help them. Hamo Beck was in that fort." She started trudging after the vanishing dragon toward the ruins below.

They didn't walk far. The dragon dropped his companions at the edge of the rubble and returned to the Zwerg, changing quickly back to his human form.

"If it please your majesty, I shall be honored to convey you hence," Jarin said, gesturing to the ruins.

"We're going to ride a dragon!" Lissy shrieked, clapping her hands together with joy. Imay, the older, looked at her mother hopefully.

Diam smiled down at her two daughters. "Yes, we're going to ride a dragon," she agreed. She turned to glance up at the tall youth. "We won't be too heavy for you?"

Jarin jerked his head up and laughed. "You're little!"

"We weigh a lot," Granno warned. "And you're exhausted, no doubt, from your efforts last night."

"Climb on," Jarin said, turning and jumping back into his dragon form, craning his now long neck back toward them, his red eyes gleaming humorously.

"I'll help the children up first, if it please your majesty," Granno offered.

"It does *not*," Diam said haughtily, raising her arms up and gesturing for him to lift her to the dragon's side. "I'll not have my daughters in danger before me."

Granno grunted in agreement and deftly hauled the small queen onto the dragon's back. Diam found a good perch and turned back to her daughters, gesturing with her hand. Granno lifted first Imay and then Lissy who both clambered forward and joined their mother at the dragon's neck. Granno looked at the three and his brow creased. "There's no more room!"

Jarin roared loudly and leapt up into the air, turning back swiftly in one tail length before reaching down and grabbing a much-surprised Granno with his front talons.

"Granno," Diam said, looking down to her surprised general, "even I know it's never wise to taunt a dragon."

"So I see," Granno said, glancing over his shoulder to the ground disappearing below them and then, hastily, back up to his queen and her daughters a-dragonback.

#

"Sir, sir!" Tortis Borkin cried, pointing up to the sky behind him. "It's a dragon!"

Captain Nevins, formerly of the airship *Warrior*, before that of the naval ship of the same name, paused in his slow trudge westward to crane his neck up to the sky.

"Probably the same one that burnt us out of the sky," Nevins said grimly, turning back to trudge onward.

"But — but — sir!" Tortis wailed.

"If it wants to burn us, or eat us, it will," Nevins said, moving one foot in front of the other with grim determination. "There's nothing we can do about it now."

"It's landing by the ruins of the fort," Tortis said a moment later. "And now it's going up again." A moment later, he added, "And landing." By his voice, Nevins could tell that the apprentice mage had stopped his forward movement to watch the dragon. "What's it picking up?" Tortis said to himself. "Children?"

Intrigued, Nevins turned back and saw that Tortis was a good twenty yards behind him. Nevins pulled out the telescope he'd somehow kept from breaking during their hellish descent and trained it on the dragon.

"Those are Zwergs," Nevins said, surprised, when he fixed the dragon in his sight.

"Zwergs?"

"One of the earth children," Nevins said. "Never thought I'd see them in daylight. Rumor says they don't like it much." He pursed his lips. "Good with metal." He trained the telescope back to where the dragon had picked up its passengers. "There are tales told that they have mountains of gold and jewels."

"And how can we carry such things?" Borkis grumbled.

"In an airship," Nevins said.

"If one *had* an airship," Borkis said.

"And a mage powerful enough to lift the weight," Nevins said. He started back to the mage, reaching him just as the dragon landed and disappeared from view. He clapped Borkis on the shoulder. "I happen to be in the presence of just such a person," he told the tired teen. He cocked his head and said, "How would you like to get very rich?"

Tortis Borkin met his look with wide eyes which narrowed quickly in thought. Slowly he nodded. "I'd like that very much," he said. "I'd like it a great deal."

Nevins waved a hand to the ruined fort. "It's not going anywhere for a while. So we'll know where to go looking for the gold. And we know where to get dragon's steel —" he pointed to the glinting long thin strips of steel — "that can be used to make most *excellent* steam engines."

Borkin's eyes widened once more and then he gulped as Nevins used his grip to turn the mage around.

"For the moment, we must report to the king," Nevins said. "He'll be most happy to hear that his plans are progressing." He tightened his grip on the mage. "And he'll be very happy with the way you learned how to lift his airships so much better than that ass Tirpin."

"I can teach others, too," Borkin said. "I know some promising lads —"

"Good," Nevins broke in. "But for the moment, let us concentrate on getting out of here alive, shall we?"

Chapter Two

"Sir, sir, two men approaching!" a private roared out from the edge of the encampment.

Brigadier General Diggory Filbert emerged from his tent and turned toward the sound. "On foot or on horse?"

"On foot, sir," the private replied, unaware of the rank of his questioner as the private was dutifully still staring out from the edge of their camp.

"Captain of the guard!" Filbert called.

"Sir!"

"Have them searched and brought to my tent," Filbert ordered. "Damned extraordinary," he muttered to himself, stepping back out of the night.

"Sir?" Gibbons, his man servant asked, scuttling anxiously toward him.

"You're no use!" Filbert swore, flashing a hand toward the man and whacking him soundly on the head. "Have something warm brought in and get my officers assembled. We've plans to make."

"Sir!" Gibbons replied, beetling out of the tent and carefully not rubbing his wounded head until safely out of sight.

Filbert swore again to the empty tent. "What a way to run a war, what?"

His father was well up in the king's favor. Filbert had earned his rank — paid for with two chests of gold — and he was looking to earn higher whenever his father could gain more gold. This ordering of troops and marching off to war was something he hadn't counted on, even less being sent out on his own to lead "the all-important eastward flank of our pincer movement" — as General Tashigg had told him. Tashigg! Where was the man? He was supposed to be coming up with the rest of the troops, the two other brigades and the heavy guns of the rest of the Second Division but all Filbert had seen arrive in the past day or so was the last of his troops — and then the trains had stopped. Something about needing them for the seaward forces.

"Just wait until Walpish tells you it's clear, then march your troops through the pass," Tashigg had ordered him.

Walpish! Some effete horseman wandering about with cavalry.

"If there's any problem, the airships will help you," Tashigg had concluded. "They'll be your eyes in the sky and their guns will drive the enemy before you!"

Well, Filbert had not seen any of these blasted *airships* everyone keep blathering about. They could hardly help if they weren't —

His tent rustled and he turned toward the intrusion.

The captain of the guard, Welless, nodded and gestured to two travel-stained men who preceded him.

"You asked to see these men, sir," Welless said, following in behind them.

"Where's the guard?" Filbert demanded. Gods! Didn't the fool know he was supposed to *guard* his general? What did the man think *Captain of the Guard* meant, anyway?

"They're our men, sir," Welless replied.

"Spies?" Filbert rasped. "They're certainly not in any uniform *I* recognize!"

"I am Captain Ismael Nevins, of his majesty's royal airship *Warrior*," the first man said, bowing slightly.

Filbert waved a hand at him. "Never heard of you!" A moment later, he added, "You've come to report, have you? Did Walpish send you?"

Nevins shook his head. "I just arrived."

"What?" Filbert growled in alarm. "I thought your ship was faster." He added, as the thought came to him, "And weren't you supposed to destroy a fort or something?"

"The East Pass Fort," Nevins said in agreement. "And we did."

"Good!" Filbert grunted. "That's something, then." He pursed his lips. "What about Walpish? Is the pass clear? Are you going to lead us?"

"The fort is destroyed, I've no doubt that the pass is clear," Nevins said, his eyes flashing. "I'm here to get transport back to the king. He'll want to hear from me."

"Transport?" Filbert repeated. "Isn't an airship transport? Like a boat but out of water?" His eyes popped as he barked a laugh at his own jest. His laughter died down when he realized that no one else had joined him. Sour lot.

"Our airships were destroyed," the other man spoke up. "The fort shot one down and the dragon destroyed the other."

"I thought you were going to fly above the fort," Captain Welless said diffidently.

"The fort flew above us!" the man replied.

"And you are?" Captain Welless demanded.

"Tortis Borkin, mage," Nevins said. "And the reason we survived."

"A *fort* flew?" Filbert said.

"Floated, actually," Borkin replied. Filbert arched an eyebrow menacingly at the man for his lack of manners but the other seemed unable to notice. "I'm thinking they might have used magnets — huge magnets —"

"Enough," Nevins said. He turned to the General. "We must get back to the king. We'll need more airships here and he'll want our knowledge."

"Well, I certainly have no use for you," Filbert allowed with an airy wave of his hand. "A captain without a ship is not much of a captain, if you ask me."

Captain Nevins gave him a hard, cold look, his fists clenched to his sides. "If you'll get us some horses and let us know where to meet the next train —"

"Train!" Filbert barked. "My good man, there'll be no more trains for the next week or so I'm told!"

"No trains?" the mage Borkis squeaked. He turned to Nevins and then back to the General. "Horses?"

"You'd have to get them off Walpish," Filbert replied, waving them off. "I've only got my string here and I'm not letting you have one of them." The mere thought of having one of these men on one of his mares!

"I've always liked horses," Nevins said politely. "How many did you bring for the campaign, sir?"

"None of your damned business, sir!" Filbert replied heatedly. "It's hard enough finding them bedding, let alone fodder, out here."

"I'm sure," Nevins said, his expression thoughtful. He turned to Borkis. "Well, we must see if we can't find another way, come along, mage."

Filbert followed their departure with his eyes and then snorted. "Really! These air people are no better than the sea people they replaced!"

"Sir," Captain Welless said in half-hearted agreement.

Filbert recoiled as though seeing him for the first time. "What are you still doing here? Get out and get back to your duty!"

With a swift salute, the captain turned and left.

"And call for my man! I'm hungry!" Filbert shouted after him.

\#

"What are we going to do now, sir?" Borkis asked when they were out of earshot of the General's tent.

"I'm going to get some food," Nevins said, turning his nose up to the air and sniffing. He brightened and pointed the direction. "It's cooking over there."

"And then?"

"A horse seems in order," Nevins allowed.

"A horse, sir?" Borkis squeaked. "But —"

"Mountains of gold, Tortin, mountains of gold," Nevins said, walking briskly toward the smell of stewing beef. "Always keep that in your mind and you'll not go wrong when tasked with a decision."

"Mountains of —"

Nevins shot a hand behind him, palm up. "Best not mention that too loudly."

\#

"We should be able to deploy the next brigade tomorrow," Major Gelicott reported to General Tashigg that evening at their headquarters near the train station outside Kingsford. The troops, of course, were billeted outside the city. Major Gelicott had heard that the lands had belonged to the traitor, Rabel Zebala. There was a forge, a stable, and the ruins of a farmhouse. Beyond, through a small stand of trees was a field of wyvern's flowers — now mostly trampled and crushed under the soldiers' tents. Not that anyone cared.

General Tashigg grunted in acknowledgement and turned back to his map.

"Any more news from Walpish?" Tashigg asked, looking at the marks that showed the location of the cavalry. "Has he got the town?"

"Nothing, sir," Gelicott replied.

"I expect he's too busy celebrating," General Tashigg said to himself. He glanced up through his bushy eyebrows at his staff officer to gage his reaction.

"Undoubtedly," Gelicott agreed. But the set of his jaw showed concern.

"What is it man," Tashigg growled. "Spit it out! You'll only make a fool of yourself here with me and that's much better than on the field where everyone will notice."

"S-sir," Gelicott began slowly, "do you think it was our best notion to send General Filbert out first?"

"Why not?" Tashigg asked, his bushy eyebrows beetling. "He's commander of the first brigade and that's the order of battle."

"But… he's a bit of a stickler, sir," Gelicott said, trying to speak as circumspectly as possible.

"He's not one of our best, I agree," Tashigg said. "But he doesn't stop when he gets going."

"Even when it's in the wrong direction," Gelicott muttered. Tashigg snorted. On their last maneuvers, General Filbert had famously led his troops in an assault on their own artillery — much to the surprise of the king, General Gorgos, General Tashigg himself and, most certainly, the artillerymen.

"With luck, he'll get himself killed and we'll be earning the king another couple of chests of gold," Tashigg replied.

"I suppose there's that, sir," Gelicott agreed glumly.

"But his orders are easy enough, even *he* shouldn't get them wrong," Tashigg said. "He's to march through Korin's Pass, take the village of the same name at the north end and await for the rest of the division." Tashigg snorted. "It's not like there's any *artillery* to distract him."

"I suppose there's that," Gelicott agreed.

"I shall turn in," Tashigg said, rising from his chair and moving toward the bedroom in the inn that spymaster Hewlitt had so obligingly provided him. "Check on the troops, check with the station, and call me at first light."

"As you wish, sir," Gelicott said, rising from his chair and giving the general a brisk salute.

General Tashigg waved away the salute and shooed him to the door.

#

"Captain of the guard!" General Filbert called out. "Drat the man, where is he?"

A sound of running boots approached and Captain Welless braced to attention. "Sir!"

"What are you still doing on duty?" Filbert demanded. Before Welless could reply, he waved a hand. "Never mind! Just report. Why were you so late?"

"I was investigating something, sir," Captain Welless reported. "I've delayed my relief while I was doing that."

"Investigating?"

"Yes, sir," Welless said.

"Aren't you supposed to be the captain of the guard?" Filbert chided. "What on earth would you be investigating, particularly at this hour!"

"My men reported noises, sir," Welless replied with a tight voice.

"So they should, they're guarding us, after all," Filbert said. A moment passed and he added, "What noises?"

"That's the problem, sir," Welless said.

"What?"

"There were three sets of noises and it took us a while to sort them out," Welless said.

"Three?" Filbert demanded. When captain nodded, he continued, "And what did you determine, captain?"

"There are noises come to the east of us and we can't figure them out, they're very faint and distant," Welless said.

"Where are they coming from?"

"Some of my men think there are coming from the ground… sir," Welless confessed.

"From the ground?" Filbert repeated. "What sorts of sounds?"

"Like people digging," Welless said.

"So you sent a party out to investigate and they found what?"

"Nothing, sir," Welless replied. "I told them to go no more than a mile from camp and return."

"And the noises stopped?"

"No sir, they grew louder but just a bit."

"So the sound is far away."

"That's my belief, sir," Welless replied. "But there has to be a lot of digging to carry this far, doesn't there, sir?"

"I wouldn't know," Filbert said with a shrug. "Do we have anyone who digs in the troops?"

"None on patrol," Welless said. He licked his lips. "Except —"

"Except what?"

"One of my men deserted," Welless said. "He never came back with the patrol. His name was Slater, sir."

"So he worked stone," Filbert guessed. Not that last names always kept their meaning. "Did he say anything before he disappeared?"

"My ensign said that he was scared out of his wits and swore that it was the Zwerg, sir," Welless said with much reluctance.

"The Zwerg?" Filbert scoffed. "They're nothing but tales to scare children."

"The ensign tells me that Slater was scared for his life," Welless said. "He left Slater where they'd stopped and went forward himself to scout the last tenth mile and, when he returned, Slater was gone."

"Should have taken him with him," Filbert declared.

"He tried, sir," Welless said in defense of his nameless ensign.

"Well, so we've one less mouth to feed," Filbert said. "You said three things?"

"Yes sir, we picked up some men who claimed to be from one of the airships," Welless said.

"I remember that," Filbert said with a dismissive wave.

"No, sir, I mean that we picked up three more men," Welless said. "There were in pretty bad shape."

"Assign them to a platoon — give them to that ensign of yours — they can't be any worse than that deserter," Filbert said.

"One of them claimed to be an officer," Welless protested.

"Was he wearing a uniform?"

"They were all in tatters," Welless said. "Two of them have broken limbs."

"Oh, bother!" Filbert growled. "Leave them for the second brigade, then."

"As you wish, sir," Welless said.

"That's two distractions," Filbert allowed. "What was the third?"

"I'm afraid there was a disturbance down at the pasture," Welless said.

"The pasture?" Filbert repeated. "My horses?"

"It seems that some of them weren't properly hobbled and they seem to have disappeared, sir," Welless told his commanding officer miserably.

"WHAT?" Filbert roared. "How many are gone?"

"There are six left," Welless reported.

"Six? Six!" Filbert shouted. "There were *twelve!*"

"I'm very sorry, sir," Welless said miserably.

"You will be," General Filbert promised. He pointed toward the opening of the tent. "Leave me." As the hangdog captain went through the canvas opening, he added, "And send for my man, Gibbons!" The canvas settled back into place hiding the miserable captain, as Filbert added, "That is, if you haven't lost him, too."

Chapter Three

"He must be dead," Jarin said as he joined the others back in human form, after ferrying them to the ruins of the fort. "Nothing could survive that."

"He is old," Rabel said with a thoughtful frown. "He might surprise you."

Jarin snorted. "Old is nothing against…" the young man swayed and crumpled to the ground.

"Jarin!" Ellen cried, rushing to his side. She nudged his shoulder and looked up to Rabel with tears in her eyes.

Rabel knelt beside the lad, joined shortly by queen Diam and Granno. Rabel felt under Jarin's nose for breath, examined the color of his skin but it was Diam who spoke first.

"He's exhausted," she said. She glanced from the teen dragon to Rabel and Ellen. "You're all exhausted."

"He saved us and he carried us," Rabel said gruffly. "He ate into his strength more than we."

"Will he die?" Ellen asked nervously. Her fingers reached to the bulge in her blouse where she kept one of the blue light demons, clearly thinking of the death of captain Ford.

"No!" Diam snorted. "He needs rest." She frowned. "A lot of it."

"He's a dragon…" Rabel began slowly.

"Oh, I know what you're thinking!" Diam said, pushing herself back up to her feet. She glanced down at the dark-haired teen fondly. She exchanged looks with Granno who did not look pleased but her expression hardened and he sighed. "We will take him," she told Rabel.

Rabel got to his knees and bowed to her. "Your majesty, you won't regret it."

"Of course," Diam said irritably, waving for Rabel to rise to his feet. She turned to Granno. "I need you to get to our people, send a party here to meet us."

"Your majesty!" Granno exclaimed, glancing from her to the others.

"Take Imay, she's got the longer legs," Diam said. She smiled at her daughter. "Granno is correct in thinking that it's unwise to leave all the royal family unguarded."

"I'll guard you!" Ellen said rising to her feet and standing protectively before the zwerg queen.

"That's very —" queen Diam began politely but stopped as Ellen produced a ball of fire in the palm of her hand. "I suppose you can, at that."

"And I," Rabel said.

"Indeed," Diam agreed. She gestured to Ellen. "Save your strength, child, in case you need it." She turned to her eldest daughter and gave her a quick hug. "We'll be safe until your return, as you have just been shown." Imay hugged her back tightly, locked eyes warningly with Rabel who nodded solemnly in response, then gestured for Granno to lead the way.

Diam watched them trudge off into the distance and then turned back to the others. "While we're waiting, we should see what we can discover." She nodded to Lissy and Ellen. "Why don't you two guard Jarin while Rabel and I look around?"

Before they could protest, queen Diam took off briskly toward the base of the ruined fort. Rabel started toward the ruins of the top.

The towers and turrets of the fort had all shattered on impact, leaving piles of rubble at the top but, surprisingly, the walls further down had survived. Rabel took himself to the nearest one and looked at the rocks. He frowned, moving one rock down from the pile and then another, looking to widen the gap enough that he could peer inside. He had just gained enough of an opening that he could see the darkness inside when a light — faint and distant — winked on far in the tunnel that was the stairs of the ruined turret.

Intrigued, he summoned a small ball of fire and sent it down the tunnel. It impacted about halfway down, brightening as it burned against the stone and then winked out.

Another light winked on for a moment deep in the tunnel.

"Hang on!" Rabel shouted through the hole. "We'll come for you! We'll get you out!"

#

"And you have no idea have far down the turret they are?" Queen Diam asked when she met Rabel.

"Not precisely, no," Rabel said with a sigh. "But I think we could start —"

"The turrets have spiral staircases, as I recall," Diam said. "How do we know they have not collapsed and will block us?"

"The light —"

"They might be open enough to let light through," Diam said, "and not humans —"

"But the zwerg —"

"It is not enough to get zwerg in, you must get whoever is there out," Diam interrupted. "And your metal man was large, even by human standards."

Rabel could only grunt in agreement.

It was getting dark. A line of lights — torches — approached from the distance.

"Ellen," Rabel said warningly. He needn't have worried, the girl stood beside him, ready to throw fireballs at his command. He turned to Diam. "Your majesty —"

"Let's see if we need worry, first," Diam said. She moved in front of the two humans and raised her voice to shout, "Identify yourselves!"

"Mother!" Imay's voice came back.

Diam turned a relieved smile toward Rabel —

"It's a trap!" Imay's voice cried, cut off suddenly with a cry of pain.

"Your majesty, stand back!" Rabel said, sweeping the zwerg queen behind him. He said to Ellen, "They were carrying the torches too high for zwerg."

Ellen nodded. "What do we do?"

"I'm going to wake Jarin," Rabel said, turning and putting his words into action. "I'll have him get the queen to safety."

"But he's too —"

"He'll do it, your majesty," Ellen cut across the queen's protests. She knelt on the far side of Jarin and gently shook him. "Jarin, the queen wants you."

Nothing.

"Tell him I'll bring him to a bed of gold," Diam said in a low voice.

Jarin's eyes popped open. "Gold?"

"Yes, brave dragon," Diam said with a laugh in her voice. "One of my treasures. You shall rest and guard it until you are well."

"When do we go?" Jarin said, rising to his feet.

"Now would be good," Rabel said, gesturing to the torches in the distance. "Someone has captured Granno and the princess."

"We're going to free them," Ellen said. She put an arm on Jarin. "You're too tired, take the queen, Lissy, and go."

Jarin gave Rabel a troubled look. "And you?"

"We're going to teach these people fear," Rabel told him grimly. He reached down and grabbed Ellen's hand. "Go on, we'll be fine!"

#

Robin Slater still couldn't believe his luck, even after he'd met the mage. The mage said his name was Tirpin and he needed help. He was escorting a seriously injured man who he claimed was the captain of the airship *Vengeance* but the injured man looked Sorian, so Slater had his doubts.

"We've got to get back to the king," Tirpin had said, forcing Slater to help him prop up the injured 'captain'.

"The railway's closed," Slater said. "They're using the trains elsewhere."

"Hmph," Tirpin grunted. "How did you get here?"

"Train," Slater said tersely. "Came up with the first brigade."

"And Walpish?"

"Who?"

"Colonel Walpish of the cavalry," Tirpin said in irritation.

Slater shrugged the shoulder that wasn't supporting the Sorian captain. "They probably came up before us. I never saw them."

"How many men are with you?"

"Me?" Slater said in surprise. "Just you two and only if you're heading my way."

"Which is?" Tirpin prodded.

"Toward the trains," Slater said. "I'm heading back home, never wanted to be a soldier."

"Deserter," the Sorian captain groaned.

"And you're lucky I am," Slater said. "Or your buddy would have to carry you himself."

"Why'd did you go?" Tirpin asked.

Slater jerked his head to indicate behind them. "I heard there were zwergs up ahead. I won't have nothing to do with them."

"Zwergs?" Tirpin repeated. "The cave dwellers?"

Slater snorted. "Their 'caves' are finer than any palace I've ever seen. They don't like us 'sky-touchers' much, particularly if we're in their territory. And I heard them digging." He picked up his pace. "Anywhere they *aren't* is where I want to be."

"Gold," the Sorian murmured.

Tirpin pulled up short, jerking Slater beside him and causing the injured captain to groan in anguish.

"What did you say?" Tirpin asked.

"Zwergs have gold," the Sorian said. "Capture one, get a fortune in ransom."

"Try to capture them and *die*," Slater said. "They're vicious and used to defending themselves."

A sound startled them and before they could react, they were surrounded by mounted men.

"Hold!" A voice called loudly in the night. "Name yourselves!"

"I am mage Tirpin of the royal airship *Vengeance*, this is Captain Martel who requires aid," Tirpin said, drawing himself up in his tattered clothes. He clamped a hand on the startled Slater. "And this man is our prisoner!"

Slater's face fell as he recognized the mounted man: Captain Welless.

"Slater!" Welless hissed. He waved to the men around him. "Take him! And have these others brought back to camp!"

#

"What are we going to do?" Ellen asked Rabel nervously when the two of them were left alone with the torches and the captive princess in the distance.

"We're going to show these people fear and a reason to leave our friends alone," Rabel told her. "First, we need to find out how many there are."

"How do we do that?"

"They have torches," Rabel said. "How many?"

"Six," Ellen said after a quick count. "So there are six of them?"

"Some of them have to be holding Imay and Granno," Rabel said.

"So… eight?" Ellen guessed.

"Perhaps as many as ten," Rabel said with a shrug. "Not more."

"Why not?"

"I think if they'd had more, they would have left a party behind with Granno and Imay to guard them and come without torches to overwhelm us," Rabel said. He cocked his head down to Ellen. "Do you think you could pretend to be Queen Diam?"

"Me?" Ellen squeaked.

"That's who they're hoping to catch," Rabel said. "Or bargain with."

"I don't look like a zwerg," Ellen said.

"They will see what they're expecting to see," Rabel told her. "And it's dark out."

"And you?"

"What will I be doing?" Rabel asked pedantically.

Ellen hated it when he made her think like that. She gave him a sour look which was barely visible in the dark. "You'll be going to the rear and killing the men from behind."

"Incapacitating them," Rabel corrected. "We might need them later."

"The dead can't fight back," Ellen said.

"And they can't lift rocks, either," Rabel replied. Ellen shrugged in acceptance of his point.

"If you get hurt…"

"I am old, I got that way by being careful," Rabel reminded her.

"You're not so old now!" Ellen protested.

"But I still have my memories," Rabel said. "Now, are we ready?"

Ellen took a deep breath and nodded shakily. She pushed him away. "Go!"

#

"Hello!" Ellen called out as she got close enough to make out the men holding the torches. "Who goes there? And where is my daughter, Princess Imay?"

"Who are you?" A gruff man's voice called back. Ellen could see that he was in the front with a torch, peering into the night.

"I am Diam, queen of the Zwerg," Ellen said, drawing herself up regally. "If you have harmed my daughter or my man —"

"They're safe," the man replied. Another added from a darker spot, "For now."

"Release them," Ellen said, "and no harm will come to you."

"Give us gold and we'll give them to you," the leader replied. He was getting close to her, soon she would be in his torch light.

"Hold!" Ellen called. "Come no closer!"

"You sound awfully young for a queen," the leader said, taking another step forward. Ellen took a step back to keep herself in shadow.

"She's a zwerg, Hevor, they all sound like children," the second man called.

"Murderous children," another man muttered. "Killed half the ship's crew."

"They're dead, we're not," Hevor said to the nameless man. He took another step forward, then stepped back. "All's we want is gold and we'll be on our way."

"And my daughter and my man?" Ellen said. "Are they unharmed?"

"A bit roughed up but no worse for the wear," one of the men holding a torch in the rear replied. He kicked at something and Ellen heard Granno grunt in pain.

"Release them and send to me, so that I know they're safe," Ellen said.

"Hah!" Hevor snorted. "Give us the gold first."

Ellen saw one of the torches furthest back from her wobble and then it steadied. Then another. She thought she saw a spark when the third torch wobbled.

"I'll not trade for nothing," Ellen said. She wondered if the men were so foolish to think that the queen of the Zwergs travelled with chests of gold strapped to her body. When would they consider that she'd have to contact her own people to get the gold? And wouldn't they think that, once alerted, the zwergs would just trade chests rather than fight? "Release my daughter as a sign of good faith."

Silence.

"Release her now!"

The men muttered among themselves. The leader moved back to a different patch of darkness and grabbed someone, hustling her forward roughly by one arm. Ellen saw another torch wobble in the distance. That was four. It still left at least six. Five, excluding Hevor, the leader.

Hevor dragged Imay up beside him, walking right up to Ellen. When his torch finally lit her face her gasped. "You're not a Zwerg! You're a girl!"

Imay crashed into him but he only slid away.

Ellen raised her hands and a ball of fire rushed from them, taking Hevor in the face. The blazing light wrapped around his face and engulfed it. He had no time to cry. His headless body fell, lifeless to the ground.

"You were warned!" Ellen shouted at the other men, sending two beams of flame into the air from her upraised hands. "Release my man and flee or you'll die like Hevor!"

Sparks rose all around the men and a voice boomed out, "Drop your weapons! Down on your knees or face the wrath of the Zwergs!"

The voice seemed to come from everywhere. The men turned in fright trying to locate it but without any luck. That was when they noticed their missing numbers.

A sword clattered to the ground. Then another. And then the rest rained on the hard plain as the last of the men rushed to surrender.

"Release Granno" Ellen ordered. "Send him up to me."

There was a rustling and movement. Granno limped forward to Ellen and Imay. Imay rushed to grab him and hugged him tightly.

"Put out your flame," Rabel's voice whispered in Ellen's ear. "I'm going to lift you on my back and when I say, you're going to pretend to be a dragon."

"A dragon?"

"To scare them away," Rabel said.

"I thought you wanted to keep them," Ellen protested.

"There are nine of them and only four of us," Rabel said. "We wouldn't last the night. Besides, they'll tell everyone they see that there's a dragon and that will keep us safe from any others."

Ellen nodded and extinguished her light, stepping to the side. She felt Rabel grab her and lift her to his shoulders. He stood up to his full height and Ellen, greatly daring, moved and squatted on his head to get up higher. Rabel grunted in encouragement and grabbed her ankles. Supported this way, Ellen took a gamble and stood to her full height on Rabel's shoulders. Below her, she heard him gasp in surprise.

"Now," Rabel said tapping one of Ellen's ankles firmly. He changed his voice — some magic, Ellen guessed — and roared. "I am the great dragon Jarin! You shall leave my land before I burn you to ash!"

Ellen called forth a huge gout of flame and flared it up into the night, above the frightened men.

The men didn't need to be told twice. In scant seconds they were out of sight, running for their lives.

With a chuckle, Rabel leaned forward, dislodged Ellen from his shoulders and caught her in his outstretched arms. Still laughing, he lowered her to the ground and hugged her tightly.

"That was perfect!" He said. "They'll never dare come back!"

"Where's my mother?" Imay asked worriedly, still holding tightly on to Granno.

"She's safe, your highness," Rabel said. "The real Jarin took her and your sister to safety. And you?"

"They caught us unawares," Imay said ruefully.

"My fault," Granno said. "I should have scouted ahead."

"I don't think it would have mattered either way," Imay said.

"Granno, how are you?" Rabel asked, popping a small bright light from the end of his fingertip and examining the zwerg bodyguard anxiously.

"Bruised, battered, and no happier," Granno replied. He unlinked his arms from around Imay and stood up to his full height. "I thought the dragon was too weak."

"Diam promised him a bed of gold," Ellen said. "He perked right up."

"A dragon?" Imay said. "She promised a dragon a bed of gold?" Imay turned to Granno, looking horrified. "We have to get back to her now!"

"Princess Imay," Rabel said, nodding to her, "there are only four of us." He waved a hand in the direction of the fleeing men. "We have just been given a potent lesson in the dangers of travelling at night." He gestured back toward the ruined fort. "I advise that we find shelter, hide, and wait for morning when we shall doubtless find reinforcements."

"He's right, Imay," Granno said solemnly.

"At least we don't have to worry about keeping warm," Imay said, nodding toward Ellen.

Just as she said that, the little girl collapsed, falling into Rabel's quick grasp.

"I was expecting that," Rabel said, raising the little girl up so that he could cradle her with one arm.

"You can't be any less tired," Granno said. "Perhaps we should make camp here."

Rabel shook his head, barely visible in the darkness. "I can make it back to the fort." He turned and started trudging off.

#

"Guards! Guards!" Diam shouted the moment Jarin touched the ground. She jumped off, clutching Lissy with her just before the dragon collapsed with a groan. "Jarin! You must become a man! We can't help you in dragon form!" Diam told the black-red dragon nervously. The dragon groaned and whimpered. Diam moved forward to its head and whispered, "I can't get you to gold unless you're human."

The dragon's eyelids fluttered and in an instant the dragon changed into a man. Diam knelt down and listened to his breathing. "Good lad!"

"Your majesty!" Kavim, the officer of the guard, rushed forward from the guard post. "Are you all right?"

"I'm fine," Diam said irritably. "This man is exhausted and needs to go to the treasury."

"The treasury?"

"And then I shall need a troop of men, we have to go to the ruins of the East Pass fort," Diam said. "Imay and Granno are in danger."

"In danger?"

"Is he okay, mother?" Lissy asked, looking at the sleeping form of Jarin.

"He's going to be just fine, little one," Diam assured her. "He's exhausted and needs to rest on a bed of gold."

"A bed of gold?" Kavim repeated, eyeing the tall human warily. "Is he a dragon?" When Diam nodded, he coughed and added, "Is that wise, your majesty?"

"He saved my life, Kavim," Diam replied in a voice that brooked no argument. "Have a cart brought here immediately. We have much to do once he's settled and safe."

"At once, your majesty," Kavim said, coming to attention and darting away, signalling for some of his soldiers to take guard around the queen and princess.

#

"Just wait, Jarin, just wait," Diam said anxiously as the guards gently placed the sleeping man on the top of a pile of gold coins. "We've got to get you placed and move away and then, when I give the word —"

Jarin's head jerked in what might be a nod. Diam gestured for her guards to finish and move away. Then she and Lissy joined them at the edge of the chamber.

"Jarin, you may rest on this gold until you are well," Diam called loudly. And in that moment, the dragon took its full form. It stretched once contentedly, spilling piles of gold as it moved and then it rolled over, on its back, stretched out its neck… and snored.

"He snores?" Lissy asked in surprise.

"He's very tired," Diam said, gesturing for them to leave the treasury.

"Shall I post a guard?" Kavim asked stiffly.

"I imagine he's going to sleep for many hours," Diam said thoughtfully. "But it is probably best that he is not disturbed." She stood at the door and withdrew a key, locking the door. "He'll be safe there. A guard could let us know when he wakes."

"It is good to have him under lock and key," Kavim said approvingly.

Diam snorted. "If you think a lock and a key will keep a dragon from going where he will, you are much mistaken!" She shook her head ruefully. "Things are changing, Kavim. He is sworn, with the girl, to Geros. We have already seen the advantages of having a dragon as a friend." She turned and started moving briskly down the corridor. "Now, do you have that troop ready?"

Kavim gave her a look of surprise. "I do," he said, "but I thought you would not want to leave until you've had some rest."

"And indeed I would," Diam agreed. She pursed her lips tightly and shook her head. "But we don't have the time. I will not leave my daughter and Granno in danger a moment longer. And, beyond that, there are people buried in the fort."

"Humans," Kavim said sourly.

"They fought as much for us as for themselves," Diam told him. "How we treat our friends says much about who will value our friendship."

Kavim absorbed this with a thoughtful expression.

Chapter Four

"You're saying that these Zwerg have piles of gold?" General Filbert said dubiously to the man who claimed to be the captain of His Majesty's airship *Vengeance*. Filbert was not inclined to believe him as the man was clearly a Sorian but the mage beside him — dressed in the ruins of some quite fine garb — said that King Markel had appointed this captain Martel himself. *It probably wouldn't do to upset the King,* Filbert thought to himself darkly. *At least, not again.*

"Everyone knows that," the injured captain replied. "They supply most of the gold and fine jewels to the kingdoms."

"Kingsland and Soria?" Filbert asked.

"And Issia, Vinik, South Vinik, Felland, Palam, Jasram, Keevar, Balu and probably many more that I've ever seen," the man replied.

"You sound like a sailor," Captain Welless said.

"I *am* a sailor," the man replied. He pulled himself upright using Tirpin as a crutch. "I am Captain Jacques Martel of his majesty's airship *Vengeance*."

"If so, where is your ship, captain?" General Filbert asked. "Or are you going to tell me, too, that it was destroyed?"

"'Too?'" Tirpin repeated, he glanced quickly around the room. "There are others?"

"Two men came by some hours ago," Captain Welless said miserably. "Shortly after, we noticed that some of the general's horses were missing."

"And one of *those* claimed to be a captain, too!" Filbert growled.

"If he claimed to be Captain Nevins, he was telling the truth," Mage Tirpin said bitterly. "Where did they go?"

"After stealing my horses?" Filbert said. "This miserable patrol was sent to find them and —" he waved the hands at the two of them, indicating the result.

"He spoke of wanting to get back to Kingsford to consult with the King," Welless offered. The general glowered at him but said nothing.

"Doubtless he will try to blame his defeat on *me*," Tirpin said bitterly. Beside him, Captain Martel drew breath to comment but decided against it at the last moment. "It is not my fault that the ships were too heavy."

"Or that the fort could fly in the sky," Captain Martel said.

"Float!" Tirpin said grumpily. "It could not fly, it merely floated."

"Like a cloud?" General Filbert said mockingly. "Tell me, mage, do you know of anyone who can do such magic? Will we be facing more of these 'floating' forts? Or should we concern ourselves with cities that rise out of our reach?"

Tirpin's face drained of color. Decisively, he said, "I have to return to Kingsford and warn the king."

"Good luck with that," Filbert said drolly. "The railway is closed for the next day or more while the armies are being transported to the west."

"If they had time to float more forts, wouldn't they have attacked in greater strength?" Captain Welless asked. General Filbert glared at him but Captain Martel grunted in surprise at the question.

"We saw large strips of metal at the base of the fort," Tirpin said.

"And at the base below," Captain Martel added.

"What sort of metal, do you suppose?" Captain Welless asked idly.

"Nothing like gold, I'm sure," Tirpin replied.

"Gold?" Filbert repeated, turning his gaze to Martel. "You say these Zwergs have mountains of gold?"

"No, general, I did not," Martel replied. "I'm sure they've got treasuries buried underground but they would be well-guarded."

"And our orders, sir," Welless piped up feebly.

"How much gold?" Filbert demanded.

"I could not say," Martel replied, spreading one hand while propping himself against Tirpin with the other. "At least one treasury. The zwerg like to work gold, it's one of their favorite metals."

"Do they work steel, too?" Tirpin asked.

Martel shook his head. "It is one of the metals they trade for," he said. "They provide ore, of course."

"Not many people know how to make steel," Welless said.

"Who asked you?" Filbert barked. He turned to Tirpin. "And what's this thing of yours with steel?"

"Steel is stronger and lighter than iron," Tirpin explained. "The first airship, *Spite*, has engines and boilers made of steel." He glowered. "We had to make do with heavier iron. It made our ships slower and kept them lower in the sky."

"*Warrior* managed to rise above the fort," Martel said thoughtfully. He looked up at Tirpin. "That was your magic, wasn't it?"

Tirpin scowled at him. "I think they threw their guns overboard to lighten their ship."

"But that was after..." Martel began but broke off as he saw Tirpin's face.

"How much gold?" General Filbert said. "Enough to pay for a duchy?"

"Sir," Welless said, "you're not thinking of going after the zwerg!"

"Captain, don't you have duties to attend?" Filber said, gesturing toward the doorway of his tent. "Are you supposed to be guarding things?"

"Sir, this — the rest of the division, sir — we should —"

"Be about your duties, captain," Filbert said. "That is an order!"

Captain Welless drew himself and up and saluted sharply. The general returned it sloppily and nodded him out. When the tent flaps had closed, General Filbert turned toward the others. "How much gold?"

#

"This is all that could be mustered on such short notice, your majesty," Kavim said apologetically to Diam as they inspected the troops readying for departure.

"How many?"

"Forty regular troops, twenty miners with carts and tools," Kavim said.

"That should be more than enough," Diam said.

"Truth be told, what with our work going on in the west —"

"Let us not talk about that, Kavim," Diam interrupted smoothly. "Some things are best as surprises."

Kavim's brows lifted in surprise. Diam nodded at him firmly and the officer returned the nod reluctantly.

"Forty troops and twenty miners should be enough," Diam allowed. "What does that leave you?"

167

"Me, Your Highness?" Kavim asked in surprise. "I was —"

"Planning on leading the troops," Diam guessed. "But Granno should be able —"

"Pardon, majesty, but wasn't he captured?" Kavim interrupted. "Is it wise to presume that he will be able to perform his duties when he's released?"

"It's *wise* to presume that I'll manage if needs be," Diam said. "As it is, I will not leave Lissy and my kingdom solely in the care of one very young dragon."

Kavim's eyes widened at the notion. "No, I suppose that's not the best idea."

"So, introduce me to the senior lieutenant of the troops and I'll leave it to you to maintain the guard here," Diam said with a firm nod.

Kavim gestured to a man at the head of the first twenty troops. "Lieutenant Minto, her majesty, Queen Diam."

"Y-your majesty!" Young lieutenant Minto replied with a sharp salute. "How may I serve you?"

"We are going to rescue Granno, my daughter, and some humans who have been helping us," Diam told him. "After, we may excavate the East Pass Fort in search of survivors."

"Of course, your majesty," Minto replied clicking the heels of his sturdy boots together. "We are at your service."

"Good!" Diam replied, gesturing toward the exit. "Then let us go, we must hurry."

Minto shot Kavim one frantic look and then turned back to his troops. "First platoon, take point. We're going to the East Pass Fort. Second platoon, take rearguard. Miners, keep to the middle. You're to guard the queen, on your honor."

"On our honor!" The voices of sixty zwerg shouted in reply.

#

Rabel was glad to finally be able to lower the exhausted Ellen to the ground in the shadow of the ruined fort. How far they had walked, he couldn't tell but he guessed they'd been walking at least an hour which meant they'd travelled about two miles through the broken and ruined terrain at the foot of the hills.

"Rest, I'll take watch," Imay said as Granno sank beside the two humans.

"Princess?" Granno said, rising to his feet. "I —"

"You took more hurt than I," Imay said, waving him back to the ground. Her eyes flashed as she added, "That's an order."

Granno knew better than to argue and sank back down gratefully. The ground was covered with scant grass and small pebbles. It was not the most comfortable place to sleep but Granno had slept on worse. In moments he was snoring gently.

Rabel settled Ellen as comfortably as he could but propped himself leaning back against the ruins of one of the fort's turrets.

"You need your sleep," Imay said to Rabel.

"I'm not one of your subjects to order around, princess," Rabel reminded her.

"No," she agreed, "you're a friend and I worry about you. I'd worry less if you rested."

Rabel was too tired to argue with her. As a compromise he closed his eyes but kept his senses alert.

Imay snorted and moved off, starting a slow circuit at the edge of their refuge. When she returned, she saw that the human had wrapped himself around the young girl. She smiled and turned back to the night, searching for a stick that might serve as a weapon.

#

Lissy insisted on sleeping with the dragon. Of course, she waited until her mother was safely away before issuing this demand to the harassed Kavim.

"Princess, I don't think that's wise," Kavim told her.

"Why?"

"Well," Kavim said with a shrug, "he's a dragon, your highness."

Lissy pointed to the sealed door and the sounds coming from within. "He's asleep, what harm is there?"

"He's safe enough there, your highness," Kavim said. "Dragons… well, they can be dangerous."

"I flew on his back," Lissy said by way of argument.

"And you were extremely lucky in that," Kavim agreed. "But still —"

"Let me in," Lissy said, eyeing the guard and Kavim both. "You can lock me in with him—"

"Never!" the two said at once.

"Or leave the door unlocked, if you wish," Lissy quickly allowed. "But if he wakes up, lonely, won't that be worse?"

Kavim and the guard exchanged glances. The little princess had a point.

"He knows me," Lissy insisted. "Besides, I owe him. He saved my life."

With a nod from Kavim, the guard unlocked the door. Lissy ran inside before they could react and turned to bow to them. "Thank you," she told them courteously. She turned back to the sleeping dragon and then back to them, giggling. "He's buried himself in the gold!"

She moved to the right of the door and found a bunch of old tapestries. Quickly she made herself a den of exquisite silk, curled up once so that she was facing the dragon and closed her eyes. She opened them long enough to say, "I'm safe here. You may close the door."

The guard closed the door and looked up expectantly at Kavim.

"She's safe there," Kavim said with a sigh.

"Safe with a dragon," the guard, Dermon, said dubiously.

"When your relief comes, be sure to tell them about the princess," Kavim said.

"Of course, sir," Demon said bracing to attention. Kavim saluted and he returned it.

As Kavim wandered back down the hall, Dermon thought he heard him muttering, "Safe with a dragon! Safe with a dragon."

From inside the treasury, the guard heard the princess chirping happily to herself for some minutes before she fell quiet and, shortly after, asleep.

#

"So, Morris, have you got all that?" General Filbert asked as he outlined the plan to the commander of the first battalion. Jeoffroy Morris was also a distant relative who owed his commission to General Filbert and, therefore, of unquestionable loyalty.

"I think so, sir," Major Morris replied slowly. "We're to take two companies of men, half of them equipped with carts and pickaxes and the other half deployed as scouts to find the entrance to this cave. Once there we will gain access, destroy any who oppose us —"

"Except for the prisoners," Filbert interjected. "You need to get them to show you the way to the treasure."

"— except for prisoners," Morris said with a grimace. How would he know which prisoners were to be trusted? "At which point we'll gain access to their treasure and our men will cart it off."

169

"There!" Filbert said, smiling. "Quite simple, isn't it?"

"Yes, sir," Morris agreed. The plan seemed simple enough but there were so many things that could go wrong…

"And your men must be short, Major," the ragged airman, 'captain' Martel, warned.

"Short, sir?"

"The zwerg are short," 'Captain' Martel explained. "So your men must be short or they won't be able to travel through the caves."

"I see," Morris said. He turned to the general. "Short men, sir?"

"You heard him, Major," General Filbert said with an airy wave of his hand.

"I'll have to comb the troops, sir," Morris said worriedly. "That might —"

"Just do your duty, Major," Filbert cut him off peremptorily. "You have your orders." As the major turned to leave, Filbert added, "And I'll be with you, of course."

"Sir?" Major Morris said, turning back. "What about the troops here, sir? And our orders?"

"We'll be back before we're needed," Filbert said airily. With a smile, he haded, "And we'll be much, much richer."

"And the troops here, sir?"

"Captain Welless is in charge of the guard, he'll let us out of the camp without any alarm being raised," General Filbert said. "And… and that fellow, what's his name again?"

"Colonel Marchant, sir?" Major Weymund asked warily.

"Yes, yes! That's the one!" Filbert said with a snap of his fingers. "He'll keep the troops in order until we return."

"Does he know where we're going, sir?"

"No, of course not!" Filbert said. He couldn't believe the man would ask such a stupid question. If Marchant knew, he'd want a cut of the treasure and that wouldn't do at all, not at all. As it was, Filbert was already considering the ways in which he could cut Morris out of the split — war was coming and accidents happened. He waved irritably toward the exit, "You have your orders, Major!"

#

"Yes, what is it?" Kavim asked as the zwerg soldier saluted him. "Where are you from? Who sent you?"

"I'm from the southern cave, sir," the young girl replied. "Listening post. I was sent to tell you that we're hearing movement coming our way."

"Coming our way?" Kavim repeated with a frown. "Not going away from us?"

"No, the sound is definitely getting louder, sir."

"What's your name, soldier?"

"Adelin, sir," the soldier replied with a salute. Kavim returned it.

"Could it be the queen coming back, Adelin?"

"I don't know, sir," Adelin said doubtfully. "We can hear footsteps and the sound of carts… I suppose it could be."

"It seems early," Kavim said to himself. "What direction did you say: south?"

"Yes sir."

"Not east?" When Adelin shook her head, Kavim said to himself. "Well they could have intercepted…" He cut himself off. "How far away?"

"Ten minutes, maybe less," Adelin replied.

"Very well, return to your post," Kavim told her. "I'll alert the reserve just in case."

"Yes sir!" Adelin braced to attention and saluted Kavim sharply. Approvingly, Kavim returned it before moving off briskly to alert the reserve forces.

A listening post was a great thing, particular with sky-touchers wondering about but Kavim had always wished that the queen had been willing to excavate more of them, in more directions, so that any sounds could be readily triangulated. But! Kavim shook his head. He knew that any such work took away from mining and, even worse, from the secret project the queen wanted no one to discover.

He paused in his stride and turned back, yelling down the corridor to the distant figure of Adelin.

"Soldier!" Kavim shouted. Then, remembering that she was a reservist, adding, "Adelin!"

The woman stopped and turned around.

"Spread the word! Have them pull up the tracks!" Kavim shouted.

"Pull up the tracks?" Adelin repeated, her eyes wide with horror. "Did you say pull up the tracks?"

"Pull up the tracks," Kavim repeated loudly. "We can always put them back down."

"As you order, sir," Adelin said, snapping a salute. Kavim returned it smartly and turned back to his many duties.

All throughout the kingdom in the caves there were tracks laid for the carts that carried workers, gems, gold, and supplies. In an emergency, pulling them up would deny an invader quick access to the kingdom. It was difficult but Diam had ordered that sections be laid that could easily be removed and hidden — usually no more than four or five feet stretches — enough to render the underground railway useless.

Putting it back together would be time consuming but Kavim decided the risk was justified. Besides, if there was nothing to worry about, he'd have it all back together before the queen returned.

#

Imay shook herself as the noise grew louder in the distance. Was she imagining it?

It had been three hours or more since they'd found their refuge beside the ruins of the East Pass fort. Rabel's gentle snores had turned harsh and then quiet again when Ellen twitched in his arms. Granno slept soundlessly and without noticing the noises of the others.

Imay, who was more used to the peaceful quiet of the dark caves, paced the perimeter restlessly, pausing at every sound, raising her hand-made spear — really, no more than a sharpened stick she'd found on her rounds — ready to attack whatever approached with a roar loud enough to — hopefully — wake the sleepers.

But now... there! Was that an axle creaking? A cart? Many carts? Men?

Imay moved forward, away from their hiding place.

"Halt!" She cried at the top of her lungs when she was convinced her ears were not deceiving her. "Who goes there?"

She was pleased to hear the sounds of Granno and the others stirring behind her, rising to their feet, wiping the sleep from their eyes, preparing — she hoped — to lend her their support. The three were not quite as mighty as a dragon, although —

The noise had stopped. Imay sensed a restlessness out on the plain west of her. Again she shouted, "Who goes there!"

A moment later a most welcome voice replied, "It's your mother, Queen Diam."

A tear streaked down Imay's eyes and a smile stretched across her face. But — protocol must be observed —

"Advance to be recognized!" she called, remembering Granno's stern injunctions on such matters.

"Very well," Diam replied, her tone both annoyed and approving at the same time. A moment later, the queen of the Silver Earth zwerg came into the sight of her eldest daughter. "I came as soon as I could."

Before she could react, Imay threw down her makeshift spear, and rushed to hug her mother tightly in her arms. "Mother!"

Diam patted her and hugged her back, letting out a deep sigh of relief.

"Your majesty, I have failed you," Granno's voice interrupted them. Diam looked down to find her chief kneeling at her feet. "I let your daughter be captured. Do with me as you will."

Diam took a deep breath and said, "Rise, Granno of the guard."

Granno rose to his feet. Diam was pleased to see Rabel and Ellen approaching from the side. She nodded to Rabel who nodded back, then she returned her attention to Granno.

"Are you prepared to meet your doom?" Diam asked him regally.

Grimly, Granno nodded.

Diam pushed Imay away who looked back at her mother in alarm. Diam awarded with a wink out of her left eye — the one Granno couldn't see — and grimly moved toward the downtrodden guard.

"Very well, then," Diam said imperiously. "Your doom, for failing me is…" she held it as long as she could and then rushed to him, wrapping her arms around him and hugging him tightly. "Shut up and never talk like that again!"

"Your majesty?" Granno replied feebly, trying to move away.

"I said, shut up," she told him again. Granno shut up. She hugged him tightly, then pushed him away with her arms on his shoulders. "You did your best, didn't you?"

Dumbly, Granno nodded.

"So why should I punish you?"

"I failed to protect —"

"You did the best you could with what you had," Diam told him. "That is all that I can ask."

"All that I asked, also," Imay interjected from the side. "And I told you the same thing."

Granno still looked crushed.

"We *learn* from our mistakes," Diam chided him. "We're no worse for the wear —" she glanced nervously toward her eldest child who nodded in hasty assurance "— so we move on."

"As you wish, your majesty," Granno replied hollowly.

"I *do* wish," Diam assured him, shaking his shoulders once before releasing him and turning toward the darkness. "And I believe that lieutenant Minto will be more than relieved to have you resume your duties as chief of the guard."

Granno grinned as he heard a relieved sound from the distance. He turned toward Diam. "How many did you bring and what is your will, majesty?"

"I brought forty troops and twenty miners —"

"Forty!" Granno protested. "That's more than half the guard —"

"Kavim has roused the reserves, there should be no problem —"

"But we were taken, majesty! Someone found us!"

"Yes, and?" Diam replied frostily.

"What if they saw our troops come out of the southern cave?" Granno asked. His eyes narrowed. "Which cave did you come from, just now?"

"The southern one," Diam said in a small voice. She turned back, peering to the far side of the valley. "We took two hours to get here, it would take us that long to return."

"Then we should return," Granno said seriously.

"What about Ibb?" Ellen asked, moving out of the darkness to join him.

"There may be others with him," Rabel added, as he approached and nodded to the queen.

"Lieutenant Minto!" Granno called.

"Sir?"

"Approach and report," Granno ordered. In the darkness they heard the trotting sound of a zwerg approaching as quickly as possible.

"Lieutenant Minto, reporting," the zwerg said, saluting Granno, bowing to the queen and nodding to the others.

"How are your men?" Granno asked.

"We've marched two hours," Minto reported. "The terrain was rugged, so we marched at rout step."

"Of course," Granno allowed. He gestured toward the looming darkness of the ruined fort. "I suggest you gather them up there and set up a light camp."

"Sir?" Minto asked.

"You'll at least need to let them rest before we try anything —"

CLACK! A sound rang from behind Granno and the others. They all turned in surprise. CLACK! clack! cla—!

"It's coming from over there!" Rabel said, pointing and moving toward the source of the sound.

"Ibb?" Diam said, peering from Granno to Imay and back.

"It could be," Granno allowed. "Or it could be rock settling. The sound died down, after all."

"Ellen!" Rabel called from the ruins. Ellen rushed off to join him.

"Let us see what we can learn," Diam said, gesturing for the others to lead the way.

"Follow the queen," Granno shouted to the others on the plain. "Prepare to make light camp."

The night filled with noise as his orders were obeyed.

#

Diam joined Rabel and Ellen, trailed by Imay. The others moved as quietly in the night as they could but the wagons were loud as they moved over the rough terrain.

Rabel was holding a finger toward the curved wall of the ruined turret which lay on its side. At the end of his fingertip flared a bright white light which he used to illuminate the wall.

"There," he said, pointing to a hole between the granite bricks. "If we could widen it enough to see and then put a light up there —" he pointed to another hole "— someone might be able to see inside."

"And then?" Diam prompted.

Rabel turned to her, lowering his finger and extinguishing his light. "We could at least get an idea of the state of the —"

"Look!" Ellen said, pointing.

A light glowed through the hole Rabel had indicated. It was feeble but enough to be visible in the darkness.

"Ibb?" Diam said, examining the light with wide eyes. She turned and shouted, "Granno! Get the miners! Get them now!"

"Inside the turret," Rabel called, putting his voice to the hole. "If you can hear me, turn off your light."

Rabel pulled his head back and looked at the hole where the thin beam of light escaped. A moment later, it went out.

Granno came rushing up with three other sturdy zwerg carrying pickaxes. He bowed to the queen and turned to Rabel. "These are Alicen, Aenor, and Ricon," he said introducing two women and one man in turn. He turned to the zwerg and told them, "This is Rabel and Ellen." The zwerg nodded at the two humans.

"What do we know?" Alicen asked, moving toward the ruined turret and running her hand over the stone work. She smiled as she finished her inspection. "Zwerg made, you know."

"So it should hold, even after the fall?" Rabel asked.

Alicen frowned and turned toward Aenor and Ricon who both made faces. "It's hard to say," she admitted. "The fall and the impact, both of those were not considered in the construction."

"But the fort was constructed to withstand cannon fire," Rabel said. The miners nodded in agreement. "So we can hope that the fall and the impact were not much more powerful than a cannon's blast."

"Perhaps," Alicen allowed with a flick of her fingers. "But humans?" She shook her head.

"It's well that Ibb is not human," Rabel said with a grin.

"How do we know it's Ibb in there?" Granno asked reluctantly.

"The light went out too quickly to be a torch," Rabel said slowly, as if thinking to himself. He put his lips to the hole and called, "Ibb, can you light a red light?"

He pulled back and waited. And waited. Around him the others stirred in discomfort. Ellen made a pained sound, like she was trying to hold back tears.

Then, faintly — "There!" Rabel cried, turning to the others. "Do you see it?"

"It *could* be a red light," Granno allowed skeptically.

"We have to save him," Ellen said, grabbing Granno by the arm. "He would do the same for you!"

"We must be careful," Alicen said slowly. Ellen gave her a surprised look, so the zwerg explained, "We can't say where he is or how stable the ruins are."

"We must be quick," Rabel said. He had his ear pressed against the hole.

"Why?" Granno asked. "Isn't Ibb immortal?"

"He is," Rabel agreed, moving his ear aside and gesturing for Granno to take his place. Granno listened and then grunted in surprise, pulling away from the hole with a jerk.

"We have to hurry," Granno said to the others.

"Why?" Alicen asked in surprise. "Didn't you just say that he's immortal?"

"I did," Granno agreed, "but I heard breathing. Faint, labored."

"Breathing?" Ellen said, shaking her head. "Ibb doesn't breathe."

"No," Granno said, "he doesn't."

Alicen's eyes widened as she realized what the zwerg chief meant and gestured to the others. "Let's build some supports, then we'll pull out those stones further up, widening as we go down until we can make an entrance."

In moments the night was rent with the sound of twenty miners working at full speed.

"Will we be in time?" Diam asked after Granno and Rabel had given her their findings.

"For Ibb?" Rabel shrugged. "Probably. But the others?"

Chapter Five

"Major, did you say something?" General Filbert asked, once again, in irritation. It was at least the fifth time he'd caught Major Morris whining and he was quite ready for the man to be done.

It had taken over two hours to assemble the troops, the horses — the general's *own* horses — the wagons, and all the other impedimenta necessary for their escapade. *Really!* Filbert fumed once more about his subordinate, *and he calls himself an* officer!

"I was wondering if we should perhaps rest the troops, sir," Morris said as he huffed alongside the horse Filbert was riding. "I'm afraid they're getting quite winded."

"Well, *Major*, if you'd trained them properly, they would certainly not be affected by this short march!"

Major Morris firmly tamped down his fury — General Filbert had repeatedly refused to allow him to drill the troops in his battalion since they disembarked from the trains nearly a week ago. In fact, with the exception of a few platoons called for guard duty, his men had been completely without employment. It was *not* the way to treat crack troops! At least, not if one wanted them to retain their edge.

And while the general had fumed, Morris had had to replace several platoon members and platoon leaders to meet the requisite height requirements — "No, no! They're too tall! By the gods, man! Don't you know what *zwerg* are?" — which not only delayed their departure but shredded the efficiency of his command as his troops were forced to work with others they hardly knew or did not know at all. Any training that had occurred with the regular formations was completely lost with this ragtag organization that had never had a chance to train together. Also, because he was *not* allowed to tell his troops their mission, he feared that his two half-companies of weeded out men felt that they were being sent on some sort of punishment detail and not selected because of their superior height which, of course, they lacked.

And, as they marched, Morris discovered — or at least guessed — that some of the men so picked had heard the same stories as the deserter, Slater, and had themselves deserted the formation, causing him and the remaining troops much distress.

Others, he feared, had heard the same stories and decided that their futures were guaranteed, although Morris was convinced that those hardy souls were also the dumbest in his ragtag formation.

"Come along, Major!" Filbert called down from his mount. "Keep those men in order! Another hour and we'll see some fighting!" The general showed his teeth in darkness. "And won't *that* be something, men?"

The men, panting as much as the major, made no sound in response — which was perhaps for the best, Morris decided glumly.

#

Adelin had passed the word onto Gisom and Alfren at the entrance before heading back to her own listening post. That had been over an hour ago. Since then, she'd been relieved and sent to quarters. She grabbed a quick bite to eat and lay in her bunk, too nervous to sleep but too tired to do anything more.

Adelin didn't like Gisom. He was one of the zwerg who held the secret belief that men were always better than women. He was handsome and knew it, skilled at mining, and knew it, too, and fancied himself a better soldier than most. Adelin didn't agree. Oh, he could march well but he had no patience and was always willing to assume that he was always right. She felt that was a danger for a soldier, particularly for a guard. Particularly when paired with someone like Alfren. Alfren was kind and considerate but more than a bit of a worrier. Gisom liked to bully Alfren which kept the other from voicing his concerns. Which meant that, together, they were the absolute *worst* soldiers to guard the cavern exit.

Adelin leaned back in her bunk, closed her eyes. A moment later she opened them again, shook her head, sat up and with an irritated growl, jumped onto the floor.

She was a soldier. She would go check on them. Maybe Gisom would growl at her but that was no reason to prevent her. On the way out of the barracks, Adelin paused by the stove and grabbed two cups. She would bring them some *kaffi*, to keep them warm and awake. Perhaps then Gisom wouldn't even growl. Perhaps.

#

The zwerg miners were quick and efficient. Queen Diam led Rabel and Ellen away from the work site, saying, "We'll just slow them down and you two need to rest."

Ellen made ready to protest but then the smells from the campfire came to her and she held her tongue. Her stomach rumbled instead, reminding her of how long it had been since she'd eaten.

"Food and rest are what you need," Diam said with a chuckle. She gestured for Imay and Granno to join them. "All of you!"

The zwerg made excellent *kaffi*, the bitter leaves turning water into an amazing aromatic delight which did much to banish their fatigue. The cook had skewered bits of meat, herbs, and vegetables and had roasted them over the open flame, serving them still on the thin stick with which they'd be cooked.

When they were full, Rabel turned his attention to the queen. "There are still roving bands from the wreck," he cautioned her.

"I'm sure," Diam agreed with a wicked grin. "But where they thought to take on a group of four, they'll think twice about a well-armed group of *forty*."

"And a group of twenty?" Rabel asked. "Would they stay clear as well?"

"Why?" Diam said giving Rabel a measuring look. "What have you in mind?"

"I was thinking about the ruins of the fort," Rabel said. "In particular, about the magnets that we made with Geros' help."

"And Ophidian's," Ellen added staunchly, leaning back against Rabel.

"Indeed," Rabel said.

"What about them?" Diam asked. "I can't imagine a survivor would even think about them, let alone…"

"They're made of dragon steel," Granno observed when the queen's voice trailed off.

"And there are some survivors who knew that they were used to lift the fort," Rabel said.

"But once they *know* it can be done, how hard will it be for them to duplicate the effort?" Imay wondered.

"Oh," Rabel said with a wave of his hand and a lazy smile, "I wouldn't want them not to *try*…"

"Just not to succeed," Queen Diam guessed. "What do you propose?"

"Could we send a party to the base of the fort and the cave where we placed the lower magnets?"

"And do what?"

"I was thinking that we could melt the steel, and liberate it," Rabel said.

"Liberate for whom?" Granno asked suspiciously.

"We could share evenly," Rabel suggested.

"That's a lot of metal," Granno said with a frown. "It would take days to move."

"If it were melted?" Rabel asked.

"Are you up to the task?" Granno asked.

"No," Rabel admitted. The others gave him a surprised look. "At least, not *all* of it."

"How much? And what about what remains? Would you let Markel's men have it?" Queen Diam asked.

"I thought that perhaps we could count on them taking it," Rabel said.

"You plan to trick them," Imay guessed. The dark-haired man rewarded her with a nod of his head and a smile. He turned to Ellen with a questioning look.

"This is not another *lesson* is it?" Ellen groaned. Rabel said nothing but his look gave her the answer. She pushed herself away from him and got to her feet, walking around the fire and glaring at her protector. Granno shot a glance toward Rabel, then looked back to Ellen, stroking his beard thoughtfully.

Imay, on the other hand, shot her mother a nervous look, asking *you aren't going to do that to me, are you?* Diam met her eldest daughter's unvoiced question was a smirk and Imay groaned.

"We used thirty-six magnets to lift the fort," Ellen said thoughtfully. She pursed her lips. "And even then it was wobbly."

Rabel nodded and waved a hand, enticing her to continue her thought.

Ellen stopped mid-stride, turned her head to Rabel and grinned maliciously. "What if they thought we only used twelve?"

Rabel smiled at her in approval and turned his eyes to the queen of the Zwerg. "What would your majesty do with twelve slabs of the finest dragon steel?"

"What would *you* do with twelve, smith?" Diam asked him in return. Then she turned her gaze to Ellen. "What would you need?"

"We'd have to make it look like we only used twelve slabs," Ellen said thoughtfully. "Your people would have to remove all evidence of the others."

"That would require not just removing them but chiseling away any sign of the supports," Granno said.

Diam nodded.

"And it would be best to remove the tunnel that leads there," Rabel said, "lest any *curious* sort find your realm."

"I agree," Diam said. She waved to the distant cavern. "And you want this done now?"

"War is coming," Rabel said. He shook his head as he corrected himself, "War has come." Diam and Granno both nodded. "It would be unwise not to take precautions."

"Of course," Diam said. She nodded toward Granno. "Are you up for this?"

Granno looked at Rabel. "Are you up for it?"

"I am," Ellen said.

"You are not," Rabel corrected her. She scowled at him. He raised a hand up, forestalling her protests.

"How long will this take?" Diam asked, glancing at the miners and their work on the ruined turret.

"It will take us ten minutes to get to the base of the fort," Granno guessed. He glanced to Rabel who nodded in agreement. "When we're there, we'll have to figure which slabs to move."

"What about the magnetic force?" Ellen said, glancing to Rabel.

"It may have dissipated," Rabel said. "If not, the force will dissolve when we melt the slabs."

"You won't need to melt them completely," Granno said. "Just make the metal soft enough that we can cut it, and we'll break it up that way."

"It would be easier if you could shatter it, like iron," Diam said with a frown.

"But this is dragon steel," Rabel reminded her, "it is not brittle."

Diam made a face. Beside her, Imay rose to her feet.

"No," Diam said, "you wait here with me."

Imay made a face but sat back down, glancing miserably toward Ellen.

"We'll be back soon," Ellen said.

"We will have released your friend by the time you do," Imay guessed.

"I certainly hope so," Rabel said, nodding toward Granno. The zwerg chief raised a hand and beckoned the guard lieutenant to his side. Minto's expression grew less and less happy as Granno explained the new mission to him. Finally, Minto nodded briskly, waved his other officer over to join them conversation and formed up one of his platoons. It took some more time to separate a number of wagons from the miners who insisted on sending five of their own but, finally, the group set off.

Granno had insisted that Ellen and Rabel ride in one of the wagons. Rabel, wisely, did not protest the order. Their driver, Hemin, was a good-natured sort and chatty. Ellen was happy to listen but also willing to explain their mission.

"That's a good idea," Hemin said when she had finished. She nodded to Rabel and Ellen. "And with you two sworn to Geros, there's no fear that you'll betray us."

"Betray you?" Ellen squeaked in surprise.

Hemin laughed, a deep, cheerful sound. "Ah, child! Do you how many sky-touchers have tried to force a zwerg to give up gold or jewels?"

"But you worked for them, didn't you?" Ellen asked. "Why should they get them?"

"Usually they catch one of us, ransom us off," Hemin said, shaking her head sadly. "And when the payment's made, like as not, some of the thieves kill their captive."

"That's horrible!"

"That's the way of the ground above," Hemin said with a sad shake of her head. She glanced toward the stricken girl. "Oh! We know that it's only a few that treat us this way —" she nodded toward Rabel "— we've had plenty of good dealings with you tall ones. It's just that the few bad ones are hard to take."

"Which is why we're planning on this," Ellen said, her spirits recovering. "They'll think that they're getting a trove of dragon steel, think that they know how to float a fort but they'll be wrong!"

Hemin chortled in agreement. "It's a good plan, worthy of master Rabel."

Rabel shook his head, pointing to Ellen. "She thought of it."

Hemin gave him a knowing look. "Of course, master Rabel, and you've taught her nothing."

Rabel could only answer the zwerg's statement with silence, then said "What if we could use the magnetism to melt the metal?"

Hemin's eyebrows rose in surprise at the notion. After a moment, he nodded. "It could be done, I think."

"Could take the magnetism from the twelve slabs we're leaving," Rabel added. "That way they'll take longer to create floating forts."

"Indeed," Hemin said, the corners of his lips turning upwards.

#

Hemin brought the wagon to a halt when Granno held up his hand. They were at the base of the fort. Rabel could see the glint of a number of the magnetic slabs in the light of Granno's torch. Rabel jumped down from the wagon, held up his hands for Ellen and caught her easily, lowering her to the ground at his side.

"How many can you see?" Rabel asked as he moved to join the zwerg chief.

"I count eighteen," Granno told him. "Some of the tops are buried, however."

"Can we get twelve of them out?" Ellen asked, peering up at the massive earth above her. She turned to Rabel in amazement. "Did we really lift that?"

"We had help," Rabel reminded her. Then he smiled. "But, yes, little one, we did."

Ellen's jaw dropped. She could remember the effort, the fear, the pain, the power but only now, having travelled the length of the fallen fort and looking up at the huge metal slabs did she truly grasp what they had done.

"Ophidian and Geros be praised," Ellen said, kneeling quickly and bowing to the two gods.

"Indeed," Granno agreed, sketching a quick bow.

"*They* had help," Rabel growled, nodding to Ellen who rose to her feet and joined him. "And tonight, we do not."

"But it's going to be much easier this time," Ellen said. Rabel raised an eyebrow demandingly. "We've only got to take the charges from twenty-four of the magnets —"

"That's the same amount that we took the last time," Rabel reminded her. "And we did that over the course of two days, if you remember."

"Oh," Ellen said, looking downcast. "But we only have to pull the magic and feed it to the ground." She pointed. "We'll be returning it to Geros."

"Actually, I'm planning on using the force to melt the slabs," Rabel said.

"How?"

Rabel smiled at her. "Watch closely." He moved toward the very bottom of the carved end of earth into which the slabs had been placed. He rubbed his hands together and placed one at the bottom of one of the magnetic steel slabs and the other on another of the metal slabs.

Ellen and the zwerg watched worriedly as Rabel began muttering the spell that Geros had taught them. Her ears perked up when she noticed the changes in the words he used and she found herself nodding in agreement with the changes — they should work.

Rabel grunted as if kicked and Ellen surprised a worried cry as sparks engulfed his hands and flowed up his arms. Carefully, Rabel drew back, sparks jumping from the two slabs onto him. With a triumphant roar, he moved forward and put his hands on the sides of the slab in the middle. The sparks flew from him and engulfed the metal slab which soon grew bright red with heat. Rabel pulled his hands away quickly and moved backwards, waving to Granno.

"That's the first one!" he said. Granno nodded and ordered the zwerg forward to attack the bright hot steel with their picks and hammers. They cried eagerly as the metal broke at their efforts and they pulled large chunks away with gloved hands, bearing them to the prepared carts.

Rabel, satisfied with the result, moved to another trio of slabs and repeated the process, pulling the magnetic force out of two and feeding it back into a third as heat. Another team of zwerg tackled the result.

"My turn," Ellen said as Rabel staggered backwards, wobbling on his feet and looking beat.

Rabel drew breath to admonish her but stopped, shaking his head and motioning her toward a set of dragon steel slabs. Ellen had to stretch her arms as wide as she could to get her fingertips to reach the two steel slabs. Rabel's words came to her and she repeated them quickly, her eyes closed, concentrating and imagining the fierce crackle of the magnetic force — like lightning — surging through her fingertips and up her shoulders. She opened her eyes as the first tendrils of power thrilled up her arms and she smiled as the lightnings sparked around her. With a cry of triumph, she placed her hands on the untouched middle slab, her face breaking into a grin as she called the energies to melt the metal. She jumped back and waved at the others when she saw that the slab had turned bright red, just as Rabel's. The zwerg shouted their praise and set to work with a will.

In short order, between Rabel and Ellen, they had pulled the magnetism from all the metal and the zwerg had hacked twelve of the eighteen slabs to small, portable pieces.

"Now you two rest while we clean up the stone to hide our work," Granno said, indicating the outcroppings of stone that had previously held the melted dragon steel slabs in place on the rock.

Neither Ellen nor Rabel needed urging, kneeling on the ground and drinking warm tea. The zwerg were quickly done and set off for the cavern where the lower set of dragon steel magnets lay buried — and where they could access the cave entrances to their underground world.

It took another twenty minutes to get there, set up another hasty camp, and open the doors to the Silver Earth kingdom.

After that, Ellen and Rabel repeated their efforts, heating twelve of the dragon steel slabs enough that the zwerg could easily slice them up and demagnetizing the remaining six. Granno sent the loaded wagons underground, retaining one for Rabel, Ellen, and the tools the zwerg retained.

In thirty minutes they were reunited with Queen Diam and the miners in their excavation of the ruined fort.

"We have a problem," Diam told them as soon they met.

#

Two arrows flew in from the night into the guardpost. Gisom and Alfren looked at each other in surprise — the arrows had hit neither of them. In fact, they had landed far behind them. Their surprise was short-lived as the arrows burst into flame and silhouetted them perfectly against the light. Two more arrows flew in. They didn't miss their marks. Another pair of arrows followed immediately. Each hit the falling bodies before they fell to the ground, lifeless.

"Very good," Major Morris said to his archers. He turned to the hand-picked squad of scouts and gestured them forward. The squad split into two, one half going to the right, the other to the left, soon lost in the shadows left by the spluttering arrows. Minutes passed and then one of the flaming arrows rose from the ground, was waved in arc and extinguished along with the other arrow. The signal.

"Move out," Morris ordered, standing up and leading his troops forward. It had been easy. The entrance was secured.

His archers waited at the entrance, nodded to their fellow soldiers and fell back to the rear of the formation, ready to lend aid as needed. Morris examined the entrance, motioned a pair of his scouts forwards — scouts chosen for their mining experience — and waited once more. He stood and waved for a messenger who approached quietly.

"Tell the general we've got the entrance," Morris said. "Tell him that we'll send word when we're inside."

The messenger nodded, saluted and took off into the night.

"Hopefully that'll keep him," Morris muttered to himself. The thought of general Filbert rushing forward with the bulk of his men to mill around — loudly — outside the zwerg's entrance was terrifying.

If they could get enough men inside with the alarm being raised, they'd have a chance. Otherwise… he was certain that the zwerg, guarding hordes of gold, must be well-versed in defending their underground home.

He glanced nervously toward the entrance, fearful lest his men report the entrance locked and barred against them. He had put Jansen and Merdoch just behind the two miners — two big burly men who'd seen war and murder close up for many years now. Once the miners had the opening, Jansen and Merdoch were to storm through and wait the rest of Morris's troops. If any two could hold their own against an army of zwerg, it was they.

#

Adelin paused at the second set of gates. The southern entrance was merely a side entrance in the Silver Earth kingdom but it was protected not just by the outside guard and the listening post but also by two stout sets of gates. When the guards were trooped, the gates would be opened one pair at a time until the guards were relieved and replaced. And then the gates would both be shut and barred, leaving the guards locked outside of the kingdom and the kingdom safe.

Adelin was one those tasked with understanding the gates and keeping them in good repair. Each pair of gates were barred by a huge metal bar that fit into two grooves — one on each door. The bar on each gate was pinned to one door and swung up and down. By a clever bit of work, there was a little outcropping on the near gate — the one with the pin that held the bar — that allowed a single person to push the bar up and open the gates. When the gates were pulled closed on the other side — hard enough — the motion would joggle the bar over the outcropping and let it fall into place, barring the gates once more.

Adelin had already made certain that the first set of gates had been properly secured but now she was about to open the second set. She listened carefully but heard nothing, so she lifted the bar up and pushed it over the outcropping. Before she could even open the gates, they were flung open, pushing Adelin to the side and two large humans rushed through.

Each were twice her height. One of them turned back to the opening and the night to shout loudly while the other spun and drew his sword, swinging it to take off her head.

But Adelin was shorter than he'd expected. She was shorter because she had trained for a long time. Trained to prove that no soldier — zwerg or human — was better than her. She dropped to the ground, kicking her feet against the stool she placed the warm mugs on, causing them to clatter and break loudly, even while she pulled her dirk from its sheath and reached over her back to grab her sword.

"Foes! Foes at the southern gate!" Adelin shouted with all her strength as she rolled out of the blade of the glaring human. "Alarm! Alarm!"

She threw her dirk toward the human who ducked it easily, leering at her lack of skill. But she hadn't been aiming for him — she'd been aiming for the bell at the back of the gate.

And she hit it. *Clang!*

She was on her feet and scurrying back toward the second gate — the last gate to guard her home — when she heard other bells ringing. She turned to face her two attackers knowing that the alarm was spreading.

The two men growled at her. More men, some with blinding torches, came rushing up to join them.

Torches! Adelin thought. She glanced upwards. There was rope hanging down, as planned. She sidled toward it, parrying the swords that hammered at her even as she realized that there were too many, that she could not prevail.

But Kavim and Granno had planned for such emergencies. They had chosen their soldiers — even those in reserve — carefully.

She would have only one chance. She kept half her thoughts on the swords beating on her and planned her path.

When the opening occurred she took it immediately, ducking under the two fierce men, jumping around the two others nearest, leaping, landing with one foot on the upturned tool and leaping higher, throwing her sword away even as the soldiers turned to follow her path and reached to pull her back to the ground.

But Adelin caught the rope and let the full weight of her armored body drag it down.

She was dead when her body hit the ground, stabbed through twice by the swords of Jansen and Merdoch.

As her eyes dimmed she was rewarded with a brilliant flare and a fierce heat — and then she knew no more as the oil that had been pulled down by her rope mixed with the soldiers' torches and turned the entire entrance into a flaming cauldron.

Chapter Six

Lissy woke to the sound of the doors to the treasury bursting open. In the distance she heard bells and cries of alarm.

"Princess, come on!" the guard cried. "We're being attacked!"

"Go," Lissy said, moving to the side of the dragon's head. "We'll follow."

The guard looked in, took in the sight of the sleeping dragon, and his eyes widened in fear.

"I have to wake him up," Lissy said, waving the guard away. "I'll be safe with a dragon to guard me."

Loud shouts distracted the guard and he looked away as a huge *BOOM!* Filled the hallways. "I'll tell Kavim," he promised, rushing off toward the source of the sound.

#

"You see!" General Filbert cried triumphantly as he waved a hand toward the smoke and debris that churned out of the entrance to the zwerg underground. "Enough gunpowder and you can solve any problem!" He waved toward Major Morris. "Now have your men charge, Major."

Major Morris ordered his men forward. He was still appalled at the loss of life of the first group of scouts, burned to char in an instant as they tried to gain entrance into the caves below. He had quickly organized parties to shovel dirt over the flames and the burnt skeletons, building a path toward the charred but still standing inner gates.

"Send a man back when you've secured the area, and I'll send the wagons forward," General Filbert shouted to Morris's retreating form. He waved his troops forward genially until all that was left was the rearguard and the wagoneers, then he rubbed his hands gleefully. "We're going to be rich!"

Of course, he didn't mean the *men*. They would have to go. But fortunately there was a war on and Major Morris had proved himself to be most unsatisfactory. Such a man would be well-treated by being placed at the head of any assault, along with his men, until they were all — sadly — lost. War, the general reflected, did have such a *marvelous* way of solving such tedious problems.

#

"What problem?" Rabel asked as he glanced around the camp and the excavation into the turret.

Diam motioned for Alicen to come forward.

"We found him," Alicen reported.

"And?" Rabel prompted.

"His eyes are a-light but he doesn't talk," Alicen explained.

"We're wondering if he's dead," Diam said.

"From what we can see, his backside is crushed, flattened under the weight of rock," Alicen continued. "If he were a zwerg or a human, I would swear that he had died of his injuries —"

"He's an immortal," Rabel said in a small voice. "He can't —" he broke off, shaking his head.

"There's more," Diam said, nodding to Alicen.

"There are others," Alicen said. "We can hear breathing but no sounds."

"Injured," Rabel guessed. "He would have protected him with his body."

"Why would he do that?" Alicen asked in surprise.

"He's an immortal," Rabel said. "He believes in life. That's why we're here."

"Let me go," Ellen said. The others looked at her. She turned her gaze to Rabel. "I've met him. I'm small and —" she held up a hand, thumb and forefinger nearly touching and spark lit between them "— I have some power."

"You wouldn't fit," Diam said before Rabel could protest. She turned to Ellen. "Are you willing to let him die, if you must?"

Ellen gulped in surprise. She glanced to Rabel, then said to the queen, "Only if I must."

Diam waved to Alicen, gesturing toward Ellen. "Take her, then."

"What about the others?" Rabel asked when the girl and miner were out of earshot.

"Ibb's body is keeping the rubble off of them," Diam said sadly. "If he is no longer alive, my people can dig past him and maybe free the others."

"But if he is?"

"Things will be harder," Diam said. "From what I'm told, it will take some work to build a scaffolding to take the weight off of his body. And we don't know if the rubble behind him won't collapse on the others when we do."

#

Ellen followed Acelin nervously though she refused to show it. She didn't mind caves or dust but the stones around her were all wrong — they wanted to go up into the sky, not lay on their sides on the ground. Acelin pointed at various dislodged stones and stepped over them carefully, Ellen following her steps. She brought a small light to the tip of her finger to help her see better, earning a surprised and then resigned look from Acelin in front.

They walked maybe twenty feet "down" the fallen turret until Acelin threw up a hand, bringing them to a halt.

"It is just up ahead," Acelin said in a small voice. "This is where the turret joined the wall — this is a weak spot and weaker now that the fort has fallen onto its side."

Ellen nodded. Acelin indicated the shapes of several zwerg miners working slowly and carefully to remove rubble and loose bricks. She recognized Aenor and Ricon among them and gave them smiles of appreciation.

"Is there room enough for me to touch him?" Ellen asked.

"You are small enough, if you're careful," Alicen said, nodding. "Everyone! Make room for our Ellen, please."

Ellen went forward carefully, watching as the zwerg pointed to where she should step and when she should duck under an archway. It was more difficult to navigate the transition from the stairs of the turret to the entrance to the hallway, itself on its side — the walls were now the floor and ceiling while its floor and ceiling were the new walls.

Ellen spotted the metal and hissed in surprise. She could just make out Ibb's head from the two glowing eyes — were they glowing, even? The rest of him seemed lost under the weight of stone and rubble.

She stared at him for a long while, trying to understand him, to see if he was alive or night.

Finally, she had a thought. She raised her finger up to his eyes and produced a faint white light.

"Ibb?" she said. "Can you see that? Can you make the same color?"

She lowered her hand and looked into the dim eyes of the mechanical man. She found herself holding her breath until she spotted the faintest of white sparks in his eyes.

She said nothing, raising her hand again and bringing forth a red spark. "And this?"

Again she waited. Perhaps the first light was a reflection, perhaps she'd imagined it. But — there! A faint red dot glowed in his eyes.

She gasped in delight and patted his cheek gently. "You're alive!" she cried joyfully. "We'll get you out, never fear! By the gods, you're alive!"

She turned back to join Acelin and share the news.

"This may make things more difficult," Acelin said sadly. "We cannot think of a way to get him out safely without endangering the others."

"We'll think of something," Ellen declared. She pointed toward the exit. "Let's go tell Rabel and the queen."

On the difficult scramble back, Ellen wracked her brains and tried out her thoughts on the zwerg miner. Acelin listened attentively but every plan Ellen suggested, the zwerg miner had to reluctantly declare impractical.

Finally, Ellen said, "We'll melt him."

"*What?*" Acelin cried in surprise.

"He's not human, he's made of metal," Ellen continued excitedly. "You can build supports to take the weight he's holding up, can't you?"

"Y-yes," Acelin allowed reluctantly.

"So we melt him, and we pull him out, letting the weight rest on your supports, and then we pull out the others," Ellen said.

"Child, if you melt him, won't he die?" Acelin asked.

"He's crushed already, isn't he?" Ellen said. "We won't melt him completely, just enough to make his body soft enough to pull out without jarring your supports."

"But how will we get him back to his proper shape?" Acelin asked.

"First, we need to get him out, then we'll worry about that problem," Ellen said.

Acelin was silent for a moment. Then she said, "I wonder what your Rabel will say."

#

"Is there any other choice?" Queen Diam asked Rabel when Ellen finished outlining her plan back outside of the ruined fort.

Rabel shrugged. "If there is, none of us have thought of it." He made a face. "Certainly, if we had days we could perhaps come up with a better plan but —"

"Those trapped with him won't last days," Diam agreement grimly. Acelin had brought the news that there seemed to be three people breathing and, from their sounds, two were humans. One had softer breathing which could mean either a zwerg or a younger human; they didn't know.

"If we go with this plan," Acelin said waving toward Ellen, "then we'll have to move quickly, getting everyone out as soon as we can. We can't say how much longer the ruins will remain stable." She turned to Rabel. "So, friend of Ibb, can you tell me?"

"Tell you what?"

"How much does the metal man *weigh?*"

Rabel gave her a surprised look. "I honestly don't know."

"In snow, his feet sink no deeper than a human's," Ellen said.

"So, let's say two hundredweight, perhaps three," Acelin said. She grew thoughtful. "And if we consider the others to be humans at as much as two hundredweight themselves — and the littler one at half that… we'd need sixteen zwerg to carry them all."

"If we arranged a relay could we get them out faster?" Diam asked.

"A relay would help," Granno agreed. "But you'd need to switch some of the people off or they'd get too tired."

"And they'll need to get out quickly."

"I can help carry them," Ellen said.

"No, little one, I'm afraid that you can't," Acelin said. Ellen pouted. "You are young and your weight is less than even the lightest of them." Acelin turned to Granno. "We should arrange that she is carried out just after the mechanical."

"What?" Rabel said, surprised.

"You're too big," Diam said. She nodded to the girl. "Ellen will have to do this." Diam turned to Granno. "We should arrange to leave as soon as we've recovered everyone." She made a face. "I'm worried about the stones that hold these ruins together."

"I agree," Granno said. "You get the troops and the miners arrayed, ready to depart when we return."

"We?"

"Am I not the strongest zwerg in the kingdom?" Granno asked her with a twinkle in his eye.

"And I," Imay spoke up for the first time. Diam shot her a look but the princess returned it regally. "I'm rested and I'm strong for my age."

Diam glanced toward Granno who jerked his head as if to say, *it's your problem*. Finally, Diam nodded.

Imay rose to her feet with a smile and jerked her head toward Ellen. "Let's go! This will be an adventure for the bards!"

#

Ellen moved quickly and more sure-footedly than she had the first time she'd been in the ruined turret. After all, she reasoned, she knew where she was going. And they didn't know how much time the humans had.

Behind her, the zwerg split off and took positions along the ruined turret, ready to haul the trapped survivors swiftly out of danger.

Imay held Ellen's hand and followed behind her, while Acelin led the way once more.

It took them ten minutes to reach the ruined form of Ibb, the metal man. It was only when they arrived that Ellen realized the flaw in her plan.

"Ibb," Ellen whispered as she approached him, "I have a plan." She waited to see if his eyes might spark in response but they didn't. "It's the only one we can think of that might save the others with you." She found her throat dry, felt Imay tense behind her as she guessed that all was not right. "I'm going to use my power to heat you up, make your metal soft enough that we can pull you out." She lifted a finger and brought forth a bright spark of light. "The zwerg will build supports that will take the weight when we melt your skin and then we'll pull you out and get the others."

This plan sounded so much better when she'd first thought of it than now, when she was trying to put it into practice.

"You two move back," Acelin ordered. "Aenor and Ricon and I are going to set the supports."

Imay tugged on her hand and Ellen backed up slowly.

It seemed to take forever before Acelin said, "We're ready."

Ellen moved forward, jerking her hand out of Imay's and put both hands on Ibb's metal body.

"Aenor and I will pull when you give the word," Acelin told her in a soft voice. "Ricon will pull you out as soon as you do, so don't be surprised."

"But how will I know if it worked?" Ellen whimpered.

"You'll know when we pull Ibb outside," Aenor said.

"Go on," Imay called softly to her. "I know you can do it."

The zwerg princess' words were all that Ellen heard as she closed her eyes and imagined flames growing along the palms of her hands, bathing Ibb's metal face with heat and fire.

#

Major Morris grunted as he cut down another zwerg and moved forward, glancing to his sides to check on his scouts. Two of them were down but two more had broken through, racing off in opposite directions as quickly as they could, searching for gold and avoiding the ground-dwellers.

He had lost both his lieutenants and countless other men. Behind him, he heard General Filbert at the gates, shouting to the wagoneers who tried to haul the carts over the metal rails that obstructed their way.

Morris was certain that somehow the rails were normally arranged to provide movement for carts similar to their own but he had no time to consider the situation as another wave of zwerg charged his men.

There were fewer zwerg than before. He noticed a knot of them to one side and decided that they were guarding the most prized two pathways — forward and to the left — but he couldn't tell whether that was the way to their homes or to their palace.

He heard a sound of running feet from behind him and pointed at the softer defences on the right, shouting, "There! Attack them!"

The new, fresh troops roared with fury and soon beat down the smaller zwerg guard, breaking through and racing down the cavern, breaking into smaller parties as they came upon crossings.

The zwerg guarding the more precious hallway groaned in despair but fought no less fiercely than before.

He heard a clatter of hooves behind him and shouted, "Take the right! We've broken through there!"

"Very well," General Filbert shouted back. "Hold the crossroads here and we'll return with the gold!"

Or abandon us and find another way out, Morris thought with a grimace. He had the measure of the general now and knew what to expect.

#

Lissy had worn herself out trying to wake the dragon. She'd shouted, begged, pleaded, whimpered, and tugged — all to no avail.

"Jarin, please, we have to go!" Lissy said. "Humans are invading, we need to get to safety!"

She pinched him, pulling down his eyelid and —

— suddenly the dragon was looking at her.

"Jarin?" Lissy asked in a small voice.

Outside the room, came a shout of surprise, the sound of swords crossing, a fight and a groan as someone lost.

"Jarin," Lissy said in a whisper, "what are we going to do?"

In answer, the dragon gently pushed her aside and dug deep into the piled gold coins until he was buried under them, completely out of sight. Lissy watched with widening eyes. Was the dragon abandoning her? She whimpered.

Just then, the dragon twisted its long neck enough to expose its head from under the coins and give her a long, slow wink.

Oh!

Lissy winked back, knelt down, pushed the gold coins back over the dragon's exposed skin and slowly climbed her way to the top of the mound of treasure.

Chapter Seven

It happened so fast that Ellen had a hard time describing it, later. One moment she was heating Ibb, the next she heard the stones above her groan and creak — and then she was jerked away, hauled by small but rough hands with a speed that left her breathless, the rumbling sounds of falling rocks growing louder in the distance.

And then she was outside, in Rabel's arms and then on the ground as the smith turned to the opening, expression fierce and guarded. She had barely time to gasp for breath before Rabel moved forward blocking her view and helping a swarm of zwerg pull a heavy burden out of the hole in the side of the turret.

"We need a wagon!" Rabel roared. Hooves clattered and the pony drew the wagon forward. "Careful, careful!"

The wagon creaked under as it took a heavy load and settled. Rabel jumped aboard. "Ellen, come along!"

Ellen had a moment to look around nervously before hands hauled her up to join Rabel next to —

— the ruined and crumpled metal form that once was Ibb the mechanical.

"Move out!" Queen Diam ordered. "Bring up the next wagon!" She turned toward the soldiers. "Be ready!"

Those sounds were lost to Ellen as she took in the ruins of Ibb's body. She rushed forward to his battered head, tears flowing down her cheeks. "Oh, Ibb, I'm so sorry!"

Rabel's arms went around, drawing her up and back. "Ellen."

She jerked against him, trying to free herself. "Let me go!"

"Ellen," he said softly, "open your eyes."

Ellen opened her eyes and looked down on the ruined form of the mechanical man.

Rabel waved a hand invitingly toward Ibb's eyes. "Look at his eyes."

Ellen took a breath and wiped her tears, leaning against Rabel's arms to crane forward and peered down. "They're — they're glowing!"

"He's alive," Rabel said. "You saved him."

Ellen pulled forward once more and Rabel released her. She flung her arms around the metal man's head and cried softly. "Ibb! Oh, Ibb!"

#

Major Morris was surprised when one of his scouts returned from the right passageway. Morris puzzled his memory for a moment, trying to recall the man's name. Kalfland. Ivon Kalfland. Good man. The scout made his way to him, ignoring the fighting and dying of soldiers and zwerg to their left and front.

"We found the treasury, sir," the scout reported wearily.

"Good work, Kalfland! Did you see the general?"

"Yes, sir, and I reported to him and he took off, telling me to come back here," Kalfland replied. He made a face. "He said you could probably use my help more than him."

"Hmmph," Morris replied. "Well, if you've found the treasury, he'll soon be back here with the gold." He jerked his head towards the exit. "Get out, scout our way away from here back to camp."

Kalfland jerked his head in a quick nod and disappeared into the mass of fighting men.

The battle had trailed off, somewhat, Morris decided. The zwerg were probably awaiting reinforcements or they were trying to contain the breakout down the right cavern — or they'd heard about the treasury. Whichever way it was, Morris was not ungrateful for the respite. He pursed his lips. If the general returned this way, he should probably arrive in the next half hour or so. If he found another way, the major might find himself on the short end of things. *The short end!* Major Morris snorted with amusement as he glanced toward the short zwerg soldiers battling in front of him.

#

Diam grunted in relief as she counted out the last of the miners from the turret. They'd rescued three humans as well as the metal man and had lost none of their own. In fact, Diam was thrilled to discover, one of the recovered was Hamo Beck, the mayor of Korin's Pass and one of Diam's kin.

All of them were severely bruised and had broken bones but they would live, thanks to Ibb who had protected them when the fort had collapsed. Hamo had managed to tell her as much. The other tall human was the captain of the fort, Captain Berold. Judging by their looks, the boy child was his son. The full story would have to wait until they could rest and recover from their ordeal.

"Let's go!" Daim said to the wagon driver as the rest of the troops assembled and moved off into the darkness. She raised a hand and pointed "We'll head to the south entrance —"

A gout of flame lit the night just where her hand was pointing.

"What happened?" Granno shouted, racing back to join his queen.

Diam peered toward the rapidly dimming flames.

"The oil," she said. "Someone attacked the south gates and we set them on fire."

Around them, the zwerg rumbled in alarm as the news spread. Diam pointed to Granno. "I want you to take both platoons back on the double —"

"But, what about you?"

"I've got twenty zwerg *miners* and Ophidian's sorcerers to protect me!" Diam shouted.

"And me!" Imay added stoutly.

"And my own eldest daughter," Diam added with an approving glance toward Imay. "We'll be fine! Go!"

"The Silver Earth will advance, on the double!" Granno shouted, pulling his sword from over his shoulder and pointing it toward the dying flames. "For the queen!"

"For the queen!" the troops shouted enthusiastically, bursting forward as though they had not already spent the whole night marching.

#

The doors to the treasury burst open, startling Lissy awake. She stood up, glancing down to the piled gold coins covering Jarin, to make certain that he was well-hidden.

Shouting came from the doorway and she heard the gruff voices of soldiers.

"General, it's here! Gold, sir! Mounds of gold!"

"Stand aside, let me in!" a harsh voice bellowed, and an old man pushed the soldiers out of his way. In the distance, Lissy could see a cart and heard others clattering to a stop outside the treasury.

"Mountains of it!' the man exclaimed. "And not a guard in sight!"

"I would not touch it, if I were you," Lissy cried down from the mountain of gold, staring down at the gruff man who was dressed with two gold stars on his shoulders. A general, Lissy guessed.

"Who are you?" the man shouted, glancing up toward her. He gestured toward his guards and they moved forward in front of him while a pair of archers moved in from outside, their bows drawn and arrows knocked.

"I am Lissy, princess of the Silver Earth," Lissy said, drawing herself up to her full height and glaring down at him. "And I tell you: leave now, while you can."

The general laughed. "You! A little girl! Who are you to stand up to my men?"

"I told you already," Lissy replied in a slightly peeved tone. "I am princess Lissy and this is my kingdom." She waved at him. "And who, sir, are you?"

"I am General Diggory Filbert," he said with a chuckle, clicking his heels like he was saluting her. "And I've killed countless of your subjects while you cowered in your gold."

"Then you'll pay," Lissy said. *Killed? Dead?* She knew such things happened but she never knew someone might *brag* about it. "Surrender."

"What?" General Filbert cried in outrage. "Surrender? Little girl, you are all alone here. Your people are dead, fleeing or dying. It's *you* who should surrender."

"I'm not alone," Lissy said easily, her anger rising. "I'll give you one more chance."

"Even if you had a hundred of your best soldiers with you —"

"No," Lissy said. "I don't have soldiers."

"No soldiers, eh?" General Filbert said, glancing around the chamber. "So what do you have, little princess? What could you possibly possess that would protect you from the might of Kingsland and my army?"

Lissy saw the general wave to the archers, saw them draw their bows back and jumped down, to the side. The arrows flew up toward where she'd been and fell harmlessly somewhere in the back of the treasury. The archers immediately reached back over their shoulders for more arrows.

"Dodging won't save you!" Filbert shouted. "Surrender, princess!"

"No!" Lissy shouted back. "You surrender!"

"Or what?" Filbert scoffed. "You're alone. You're helpless. Nothing can save you."

"I'm not alone," Lissy said, raising her voice and nudging the coins beside her. They started to cascade away. Filbert's brows furrowed when the trickle grew into a torrent. Lissy said to the rising figure beside her, "These are bad people. Please deal with them."

Filbert's eyes widened as quickly as his jaw gaped. Slowly he raised his arm and managed to jibber, "What's that?"

"That is a dragon," Lissy said. "He's my friend."

#

Major Morris turned his head as he caught a brilliant sight out of the corner of his eye. He gasped as he saw a flaming cart rushing toward him only to collapse in a ball of flame that emerged from the same corridor.

"Dragon!" a man shouted, rushing from the ruins of the cart. "There's a —" another ball of flame silenced him.

"Retreat!" Morris shouted, pushing his men back from the zwerg. "Retreat!"

In a moment the retreat became a rout and Morris found himself carried along in a wave of panicked men even as the zwerg cheered and rushed forward to cut them down.

Somehow the major managed to push his way through the doors and out into the night —

— where he was met by two brilliant flashes of light that left him night-blinded.

"Surrender or die!" a woman's voice called from the night.

Morris was the first to throw his sword to the ground.

Epilog

"Halt! Who goes there?" Captain Welless called out in the dim light of dawn. He'd expected to hear from one of General Filbert's scouts hours ago but there'd been no report. Doubtless Colonel Marchant would soon be waking and wondering where his superior was. Captain Welless had mixed emotions about his report on the matter. The colonel was many things but he was loyal to the king — and would not take kindly to being abandoned by his general.

"Help!" came the reply. "By all the gods, help!"

"Major Morris?" Captain Welless cried in surprise as figures resolved themselves in the morning mist to a cart and some lame soldiers walking beside it. The major was slumped in the front seat of the cart, propping up an injured soldier whose eyes were bandaged. The major looked no better, his arm in a sling.

"Get the healers," Morris ordered. "I've got many injured men."

Welless issued the order and moved up to the cart. He glanced to the back and saw a huddled mass of troops — not more than a dozen.

"Are there others?" Welless asked. Morris shook his head. "And the general?"

"The general is with the Ferryman," Morris said bitterly. He waved a hand. "Let us pass, the men need rest."

#

Ellen rushed to the treasury, looking for Lissy and Jarin while Rabel and the others tended to the injured and helped repair the ruin at the south entrance to the Silver Earth kingdom.

A gruff zwerg guard halted her at the entrance. "No one's to enter, miss," the man told her. He was wounded, a fresh scar on his face and one arm in a sling.

"But I've got to see Lissy!" Ellen cried.

From behind the doors, Ellen heard, "Ellen?"

"Lissy, let me in!"

"Let her in, Dermon, her and no other," Lissy's voice carried wearily through the door.

"Princess, are you certain?" Dermon asked uncertainly.

"Let her in!"

Dermon fumbled for the keys, grumbling to Ellen, "I'm going to have to lock you in."

"Lock me in?" Ellen repeated in surprise. "Why?"

"The princess' orders," Dermon told her bluntly. He jerked a nod toward the door. "You'll see." He paused for a moment, then blurted, "Are you sure?"

Ellen frowned. "Of course I'm sure!"

"Very well," Dermon let her enter and closed the door quickly behind her, the keys rattling as the lock was set.

Ellen turned from glancing back at the door to the dimly lit room. She found Lissy at the top of a mound, resting her head on a pile of gold coins. Ellen sniffed — the air was hot and dry. Well, she'd been told that Jarin —

"Where's Jarin?"

"Not a word to anyone!" Lissy called back, gesturing for Ellen to join her.

"What?"

"Promise, you must promise or leave!" Lissy declared imperiously. Ellen had never heard the zwerg princess so determined.

"Lissy —"

"Promise! Not a word!" The princess sounded like she was ready to cry.

"I promise," Ellen said heavily, climbing up the mound of coins slowly. She kept looking around, looking for a familiar shape, expecting to be pounced and pranked at any moment.

When she reached Lissy, she grabbed the princess in a quick hug and then looked around. "Jarin? Where are you? Everyone says that you saved them, that you're a hero!" She glanced around, her brows furrowed. "Where are you?"

Beside her a pile of gold coins shuddered and slid away.

"There you are!" Ellen said, crouching down beside a single glowing red eye. "Jarin?" She looked over nervously to princess Lissy who knelt down beside her, tears streaming from her face.

"He's not there, is he?" Lissy said in a small voice. Ellen's eyes widened and she glanced from the burning dragon's eye to the princess and back. As Ellen's eyes grew wider and wider in fright, Lissy whispered, "Ellen, what do you know about dragons? They're twin souls, right?"

Ellen nodded, afraid to look at the dragon breathing harshly beside them.

"Do you know," Lissy whispered right against Ellen's ear, "what happens when the human part dies?"

Healing Fire

Book 10

Twin Soul series

Chapter One

The healer was an old zwerg and looked up at her queen with sorrow in her eyes. "He is too human to take the healing," she said.

Diam turned to Rabel. "What do you know of healing?"

Rabel shrugged. "Not much," he said, moving forward to kneel beside the low bed in which Hamo Beck had been placed. "But let me see what I can learn."

Diam turned to Imay. "Find Lissy and Ellen." Imay glanced once at the injured and dipped her head in acceptance, turning lithely and moving away swiftly.

Rabel murmured into Hamo's ear, "It's me, Rabel. I'm a friend of Ibb's. I'd like to check you for broken bones and injuries."

A small, faint noise came back from the injured man which Rabel took for assent. He gave a small nod of his own.

He glanced warningly to Diam, then the healer but neither dropped their gaze, so he returned to his examination. With help from the healer, whose name was Molle, Rabel removed the remainder of the rags that had once been Hamo's clothes. He winced as the man groaned in pain and at the sight of the huge purpling bruises over much of his body.

"Hamo," Rabel said as he leaned back so that he could look at the man's face, "I'm going to do some magic I know, to see if I can find any broken bones. Please don't be startled, it might feel hot or tingle even."

"What are you planning to do?" Molle asked critically, glancing up to her queen in alarm.

"It's something I learned from Ibb many years ago," Rabel said.

The healer, Molle, sniffed. "You hardly have that many years yet."

"I've more than appears," Rabel assured her. He glanced toward Diam whose eyes darted from the healer to him and back thoughtfully before she nodded her assent.

Rabel drew in a deep breath and closed his eyes, rubbing his hands together as if to warm them and then spreading them out to hover over Hamo's body. A thin glow spread from his hands, a purplish yellow, like some strange flame. It lingered over the body, hovering where he'd left it but some of the glow darkened and seemed to coalesce into knots.

Molle gasped in amazement. Diam glanced at her. The healer pointed to one dark knot and whispered, "That's a broken bone, I know it!" With renewed respect and interest, she followed the glow that Rabel spread over Hamo's body and made noises of surprise and interest whenever a new knot formed.

Finally, Rabel leaned back, opening his eyes and grunting in surprise as he counted the knots. There were no less than twelve.

"Is this just for the front or does your magic see wounds on his back as well?" Molle asked.

"Both," Rabel said, taking a deep breath to restore his powers. "The darkness of the knots indicates both degree and depth of injury if you know how to read them."

"And do you —?"

Rabel shook his head quickly. "Not as well as Ibb."

"Well enough," Molle said, gesturing for her apprentices to approach. She gave Rabel a worried look. "You are exhausted. Not just from these efforts but from those prior."

Rabel shook her concern away with a wave of his hand. "I need to check on the others."

"I shall accompany you," Molle said, issuing quick orders to her apprentices who began, carefully, to deal with the illuminated wounds on the half-human. She turned to Diam and nodded deferentially. "If it pleases your majesty, I think this man and I can see to the injured."

Diam jerked her head in a quick but worried agreement.

"It's too early to tell, your majesty," Molle said, guessing the queen's fears. "If none are more injured than this, I think we can heal them, in time."

"Thank you," Diam said. "But there are many others, from the fight."

Molle allowed herself a small smile. "I am not your only healer, your majesty," she waved a hand to the large hall beyond. "But breaks and bruises are my specialty. Hallo, Nenden, and Verek are here already and we've the rest of our healers alerted and on their way to help us."

"You have burn injuries?" Rabel asked sharply, turning his head toward Diam. Healer Molle nodded before the queen could respond. "Send for Jarin and Ellen, they know how to pull the burn out."

"Pull the burn out?" Molle squeaked in amazement. When she saw that Rabel was deadly serious, she added, "Can you teach us, please?"

"I can try," Rabel said. "But the three of us have given oaths to Ophidian and that may be the source of our power."

Granno came through a doorway, looking grim and bending his knee to his queen. Diam gestured for him to rise with one wave of her hand, asking wearily, "How bad is it?"

"Kavim did an excellent job, your majesty," Granno began.

"I know," Diam said, "but *tell me* — how bad?"

Granno's lips thinned into a tight line. "Forty dead, eighty injured. Twenty of them seriously."

Diam pressed a hand to her eyes and closed them tightly. When she opened them again, there was no sign of the sorrow she felt. She was a ruler: she knew her duty.

"We will close the entrances, collapse the caves, and move west, as planned," Diam declared. She nodded to Granno. "Get that started at once and get back when you have news."

Granno drew himself up to attention and gave her a crisp salute before turning and trotting out of the healer hall, his face full of grim determination. "Minto! Kavim! To me!"

Molle hissed in surprise but, glancing toward Rabel, gestured for him to precede her to the next patient.

"The father first," Rabel said, "then the boy."

Molle agreed. "The father has the greater injuries."

"And I'd like his permission to examine the boy," Rabel told her. She accepted that with a firm nod.

#

"Lissy!" Imay shouted in growing frustration. "Lissy, open the door!" She glared at the wounded guard outside the treasury, gesturing for him to add his voice and authority.

Dermon shook his head. "She said no one was to enter," he told her firmly, "on pain of death."

"Yet she let the human, Ellen, enter," Imay said curtly. She pounded on the door again. "Lissy! Lissy, Rabel needs Ellen and Jarin to help him! He said they can heal burns! Open the door!"

"I can't!" Lissy called back miserably. "By my word, Imay, I *can't!*" In the distance, Imay could hear Ellen sobbing.

Worriedly, Imay put her face to the small opening in the door. She could see nothing but gold and that only faintly in the dim light.

"*Please* don't scold me," Lissy begged her older sister.

"Lissy, there isn't time," Imay said. She continued with a heartfelt plea, "There isn't time for this. People are dying. Jarin and Ellen could help Rabel save them."

"I'm sorry," Ellen's voice came to her, sobbing. "We can't. You have to believe me. We can't."

"If that's so," Imay said slowly, "I pity you. People will die that you could have saved."

"More would die," Ellen murmured so quietly that Imay wasn't certain she'd heard — and she was convinced that Ellen didn't expect to be heard.

"I must report this to our mother, the queen," Imay said in a resigned voice.

"We would come if we could, Imay, I swear!" Lissy called back tearfully.

#

"We have to do something," Ellen said, still sobbing miserably as Imay's footsteps faded in the hallway outside. She turned to Lissy. "We can't let people die."

"We may have no choice," Lissy said in a hard voice. She gestured to the mound of gold. "You did not see what he did."

"He won't hurt me," Ellen swore, pulling a pile of coins away until it exposed a dark dragon hide. She patted it affectionately. "I know you're scared, Jarin, but we're here. We're here for you."

From the dragon's nose came a snort of despair.

Ellen wiped her dripping nose on her sleeve and patted around in her shirt. "We must send for help," she said.

"How?" Lissy squeaked.

Ellen pulled forth a blue-white light. She showed it to Issy. "I'll send this off to get help," Ellen said bravely.

"How many do you have?" Lissy asked. "You lent one to me and one to Imay."

"I have three," Ellen said, throwing the blue-white demon up into the air.

In a flash, the small thing started toward the door but before it got more than an arm's length from the two humans, a dark shape lunged out of the gold, red eyes flaring, and snapped in the air — taking the blue demon in one quick gulp.

Ellen and Lissy stared at each other in horror.

#

"And you're *certain* that General Filbert is dead?" Colonel Marchant repeated as he eyed the swaying form of Major Morris in the healer's tent. There were only nine others there with him — two had died of their wounds in the past hour — *nine* out of nearly two hundred!

"I did not see the body, sir," Major Morris said carefully. "And none of the men who went with him returned. But there was a *dragon*, sir. I saw its flames consume one of the carts — and the carter — who'd gone with the general. I can only assume he met the same fate."

Colonel Marchant fumed as he considered the major's statement. Finally he said, "General Tashigg and the rest of the division should de-train tomorrow. I'll leave the final decision to him."

Morris nodded wearily at the colonel's words. Really, *he* didn't care what the colonel did.

"Who's next in command of your battalion, Major?" Colonel Marchant said.

"Captain Baker, sir," Morris told him wearily. Baker was a steady sort, he'd neither shine nor dim in his new position. "The men like him."

Colonel Marchant grunted in acknowledgement, patted Morris feebly on the shoulder and turned to the healer. "How soon until he recovers?"

"Weeks, at least, sir," the healer said, frowning down at Morris. "He'll probably need some leave to rest and recuperate."

"Very well," Marchant said, turning toward the door, "we'll proceed without him."

Once the colonel was out of earshot, the healer turned to the major and muttered, "Did what I could for you, sir." He eyed the major a moment longer, nodded to himself and turned away. "I'll see to the others, now, if you don't mind."

Chapter Two

"Form up by battalions, and have them move off to join Filbert's camp," General Tashigg said to his aide. The aide nodded, saluted, and marched off to carry out the general's orders. General Tashigg nodded to himself: things were proceeding nicely. Second and Third brigade would be fully formed by nightfall and then the First Division would move through Korin's Pass and take up positions on the far side, waiting to hear from the cavalry.

The air was cold and brisk and general Tashigg waved his arms about him to keep warm. The troops nudged each other and smiled at his antics. Tashigg saw them and waved them on, shouting, "Good show! Forward to victory!"

Orders were shouted, men jumped down from the carriages, others led staff horses and brought them to their officers. The troops formed up and moved off briskly. The moment the train was clear, another officer shouted to the driver who engaged the steam and the wheels, pulling the train forward toward the siding where it would turn around for another load.

Might do to lay two sets of tracks, Tashigg noted to himself idly. A shout from the distance caught his attention and he saw two horsemen trotting up, waving at the train driver and shouting furiously. *Whatever did they want?*

Presently the driver, who'd turned the train around was ready to start back to Kingsford, noticed them and waved them to approach. To Tashigg's surprise, moments after they spoke with the driver, they pulled their horses to the gap between two train cars and jumped aboard, letting the poor horses dash about uncontrolled.

"Someone get those horses!" Tashigg shouted, waving toward a number of mounted men nearby. Two nodded in acknowledgement and set off. Those horses had been ridden hard, might even be winded, but they *looked* to be of good stock. Familiar, even.

"Sir!" one of the mounted men rode back with his hands on the reins of one of the abandoned horses, pulling it along behind him.

"Bring it over here," Tashigg said, stepping down from the platform. "Let's have a look at it."

"This mare's pretty far gone, sir," the mounted officer said sadly, pulling the horse up to the side of his own and offering the reins to the general.

General Tashigg took the reins with a quick nod of thanks, and ran his hands over the flanks of the panting mare. "There, there," he said soothingly. "We'll get you rested and back on your way —" he broke off as he noticed the saddle. "By the gods! This is one of Filbert's finest mares!"

"Were they dispatch riders, sir?" one of the mounted ensigns asked. "With dispatches for the king?"

"If they were," Tashigg said with a thunderous look, "they should have reported to *me* first!" He glanced at the retreating train and decided it was moving too fast and was too far to stop. He turned around to examine his assembling troops. "Never mind, let us be off!"

#

General Georgos Gergen, the general in command of the army and now in command of the two divisions about to stage an assault against the Sorian Sea Pass, gave the mage a disgruntled look as he repeated, "And *still* no word?"

"Yes, general," mage Margen replied testily, "I would have informed you *immediately* of any contact."

"I'm sure," the general muttered, his tone belying his words. *Old doddering fool probably would have forgot!* He sighed. "Until we know, we can't begin our demonstration against the enemy."

"Surely, with your numbers, general, and our magic, we should have no trouble overwhelming the Sorian forces," Margen said acerbically.

"If I believed that, mage, I would have already done so," Gergen replied. "Perhaps, given that I am King Markel's ranking soldier, you might consider that I have more training in the art of war than you."

"Oh, I'm certain of it," Margen said, making it clear how highly he valued military arts, his face just short of a sneer.

"When is the next train due?" Gergen asked idly, thinking of sending a messenger back to the king.

"I wouldn't know, I am not a mechanic," Margen sniffed.

Gergen glared at him, signalled to one of his aides who, refreshingly, came at a trot to answer his summons. "Find out when the next train is heading back to the capital. I may want to send a message to the king."

The ensign clicked his heels, glared at the mage, saluted the general, turned briskly and trotted off in pursuit of his duties.

That's how it should be done, Gergen thought to himself smugly.

"If you'll excuse me, general, I must see to my magics," Margen said with a vague nod.

"Please see that you do," Gergen said, returning the nod in dismissal. "I understand that your bangs and booms will help us in startling the enemy."

"My magic is what powers your weapons, general," Margen said with a haughty look.

"Wonderful," Gergen said without any feeling. He waved the mage away. When he was reasonably sure the old man was out of earshot, he added to himself, "That explains all the misfires, then."

#

"Your majesty, I was told that we should expect such things," first minister Mannevy told his king firmly when they got the news.

"Then we should have built more!" King Markel roared in pure fury. "How are we going to defeat Soria if our damned trains won't roll?"

"I can get mechanic Newman on the problem immediately," Mannevy offered with a wave of his hands. "He helped perfect the machines, he'll certainly know what to do."

"It just *stopped!*" Markel roared. "Right there, halfway between us and the south!"

"At first we thought it was for lack of water, then for lack of coal," Mannevy said in explanation. "Now that we've solved both lacks, we think it might be something with the engine itself." He paused for a moment, then added, "Or the boiler."

"*Think!* You *think!*" the king roared. "How come no one *knows?*"

"We're getting our best man on it, sire," Mannevy said. He glanced toward Peter Hewlitt, the spymaster to see if perhaps he would add some placating words. Hewlitt gave him a bland look and said nothing. "We knew that we were trying something new when we came up with this plan, sire. When trying new ways, errors are always possible."

"What if they find out?" Markel asked, his anger receding. "What then, eh?"

"I have heard nothing from the Sorians, sire," Peter Hewlitt spoke up soothingly. "My spies have intercepted all dispatches northward from Korin's Pass —"

"And what happened there?" Markel demanded, glaring first at Mannevy and then at Hewlitt. Neither had an answer. "Shouldn't we have *heard* something by now?"

"Make way! Make way!" a man from outside the king's chambers bellowed. "I've no time for this idiocy!"

Mannevy's brows furrowed at the interruption. He couldn't quite place the voice but it sounded familiar. The doors burst open and his confusion deepened as two dirty, bedraggled men came marching up to the throne. In unison they paused and bowed before the king. The first one lifted his head and spoke before the king gave him permission, "Sire, I have news from the east."

"Who are you?" Markel bellowed.

The man rose to his feet and bowed. "Captain Nevins, sire. I have returned from our attack on the East Pass Fort."

"You have?"

"What news do you bring us, captain?" Mannevy asked, moving to the man's side.

"The East Pass Fort is destroyed, sire," Nevins said, bowing to the king and ignoring Mannevy. "They used some new magic against us however and destroyed our ships."

"Destroyed?" King Markel asked, aghast. "How?"

"*Vengeance* with cannon fire and *Warrior* with dragon's fire," Nevins replied, glancing toward the other bedraggled man for confirmation. The other man nodded in hasty agreement.

"A dragon?" Markel repeated. His eyes narrowed as he glared at Mannevy.

"What color was the dragon, captain?" Mannevy asked with an intent expression.

"Black, black as night," Nevins replied immediately. "Although we didn't see it well as it flamed our hull to ash flying up from the ground."

"Was it the same one that attacked *Spite* on her maiden voyage?" the king demanded.

"I don't know," Nevins said with a shrug. "Perhaps."

"It wanted revenge," Markel said. He turned to Mannevy. "That fool Ford should have killed it."

"He got the wyvern, instead, sire," Mannevy reminded his ruler.

"And we know how well *that* turned out!" Markel roared. Mannevy suppressed a wince. It was true that even now, the royal airship *Spite* had not returned from its mission to kill or capture the wyvern that had been reborn.

"Sire," Captain Nevins said hurriedly, going to one knee in obeisance, "if you will give me another airship, I will guarantee that you will hear no more of this dragon."

Markel thought on that for a moment but before he could reply, spymaster Hewlitt spoke up, "And how exactly, captain, did you lose your ship?"

"The fort flew, sire," the other man spoke up, his eyes wide and frightened.

"And who are you, sir?" King Markel asked sourly.

"Tortis Borkin, sire," the man said, bowing and rising again. "I served as mage aboard the captain's ship."

Markel's eyes narrowed. "Didn't we fire you?" He turned to Mannevy. "Isn't this that apprentice that couldn't lift a ship?"

"He did more than lift a ship, sire," Nevins spoke up stoutly. The king turned his attention to him. "When *Vengeance* was destroyed because mage Tirpin could not lift it above the flying fort, Mage Borkin *jumped* our ship a hundred feet up into the sky, putting us once again above the fort." Nevins allowed himself a smug look, as he continued, "And from there we bombarded the fort as ordered and caused it to fall to its destruction."

"And how did the fort fly in the first place?" Peter Hewlitt demanded intently.

"Did the dragon lift it?" the king added.

"There were large metal slabs placed around its foundations," Mage Borkin replied thoughtfully, "and I felt there was some magic at work."

"Magic?" Mannevy asked, turning to Hewlitt and raising his eyebrows speculatively. The spymaster returned his look with a shrug. But he looked thoughtful.

"And it didn't fly as much as it floated, sire," Nevins added. "Like it was floating on the magic in the metal."

"That was my opinion, too," Borkin said.

"Mage Borkin and I are familiar with the dragon, as well as the floating forts, sire," Nevins put in hastily. "Give us a ship and nothing will stand in our way."

The king glanced to his first minister who pursed his lips before saying, "We could use both captains and mages for our airships, sire."

"And do you, mage, know how to lift an airship?" the king said to Borkin. "It seems to me you had trouble before."

"Magic and the way it works is different for each mage, sire," Borkin replied. "Mage Tirpin had different magic from mine and I could not adapt mine to his."

"Are you saying you can't?" the king asked in confusion.

"No, sire," Nevins spoke up in the young man's defense, "he's saying that he couldn't do it Tirpin's way." Nevins gave Borkin an approving nod as he continued, "He can do it *better*."

"And I know others I can teach, sire," Borkin put in quickly.

"Better, eh?" the king repeated. "And teach?" He glanced to Mannevy.

"Give us the ships, sire, we'll find the crews," Nevins implored.

"Ships?" the king repeated. "You want more than one, now?"

"I am the only captain who has fought a floating fort and a dragon, sire, and lived to report back to you," Nevins said. "I would be happy to teach others my knowledge."

"*Harbinger* and *Pace* are ready for commissioning, sire," Mannevy said in oblique support.

"I thought there were four readying completion," Nevins remarked.

"And you want them *all?*" Mannevy asked in complete surprise.

"There's one other thing," Nevins said, slowly. He glanced toward mage Borkin, then continued, "We believe that those metal supports, the ones that floated the fort, were made of *steel*, sire."

"Steel?" the king repeated, brows furrowed. He vaguely recalled that steel was important but couldn't quite remember why. He glanced to Mannevy for help.

"Steel is better for building airship engines and boilers, sire," Mannevy reminded him. "The lack of it partly explains the performance of our last two airships."

"We could take an airship, fly to the ruins and return with steel in less than four days, sire," Nevins offered. He glanced to Mannevy, adding, "Wouldn't that help in the construction of more airships?"

Mannevy stroked his goatee. After a moment he nodded. "I do believe it would," he said. "Of course I would have to check with Mechanic Newman to be certain."

The king came to a decision, waving a hand to Mannevy. "Send them to get the steel." He turned his eyes to Nevins. "Get it, get back, and then we'll see about more ships, captain."

Captain Nevins bowed, reaching out to nudge the bemused Borkin to do the same. When he rose, the king waved him off.

When they were gone, the king turned to Mannevy, "I think that could work out very well, don't you?"

Chapter Three

Imay came back into the healing hall just as Rabel bent over a hideously burnt zwerg, murmured some soothing words, and reaching a finger to the worst burn. Imay's eyes widened in wonder as she saw the burnt skin turn bright red and then back to normal as the flame was absorbed into the nail of Rabel's finger and, as his finger and hand brightened, seemed to diffuse through the rest of the man. It was then that Imay realized that Rabel was glowing brighter than the others in the room.

Imay could see that Molle, the head healer, was overwhelmed by the dragon-sworn smith's abilities. Imay grunted in agreement and the other two turned to her, expectantly.

Not seeing Ellen with her, Rabel's face fell and Imay could see how tired the man was. From all that she'd seen and heard, he deserved a day's sleep, at the very least.

"Where's Ellen?" Rabel asked.

"Lissy said she couldn't come," Imay said hurriedly. She glanced apologetically to Molle, then back to Rabel. "She said that they had to stay with Jarin."

"I wanted him, too," Rabel said pursing his lips in a frown. He started to rise, turned back to the long line of cots with burnt zwerg in them and looked — for the first time to Imay's eyes — lost.

"You taught Ellen how to do this?" Imay said, gesturing toward the now uninjured zwerg whose burns had been absorbed into Rabel's body.

Rabel nodded. "Jarin knows how to do it instinctively, being a dragon."

"He can breathe fire, so he can take fire back," Imay guessed. Rabel gave her an appraising look and nodded.

"Can all the fire-touched do this?" Imay asked. Rabel shrugged. Imay felt her heart race as she continued in a rush, "Could you teach me?"

"Princess!" Molle squeaked in surprise.

"Ellen and I are oath-sworn to Ophidian," Rabel said slowly. "I think this ability comes from him."

"Can you teach it to me?" Imay reiterated. "If I take an oath to the dragon-god?"

"My princess, this is not a good time," Molle began thoughtfully.

"I disagree," Imay cut her off. "I think this is the perfect time. Rabel is tired, Ellen and Jarin are indisposed and there are injured who need our help."

"Your mother, the queen —"

"Is not here, and I am here daughter, her heir, and her representative," Imay said. "I am old enough to speak for myself."

"I thought you were a child," Rabel said, glancing from her to Molle and back.

"I have been in the world for twenty years only, it is true," Imay said. "And a zwerg can expect to live for several hundred, so I am considered still a youngster by most." She glanced to Molle, saying, "But it is my right to declare myself of age." The healer nodded in reluctant agreement. Imay waved a hand at the injured. "These people need my help and I am their princess." She glanced to Rabel. "Your Ellen is very young, and yet she is sworn to Ophidian."

"That's true," Rabel agreed somberly. "But —"

"Princess, it's bad enough to have a dragon with our gold!" Molle declared. "You are now offering Ophidian all our riches and our kingdom."

"No," Imay declared, "I am offering him my help for his help." A slight smile flicked across her lips. "Given what I know of our friend here," she nodded toward Rabel, "and his apprentice, I rather suspect that Ophidian and I will be well-matched."

Rabel snorted, eyes dancing in amusement.

"You were going to teach us how to make dragon-steel, what makes this any different?" Imay asked him.

Rabel shook his head. "As you say, princess, it's your life." He glanced toward the healer. "Healer Molle, do you have any further objections?"

The old healer shook her head.

"If so, then I suggest you tend other patients," Rabel said, "while I lead your princess through the oath."

Molle glanced at Imay, biting her lips. "Princess?"

Imay waved her away. "Go! These people need our help and we cannot wait."

With a final nod to the princess and a reluctant glance toward Rabel, Molle moved away.

"The oath we swore to Ophidian was special," Rabel said to Imay in a low voice. "And it required blood and an image of the dragon-god."

"Does the image have to be physical?" Imay asked.

Rabel pursed his lips, then shrugged. "Can you imagine him fully?"

"Well enough," Imay said. "And if I can't the oath won't work, will it?"

"Take my hand," Rabel said. Imay grabbed his hand in hers.

"Please hurry," Imay said, gesturing toward the burn victims. "I fear they cannot wait much longer."

"No," Rabel agreed with a tired sigh. He locked his eyes with Imay. "I cannot use the same oath for you, so I'm going to have to make it up."

"I understand," Imay said. "What do I need to say?"

"I don't know," Rabel admitted with a heavy sigh. Imay gasped. He turned his eyes to meet hers. "What I swore to him was…" he paused, then continued in a different tone: "'Ophidian, I, Rabel Zebala, wielder of the dragon's fire do accept your bargain. Life given, lives guarded. Three lives I'll guard for you, even beyond death.'"

"Which lives?" Imay asked.

"Ellen, Jarin, and Krea Wymarc," Rabel said, his lips twisting as he added, "My daughter and his daughter."

"I see," Imay replied. "And the blood?"

"You must prick your finger and offer him your blood," Rabel said.

#

Ellen woke with a start and looked wildly around the darkened chamber, confused. She raised a finger and started to call forth a light — but her hand was knocked down. Her eyes widened as she saw the darkened form beide her, eyes gleaming fearfully, put her finger to her lips and whisper, "Don't wake him."

Jarin. Ellen's memories flooded back and she recalled vividly the moment the black dragon gobbled up her blue-white demon. She had two left. The last would only leave on her death.

The black dragon was snoring, hidden under a layer of gold coins in the treasury of the zwerg queen, Diam's, underground city. Next to her was Lissy, the queen's youngest daughter.

"Do you have the demon I loaned you?" Ellen said, reaching a hand toward Lissy. Lissy nodded in a quick jerk and shook her head as she grasped Ellen's demand. "I'm going to get help," Ellen assured her.

"Captain Ford?" Lissy wondered, dimly recalling the name from her memory. "Isn't he dead?"

"The one who bound them," Ellen said. "Even Ophidian was impressed."

Lissy reached into her top and pulled forth a bright, blue-white demon which she cupped quickly in her hands to reduce the glare.

Ellen took it, leaned her head down and said, "Send help." Then she threw the demon into the air.

The dragon's snores stopped and the two girls looked at each other in alarm. The blue-white demon headed toward the door, paused, and disappeared.

The two girls clutched at each other for support and waited wide-eyed while the dragon twitched under its pile of gold, twitched again — and started snoring.

The two girls sighed in unison, still holding each other tightly.

#

"I think I have it," Imay said, reaching her finger up to her mouth and biting hard. A steady drip of blood poured from the wound. "Ophidian, hear my oath. I, Imay, Princess of the Silver Earth zwerg, do offer you this bargain: for your gift of dragon's fire and dragon's healing, I swear to you to guard my people and my friends, to protect them with my life, particularly to protect, aid, and guard Ellen Ford, Rabel Zebala, Ibb the Immortal, Krea Wymarc and Jarin the dragon —"

"Accepted!" A voice spoke from nowhere. And suddenly the room was crowded with three more people.

"That was quick," Rabel said, glancing toward the dragon-god in surprise. Then his brows drew together as he added, "Who are these two?"

Ophidian ignored him, turning to Imay. "Your offer is accepted," he reached forward to her bleeding wound and light flared from his fingertip. The wound glowed brightly and the color raced up Imay's arm and into her body, causing her to glow slightly in the room. "In addition, I'll heal all these wounds, just —"

"Just what?" Rabel asked.

"Where is my son?" Ophidian said, turning his fire-red eyes on the sorcerer. "What have you done with him?"

"He's —" Rabel began easily, then stopped, turning a horrified look to Imay. "*That's* why they didn't come!"

"Who?" the new man demanded. He glanced around. "Where are we?"

"In the Silver Earth kingdom of the zwerg," Ophidian told him. He glanced back to Rabel. "Where is Jarin?"

"Underground?" the man looked like he was going to faint. "We're underground!"

Ophidian's brows creased. "And that is a problem?"

The man licked his lips nervously. "I don't do well underground."

"I'm afraid you're going to have to cope for the foreseeable future," Rabel said, toward the man with his hand extended. "I'm Rabel."

"Rabel?" The man repeated in surprise. "You're not related to Krea Wymarc are you?"

"If you're referring to the same Krea who was Krea Zebala not long ago, yes," Rabel replied.

The man pulled his hand back hastily and raised both arms, ready to cast a spell. "You can't be!"

"I am," Rabel replied, looking at the mage in surprise. "Why can't I be?"

"Krea said you were *old!*"

"I was," Rabel agreed, jerking his head toward Ophidian. "We came to an arrangement."

"He made you younger?"

"Not the first time," Ophidian added with a glance toward Rabel, his eyes lidded in secret amusement. "He swore to protect three lives with his own, even beyond death." He jerked a finger toward the woman. "Rabel, this is Annabelle. She's sworn in service to me —"

"Only for the next few days!" Annabelle said.

"— for the next *three* days," Ophidian corrected. He pointed to the man. "And this is mage Reedis, formerly of the airship *Spite* and an acquaintance of the late Captain Ford." He pointed back to Rabel. "And this man *is* Krea's father, Rabel. He's young because he took an oath —"

"*Another* oath," Rabel interjected.

"— to me," Ophidian finished.

"You did?" Reedis said giving Rabel a look of surprise. "An oath beyond death? That seems a bit difficult…"

"In fairness, he probably won't need that part," Ophidian said. "He has only to protect them to adulthood."

"Krea would be one, I imagine," Reedis said. "May I ask about the others?"

"Ellen, an urchin with great potential," Rabel replied, "now called Ellen Ford —"

"After Captain Ford?" Reedis interrupted. "Why?"

"He was the first person to help her," Rabel said. "When he died —"

"How did you know?"

"I told them," Ophidian said. "The girl had been given spy demons and she needed to understand why they were free."

"Annabelle made those," Reedis said, glancing toward his silent companion who nodded in affirmation. "And the third?"

"Jarin," Ophidian said, "my son." He glared at Rabel. "And where is he?"

"Last I heard, he was in one of the treasuries, resting on a bed of gold," Rabel replied. "Ellen and Lissy, the queen's youngest, were attending him."

"That is not all," Ophidian said angrily. He started for the door, turned back to Rabel, saying, "Well?"

"Great god, the injured?" Imay asked in a small voice.

Ophidian paused, visibly torn. He turned around and went back toward the row of burn victims. He glanced at Imay. "Are you ready to learn?"

"Yes," she said without hesitation.

"Good," Ophidian said. He pointed to the first victim. "His wounds are all over his body, you know that, don't you?"

"I do," Imay said. She knelt beside the burned man. "What do I need to do?"

"You must think of fire," Rabel said, moving back to stand behind her. "Close your eyes and imagine the tip of your finger on fire, burning brightly but not hurting." He glanced to Ophidian. The dragon-god nodded. "Do it now."

Imay took a shaky breath, closed her eyes and held up her left hand.

"It must be the hand you favor," Ophidian said.

Imay switched hands. She closed her eyes, held up her index finger and — a brilliant white light flared at the tip.

"Open your eyes," Rabel said. "Slowly."

Imay did as instructed. Her eyes widened as she saw her burning finger but her surprise faded and, intrigued, she brought the burning fingertip closer to her eyes, examining it from all angles, her mouth agape with wonder. Finally, she turned to Ophidian, "Now what?"

"Ask your teacher," Ophidian said, gesturing to Rabel.

"As you make fire, you can pull it," Rabel told her gently. "First, kill the flame in your finger."

Imay glanced at her finger, blinked, and the light went out.

"Good," Rabel said. "Now, you need to imagine the fire of the burns, the fire that made the burns. And then reach forward — but don't touch — toward the burns. Imagine the fire flowing into you, warming you and cooling the injured, making their flesh whole and unharmed."

Imay took a deep breath, looked carefully at the burns on the zwerg lying unconscious before her and gently lifted her finger toward him. In a moment, the man's body was bathed in light which coalesced into a brilliant flame. The flame raced up her finger, through her hand, her arm, and into her body. With a gasp of surprise, Imay rocked back on her heels.

"I did it!" She sat back up again and looked at the injured zwerg, his burns all gone, skin healthy. She turned to Ophidian. "Thank you."

Ophidian gave her a small nod. "Now, the others."

"I don't know if she has the strength," Rabel cautioned.

"Now is the time to find out," Imay said, moving to the next injured person.

"Sometimes you have to put your finger near the worst burns," Rabel warned.

"She did well enough," Ophidian said, "perhaps her gift is stronger than yours."

Rabel returned the dragon-god's taunt with a quirk of his lips but nothing more.

"It will go quicker if two sets of hands are helping," Ophidian said to Rabel.

"Indeed," Rabel said, stifling a yawn. "But I am at the end of my strength. I must rest."

"Oh!" Ophidian said, raising a hand and dropping it on Rabel's shoulder. "I can fix that."

Rabel gasped as the god filled him with strength, standing taller and looking a full year younger. He turned to the dragon-god, shaking his head, and said, "A little warning, next time."

"As you wish," Ophidian said. "Now, the injured?"

Between Imay and Rabel it took twenty minutes to heal the forty injured zwerg. Their bodies were bright with the retrieved energy and Imay smiled and laughed with delight as she healed the last of the wounded.

"Now," Ophidian said with a tone of great forbearance, "perhaps we can see to my son?"

"What of these two?" Rabel asked, pointing to the newcomers Ophidian had brought with him.

"They come with us," Ophidian said. "He's a mage of hot and cold, she's a witch." When he heard Imay's gasp, he added, "Rabel's a sorcerer which makes him the worst of the three."

"What am I, great god?" Imay asked in a small voice.

"Untrained," Ophidian said. "Rabel…?"

"Until we leave, I'll train you," Rabel told the princess with a poorly veiled sigh. "You have great potential, you know."

"Now, where's my son?" Ophidian repeated in a dangerous tone.

"I'll take you," Imay said, moving to the fore.

Chapter Four

Captain Nevins growled as he beckoned the young apprentice toward him. "What's your name, again?"

"Mage Marten, sir," the pimply-faced lad supplied with a pitiful attempt at a salute.

Nevins raised a hand to his hand in acknowledgement. He turned to the mechanic, another apprentice. "And your name?"

"Dalton, sir," the mechanic said. He was an older man, grizzled, grimy. He smelled, too. Mostly of coal and oil, so Nevins didn't complain. Besides, he seemed to know what he was doing. "Aldis Dalton."

"Very good, Mr. Dalton," Nevins said. "Is the ship ready?"

"The engines and propellers, sir," Dalton said. "That's all I speak to."

"And the coal? And the boiler?" Nevins prompted with a bite in his voice.

Dalton blinked. "Them, too, of course."

Nevins glared at him, waiting. The mechanic frowned, then added, "Sir."

"Good," Nevins allowed. He turned to the mage. "And the spell?"

"At your command, sir," Bill Marten replied with another botched salute.

Nevins nodded and gestured the two to their stations. He turned to the first mate, a lieutenant "on loan" from the King's Navy. His name was Walter. Nevins was keeping a stern eye on him — *Harbinger's* captain wasn't up to snuff and if Walter worked out right, Nevins would give him *Pace* and take *Harbinger* himself, bumping the bumbler down to first mate. Besides, both ships were light on crew.

Fortunately, what crew they had aside from the 'specials' — mages and mechanics — were "on loan" from the Navy. Nevins hid a bitter smile. He'd been Navy, too, not that long ago. But he could tell which way the wind was blowing — and it was blowing upwards, from ships to airships. They would be the wave of the future. Nevins snorted as he recognized his un-intended witticism — no! *Two* by Ametza! *I'm becoming quite the wit*, he thought to himself.

He went to the stern, grabbed his speaking trumpet and bellowed across to the other ship, *Harbinger*. "Ahoy, *Harbinger*! Are you ready to lift?"

"What?" a querulous voice came back to him.

"Ready, sir!" Tortis Borkin shouted above the voice of the captain.

"Very well, follow us in turn," Nevins called. He turned to his crew. "Lift ship! All hands, lift ship!"

"Lift ship, aye sir!" Lieutenant Walter called, cupping his hands to bellow forward. "Release lines forward!" He turned to the mechanic. "Prepare to deploy the propellers! Full steam!"

"Full steam, aye sir!" One of the mechanic's men called back.

"Propellers at the ready!" Dalton called back.

"Mage, give us lift!" Walter called to mage Borkin.

"Aye, sir!" Tortis Borkin called back, lifting his purple sorcerer's hat and waving it once in acknowledgement before returning it again to his head. He closed his eyes, raised his arms, and chanted his spell.

And *Pace* rose into the sky.

"Release rear lines!" Lieutenant Walter called. "Dalton, you may deploy when ready!"

"Aye, sir!"

"What speed and heading, sir?" Lieutenant Walter asked Nevins when the ship was level.

"Head to the sea, two-thirds power," Nevins said.

"Aye, sir!" Walter called back smartly. "Helmsman! Port rudder, bring us about due west."

"Due west, aye sir!" the helmsman called back.

Nevins moved forward to Lieutenant Walter, saying, "That was smartly done."

Walter beamed. "Thank you, sir!"

Nevins turned without comment heading back to the stern rails. He gazed down below and shook his head at the sight of *Harbinger*, dangling half-up, half-down just above their land dock. Someone had forgotten to order the rear lines released and the poor ship was all a-kilter, straining skywards, her propellers still un-deployed. "Mr. Walter!"

"Sir?"

"Reduce speed, and set up station just north of the palace," Nevins called back.

"Sir?" the lieutenant sounded confused.

Nevins pointed downwards. "Let us wait for our sister ship to join us."

The lieutenant gave him a surprised look, went to the side rail and peered overboard. His eyes widened in surprise as he took in the sight below him. When he straightened, his eyes were dancing with delight. He saluted Nevins and turned to bellow, "Mechanic! Reduce steam! Helm, set course for the palace. We're going to wait for *Harbinger* to join us."

"Aye sir!" came the replies.

Captain Nevins turned to the hatchway. "I'll be in my cabin," he called to the lieutenant. "Let me know when we are ready to proceed."

"Aye, sir!"

#

"Colonel, sir," Jenthen Barros said as he entered colonel Walpish's tent. He didn't salute. Walpish still abhorred the man's presence, his smell, his manners, and his tone but he could not deny the value of the man's intelligence.

"Sit," Walpish said, gesturing to the rough-hewn wooden stool next to his camp table.

"I'll stand," Barros replied, eyeing the stool and the colonel — seated in a well-built camp chair — with disdain.

"Very well," Walpish said sourly. "I've drink if you want it. Warm tea, coffee?"

"I'm doing well, sir," Barros replied.

"What have you to report?"

Barros hid a smile. *That* was his value to this cavalry colonel.

"The enemy has no knowledge of your movements," Barros said, tapping the bow slung over his shoulder with a vulpine smile.

"Surely they sent messengers?" Lieutenant Marless, sitting opposite his colonel, asked in surprise.

"Oh, about twenty or more," Barros replied with an evil leer. "And that's just the humans." He paused for that to sink in before patting his bow again. "None of them got through."

"Good," Walpish said, exchanging a quelling look with his lieutenant before turning back to the spy. "And South Pass?"

Barros shook his head. "I was told to keep here, stop messengers, until the musketeers arrive."

"But nothing coming from that way?" Marless pressed.

"You've sent scouts, what do they say?" Barros asked.

"We were just wondering if you had anything to add," Colonel Walpish said soothingly. He spread his hand over the map laid out on his table. "So far, aside from the garrison in the fort, we've met no soldiers."

"And you didn't meet them, either," Barros replied. Walpish shot him an angry look but the spy shrugged. "It was the airships that 'met' them and they all died, didn't they?"

"I believe some survivors joined the soldiers," Lieutenant Marless replied. "But our orders were clear: we were to take this town and await reinforcements."

Barros grunted: there was nothing to say.

Walpish frowned at him for a moment, and then rose. "Very well, Barros, you've been a great service." He gestured toward the cook's tent. "If you've need of any supplies, feel free."

"Thankee, sir," Barros said. He turned his head toward the armory. "It's more arrows, I need." He turned back to Walpish, smiling murderously, as he said, "Arrows and poison. It's the poison that does the job, as it were."

"I'm sure our armorer will give you all the help he has in the past," Walpish allowed, turning back to the lieutenant and dismissing the spy from his sight. "Now, Marless, we must see about sending some scouts eastward, just to extend our perimeter. And then we have to set a detail hold the town until the soldiers arrive."

"You're thinking of starting westwards, sir?"

"I am," Walpish replied. "I believe we're safe enough now to send a troop or more down the road some miles, just to keep an eye on things."

"I see, sir," Marless replied. "Shall I get Captain Lewis, sir?"

"Yes," Walpish said. "He will do excellently!"

Barros ignored the colonel just as thoroughly as the colonel now ignored him. He moved quickly to the armorer's tent, got his supplies and left the camp as silently as he'd entered. There were more things to kill. He liked killing.

#

"Gold?" General Tashigg roared. "I don't care a fig about gold! We've a war to win!"

The young ensign riding beside him wilted. "Sir, it's just that's what I'd heard, sir. About those two who left the horses."

"General Diggory and I will be talking about that, just as soon as we —" he broke off, pointing to lights in the distance. "We'll be meeting him shortly."

It had taken the better part of the day to form the division and set on the road to Korin's Pass. He expected to join the first brigade to the rest of his division, meet up with scouts from Walpish, the cavalry commander, and move immediately through the pass to secure the town of Korin's Pass.

Then he'd be ready to start his part of the trap that would destroy the Sorian army completely. After that, there would be plenty of *gold*.

The King's spymaster, Hewlitt, had sworn that the Sorians only had five divisions at the ready and most of them would be waiting for Gergen's two divisions at South Pass. Everyone *knew* that Korin's Pass was unbreachable — because of the fort that guarded it.

And that had been true. No canon shot could hope to reach the height of the fort — until airships were built that could fly *above* it and fire *down*.

213

General Tashigg smiled to himself. He knew some of the Sorian generals. They were smug and thought that, since their triumph in the Pinch, no one would dare assault them. They were about to find out that they were wrong.

#

"Captain of the guard!" a private called from the darkness. Captain Welless jerked in his cot and jumped out of it. *Now what?* "I've got someone here claiming to be General Tashigg — oh, wait! First Division approaching!"

Whew, Welless thought to himself as he raced from his tent. The rest of the division has arrived.

He caught a glimpse of a large party of officers entering the command tent and decided that he might as well rest up. *It's not as if —*

"Captain Welless!" a voice shouted. "Report to General Tashigg!"

Welless suppressed a groan and turned sharply back to his tent, gathering his helmet and sword before rushing off to the command tent.

Inside, he found Colonel Marchant, newly-promoted Major Baker, and other officers he didn't recognize all gathered around the small figure of General Tashigg.

"Captain Welless reports!" he said as he entered, saluting toward the general.

"You are the captain of the watch?" General Tashigg said, beckoning for him to approach.

"Yes, sir," Welless replied.

"And you had the watch when these… unpleasantries occured?" Tashigg asked.

"Sir?"

"I believe the general is referring to General Filbert, captain," Colonel Marchant told him.

"And his missing horses, too," General Tashigg added tartly.

"Yes sir," Welless admittedly glumly.

General Tashigg beckoned him forward with a wave of his fingers and gestured toward a seat opposite him. He gave the captain a probing look then turned to the rest of the room. "Gentlemen, you may leave."

"Sir?"

"The captain and I are going to have a long talk," General Tashigg said frostily. "We do not require company."

Reluctantly the others left, Colonel Marchant lingering long enough to give Welless a warning look.

When they were all gone, General Tashigg heaved a deep sigh and turned to the luckless captain. "If you ever repeat this, I'll break down to private," the general warned.

"Sir?"

"General Filbert was an ass, and I'm neither surprised he tried the stunt I've heard about or got his justly deserved reward," General Tashigg told the bewildered captain quickly. "But I want to know *everything* you can recall about the events up to and after his demise."

"Sir?"

"Off the record, captain," the general affirmed. "Just talk, answer my questions, and you'll do fine."

"Very well, sir," Welless replied slowly. "Where would you like me to start?"

"Tell me when you first had difficulties on your watch," the general said, leaning back in his chair and tenting his hands attentively. "Don't leave out any detail. There will be reports to write, and I want to know where to start."

Chapter Five

"My orders are no one is to enter," Dermon, the injured zwerg guard insisted staunchly when Imay asked him to open the door. Imay opened her mouth to protest but he cut her off. "Miss Lissy told me herself. No one can counter that order, except the queen."

"How about a god?" Ophidian asked, raising his claws up to his chest and buffing them idly as he leaned against the corridor in the back of the group.

"Well," Dermon allowed, "I suppose I'd *have* to defer to a god but, really, do you expect Geros or Granna to come give me orders?"

"No," Ophidian replied, stepping forward so that Dermon could get a good look at his face. "I'm pretty sure I can do it myself."

Dermon's eyes bugged out of his head and he dropped his sword before dropping to his knees. "God Ophidian! I didn't know — I'm terribly —"

"Just open the door, please," Ophidian said, gesturing for the guard to rise. "I want to see my son."

Dermon rose, grabbed the keys but paused and turned back. "I'm not sure that's wise, your greatness."

"What?"

"Miss Lissy and her friend seemed very firm that they were the only ones who could stay with him," Dermon went on quickly. "He's in his dragon form —"

"Well, he's in a room full of gold," Imay said, "isn't that the sort of thing that dragons adore?"

"Ellen!" Rabel called through the doorway. "Ophidian is here! We need to speak with Jarin."

After a moment, they heard the sounds of feet dislodging coins and other trinkets. The feet stopped just before the door. Her voice muffled by the thick door, Ellen said with a sniffle, "I don't think you can."

"Oh," Ophidian said. He turned to Rabel with a look that combined anger and sorrow. After a moment he turned back to the door. "Are you going to be all right?"

"He swore he would never harm me," Ellen said softly. "And I think he loves Lissy the same way."

"We will be back," Ophidian said, gesturing to the others to follow him. He turned his head back to Dermon, ordering, "No one enters or leaves that room."

"The queen —"

"No one," Ophidian said, his voice full of menace.

"As you say," Dermon replied.

\#

"Is my sister in danger?" Imay asked as they walked back down the corridor.

"We all are," Rabel said. He turned his head toward Ophidian. "They were coming for me."

Ophidian his head twitched in the merest nod.

"We must find my mother," Imay declared. "She has to be warned."

"Yes," Ophidian agreed. "Please take us to her."

They found her just outside the infirmary, consulting with Molle and Granno. Another zwerg was with them, dressed for combat, looking grimey, injured, and sorrowful.

"This is Colonel Kavim," Diam said, waving a hand to introduce him to the rest. She raised an eyebrow as she took in the others. "God Ophidian, you grace our halls."

"I do," Ophidian agreed. "My son is in your treasury and one of my oath-sworn and your youngest are refusing entry."

"What?" Diam exclaimed. "Great god, I cannot understand —"

"I can," Ophidian cut through her nascent apology. He waved a hand toward the others. "These are mage Reedis, formerly of the airship *Spite*, and the witch, Annabelle, also from same."

Diam nodded warily to the newcomers. Reedis bowed deeply and Annabelle gave the queen a deep, respectful curtsy.

"Are they also your oath-sworn, great god?" Diam asked.

"Annabelle is," Ophidian allowed. He gave Reedis a measuring look. "The mage has not declared himself one way or the other."

"Although I *am* most interested in why I'm here," Reedis told the god. He nodded toward Annabelle. "I understand that Annabelle owes you service but —"

"Consider it a courtesy," Ophidian cut across him with a warning tone. "How else would you have returned from such a great distance?"

"Where did you come from?" Diam asked with sudden interest, glancing between Reedis and Annabelle.

"They came from the bitter north," Ophidian answered with a tone of finality, his eyes briefly catching those of Reedis in warning.

Reedis swallowed quickly and nodded. "As the dragon-god says."

"Indeed," Diam agreed, her eyes bright. She swayed on her feet.

"Ophidian, the queen has suffered several long and tiring days," Rabel warned.

"Perhaps we should find a better place to converse," Ophidian allowed. "One with food."

"My office is at your disposal," Molle said to the queen. She added, "Although it might be cramped."

"Perhaps the barracks?" Kavim suggested.

"I am a queen," Diam replied haughtily, "I have a court and a throne."

"Does it have a table and chairs for others?" Ophidian asked smugly.

"I keep a council room next door," Diam replied quickly. "It is well suited to consultations."

"Then, by all means, let us retire there," Ophidian allowed. "We have much to speak about."

#

Diam left Colonel Kavim go about his duties and gave her thanks to Molle and Rabel for their efforts. She gave Imay a thoughtful look, trying to determine what was different about her daughter but was too tired and too worried to tackle the issue before they were assembled in the council room.

Servants brought in two trolleys loaded with a hastily assembled assortment of sustenance: cold meats, breads, fruits, pastries, tea, and coffee.

There was a long silence while everyone filled plates and found seats. Ophidian delighted the others by acquiring several large slices of meat and roasting them with his breath.

Imay turned to Rabel and asked in a whisper, "Can I learn to do that?"

Rabel grinned at her.

Diam noticed the byplay from where she sat at the head of the table and inquired acerbically, "Daughter, what were you joking about with our friend?"

Imay blushed bright red and ducked her head, not willing to meet her mother's eyes.

"Please, your majesty, let us eat first, and then we'll answer all questions," Ophidian implored.

"As you wish, god Ophidian," Diam replied with a tilt of her head. But she kept her eyes on Rabel and Imay whenever she could.

Plates emptied, were refilled, cups were topped off, and finally everyone was sated.

Ophidian coughed politely and all eyes turned to him. "Queen Diam, thank you for your hospitality," he said. He gestured toward Reedis and Annabelle. "I thank you for allowing me to bring guests, uninvited into your underground kingdom."

Beside the queen, Granno frowned darkly.

Ophidian noticed and said to him, "I would only have done this under the direst of circumstances."

"Worse than an invasion by humans?" Granno asked.

"*I* think so," the dragon-god replied. He glanced to Diam. "Please, has my son been any help to you?"

"Yes," Diam replied, her eyes clearly showing her surprise at the question and the rapid calculations that it inspired. "In fact, all four have been most helpful."

"I am glad," Ophidian replied. He sighed and dropped his eyes in a manner most uncharacteristic of the always-cocky dragon god. "Jarin is special to me."

Rabel glanced at him and then away.

"All my children are special to me," Ophidian continued. "But some manage to find a special place in my affections."

"I understand," Diam said quietly. "I feel the same about my girls." She glanced sharply toward Imay. "I would be most upset if anything were to affect them unexpectedly."

"Imay asked for the gift of burn healing," Rabel spoke up, meeting Diam's eyes directly. He glanced toward Ophidian who was watching him with a smoldering look. "Ophidian has accepted her oath." He tapped Imay's shoulder. "Your daughter saved half the burn victims in your infirmary." Imay turned her eyes toward her mother. "She is going to be a great healer."

"She has the gift of fire," Ophidian agreed. "Healing, burning…" he met Diam's eyes firmly as he continued, "steel-making."

"You took Ophidian's oath?" Diam demanded of her eldest daughter.

"I did," Imay told her, raising her chin high. "Our people were dying. Rabel was at his last strength —"

"He looks fine now!" Diam interjected.

"Ophidian," Rabel explained, cocking his head toward the dragon-god.

"I asked for this, mother," Imay persisted. "And I'm glad I did."

"You are my daughter, my subject —"

"I am a princess of the realm," Imay interjected. "Our people were in danger, dying. I did what I felt was right."

Diam regarded her eldest daughter for a long moment, speechless. A tear slid down her cheek. She wiped it away and nodded. She turned her gaze toward Ophidian and then to Rabel.

"You approved?" she asked them.

"Yes," Rabel said. "She has a gift, your majesty." He allowed himself a wry smile. "Along with your… determination… she has all the other gifts you gave her."

"And, god Ophidian, what is it you demand in return?" Diam asked, glaring at her daughter. "All our gold? Our treasures?"

"I swore this, mother," Imay said. "'I, Imay, Princess of the Silver Earth zwerg, do offer you this bargain: for your gift of dragon's fire and dragon's healing, I swear to you to guard my people and my friends, to protect them with my life, particularly to protect, aid, and guard Ellen Ford, Rabel Zebala, Ibb the Immortal, Krea Wymarc, and Jarin the dragon.'"

"And I accepted," Ophidian said. He cocked his head toward Diam. "Although, if you wish, your majesty, I may consider a different bargain."

Diam leaned back in her chair and laughed. Ophidian gave her a surprised look. Beside her, Granno looked from his queen to the dragon-god back in alarm, uncertain what to do. Diam waved his worries aside and recovered. "Imay, my first-born, I am so proud of you!" she said to her daughter. She glanced down the table to Ophidian. "I am pleased, dragon-god, that you will take my daughter under your protection."

Ophidian gave her a slow nod. "The gifts that Geros has granted my oath-sworn have been reciprocated with your daughter."

"Geros gave his gifts to three of yours," Diam observed sharply.

Ophidian accepted her observation with a slight nod of his head. "I would be happy to extend the same to your other daughter and any other of your subjects if you so desire."

"I shall consider this kind offer," Diam said politically. Ophidian lidded his eyes in acknowledgement. She took a breath to focus herself and then said, "But, I gather, you also accepted my daughter's oath as a way to gain access to my kingdom."

Ophidian nodded.

"Why?" Diam asked. "Is this connected with your son, Jarin?"

"He's dead, isn't he?" Reedis said, lifting his eyes up from where he sat, opposite Ophidian, to gaze at the dragon-god directly. "He never had a second name."

Ophidian nodded slowly. He closed his eyes and said, "All dragons were formed from drops of my blood. Wyverns come from my tears." He took a deep breath and opened his eyes, meeting and holding Reedis' eyes with his. "There was a war. Long, long ago. Lost to the memory of men. Perhaps even before men could write. It doesn't matter. I was wounded, cut with many cuts.

"When I recovered, I discovered that my blood had made dragons, and my tears, wyverns," Ophidian continued. "I tracked down my children born in this manner but I could not track them all. The ones I found had all found souls to twin with, perhaps for safety or perhaps because it filled the void in them that I had left, I don't know. I only knew of so many."

"Like Wymarc?" Rabel asked. The dragon-god nodded.

"She was one of the first I discovered," Ophidian allowed. He smiled at some distant memory. "She was not the last."

"Jarin was," Reedis guessed. Ophidian gave him a piercing look but nodded.

"We discovered him in the frozen wastes, like your friend, Pallas," Ophidian replied. "I took him —" he paused, continuing "— I took him to a place some of you know."

Annabelle and Reedis exchanged looks.

"Don't say it," Ophidian told them warningly. He waited until he caught their agreement, then continued, "There was a child there. The dragon needed a twin soul. The child was near death. They bound to each other."

"But the child died," Rabel guessed. "He died and Jarin has been alone for…" his brows creased and he turned to Ophidian. "… how long, now?"

"I sent him with Wymarc," Ophidian said obliquely.

"You sent him to me," Rabel said, his expression bleak. "You wanted me to twin with a dragon?"

"You are more than worthy," Ophidian said.

"What about *my* daughter?" Rabel demanded angrily, jumping out of his chair.

In a pained voice, Ophidian replied, "Forgive me. I hadn't thought… I was desperate."

Rabel took a deep breath and met the dragon-god's eyes. He sat back down with a sigh, raising a hand toward Ophidian. "You thought of your son."

"I think of your daughter now, too," Ophidian allowed. "I learned a lesson."

"But—" Annabelle glanced over to the dragon-god "— Jarin is now like Pallas?"

Ophidian gave the barest nod of his head.

"And if we cannot help him?" Rabel asked. He frowned, turning to Annabelle. "Who is Pallas?"

"Another one of Ophidian's get," Reedis replied. He glanced toward Rabel, his lips twisting into a smile, "Do you recall Crown Prince Nestor?"

"That fool!" Rabel roared. "What of him? Did he outlive Captain Ford?"

"Very much so," Annabelle said. She made a face. "And you might not think him so foolish these days."

"Indeed," Ophidian agreed, turning to Rabel, "even *I* was surprised by his actions."

Rabel raised an eyebrow in response: the dragon-god had lived a very long time — surprising him was rare.

Annabelle glared at the dragon-god as she guessed his plan. "You want one of *us* to twin with Jarin?"

"And live forever," Ophidian offered. "Ellen, Imay, Rabel, mage Reedis, and Annabelle are all very suitable candidates."

"Captain *Ford* was a suitable candidate," Reedis muttered darkly.

"Was?" Diam said, glancing to the others. "And what happened to him?"

"Pallas was angry and hurt," Annabelle said defensively.

"She ate him," Reedis explained, using his hands to illustrate jaws snapping shut. He shook his head. "Took two bites."

"Perhaps, mage," Ophidian said, his eyes glaring, "it would be best if you were quiet."

Reedis gave him a look of alarm and snapped his mouth shut.

"Actually," Annabelle said, "I think that everyone should know what they're getting into."

"Ellen is too young," Rabel said. He pursed his lips and glanced at Imay.

"I have obtained my majority," the zwerg princess told him levelly. She nodded to Ophidian. "What must we do?"

"Jarin is male, is he not?" Queen Diam said, glancing to her daughter.

"Pallas is female and it didn't stop her twinning with Nestor," Annabelle said brightly.

"Gender is not an issue," Ophidian said. "In most instances, the difference proves advantageous to both."

"Should I make another love potion?" Annabelle asked the dragon-god. Ophidian shook his head. "Why not?"

"Let us go see my son first," Ophidian said, rising from his chair.

"Ophidian," Queen Diam remained seating. The dragon-god turned back to her. "What if you can't find a twin soul for him?"

"In time, I am sure that he will be united," Ophidian said slowly. He cocked an eyebrow. "Perhaps he can stay in your treasury until then?"

"My treasury will be moving shortly," Diam said. Beside her, Granno sounded surprised. She turned to him, saying, "He's a god, Granno. He'll figure it out."

Ophidian's eyes lit with some hidden amusement but he nodded sternly to the zwerg guard. With a nod to the queen, Ophidian headed for the door, expecting that the others would follow him.

"You know," Reedis called calmly from his chair at the table, "I'm not sworn to you."

Ophidian nodded and spoke, without turning his head. "You're a mage of hot and cold."

Reedis acknowledged this with a quick nod and appreciative smile. As Ophidian and the others exited, his smile grew slack and then an expression of alarm overtook his face. He jumped up and raced to join the others, elbowing them aside until he was just behind Ophidian.

"Glad to see that you can think," Ophidian muttered as he pressed on toward the treasury.

Chapter Six

"Set course nor'-nor'-east," Captain Nevins told the helmsman as *Harbinger* rose above the rooftops of Kingsford at the fall of night two days after her maiden voyage.

"Nor'-nor'-east, aye, sir," the helmsman repeated.

"What speed, sir?"

"One third power, if you please," Nevins told the mechanic, Dalton, whom he'd pilfered from *Pace* when he'd switched commands after proving that the old Navy captain was a complete incompetent. He smiled briefly as he turned to the taffrail, removed his cocked hat and waved it to the ship following behind.

Captain Walter strode to the bow, removed his hat and waved it back in reply. The former lieutenant was more than grateful for his promotion and, being also competent, was a welcome addition to Nevins' little fleet.

Besides, Nevins thought to himself, *with him there by my hand, he'll not question my orders.*

"Mage Borkin," Nevins called softly in the night air. A rush of feet brought the young mage into his sight. "Is everything in order?"

"Yes sir," Tortis Borkin said with a salute that nearly knocked his brimless sorcerer's hat off his head.

Nevins lowered his voice. "And... the men?"

"Ready when you are, sir," Borkin replied in the same low voice.

"And they've been getting their drink?" Nevins asked with hooded eyes. "I wouldn't want anything untoward to happen to them before we complete our mission."

"Watered and fed as you requested, sir," Borkin replied. "And I've had them prepare a special part of the hold and spelled it with alarms and charms."

"Very good," Nevins said, allowing his lips to curve upwards. "It will take us a day or more to reach our destination."

"And then, sir?"

"*Pace* will begin collecting the dragon-steel while we undertake our own... investigations," Nevins told him.

"Half the men are miners, sir," Borkin told him, "just as you requested."

"We'll draw powder and shot as needed," Nevins said. "I don't doubt we'll have to blast our way in."

Mage Borkin frowned. "And then, sir? The zwerg won't like us taking their gold."

"I doubt they can fly," Nevins said.

"It'll take a lot of gold to satisfy a dozen men, sir," Borkin said uneasily. "Maybe more than I can lift."

"Then it is just as well that I only need you to lift enough for two," Nevins told him. He pointed to the mage and himself.

"And the others?"

"Just see that they're fed their drink regularly," Nevins told him. "Leave the rest to me."

#

"Make way, make way!" the guard bellowed. "All bow before his majesty! Bow before King Wendel, Prince of the Pinch, ruler of the rightful kingdom of Soria, and mayor of Sarskar by the grace of the gods!"

The mob moved out of the way or were trampled as the king's guard broke way for the royal presence.

"Ruling the capital seems awfully complicated if you ask me," Queen Rassa said as she rode side by side with her young king. Wendel inclined his head towards hers. "Why not let Sarsal take that burden off your hands?"

Wendel frowned in thought and shrugged. "He's young, why add to his burdens?"

"He'll be king someday, as you promised," Rassa replied. "Why not let him have a taste of power now?"

Wendel waved a hand at her in acknowledgement. "I'll consider it."

"That's all I ask, dear," Queen Rassa purred in response. She knew that she had only to ask three or four more times and Sarsal would rule the capital. She eyed Wendel fondly, wondering if the King had any inkling of the doom that would soon befall him. "That's all I ask."

"Very well," Wendel replied. They entered the courtyard of the palace and drew to a halt. Wendel jumped down from his mount, tossed the reins to his squire and turned to face his queen. "I'm very sorry, but I am going to be stuck with the generals this afternoon."

"Oh, dear!"

"Will you cope?" Wendel asked solicitously.

"I worry about you more than I," Queen Rassa replied easily. "After all, heavy hangs the head that wears the crown."

Wendel smiled up at her. "It is a crown I am glad to wear as it makes me your king."

"Always," Rassa swore. She waved a hand. "Go! Seeing you return will lighten my heart!"

Wendel bowed to her, turned on his heel and strode quickly up the stairs to the castle proper, certain to complete his meeting with all the haste that a randy young lover could compel.

Rassa smiled until he was out of her sight, then she dropped her reins and called to the servants below her. "Someone help me down!"

#

Wendel's spymaster met him outside the great hall.

"I'm worried about the border, sire," the man said. He was the second to hold the post in the past year — the other had tediously implied that Queen Rassa might not love the king as much as he was *certain* she did and so had been replaced. The one before that... well, Rassa was certain that he was in league with those loyal to the old king... so he went, too. He was a good actor, too: he pled his innocence all the way to the point where the executioner separated his head from his body.

Wendel had grown up in the Pinch: the open valley between the mountains of the three kingdoms. The Pinch was the heart of all rootlessness, treachery, and betrayal. He knew how such things worked. When he met Rassa it was to discover that she was not only above such things but so pure of heart that he just *had* to free her from horrid old Sorgal. Besides, the king was not a good fighter and Wendel had no respect for those who couldn't fight.

So, with Rassa's fervent urging, Wendel found a way to kill the king and make it look like some of the villains of the Pinch had been responsible. Queen Rassa, in her grief, had begged him to take the throne. And so now Wendel was King of all Soria. And he had plans.

Plans that did not include getting tied up with boring spies and generals. Plans that had more to do with ensuring the royal line. Or, at least, attempting to continue the royal line. Sarsal was a stand-in until he and Rassa could create a better prince. He smiled to himself as he considered how he might ensure such a creation later that evening.

"Which border?" Wendel asked testily. "Aside from the Pinch, which *I* rule, all our other borders are mountain passes and our neighbors too small and fearful of our might and prowess."

"I have heard nothing from the south for nearly a week now, sire," the spy told him solemnly.

"What?" Wendel roared. "You are complaining when no one gives you *work?*" *Drat, what* was *the man's name again?* Wendel thought in irritation. *Something vital. And trying. Trystan Vitel, that was it!* "Spymaster Vitel, I don't know about you but when I have a chance to relax, I take it." He peered down at the thin, nervous man. "And if I were you, I'd definitely take any chance to look after my health."

"Sire, you are too kind," Spymaster Vitel returned smoothly. "And it is in the interest of my health that I bring this matter to you."

"Which matter?"

"The matter of the south, sire," Vitel said. "We usually get messages once a day, particularly from Korin's Pass."

"Korin's Pass?" Wendel frowned trying to recall where it was. He was very intimate with the tumbled geography of the hills and mountains around the Pinch and he was becoming used to the streets of hill-high Sarskar but the rest of the kingdom was still a bit of a blur and a bore to him. "Don't we have guards at the Pass?"

"Not only guards but the East Pass Fort, sire," Vitel assured him, politely filling in the gaps in the king's knowledge. "Captain Berold is constantly in communication, as is the mayor of the village of the same name."

"What, there's a village named East Pass Fort?"

"No, sire," Vitel replied easily. "There is a village named Korin's Pass. It's on our side of the pass and we have a customs patrol there to tax any goods coming into the kingdom."

"Good," Wendel said. He turned toward the doors of the great hall. "Now, if you'll excuse me, my generals await."

"That's why I wanted to talk to you, sire," Vitel pressed.

"Well, you have, thank you very much," Wendel replied, stepping past him and into the room where several generals looked up with interest. Wendel shut the door firmly and stepped down into the room. "Pardon me, generals, but there was a man who had to talk with me." They all dutifully rose as he moved to the head of the table and took his seat. "I hope this won't take long."

General Armand, who sat at his right, glared at the other generals in warning before turning to the king. "I'm sure we can expedite, sire."

"Excellent!" Wendel said, beaming. He nodded to his senior general. "So, what news?"

"I'm afraid we're not getting much news from the South Pass, sire," General Armand spoke quickly. "I think that Vitel has informed you of *his* concerns regarding Korin's Pass—"

"He said something about it, yes," King Wendel said with a frown. He tried to recall the conversation but was distracted by the thought of his queen. Rassa would be *so* pleased to see him. She always said so. He shook himself back to his duties. "This South Pass, where is it?"

#

"You look troubled," Crown Prince Sarsal said as he spotted the spymaster loitering outside the grand hall. "What is it, my friend?"

"Sire," Spymaster Vitel said, giving the crown prince a quick bow. He glanced toward the doors of the grand hall and back to the prince. "I really need to tell the king —"

"I am his heir, I can speak with him," Sarsal said quickly. He gave the spy a conspiratorial smile. "Sometimes I think our liege is perhaps too happy to have my mother's affections to pay attention to much else."

"He does seem… very attached," Vitel said diplomatically. "But I worry…"

"About what?" Sarsal said, moving to the spy and gesturing for them to walk together. "Tell me your concerns and I'll relay them to our lord, you have my word."

"Well…" Vitel began hesitantly. "If you insist, my prince."

"I insist," Sarsal assured him with a quick smile. "Now, tell me what is gnawing at you so?"

#

"So, Baker, can you handle it?" Colonel Marchant asked his newest battalion commander as they prepared to march through the five-mile stretch known as Korin's Pass the next day.

"Yes, sir," Major Baker replied curtly. "My men are to act as skirmishers, moving forward as swiftly as possible and masking any opposition."

"And we don't expect any opposition," Colonel Marchant said. "Unless the zwerg attack us."

"Of course, sir," Major Baker said, finding nothing else to say.

Colonel Marchant clapped him on the shoulder. "Good man, you're to be the eyes and ears of the division. Don't fail us."

"Of course not, sir," Major Baker replied. He nodded toward his officers and, with a final salute, turned to join them.

Colonel Marchant and his staff watched while the depleted battalion formed up and moved off quickly, their ranks oddly depleted by the General Filbert's treasonous debacle.

He turned to the troops forming behind him and bellowed, "The First Brigade will advance! At the rout step, march!"

Further in the distance, he heard orders relayed and the bugles of the other two brigades calling them to formation and on to the march.

The First Division was moving through Korin's Pass. They would be through and throwing a hasty fortification around the village of the same name before evening.

And then, if all went well, they'd march west. Onto the Sorian Army's rear.

If First Brigade did as well as he expected, Colonel Marchant could soon be General Marchant. He nodded to his aides, mounted his horse and started it forward at a slow walk. Behind him, the rest of the division moved out.

#

"Even if you haven't heard anything, what could happen?" Prince Sarsal asked spymaster Vitel as they sat in his small day chamber, sipping tea.

Vitel frowned. "Normally, my prince, nothing."

"Normally?"

"I'm concerned about recent developments my spies have reported from Kingsland," Vitel said.

"Kingsland is a small kingdom with a small army," Sarsal said. "What could it do against our armies?"

"Their mages are good and they've been working on some new projects," Vitel said slowly. The prince waved him on with an encouraging hand. "You may not have heard but they've developed some method of moving things with steam."

"I've heard about their railways," Sarsal said with a nod. "They bring goods between their capital and the border at South Pass."

"And, recently, to their side of Korin's Pass," Vitel told him.

Sarsal's eyebrows rose in surprise, then he shrugged. "Those are our two most common trading places, it would make sense to speed up commerce."

"Indeed," Vitel agreed. "And I've been urging the king to consider doing the same with Soria."

"Build these steam tractors?"

"They call them locomotives," Vitel said with a sniff. "They run on iron rails and can haul many carriages behind them at the same time." He made a face. "It is most efficient and far more economic than carrying goods by road." He paused a moment, in thought. "And, I think, even more beneficial to commerce than carrying goods by sea."

"Really?" Sarsal seemed impressed.

"A while back King Markel asked if Soria was interested in acquiring 'rail lines' of our own, perhaps even linking ours with his," Vitel said.

"They are tracks of metal, are they not?"

Vitel nodded.

"So it would not be difficult to destroy one of these lines if the need arose," Sarsal guessed. Vitel nodded again, this time, grudgingly. "So why did not our king accept Markel's offer? Surely it makes sense to let them do the work for us."

Vitel drew breath, then paused. "I had not considered this, my prince."

"But you were worried about these 'locomotives' and Markel's army?" Vitel nodded in agreement. Sarsal frowned. "Why?"

"It occurred to me that goods can include soldiers," Vitel replied. "If Markel used his locomotives to move his army to our borders quickly, he might gain some surprise."

"He might," Sarsal agreed slowly. "But our army is stronger, why would that matter?"

"Our army is spread out and would take time to gather," Vitel said. "We have two full divisions at the South Pass, it's true, but only the garrison in the fort to guard Korin's Pass —" Vitel gasped, eyes going wide. "And we haven't heard from them in nearly a week!" He jumped from his chair and turned to the door.

"Where are you going?" Sarsal demanded imperiously.

"I must warn the king!" Vitel cried, moving quickly. "Kingsland may be attacking!"

"No," Sarsal said, rising from his chair and moving quickly, drawing his belt knife and grabbing for the spymaster's shoulder. He spun the surprised man quickly and struck with his knife — once, twice, three times. Vitel had no time to defend himself. As the blood spurted from the wounds in his throat and chest, his vision darkened and the last words he heard were from the prince, "I can't have you doing that."

Sarsal eyed the bloody mess with a frown, flicking the dead spy's leg with his foot to be certain. He leaned down and drew the spy's knife from its sheath. He smelled it quickly to determine if it was poisoned. Satisfied that it wasn't, he took a deep breath and ripped the knife across his chest, tearing his silk shirt and drawing a long line of blood to drip down his chest. He knelt and placed the knife in Vitel's dead hand, dropped his knife artfully beside the body, drew a deep breath and roared, "Guards, guards! I've been attacked!"

As he heard the alarm spread, he looked down at the dead spy and told the corpse venomously, "You're lucky I only killed you. You cost me my favorite shirt."

Chapter Seven

Ophidian and the others were out of sight, their footsteps faded to silence before Queen Diam turned to Granno, her trusted aid, general, and friend.

"Would the kingdom follow a dragon?" she asked him in a small voice.

"The kingdom would follow Imay, your majesty," Granno assured her. He saw the queen's distraught look and added, "She is your daughter and she is more than a match for an immature dragon."

Diam snorted. "I suppose." She sniffed, before adding, "She took an oath to Ophidian."

"*That*, I think, was masterful," Granno said. Queen Diam nodded in agreement. Then she shook herself.

"Back to work," she said sternly. "How quickly can we close the old entrances?"

"I've got crews working now, your majesty," Granno told her. "But we have many entrances to close and new ones to open. For the moment we can only close the old ones for a short span."

"Good," Diam said decisively. "We might need them again. Remember, we must always have four openings."

"I remember, your majesty," Granno replied gravely. "Does the new work count?"

"No," Diam said. "Our escape must be to the air." She gave him a grim smile. "Too many sky-touchers think that we can only live underground. Our safety has always been to come above ground."

Granno nodded in agreement, adding slyly, "And remind them of their errors."

Diam smiled fiercely. "We should keep the rails up near the entrances, just in case," Diam said. "And have a company at the ready."

"Already done, your majesty," Granno said with a nod.

"Excellent!" Diam said, her eyes cutting to the door.

"Your majesty," Granno said with an amused look, "I think the kingdom's affairs can wait while you check on your treasury."

Diam was out the door before he finished speaking. Chuckling, Granno rose and followed.

#

"So what is our plan, great god?" Reedis asked as they once again entered the corridor toward the locked treasury. Ophidian turned to glare at him with red eyes. Reedis sighed. "So… no plan, as before."

"Reedis," Annabelle said in a warning tone, shaking her head. "He can kill you."

"Only once," Reedis said.

"Really?" Ophidian asked him silkily. "Are you certain of that?"

Reedis' face went white. He gulped. "It's just that — god Ophidian — I always work better with a plan."

"How about this?" Rabel said. "We do our best. No one dies."

"That sounds more like a wish than a plan," Ophidian remarked.

"It was the best I could do on such short notice," Rabel allowed. After a moment, he continued, "If anything happens to me, please revive Ibb."

"The metal man?" Ophidian said, cocking his head. "Who else has the knowledge?"

"I believe he might have been training an apprentice," Rabel said.

"Lyric?" Annabelle and Reedis said in unison. "The one who stole Krea?"

"*Stole* Krea?" Rabel repeated, turning his gaze back to the dragon-god.

"It didn't last," Ophidian said with a wave of his fingers. "But if she was the one he was training, she'll not be available any time soon."

"She stole a *kitsune* and fled," Reedis said.

Rabel glanced toward him. "I'd like to learn all about this."

"Later," Ophidian said. They halted in front of the treasury and the nervous guard, Dermon. "For the moment, we have a different issue."

"Actually," Rabel said slowly, "perhaps not."

"My son is in danger," Ophidian said warningly.

"I know," Rabel said. "But if something happens to me, there is no one who has the knowledge to restore Ibb."

Ophidian's jaw worked as he considered this. Finally, he said, "What is your plan? Remember that there are two girls — humans —"

"One human, one zwerg," Annabelle corrected. Ophidian glared at her. She shrugged it off. "Just wanted to be accurate, especially as one of them is a princess and all."

"Are you done?" Ophidian demanded.

"Well," Anabelle said slowly, "they're girls, right?" The dragon-god nodded, fighting to keep his temper in check. "So, like all girls, they can't stay in that room forever, can they?"

"And they've been in there for a while," Rabel said in agreement. "They'll be getting hungry and they'll need —"

"A rest break," Reedis said, glancing to Ophidian who accepted the reality with ill grace. Reedis turned to Rabel. "That puts a limit on how much longer we can leave them unrelieved."

"Can you fix Ibb?" Rabel said, looking at Ophidian. "You're the god of fire and changes."

"And tricks," Annabelle added with feeling.

"I cannot fix Ibb," Ophidian said. "Even with the zwerg, even with Geros, I cannot fix Ibb."

"So, we now know that we can't allow Rabel to die," Annabelle said.

"I like the plan where no one dies," Reedis said in a small voice.

"Ophidian," Rabel said, moving around the zwerg guard, "open the door."

Dermon, the zwerg guard looked from Rabel to Ophidian and back again before, pulling the key out of his pocket and passing it to the black-haired smith.

Rabel nodded in thanks, put the key in the lock and turned it quickly.

It made a loud noise. Beyond it, they could hear the sounds of coins and treasures spilling and moving in the treasury. From the amount, Rabel had no doubt that the major contributor was Jarin, in dragon form.

Rabel turned back to Ophidian, gesturing grandly toward the door. "You're his father."

Fast moving footsteps approached around the corner and they all paused to see who owned them. It was Diam and Granno.

"You're going in?" the queen of the zwerg asked. She raised an eyebrow as she saw Imay. "All of you?"

"We're sworn to Ophidian," Imay said.

"Well, not *all* of us," Reedis said, pointing at himself. "Some of us were drafted."

"I rather imagine that Ophidian will find some suitable reward for your services," Granno remarked.

"The last reward was bringing me *here*," Reedis grumbled.

"See?" Rabel said. "You are enjoying the benevolence of the great god."

"Come on," Ophidian said, pushing the door open. He glanced to Diam. "Except you."

Rabel was the first through, followed quickly by Imay, then Annabelle who tugged Reedis along after her.

"Ellen, how is he?" Rabel called softly as he spied the young girl, raising her head from under a mound of gold coins.

A gout of flame answered him. Ophidian moved in front of the smith and waved the flames into the ground.

"Not well," Ellen said, moving hastily away from the larger mound which contained the dragon.

"He is confused and in pain," Annabelle said, sounding concerned.

"Jarin, what can we do to help?" Imay asked, moving up to stand to the left side of Ophidian. "Are you in pain?"

The dragon replied with a piercing moan of despair.

"I'm sorry, my son," Ophidian said, moving forward. "I didn't know."

"They got here as soon as they could," Rabel said, moving up to stand on Ophidian's right side.

"Mother!" Lissy cried, rushing out from under a pile of coin and treasure.

The dragon bellowed in terror and rage and opened its mouth —

"No!" Reedis shouted, racing forward to bat the dragon on its snout. "We do *not* harm children!"

Jarin's head reared back in surprise. His eyes narrowed at the small human in front of him. He snapped his jaws, swallowing Reedis whole in one blinding motion.

The others were shocked to silence. Annabelle found breath to sob, her hand going to her mouth. Ophidian looked imploringly to Rabel who stared, wide-eyed at the black dragon, unable to speak.

And then the dragon disappeared. It collapsed on itself in a flash of white light which coalesced down and down, darker and darker, becoming a solid —

"Well, I showed him," Reedis said proudly, turning back to the others. "He only needed to be told — he didn't mean any harm…" He broke off as he caught their expressions. "What are you all looking at?"

"Reedis," Annabelle began slowly, "where's the dragon?"

"What?" Reedis twisted around, staring toward the empty mound of gold. Idly he picked one coin up and pocketed it before turning around again to stare at the others. "Well, he was just here. I'm sure he'll turn up soon enough."

Ellen rushed back up the mound of coins and stood in front of the mage, her hands planted firmly on her hips as she demanded, "What did you do with Jarin?"

"What?" Reedis began worriedly, looking down at the young girl. "You're just a girl, don't you know it's rude to —"

"Where's Jarin?" Ellen cried, looking around the man, her eyes filling with tears. "He was just here. I was guarding him." She rounded on Reedis once more and shouted, "*What* did you do to him?"

"You were guarding me?" the voice belonged to Reedis, the expression did not. Ellen's eyes widened as the mage wrapped her arms around her and hugged her tightly. "It's okay. I'm here. I'm here, Ellen, this is me."

Ellen broke up, looking up in awe. "Jarin?"

"Have we met?" Reedis asked her.

Ellen's eyes widened once more. "What did you do with my friend?"

"Ellen," Ophidian's voice came from behind her. "He *is* your friend."

"I am?" Reedis asked, looking pale. His eyes rolled up and he fainted onto the mound of coins and treasure.

"Becoming a twin soul is difficult," Imay said, moving up toward Ellen.

"That man?" Ellen said, pointing to the unconscious mage. "He's *Jarin?*"

"Technically, he's Reedis Jarin, now," Annabelle said, moving forward and looking down to the unconscious mage, a slight smile tugging at the corners of her lips.

"Jarin Reedis," Ophidian rumbled in correction. The others stared at him. "I'm given to understand that Reedis is the mage's last name." He leaned down, grabbed the unconscious form's right arm and threw the man over his back. The others stared at him in surprise. "May I bring him to your infirmary?"

"Of course," Diam said. She held a hand out to Lissy who ran to take it, before saying to the dragon god, "He'll need rest."

"And we'll need to work on Ibb," Rabel said. He looked over at Imay and winked. "Would you like to learn some ancient secrets?"

Imay's eyes bulged and she nodded eagerly.

About The Twin Soul Series

Currently spanning 19 books and over 200 characters, the Twin Soul Series keeps on growing!

If you'd like a list of characters, scan the QR Code below, it'll take you to the characters page on our website, http://www.twinsoulseries.com

Acknowledgements

No book gets done without a lot of outside help.

We are so grateful to Jeff Winner for his marvelous cover art work.

We'd like to thank all our first readers for their support, encouragement, and valuable feedback.

Any mistakes or omissions are, of course, all our own.

About the Authors

Award-winning authors The Winner Twins, Brit and Brianna, have been writing for over ten years, with their first novel (*The Strand*) published when they were twelve years old.

New York Times bestselling author Todd McCaffrey has written over a dozen books, including eight in the Dragonriders of Pern® universe.

http://www.twinsoulseries.com

Printed in Great Britain
by Amazon